I0766071

DARK SOVEREIGNTY

COMPLETE SERIES

USA TODAY BESTSELLING AUTHOR

ANNA EDWARDS

DARK SOVEREIGNTY, The Complete Series
© 2023 by Anna Edwards
Cover Design © 2023 by Charity Hendry Designs
Logo Design © 2021 by Charity Hendry Designs
Editing by Tracy Roelle
Formatting by Charity Hendry Designs
Proofreading by Sheena Taylor
ASIN: B07X43CQFG
ISBN: 978-1-3999-6192-9

Excerpt: **MINE**
© 2023 by Anna Edwards
Cover Design © 2023 by Dani René at Raven Designs
ISBN: 979-8-85670-900-0

Excerpt: **SURRENDERED CONTROL**
© 2016 by Anna Edwards
Cover Design © 2016 by Charity Hendry Designs
ISBN: 978-1-5393-8091-7

Excerpt: **THE TOUCH OF SNOW**
© 2017 by Anna Edwards
Cover Design © 2017 by Charity Hendry Designs
ISBN: 978-1-5481-3514-0

adults only, as defined by the laws of the country in which you made your purchase.

Disclaimer: Please do not try any sexual practice without the guidance of an experienced practitioner. Neither the publisher nor the author will be responsible for any loss, harm, injury, or death resulting from the use of the information contained in this book.

Dark Sovereignty / Anna Edwards -- 1st ed.

www.AuthorAnnaEdwards.com

Please note this is an unconventional dark romance.
There will be triggers.
Thank you for understanding.
I hope you enjoy reading.

Anna xx

ACKNOWLEDGMENTS

First and always to my great friend, Charity Hendry, for always being there for me. For entertaining my crazy ideas and helping me bring them to fruition. Love you to bits.

To my editor, Tracy Roelle, and proofreader, Sheena Taylor, you polish my books so that they shine brightly. I'm lucky to have such a good team.

To my street team, thank you so much for all you that you do to get my books out in the reader world.

To Yvonne, for not only beta reading and offering me advice but for organizing so much when it comes to conventions. I'd be lost without you.

To my family, thank you for all the support that you give me.

To Debbie Pothin for naming my Duke in a competition in my Facebook group. Thank you. It's given me so many ideas.

Finally, to all the readers who have embraced me as an author. I'm so glad that you enjoy the stories my mind creates. I hope I'm able to give you many more years of pleasure.

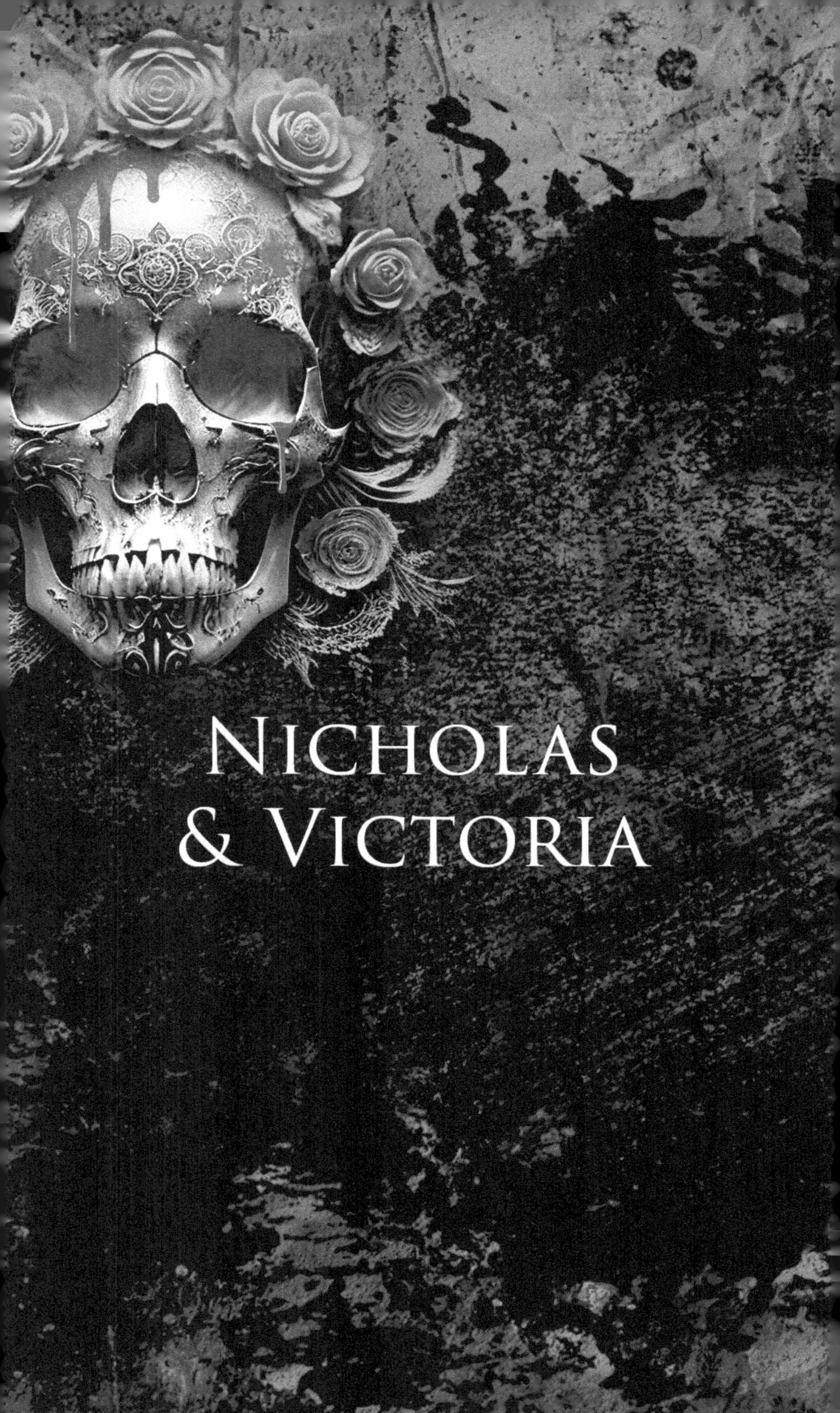

Nicholas
& Victoria

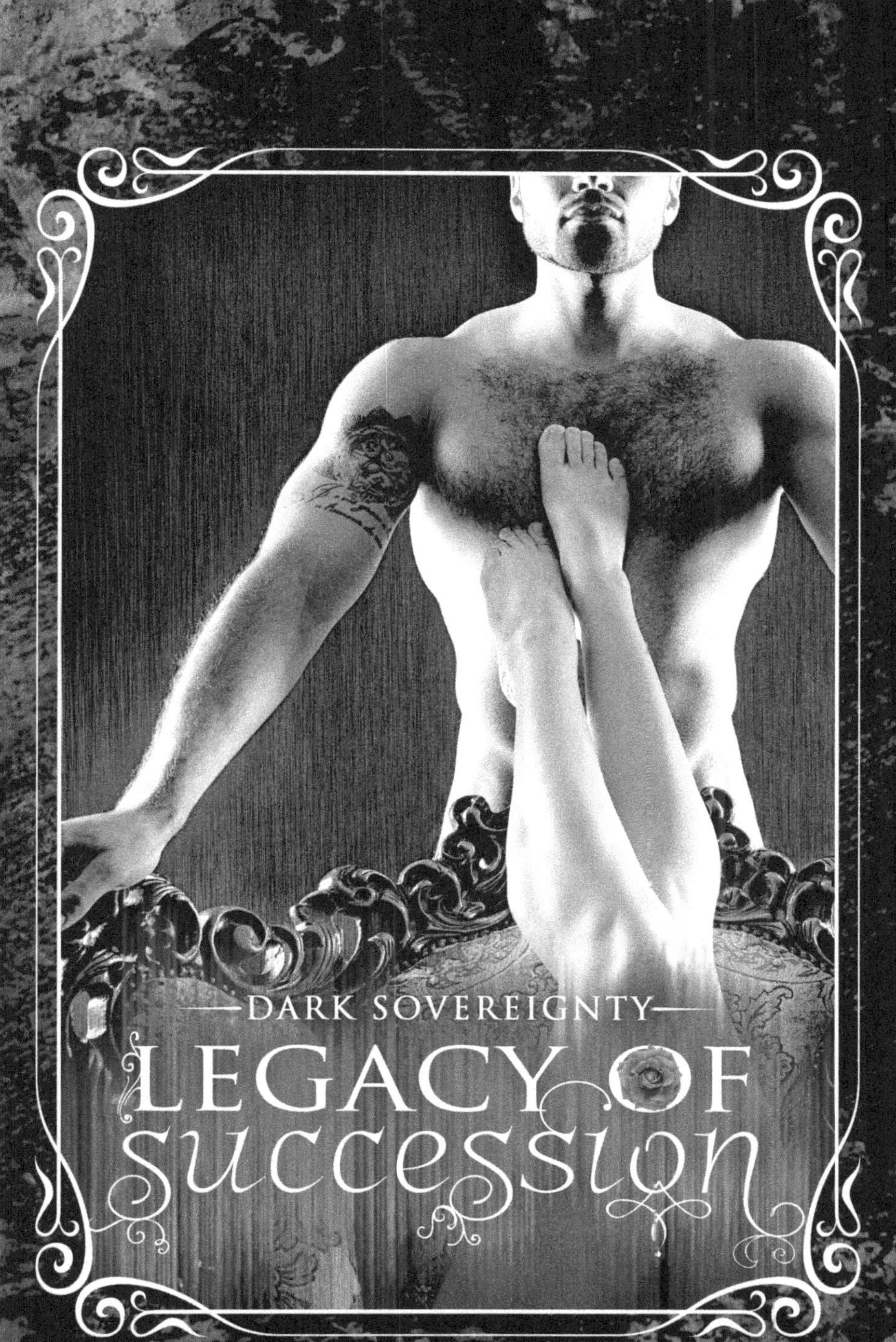
DARK SOVEREIGNTY
LEGACY OF
succession

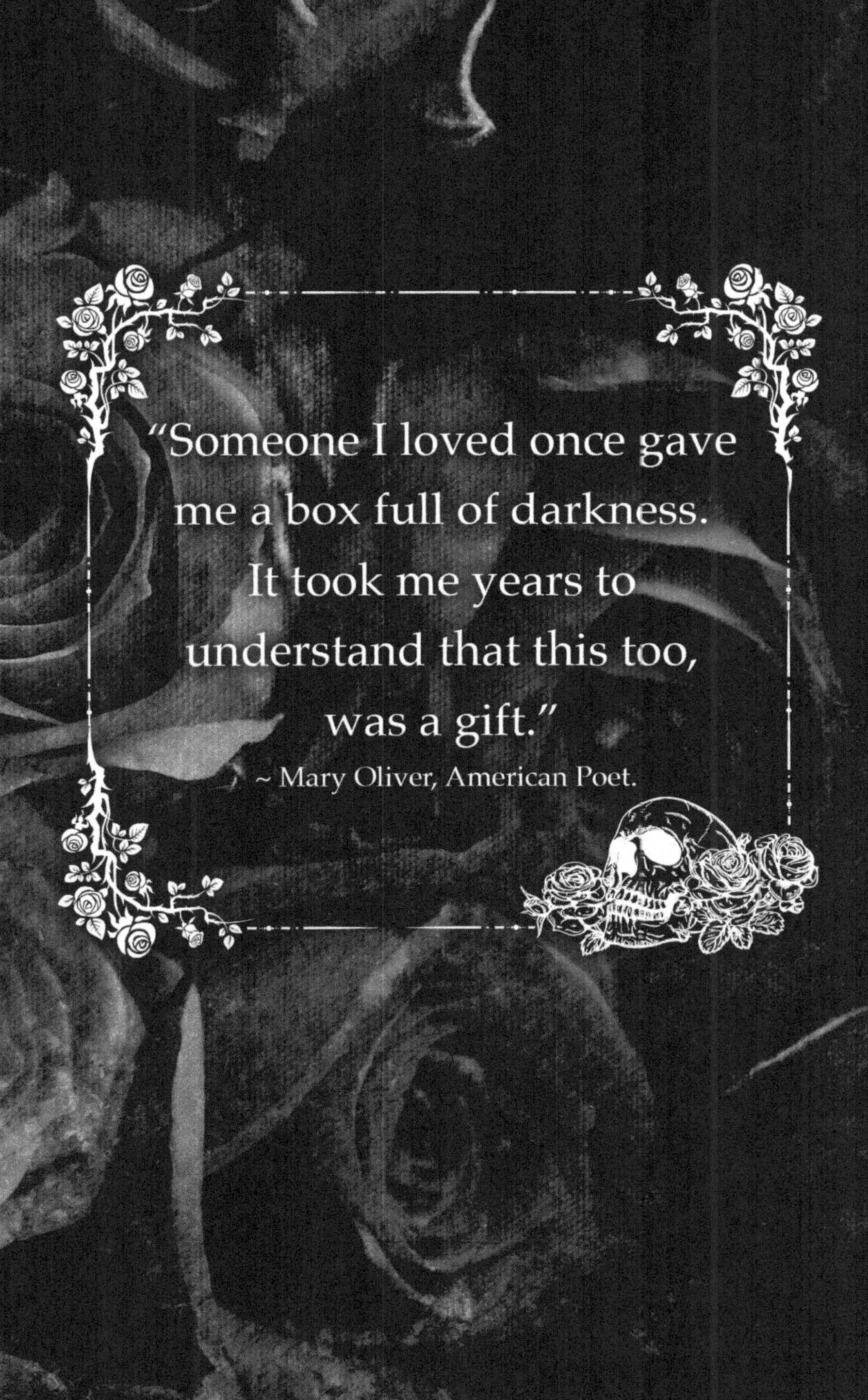

"Someone I loved once gave me a box full of darkness. It took me years to understand that this too, was a gift."
~ Mary Oliver, American Poet.

I swear I must have read the same page in this high society gossip magazine at least five times. You know the sort: who's marrying who, which couples are divorcing, and who's running around Chelsea in nothing but their bra and knickers. It's boring! But then again, it's more interesting than the life I have. The highlight of my day would be if the cook changed the strictly ordered meal plan that I've eaten every week, without fail, since I turned sixteen. Five years of the same food is enough to send anyone crazy. But I shouldn't complain. My father, Arthur Cortland Hamilton, Viscount Mayfield, is a wealthy man, and I lead a life of privilege. I've never wanted for anything: clothes, makeup, books, they've all been produced within hours of asking. My days are often spent lounging around by the indoor pool after swimming a hundred lengths, as I am now, but I want something more. I didn't go to regular school like normal people — I was educated at home by a governess. My brother, Theodore, Theo for short, went to a local private school. He would always come home with tales of the friends he'd made and the games that he'd played. My games would consist of reciting my times tables, so I didn't fall asleep from the monotony of the day. I once asked my mother why I wasn't allowed to go to school, and all she would say was 'to protect your reputation'. I have no doubt my gravestone will read, 'Here lies, the honorable Victoria Hamilton. She died from boredom, but at least, her reputation was intact.'

I give up on the magazine and place it down on the ornately carved sixteenth-century table. I take off the towel, which I'd wrapped around me after my swim. I'm dressed in only a small black bikini. It's the one I always try to choose because of the inlaid embroidery of a rose on it. It's my favorite flower.

"Miss Hamilton?" I turn my head toward the middle-aged butler when he addresses me. He bows.

"Yes."

"Miss Bennett is on the telephone for you." He hands me the phone, and I wave him away before squealing into the receiver.

"Tammy, how are you?"

She's excited about something. I can tell from the hyper-ventilating breaths coming from the other end of the phone.

"I did it. I've taken my last exam, and it feels so good. I'm sure I passed it. I answered nearly every question."

"I'm so happy for you. That's amazing news."

Tamara Bennett is my only friend. She's the same age as me. We grew up together. She made life tolerable in this mansion of no fun. Her mother, Elsie, is lady's maid to my mother and me. She doesn't know who her father is. Her mother tells her it isn't important. We used to make up stories that he was a hero off fighting for his country, and one day, he would come back for her and Elsie. He never did though, and the truth, about him being a father who abandoned a pregnant woman, seems a lot less exciting. Still, I'm glad she came to live with me because it means I can live vicariously through her. She's been at Oxford University for the last three years, studying law. I've missed her so much.

"All I need to do is pack up all my stuff and I'll be coming back to London."

"When?" I try to temper down my excitement a little bit, but her giggle tells me she knows I'm practically climbing the walls without her here.

"I've got a few end-of-term parties first, so a couple of weeks."

"A couple of weeks," I say sadly.

"I know. It'll go quickly. You'll see."

"I wonder if Daddy would let me come up to see you at the parties? Theo could accompany me. That way, I wouldn't get into any of the trouble he thinks would befall me if I happened to leave the house."

"Victoria." Her answer is ominous. Not because she doesn't want me to come, but she knows my father would say 'no' immediately.

"I just wish for once he would trust me."

"He does trust you."

"He doesn't," I interrupt. "He thinks that if I see a man, who isn't a relative, all my morals will go down the drain, and I'll hump him like a wild dog."

"He's doesn't think that!"

"Then, why didn't he allow me to go to University to study the History of Art? I obtained a place at Oxford. You don't get higher than that. I also had a place at Goldsmiths, which is just down the road, so I'd still be able to live at home. Every time I asked, the answer was 'no'. If he'd trusted me, he'd have let me go."

"He just doesn't want to see any harm come to you. Some parties can get a little bit rowdy." Tammy's voice went quiet on the other end of the phone.

"You've been to them?" I ask.

"A few times."

"What happens, tell me?" My living by proxy is all done through my friend, and I'm not going to let her keep details from me.

"Ria." My nickname since we were toddlers. She struggled to say Victoria when she was younger, so it was just shortened to Ria, and it stuck.

"Please," I beg.

"Ok, there was this one party when I was in my second year. It was after the end of the final year exams. Some of my mates brought in some kegs of beer. They were paid for by one of the final years, he was a billionaire's son. He had more money than sense. We spent most of the day drinking and ordering in pizza when we got hungry. By the evening, we were all pretty merry."

"Drunk?" I interrupt, not knowing what that feels like. I'm allowed a glass of wine with my dinner and champagne at the functions Daddy throws. I've never been drunk.

"I was on my way to drunk. I wasn't drunk. My inhibitions were lowered. There was this guy. We'd been working together on our final project for the term."

"Did you have sex with him?" I know Tammy isn't a virgin. She lost her cherry, when she was at school, to a guy she'd been dating for a year. She came home and told me all the details.

"Eventually. But first, we played Twister with another couple. Every time someone fell over, they had to remove an item of clothing. You know how clumsy I am. I was naked with my backside in the air in no time. One of the moves put him behind me. He got hard, so we stopped playing and fucked right there on the lounge floor. Most of the party were watching us, but we weren't the only ones naked. Lots of couples were having sex around us."

"Wow." It's all I can say. I mean I've read books about sex and looked at videos on the internet, when I've wanted to get myself off, but to be involved in a real-life orgy sounds amazing. Jesus, Tammy had such a good life. "What happened next?"

"Yeah. Next wasn't good." She goes quiet. "I found him having sex with some other girl later that evening."

"The bastard."

"It was an evening of free love. I went and found another partner."

"I wish I could do it for once."

"No, you don't. Your saving yourself for your husband."

"What husband!" I exclaim indignantly. "Don't I actually have to be allowed to leave the house to find one?"

"Have you spoken to your father again about getting a job?"

"What's the point?"

"You told me about the volunteering position at the art gallery. Maybe since you won't be getting paid, he'll let you?" she asks, hopefully.

"Oh that, I left the information on his desk. I went in the

next day and found it in the bin. He wouldn't even entertain it, money or not." I stand up and walk around the pool to the French doors that open over our manicured gardens. We're on the outskirts of London so have a large plot compared to some, and I welcome it because it means I can escape and walk. I open them and take a breath of air.

"I'm sure he'll allow something soon. Maybe when I move back, we can persuade him to allow you to come out with me more."

"It won't happen, there's no point in asking. I'm stuck in this place. Probably until he chooses a husband for me, and then, I'll be stuck doing what another man wants me to do." I'm so down with my life at the moment, I just want to have a purpose.

"We'll think of something," Tammy offers. She knows how sad I get. "What about asking him if you can help him with his business affairs again? He was more than happy for you to help him arrange the functions when your mother was ill. Maybe you could take some of the running of the estates away from her. Talk to her."

"That's a good idea. She's been busy with Theodore and his new business venture recently, and she still looks weak after the flu." Her mother had caught flu the previous winter and had been bedridden for weeks. She had problems with her lungs anyway, from an iron deficiency at birth. It really hit her hard. She spent time in the hospital and took months to recover. "I'll ask him when I next see him. Mother can concentrate on Theo, and I'll run the estates. At least I'll get to talk to people. "

"Great idea." I can hear voices, in the background, on the

other end of the phone. They're calling my friend. "I'm going to have to go, Ria."

"Going on another drinking fest?" I laugh, but she goes silent. "Have fun and be careful."

"I'll be home soon, and we'll work on you being allowed out more. I promise. Go talk to your father about the estate."

She hangs up, and I go back to staring out of the window. Our gardens are formal in style. A rose border dominates the vista from the pool. It's June, and the beautiful pink and red petals of the climber's contrast stunningly with the crisp white of the fragrant tea roses. The gardener appears from behind a hedge, and he sees me standing there. I go to ask him to cut a rose for me, but he puts his head down and hurries away back into the depths of the woodland area. Oops, I remember that I'm in a bikini. Awkward.

"Victoria," my father calls me. I stroll back to the lounger and pick up my dressing gown. I've just finished wrapping it around me and tying the cord when he enters the room.

"Father." I smile.

"I've been looking for you everywhere."

"You know I *always* swim at this time," I offer with a hint of sarcasm, alluding to the fact that I don't have anything else to do.

"We don't have much time." He seems flustered.

"Time for what?" I come over to his side and place my arm through the crook of his. For all my father's overprotective faults, I do love him. I remember once, as a child, him building Theo and me this tent in his office and having afternoon tea with us in it. Theo, of course, being a lively boy wanted to use the shelter as a place to hide from the enemies who were chasing him. He didn't really want to have a girly tea party, but my father insisted that it was my turn to choose the game, we sat with our pinkies out and pretended to drink tea.

"You have to get changed. We're going out."

"Out? Where?" I enquire with a great deal of excitement in my voice.

"It's time," he says and brushes me off, striding away through the house. I follow him as he heads toward my bedroom. Elsie's waiting in the room for us when we walk in. She looks sad. There's a definite air of tension in the room. Elsie steps aside and on the bed is a pure white linen dress. It's plain in design except for a small crest on the breast. I don't recognize it. Are those oak leaves? I try to think to whom it might belong but come up blank.

"Father, will you please tell me what's going on? I'm worried." I take his hand and squeeze it. He looks down at the floor.

"It's time for you to enter society. Put the dress on. No make-up. No undergarments. Just the dress. Elsie knows how your hair should be. We leave within the hour." I stand there in shock. Society? The door slams before I even realize he's left. I get to go and meet people. This is it — I finally get the freedom I crave. Alright, it'll be in probably the most unflattering dress I've ever seen, but at least it's going out. I squeal inwardly with barely contained excitement. My wish is going to come true.

CHAPTER TWO

NICHOLAS

The Ferrari 448GTB, in the obligatory red color, skids to a halt, and I'm out of the vehicle before the footman even has a chance to react. I throw him the keys and stomp into the house. I need coffee, preferably intravenously. I've got a herd of fucking elephants in my head along with a severe case of flashbacks to what was the best twenty-ninth birthday party, ever. Another one hits me when I shut my eyes and slump down into my favorite comfortable chair in the ostentatious room that my father calls the waiting room. It's a blonde this time and a brunette. The blonde is riding my dick like a cowgirl while my friend, Prince John, is doing her up the ass. I've got the brunette on my face, and she's bathing me in her cum. I love a woman's orgasm — it's the sweetest flavor in the world, especially when she's soaking your chin. My dick gets hard again at the thought.

"Down boy," I tell him. "Any more action for you, and

you're going to end up with burns. We're taking the day off."
I'm sure he's sulking in my pants.

"Lord Lullington." I reluctantly open my bloodshot eyes to see my elderly butler standing over me with the ever-present stern expression on his face.

"This had better be good, Reggie, and it better come with coffee."

"It comes with a bacon sandwich, My Lord." He steps back to reveal the glorious delicacy placed on fine china and resting on my father's sixteenth century, carved oak chest.

"You're sent from heaven." I jump up and sink my teeth into the first juicy bite. "Hmm. Ketchup. This is the best."

"You'll need the strength it gives you." I finish the sandwich in a few bites and pick up the cup of steaming coffee. I know it'll be the King's blend, from Fortnum & Mason, because that's the only one I'll drink since I discovered it at fourteen. I'm not a tea person, unlike the rest of my family.

"Are you going to tell me that my father wants me?"

"He's been shouting obscenities and then your name since the sun rose. He says I'm to inform him the minute you return home." I rub a hand over my unshaven chin and groan.

"I better go and find him before he has an aneurysm."

"It would be wise, My Lord."

Reginald coughs.

"What is it?" I ask, knowing the sudden frog in his throat means he wants to voice his opinion on something.

"May I speak without consequence?" He bows his head.

"Don't you usually around me?" I chuckle and grab my head when it hurts.

"Only when I know you need a bit of fatherly advice."

"Go ahead."

"Don't fight your father on this. You can't stop what's about to happen. It's bigger than anything you know. It's the future of your name and of what governs us."

"Why does it have to be, though?" I sit back in the chair and place my head in my hands. My mahogany hair hasn't been brushed and has a definite recently fucked look.

"History, Nicholas. It's too ingrained in your family to change. To try now would destroy everything. You're implicit in the crimes of the generations past. Blood stains your hands — it can never be cleaned off."

I know that the old man, who's been within my household since I can remember, is right. I have no choice, and I nod acceptance.

"To my death, I go." I get back to my feet and leave him to clear up my empty plate while I search for the man who holds my future in his hands. No sooner do I think of the devil than he appears in front of me, from his office.

"Nicholas, finally. Where have you been?" He stares at me from behind dead eyes. No emotion belies the torture that he's, likely, about to commit.

"My apologies, Your Grace." I've never once called him Father. I was taught at an early age with a wooden cane that he would demand his title, even from his son. "I was enjoying the celebrations for my birthday. I knew it would be the last one I can enjoy as a free man — they may have gone on longer than I'd anticipated."

"You mean that you were sticking your cock in as many women as possible." He raises an eyebrow, which makes me feel like a ten-year-old boy about to get the cane again for stealing a sweet. I'm not, though, I'm a grown man of twenty-nine and should be able to make my own decisions.

"Only two women. My friends shared the other ones."

"You're disgusting," he scoffs.

"Don't tell me you didn't do the same when you were younger, or indeed that you wouldn't do it still, given half the chance." I go to walk away. I've had enough of this. I need a shit, shave, and shower before a long sleep.

"The difference is I do it with decorum and restraint. I don't risk my male parts being posted all over social media with full commentary on how good I am in bed."

"That was one time." I stop and turn back to face him with my fists clenched.

"And it cost me a good million to silence the little bitch. We have a reputation to maintain, and you're going to throw it all away." My father stands up to my anger, but I'm so livid I'm not about to back down and act sensibly.

"No, we can't damage your reputation as the leader of your little secret society, can we?"

"Jesus, Nicholas, will you grow up?"

"Why? What's the point?"

"Because by your next birthday, you'll be married, the Duke of Oakfield, and the leader of my, 'little secret society', as you put it. This isn't a bad thing I'm asking you to do. I've left you alone, to do as you please with your life, since you turned eighteen. That's eleven years of fun. Do you not find it monotonous? All I'm asking is that you start to take on some responsibility." My father lowers his voice from one full of disappointment and anguish to one I vaguely remember. The one that holds compassion and fondness in it. "You're my son, my heir. I want what's best for you, and I know this is it."

"But why this way?" I state.

"It's the rules. Our forefathers signed the documents governing how we must prove that we're worthy of the title. It's not possible to change them."

"It's possible to change anything if you put your mind to it."

"Not this, Nicholas. There's too much at stake. Oakfield Hall for one."

"This is our ancestors' home since before the time of the society," I protest. "They surely can't take it."

"It was written into the founding documents that all this can be taken from us. The money was needed when it fell into disrepair before your four times great-grandfather came into his inheritance. He was a brave man who was prepared to risk everything for the sake of protecting the name and estates. You can't let him down."

This founding document has been the bane of my life ever since I heard about it, for the first time, at the age of ten. That was when I found out how much my life was mapped out for me. My four times great grandfather needed funds to live. It was around the time that the cost of living went through the roof for the elite, and it became increasingly difficult for them to afford to run a stately home, like the one we now live in. It became even harder for them to pay their way at lavish court functions, which were a pre-requisite for those having a title such as Duke, whether it was a royal title or not. It was neces-sary to make an appearance, and if the King wanted money then it had to be given to him. Drugs, prostitution, high levels of alcohol consumption, it was all rife then. The elite had to be seen to be partaking. Along with some of the other title holders in the country, my ancestor formed a pact. They'd work together to be able to live the lifestyles they wanted, but in return they had to give up something. My ancestor was designated the leader as he was the highest ranked and also a close confidant of the King. It was decided that should he forfeit his position then Oakfield Hall and any other assets, owned by the Cavendish family, would be sold and distributed between the remaining members of the society. A pretty big forfeiture, considering that in addition he had no say on when or to whom he got married! Because every eldest son on his thirtieth birthday, going down in perpetuity, takes over the title and leadership of the society, on the proviso that he is married. I guess that the position means power and a casting vote in the way the organization's run, but to me, it just takes away my free will.

"Nicholas!" my father shouts at me, and I realize that I'd disappeared into a dream world. "Are you listening to a word I'm saying?"

"Sorry, Your Grace."

"You've been training for this your entire life. You've known it was coming. Think of the power you'll wield, this time next year. You'll be responsible for the business behind the scenes."

"I'm not entirely sure that's something to be proud of." I roll my eyes.

"It is if it keeps a roof over our heads."

"Theft, murder, god knows what else." My father's face reddens as I speak, partly through anger, I think, but also through the embarrassment of knowing that he has the life he leads because of the hardship he puts others through. Actually, no, scrap that. It's all anger because my father doesn't think about anyone else but himself.

"I sometimes wonder what I did to raise such an ungrateful child. Hear me out, Nicholas, enough arguing. You'll shut that intolerable mouth of yours until you can learn to use it for something that's actually important. You'll go to your quarters, and you'll make yourself presentable rather than looking like you have just crawled off the street or out of a barrel of wine. If you don't, you won't like the consequences that I'll be forced to bring down on you." He's seething. The whites of his eyes are showing as he stands face to face with me. My father's a strong man. He may be sixty, but he keeps himself healthy. "The ladies are on their way, and you'll be ready to meet them. You'll show them what it means to be in Oakfield Hall, and you'll embrace your birthright because if you don't then I'll make the decisions for you. I'll make you sit back and watch, while I do your duty!"

My stomach turns — I wish I'd not drunk so much last night. I knew this was coming today, and I knew what I'd have to do. I don't want to marry. I want to fuck my way around England, but my father's right: I have a duty to my family name and my future. Last night was the end of my old life, and today is the first of my new one. I'll embrace the monster that I must become.

CHAPTER THREE

VICTORIA

I stare up at the imposing mansion on the outskirts of London. I thought I lived in a big house, but this place must be more imposing than Buckingham Palace. You can tell that part of it dates back to Tudor times, but the majority of the brickwork and style is gothic in nature, and thus from the Victorian era. I bet these walls can tell a few stories, and I'd love to hear them.

"Hurry up, Victoria," my father calls. I scamper quickly to his side, and we enter together through the grand arch of the welcoming chamber.

"Sorry, Father, I was just admiring the house. Who lives here?"

"The Duke of Oakfield," he replies curtly.

I scan my memory for details on who that is. I've heard that name before — I'm sure of it. Yes, he's the patron of my favorite art museum in London. I'm even more excited for my debut into society because I wonder if he has artwork in his home, which I can study.

The heavy oak doors are opened for us, and we're shown into a room with several other girls wearing the same linen dress as I am. I smile at one of them, but she just raises an eyebrow at me and walks off after a man who must be her father. Fine, I'll avoid her then. My coat and my father's are taken. He's presented with a glass of Champagne. I'm offered one but respectively decline. I want to make sure I remember every moment of what's about to happen.

"Father." He turns to me, when I address him, and takes a sip of his drink.

"Yes."

"Are we to attend a banquet?" I look around the room at the paintings on the wall while I speak.

"There'll be food later."

"Will gentlemen be attending?"

"Just one."

"Just one?" I repeat and face him.

"The Duke's son, Earl Lullington."

"Oh."

The conversation stops, and my father nods to another man as he walks near.

"My Lord Linton."

"Mayfield."

"Is Lady Joanna ready?" my father asks.

"She's with my wife trying to tame her unruly hair."

"I'm blessed, Victoria has straight hair even if it's as red as a cherry. It must be the Irish blood in Cecilia." I take hold of my hair, which is neatly tied back in a French plait. The end of the braid comes down to my waist. When hanging loose, my hair reaches the middle of my back. I've always loved it long, and the color I find unique. I'm not ginger but a natural dark red. Nobody knows where it came from even if my father blames my mother's ancestry.

"I guess I should blame the Celtic blood for Joanna's curly hair, then. It's as wild as one of the bare-chested brutes who used to run wild over our lands," Lord Linton replies with a chuckle. His attention is taken when a girl the same age as me hurries up to him and bows her head low, so he can see the top of it.

"Is this alright Father," she asks.

He inspects it. Her hair looks fine to me, but then, I don't see why we all need to be dressed the same and so plainly. I don't wear a lot of makeup usually, but I do like mascara and a spot of lipstick. I had all of that scrubbed off my face before I left. This isn't exactly the debut into society I'd dreamed of. I expected lavish gowns, and an evening full of dancing with handsome men. The sort of thing that comes straight from the pages of Pride and Prejudice. Instead, I've got no make-up, no underwear, and a dress that looks like a white bin liner. I pray to god that I don't get it wet because everything will be on display if I do. I can't let a fashion disaster get me down. I'm out of the house — ok, there are not as many people as I expected, but there are still people to talk to.

Joanna's father gives her his seal of approval, and she turns to face me.

"Hello, I'm Lady Joanna Nethercutt," she smiles.

"Victoria Hamilton," I respond.

"The Honorable," my father adds. I never use the title that precedes my name. My father is a Viscount — as his daughter, I am not entitled to use 'Lady' only 'The Honorable'. What's the point? I'm not pretentious. Well having said that, if it were Duchess or Countess, then I'd probably use it.

"Are you excited?" I ask.

"Excited?" She narrows her eyes at me.

"Yes, for your debut."

"We should take our places," my father interrupts and pulls me away toward the front of the room.

"That was rude," I exclaim and look back to Joanna with an apologetic nod.

"You don't need to make small talk and get yourself all flustered. You need to remember your manners and behave." He raises his voice but not so much that anyone else in the room can hear him.

"Sorry, Father." I look down at the ground and wish it would swallow me up. Why do I have a feeling that this evening isn't going to be as much fun as I was hoping for?

My father pulls out his phone and starts to scroll through his emails. I'm dismissed from any further conversation. I take another look around the room that we're in. It's some sort of banqueting hall. Swords, armor, and stags' horns adorn the wood-paneled walls. Any space that isn't wooden is painted cream. There are three paintings on the wall, and I take a step closer to get a better look at them. My father tuts, but I ignore him.

One is a Rembrandt and another a Caravaggio. I'd read about them being bought by a private collector for millions. Wow, the Cavendish family must be loaded if they can afford these. My attention is drawn to the third. I can't place the artist at first, I take a step even closer.

"Victoria," my father admonishes me, but I ignore him again because I can see the signature. Van Gogh's Poppy Flowers. I smirk, knowing that the original of this painting was stolen in two thousand and ten. This must be a fake. I take another quick look at the Rembrandt and Caravaggio. Nothing distinguishes them as fakes at this distance, but given the Van Gogh must be then I'm sure the others are too. The residents of Oakfield Hall aren't as affluent as they like to portray. I stand back and smile, knowingly. It's then that I feel the heat of eyes burning into me.

I turn towards the source of this overwhelming sense of being observed and find a gentleman staring at me. He's tall, about six foot three, and wears a three-piece suit with a crisp white open-necked shirt. His brown hair is long but brushed and neatly gelled in place. His eyes are a cerulean blue like the sky, but a shade darker. He's looking directly at me. My heart flutters, and my breath quickens. I've not seen many men, due to a life spent in relative solitude, but I know instantly that this man screams sex, and by the way he's looking at me, I'm the next delicacy on his menu. I can feel my cheeks heat and want to look away, but I can't. He's captured me in his spell and taken my breath away. He winks and directs his attention back to an older gentleman at his side. They have a similar look about each other, I surmise they must be father and son.

"Victoria, come here," my father orders, and I snap to attention this time. A gong rings out in the room, and the older gentleman steps up onto a makeshift stage. I hadn't noticed before, as I was too interested in the walls, but a fire pit sits on the staging. I can't help but think that a little odd.

"Welcome everyone," the man speaks. "Are we all ready to begin?"

The crowd murmurs a resounding 'yes', and I wait for the music to start.

"For those who don't know me, I'm the Duke of Oakfield

and the leader of this society. We're here today to continue traditions our forbearers have handed down to us, for generations." He steps toward the fire pit and pulls out a metal rod. A couple of the men in the room cheer. I look at my father, but he pales and refuses to meet my eyes. "Bring the first one up."

Two men jump down from the stage and take one of the girls by the arms. She screams, "No", but is manhandled onto the stage with little effort. I can feel a heated gaze on me again, and I look to the man who was watching me before. He's watching me again. He smiles — though this time it isn't the sweet one from before but an arrogant one. He steps forward and takes the rod from his father and, without hesitating, brands the screaming girl with a sickening sizzle of burning flesh. I stumble backward, trying to catch my breath, but my father grabs me and causes the world that I know to collapse when he says,

"Your turn."

NICHOLAS

My father holds up the arm of the girl who has just been branded. I know her, from the files I've been given about each of them, as Daphne Knight. She's the daughter of a member of the House of Lords. She sobs with the pain, that she must be experiencing, from where the society's crest is forever branded onto her porcelain flesh. I should feel regret, for what I've just done, but I know that I had no choice. I can't show weakness in front of these people who, this time next year, I'll govern. Another girl is brought forward. This one isn't dragged. She comes willingly to her fate. Elizabeth Sandford, a Lord Bishop's daughter, no less. Judging by the fact that she's pushing her lips together in a sexy pout, she's looking forward to what's about to happen. She pulls the material of her dress up and reveals a toned and tanned thigh. She's definitely been preparing. She pulls it a little too high and exposes the edge of a bare pussy. I ignore the blatant flirting and brand her. She whimpers but doesn't break down like the first girl.

She has spirit — I like it. I bet she would fuck like a dog in heat.

My father drags the first girl forward to the front of the stage.

"As first declared in eighteen hundred and eight, during the reign of the mad King George III — all girls born to members of the society, in the eighth year after the birth of the son of the incumbent Duke of Oakfield, are to be handed over to the society. This tradition has continued, in perpetuity, down the family lines since that date. My son, Nicholas, has reached the required age, and thus, all girls born in nineteen ninety-seven must be given to us. It's in our ruling documentation and to deny this clause will lead to dire consequences."

I brand another two girls while he speaks. Both sit on the stage, crying tears of pain from the imprint of the society's crest.

"We have five girls here today — five virgins from which my son will choose his wife."

I cringe at that bit of my father's speech. I don't want to marry even if all five of the girls before me are fuckable. I'm a playboy and would rather continue in that vein than be tied to one woman for the rest of my life. A woman who'd most probably hate my guts anyway. Mind you, if my own mother is an example to go by, then my wife is unlikely to be around for long. She died when I was five. They say she slipped while walking on the battlements at the top of the house. I'm not stupid, though. Presuming she'd gone through what I'm about to subject these women to, then it is more likely that she ended up insane and took her own life. My father didn't really care about her death.

There was no grief — he couldn't remarry as per the rules of the society, but he could fuck every bit of skirt willing to open her legs for a Duke. The best-case scenario might even be that the woman I marry kills herself before I get her pregnant, and I don't have to subject my children to this ritual crap.

"If any person here doesn't hand over their daughter, then they'll be cast out of the society and all their assets taken away. These are the rules we live by."

The room falls silent. No man will dare go against the society. Nobody of rank within it ever has, and nobody ever will. Money, it's the one thing we all crave, and we'd even sell our daughters just to get it or, in this case, to keep it. The silence is broken when the next girl is called up.

"No fucking way." Her sultry swear has me turning my head toward the commotion. Several of my father's bodyguards, or as I prefer to call them 'hired goons', surround the girl, so I can't see her. "If you think I'm going to let him do that, then you're fucking insane."

Damn, she needs to stop swearing — it's turning me on with the raspy melody of her tone. The guards part when a punch comes flying through the air. I see the vibrant red tresses that follow it, and I know this is the girl who was looking at the paintings. She is exquisite to the eye. All curves and breasts even in the most unflattering dress. Her big eyes are almost emerald in color. I'd immediately wanted to savor her flesh, knowing that it would taste like perfection. But as she's dragged toward me, I see the hatred in her eyes and know that she'll never willingly give herself to me, and I don't take what isn't offered. I don't need to.

"You're all mad. The lot of you. I don't consent to this. My father may have, but I never will. Let me go, or I'll scream so loudly that someone will call the police."

My father laughs before addressing the assembled crowd.

"There's always one who thinks that she's bigger and better than her fate. I don't know why they bother to fight it."

"Fuck you, you freak." She swears again, and my cock lengthens.

"Enough time wasting, we've a long evening ahead of us, and we need to get on with it. Hold her down. Nicholas, the iron. Brand her," my father orders. The men descend on the poor girl, and they grab her hands and legs to pin her to the floor. She has no decorum or grace, at this moment. She's a wild animal fighting for her life. She's a scared antelope to my savage predator. I stalk her like the ferocious animal I am — a lion hungry for its dinner, and the smell of her fear entices me. Panic overrides modesty, and her sex is bared to me. Fuck, I want her. I'll have her. No, I need to concentrate. I can't allow her femininity to cloud my judgment. I need to succeed. I'm the next Duke of Oakfield. I'll rule this society as soon as I choose a wife. She needs to be shown she's nothing now — a pawn in a fight she can't win. I take the poker and place it hard into the flesh of her thigh. The gossamer skin burns with an acrid smell, and she screams and screams. It's not a cry of ecstasy but one of agony. My throat clenches, and the guilt I feel wraps me tightly in a blanket of disgust. I throw it off, though. She's the one at fault and should just accept her fate. There's no point in fighting what's happening here — it will happen even if we say we don't want it to. Nothing can change what's about to occur — least of all the screams of a girl too young to know better. I look down at her as tears stream from her eyes.

"Stupid girl. You'd be better to accept your fate rather than fight it."

"Go to hell," she whimpers.

I laugh.

"Don't you realize? You just entered hell, and there's no chance of leaving."

CHAPTER FIVE

VICTORIA

The four men holding me let go, and I scramble to my feet. However, not before kicking the freak with the branding iron in the kneecap. The mark inflicted on my skin might only be small, but it hurts so much. It feels as though they've ripped the skin from my body and carved the inside with knives. I tried to cook dinner for my mother once, when I was fifteen, and I burned my hand on the oven. It had barely touched the flesh, but at the time, I thought *that* had hurt badly. Now, I know a lot differently. I move as far away from the staging and all the men as I can. I refuse to let tears fall from my eyes, even though several of the other girls are crying. I won't let them have the honor of seeing my tears. I glare at them instead with an evil stare. If only I had magical powers, they would drop dead in an instant. Has the world I'm living in gone insane? Have I fallen asleep on my sun lounger, and this is a terrible nightmare? Please, let me wake up. I know this isn't a dream when I look at my father. There isn't an ounce of guilt written on his face. He steps forward, signs a document, and shakes the hand of the man who now owns me. I gulp and try to swallow back down the bile forming in the pit of my stomach. The other men handing over their daughters do the same. None of them show remorse. They're clearly happy to commit crimes against the fundamental human right to freedom.

"Nicholas."

The prick who branded me steps forward with a limp. He bends down and rubs his knee where I kicked him. I wish I could have got him in the balls before he can do any worse damage.

"Your Grace," He addresses his father with a formal title, in a stuck up tone. Ok, it's a deep masculine voice of the type that I might have once dreamed of, but now, I wouldn't touch him with a barge pole. A man's the last thing on my mind. Getting the hell out of this place and as far away as possible from these nutcases, is all I want to do. I survey my surroundings while the men continue to procrastinate and congratulate themselves on being chauvinist pigs. There's the door I came in, but I can't get to it from the stage with the crowd of people surrounding me. There are no windows in this room. What the hell? What kind of place has no windows? Oh yeah, secret society, a room that a bunch of freaks want to keep hidden. I shake my head. I never thought I'd use the language that's running through my head, but I'm pissed off. How could my father do this to me? He's always been strict, but I didn't realize why. I, at least, thought he loved me. He can't if he's willing to put me through this. Does my mother know what's happening? Is she a part of this? She'll be so distraught if she doesn't. Theo, oh god. I don't think I can do this. Despite trying my hardest to keep it in, a tear escapes and tumbles down my cheek. I wipe it away with the back of my hand. I can't allow them to see weakness in me. I tell myself to bide my time. I'll escape this.

The Duke's penetrating voice refocuses my thoughts onto what's happening in the room.

"Welcome, ladies, the next few weeks will decide your future, but before all that, let me introduce you to my son, Nicholas, Earl Lullington. To one of you, he'll be a future husband. To the rest, a nightmare that will haunt your dreams for whatever time you have left." The smile adorning the Duke's face, as he speaks, sends shivers down my spine. How can a man be so evil?

Nicholas stands proudly next to his father with an equally arrogant expression on his face.

"Good evening, ladies. I'm glad to meet you all. Over the next few weeks, you'll be living here at Oakfield Hall and perform tasks to determine which one of you is suitable to be my wife. I have high expectations and will demand complete acquiescence. Any defiance will be dealt with severely. You're mine, to do whatever I wish with. That's the power of my succession. I hope that you'll be able to relax and enjoy yourselves, though."

What, before or after the brand on my leg stops hurting and heals? I think but keep my mouth shut. Now isn't the time to insult my wonderfully hospitable hosts.

"Thank you, Nicholas, we have five girls here. The rules state only three are allowed to enter the final stages of marriage choice. I need you to, now, choose two girls who'll not go any further." My heart starts to beat faster. I have a way out of this nightmare. I can hope he doesn't choose me, and I can leave this place and London. I'm not going back home with my father. I'll go to Oxford and find Tammy. She'll look after me until I can figure something else out.

"Ladies on your feet and form a line for inspection," the Duke orders, and one of the men who held me down comes my way. I'm not going to be manhandled again. I get to my feet and form a line with the other girls. I'm standing next to Lady Joanna Nethercutt. She stands with her weight balanced on the leg not branded. Her eyes are red from crying, but she tries her hardest, now, to suppress the tears.

Nicholas struts over to us with a confident swagger. I want to dig my nails into his eyes and rip the balls from his body. He walks up and down the line, taking in everything about us. When he gets to me, I face him down. I'll not be shown to be weak in his eyes. I'm not a feeble woman as these men clearly think. If he chooses me to stay, I'll make his life hell and not the other way round. He'd do better to get rid of me, now, if he wants the meek and mild little wife, who'll go to his bed willingly, because I never will. Even when hell freezes over. He shakes his head and laughs.

"There are five girls: Amelia, Daphne, Elizabeth, Joanne and Victoria. Which three do you choose to take forward?" the Duke asks of his son.

"Elizabeth," he names the first one, and it figures, she's the bitch who ignored me at the start. They'd make a good couple. Why doesn't he just choose her now, and the rest of us can go home?

"Amelia." A small girl with blonde hair whimpers when her name is spoken. I feel sorry for her but not *that* sorry, since it means there's only a one in three chance of me having to stay here any longer. I can find somewhere with a rose garden and lose myself in the scent. Maybe, I could get a rose tattoo over this thing on my thigh.

"Daphne is free to go." Nicholas states, and the girl screams with delight. Her father curses out loudly — the language coming out of his mouth a complete contrast from the religious ropes he wears.

"So I'm down to two." Nicholas stands in front of Joanna and myself. I think I can hear my heart beating out of my chest. I'm praying my name isn't spoken.

"Victoria you may…" He pauses. Go, say go, I'm pleading within my head.

"Not go anywhere. Joanna's free to go."

I groan long and low with frustration and fear for what comes next. The women named are pushed to the side, and the two not named are grabbed. I try to jostle the guys off Joanna.

"Leave her alone. She wasn't chosen — she's free to go." I ball my fist and punch one of the men. He goes to slap me back, but Nicholas catches his hand and sends him flying off the stage.

"Stop!" the Duke commands, and everyone freezes. He comes up to me and, in a smooth movement, throws me to the floor. I land on my burn, and agony cascades through me. I scream.

"You had to pick the one who's going to cause trouble, didn't you?" he addresses his son with a scowl.

"Why would I want a meek and mild wife when I can have one who puts up a fight?" Nicholas responds, and I try to kick out at him, again. Bastard.

"You…" the Duke addresses me. "Unless you want to spend the rest of the evening locked in the dungeon, I suggest you keep quiet and let me finish this part of the ceremony."

I go to tell him to fuck off, but I think better of it and silence myself with a no-nonsense pout.

"Thank you."

Lady Joanna, Miss Daphne. I'm afraid my son was wrong with his words that you are free to go. You belong to the society now. You may not be in the running to be his wife, but we still own you, and as such, you'll be taken from this place to rooms for rest. Tomorrow evening, you'll be sold to the highest bidder to do with as they please. Take them away."

I gasp, and both girls start to cry. He's going to sell them like slaves. I look to the man who was complaining about Joanna earlier. He's expressionless. This is his daughter — he's going to allow her to be sold to god knows who. I want to scream at him to help her, but when he turns away and leaves the room, I know that it'll make no difference. The men in this room have no respect for women. We're back in centuries of old when women were chattels: bought and sold for gain. I'm pulled to my feet by one of the guards. I don't fight him — I'm tired and weak. I look over my shoulder to Nicholas. He's watching me be dragged away. He wears the mask of many others in this room. I've died and gone to hell.

CHAPTER SIX

NICHOLAS

"Here is your drink, Sir." Reggie places the fine brandy next to me. I need this, after the events of the day. I want nothing more than to jump in my Ferrari and find a warm pussy to pound away my worries. I know that if I leave the house, my father will have his guards find me and drag me back. These women think they have it hard. I'm just as confined by the damn founding documentation of the society as they are. My head is in my hands, and I rub at my temples. I'm shaking.

"Nicholas, drink it." Reggie urges, and I pick the glass up and drain it in one long gulp. I wonder if the burning in my throat compares to the pain, which I inflicted on the girls' legs. How can I be so callous? It'll be nothing compared to the agony ripping through their bodies that they have yet to experience. Reggie pours me another drink and hands me a cigarette. I'm not a big smoker, but I like one with my glass in the evening. I'm sure it should be a cigar, but a cigarette suffices for me. I puff on the nicotine, killing stick, and the smoke mixing with the amber nectar of my drink starts to relax my body. I wave Reggie away, and he disappears to do whatever task he has next on his list. The man is sixty and should be slowing down, not having to deal with this shit.

I pick up the remote and turn on the televisions in front of me. There are three of them, one for each girl. I look at the one labeled Amelia, first. The guards throw her into her room. She's been washed and provided with a long night-gown to sleep in. You know the sort, the ones that your great-grandparents wore in the Victorian ages. Why we have to continue with the awful fashion, I'll never know. Give the girls one of my t-shirts or some pajamas, anything but those lace doilies for god's sake. I make it my mission, tomorrow, to give them some sensible clothes. Amelia looks around the room, and I notice she's still crying. I wonder whether I should have chosen her or not. She's pretty with her blonde hair and blue eyes. I don't lust after her. In fact, I wanted to protect her more, and that's why I chose her. I knew my father would never let the other two girls go. They know too much, now. The society will own them until the day they die — whether that is sooner or later. I saw strength in them, but in Amelia, I see a terrified little girl who needs someone to watch over her. She climbs onto her bed and pulls the covers over her head. I know she won't sleep a wink tonight not until she's exhausted herself with her tears. A strange feeling of guilt sits on my shoulders. I drink it away with another sip of the brandy and turn off that television. I turn to the one labeled Elizabeth, next.

For a girl who's about to be sold into slavery for the rest of her life, Elizabeth's surprisingly happy about being here. It's the reason I chose her. She's been prepared properly.

When the girls are born, they're brought together and christened into the society. Their fathers may raise them telling them of their futures or may keep it a secret. That is their choice, but they must adhere to several rules. The most important being their daughters must remain virgins. If any of them are found not to be, then the girl is disqualified and, from what I've heard of previously, killed. The body is then delivered back to the father who has all his assets taken by the society. What gets me is that nobody has ever talked or gone to a higher authority about what happens here. If my daughter were killed, I'd report it. But then again, my father controls most of the criminal courts in London as well as managing the majority of the government. The culture of fear surrounding us prevents any defectors.

I drink a little more and watch Elizabeth. She, too, wears the ridiculous nightgown but, with a wink to the camera hidden in the wooden paneling of her room, strips it off. How does she know I'm watching? I think she's been a little too well prepared by her father, Lord Bishop of Monchelsea. She climbs into the bed but doesn't get under the covers. Instead, she lays back and parts her legs. I can see everything: her neatly shaved pussy already gleaming with her juices. She runs a finger over her slit from front to back and dips it inside. My cock hardens, but I don't want to touch it. Instead, I make a mental note to check on the validity of this one being a virgin. I turn the screen off and leave her to her intimate act, despite the fact she obviously wanted an audience. I flick the button for the last screen, and the woman who captured my attention in the initial meeting fills it. She's wearing the gown and, apparently, isn't happy with it. I stare intently as she finds what must be a loose seam and pulls it so she can shorten it. The material rips and bares her shapely legs. I find myself leaning forward and hoping she tears too far, and I can get sight of her pussy again. I had a glimpse when she was struggling to prevent herself from being branded. It wasn't bare like Elizabeth's, but it was neatly trimmed. She stops when the gown reaches thigh high, though. Damn it. She goes over to the dressing table and looks at the bottle placed there. We aren't horrible — we make sure that the fathers pack a bag of things that'll make the girls feel at home. Victoria picks up a bottle, and I can just make out that it's aloe vera gel. She smears some over the burn and wraps the torn material around the brand. I shake my head at the care she takes. None of the other girls even thought about dressing the wound. It was the first thing she thought of. I'm sure it's some false hope that it won't leave a mark. She finishes treating her leg and takes out the French plait in her hair. Her red waves tumble out, and she sees the brush on the table and uses it to pull her hair back into a neat ponytail. She's exquisite to watch. Calm but with the slight tremor in her hand, I can see her apprehension. I pick up my brandy glass and noticing it's empty, I ring the bell for Reggie. He appears almost immediately and tops me up.

"Are they doing alright?" he asks and motions toward the screen.

"As can be expected," I reply, still engrossed in Victoria. She's looking around the room for an escape route now. She tries the bedroom door — it's locked, and the window is the same. She stamps her foot in frustration.

"Which one is that?" Reggie queries.

"Victoria Hamilton."

"Viscount Mayfield's daughter?"

"Yes."

"She seems braver than your mother. I remember standing here with your father watching her. I'd just been promoted to butler, despite being young. He was laughing at the girls as he watched them cry and try to find their way out. He picked your mother out immediately as the weakest of the three. I knew she wouldn't last long, from that moment." He goes quiet and becomes lost in his private thoughts. I don't ask him to share them. I know he'll clam up. He always does — small snippets about my mother are all I'll ever get out of him. He bows and leaves me alone again.

My attention re-focuses on Victoria. She's at the bookcase. As her fingers skim the titles, she stops on one and pulls it out — I can't make out the name from the angle I have. It doesn't matter because she pushes that one back in when she sees another that captures her attention. I recognize this one. It's a book on art. It's one of my personal favorites, and we have several copies around the house. It lists the more obscure paintings by some of the most famous artists in the world.

She looks between a Queen Anne chair, in the corner of the room, and the four poster bed as she debates on which one to choose. She finally decides on the chair and settles in it with the book. I pull up the file on her, on my phone.

The Honorable Victoria Hamilton
    Born: 25th July 1997

I skip past the bit that tells me about her breeding, education, and physical attributes to the hobbies part.

Hobbies:

Victoria swims regularly, at least one hundred lengths a day. She doesn't have many interests that allow her to leave the house as has been specified in the documentation regarding the raising of a chosen girl. She enjoys baking with Viscountess Mayfield and has been painting since a young age. The only time I allow her out, under my strict supervision, is to visit the art galleries of London. She reads an abundance of material on the subject. I'm sure this will be of interest to Earl Lullington.

The passage written by her father does indeed interest me. Art is my life. The pictures in the hallway — she was studying them. I smirk at my intelligent little girl.

Victoria yawns in her chair, and her eyelids flutter. She's becoming exhausted from her long day, no matter how much she wants to continue reading the book that interests her. She yawns again, and her head falls forward. A few seconds later the book drops to the floor open on the page showing Van Gogh's Poppies. I knew it. I turn the screen off and let her sleep peacefully. Tomorrow is a new day, and I think my father is correct: Victoria Hamilton is going to cause a great deal of trouble.

CHAPTER SEVEN

VICTORIA

’m out at a party with Tammy. We're dancing away to the latest craze, and two guys are behind us with their hands on our backsides. I turn around and lock lips with my man. His deep, raspy voice tells me he wants to fuck me hard tonight. I won't be able to walk the next day. I pull away, and the face of Nicholas Cavendish greets me.

I sit bolt upright in the bed when the door slams, and men flood in, I realize I was dreaming. I'm confused. I'm in bed, but I fell asleep in the chair. I look at the dressing table, and the book I was reading is placed on it. How did I get here?

"Good morning, Miss Hamilton." It's then I realize that the Duke of Oakfield stands at the foot of my bed. My eyes widen as I take in him and Nicholas, plus two other men.

"Get out," I shout.

"Manners. When you address me, you'll call me, Your Grace."

"Get out, you fucking pervert."

I see the little smirk on Nicholas' face, but the Duke's far from having a sense of humor. If steam could come out of his ears, I think it would be right now.

"Playing the little bitch won't get you anywhere." He rips the sheets from my grasp and throws them onto the floor. I'm left on the bed in only the nightgown, which I made shorter yesterday. I'm beginning to regret that decision.

"If you've brought him here to try and take me for his wife" –I look at Nicholas who is motionless– "then, it'll be rape because I don't consent to this."

The Duke laughs.

"What kind of savages do you take us for."

"Err. The type that kidnaps and brands girls for their pleasure."

He steps forward and slaps me hard on the cheek. I see stars but also see Nicholas' fists clench.

"If I didn't need you pure because my son chose you, I would teach you a few lessons about just what type of man I am, and why you need to respect me," the duke snarls. "This is my private physician, Dr. Fredrick Fallen, and this is my lawyer, Sir Percy Cleveland. When your father gave you to us, he made assurances as to your virginity. As part of the requirements of the rules governing our society, you'll be tested to ensure that is, in fact, the case."

"I'll what?" I pull my legs up to my chest and use the pillow to hide my modesty.

"Don't play dumb. Dr. Fallen here will check to see that your hymen is still intact."

"Hell no." I scramble from the bed and grab the nearest implement to protect myself. A lamp. "If any of you try to come near me, Dr. Fallen will need to spend his time stitching your head back together rather than sticking his fingers up my vagina."

The Duke sighs, "Nicholas, why couldn't you have chosen the docile one?"

"Less fun to break," he replies and steps closer to me.

"Try it, and there won't be anyone for us to marry."

He picks up the book on my table instead.

"Interesting book choice." He opens it to the page that shows the Van Gogh painting. It's then I realize he was the one to move me. I do a mental tally in my head to see if it feels as though I've been violated anywhere. Maybe he drugged me.

"You get your kicks from sneaking into a sleeping lady's room? Mind you, it's probably the only way you can get someone near that small dick, you're no doubt packing."

"My dick's the thing of your dreams, Victoria." He gives me an arrogant grin.

"Get a life." I roll my eyes.

"I've got three to play with at the moment, thank you."

"Enough." The Duke interrupts our bickering. "Guards."

Four men file into the room.

"We don't have time for this. We need to see the other two girls, and then, we have the sale. Disarm her and hold her down."

"Is that the only way you can get a woman?" I make a swing for the Duke, but one of the guards rips the lamp from my hand. The others grab for me, and I'm dragged, kicking and screaming, toward the bed. I don't want this. I want to disappear back into my dream, preferably without Nicholas Cavendish in it. Actually, no, I could happily be dreaming of him and his father getting castrated. Instead, I'm thrown face down on the bed. The guards each pin one of my legs and arms down. I thrash my head around, trying to shift enough to sink my teeth into flesh, but a massive hand pushes it down so I can no longer move. I flick my eyes up to see that it belongs to the Duke. He's sadistic in his triumph over me. I feel my hips lifted and my gown pulled around my waist, bared to the eight men in the room. My ass in the air like a wild animal ready for the taking. Nicholas comes to the head of the bed. I watch his every move. He's like a stalking lion, surveying his prey. He plays with the cufflinks that peep out from his suit jacket. They are gold in color and emblazoned with the symbol, which will forever scar my skin. In this position, I have no dignity, and he's enjoying it.

"Don't fight — relax, and it won't hurt so much." He orders. I spit at him in a fury, and he wipes it away with a smirk. His eyes never leave mine as two fingers are inserted into my body. I experience severe pain because I'm dry and not prepared — the doctor is tearing me apart. I screw my face up, but I can't take my eyes off Nicholas'. I want him to die, painfully, slowly, and maybe, with two fingers stuck up his ass. No, make that a whole fist.

The doctor gropes around inside me, and I can't help but feel violated.

"She's a virgin," he announces and withdraws his fingers. I breathe a sigh of relief. Nicholas looks pleased.

"I could've told you that without the need for all of this." I try to struggle, but they still hold me down.

"Give her the injection." The Duke's voice comes from behind me. There's silence for a few moments except for the movement of the doctor, and then, I feel a sharp jab in my bottom. Everyone holding me lets me go, and I scramble as far away, to the other side of the room, as possible.

"What did you do to me?"

"A contraception injection. No babies before marriage allowed here. It wouldn't be proper," the Duke answers me.

"Proper? After what you just did, you're talking to me about what's proper and what isn't."

The Duke ignores me.

"Is there anything you can give her to calm her down a bit? Her constant moaning has given me a migraine and become far too tedious." He glares at me, but I stick my tongue out and look for another weapon. If any of them come near me, then they're going to lose their heads.

"Leave her, Your Grace," Nicholas interrupts. "I think that when she sees what happens next, she'll behave." He turns on his heels with no further explanation and leaves. The Duke looks at me and cackles, making my blood freeze, and my body slump to the floor in defeat.

CHAPTER EIGHT

NICHOLAS

I watch the girls file into the room. Those to be sold are led to the stage while the ones I chose to keep, for now, are being ushered to seats and told to sit. I watch them. Elizabeth's her usual confident self and flashes a seductive smile in my direction when she walks in. Amelia's barely holding it together — she seems like she's a zombie. Victoria's quieter than usual. I think I'm getting used to her having a mouth on her and miss the backchat. She doesn't curse the guard who pushes her down on the chair, and I notice she's walking a little stiffly. She struggled a lot this morning. Her muscles must be hurting from the exertion. She needs to learn to go with what's happening here. Nothing can change the future.

"Welcome back, gentlemen." My father starts proceedings with his confident address. The room instantly silences, and we all focus our attention on him. "Let's get straight down to business. We have two ladies here, Lady Joanna Nethercutt and Daphne Knight. I'm going to start with Miss Knight. Daphne step forward please."

The small brunette does as she's told — her eyes are red-rimmed with tears. What is it with all these women and tears? Why don't they just accept what's happening and get on with it? None of us have a choice in this farce. At least they'll have a roof over their head at the end of it. There are plenty of people on the streets of England who have nothing. That's what we all fear, after all, nothing — no life, no wealth, no love. I snort at the last one. Oakfield Hall has never had any love within its walls.

I look over at Victoria again. I can see her cheeks are flushed red — she's getting angry. I find myself wanting her to scream and shout and interrupt the proceedings. I like her spirit. She must feel me watching her because she turns her attention in my direction. She rolls her eyes in derision. I smirk, and she focuses back on the sale.

"Daphne's an accomplished musician. She plays a variety of instruments including the piano, violin, and harp. She's been privately educated to a high standard and particularly enjoys reading classics. She'd make a good governess and tutor for the next generation of our society." My father pauses and Laird McGuire, a despicable man from the Scottish Borders, calls out.

"Enough with the tedious facts. What aboot the interesting ones. How big are her boobs? I'm assuming ye've checked she's a virgin. A dinnae want sloppy seconds from yer son."

"Laird McGuire, I can assure you that she's been checked and is innocent. Her vital statistics are in the pack, which you were handed on arrival." My father doesn't like this man. In fact, he has a thing against most Scots. He believes them brutish and uncouth. I hear him often chastising my ancestors for allowing them into the society. Thankfully, Laird McGuire and Laird McDonald, who is also loud but less of an oaf, are the only two of Scottish origin.

"A bet she takes a good whipping. Her skin is pasty white. Will color red in a matter o' moments. A think I'll be bidding on this one. Get ma cock up her ass within the hour and fuck her senseless."

Daphne lets out a whimpering cry at his comment, and Joanna steps forward and holds her up.

"Laird McGuire. These are ladies, not whores. Please, have some decorum if, that is, you intend to place a bid on Miss Knight. If you simply want a body to engage in sadistic acts, then my butler will provide you with a number to contact."

"We have a right to bid on these pieces of meat. Ye canae be telling me how to treat them." Laird McGuire is on his feet and waving his fist at my father.

"No, I can't tell you how to treat them, but I can outbid you and see that you don't win."

I chuckle under my breath. My father doesn't want this girl. He doesn't care what happens to her. If he did buy her, he'd be the one fucking her up the ass within the hour. He just wants to put this man, that he hates, in his place.

"Should we continue, Your Grace."

I step up onto the stage and link my arm around Daphne's. Her legs are weak, and she leans on me.

"Please, don't sell me to him," she whispers to me.

"You'll be sold to the highest bidder, no matter who it is. Those are the rules. Accept it," I reply heartlessly.

My father comes to stand on the other side of her, and Laird McGuire sits down with a scowl on his face.

"Shall we start at one hundred thousand?" my father offers to the crowd.

Laird McGuire puts his hand up.

"Two hundred thousand." Comes from Earl Winters, an older man with a penchant for young girls. He's kind though, and she'll be treated like a princess. He has a daddy complex. Don't get me wrong — he'll fuck her, but she'll be looked after.

"Three," Lord McGuire counters.

"Four," Winters offers in reply.

"Five," A new voice enters the fray. I don't recognize it at first but purse my lips in a smile when I see that it's one of my old friends, Viscount West. This just got interesting.

Lord McGuire waves his hand in defeat, and my father smirks with triumph. West must be bidding on his behalf. Fuck, the poor girl's screwed.

"Earl Winters?" my father asks.

"Five and a half."

"Six." West counters right back.

"She's not worth anything more. I'm out." Earl Winters accepts defeat, and the hammer comes down on Daphne Knight. I can't help feeling a little sick. If my father has anything to do with this purchase, then the girl wrapped tightly around my arm has little time left to live. There's nothing I can do, though. I hand her over to West and go to the next girl.

Lady Joanna Nethercutt was a difficult one to give up. If Victoria hadn't intrigued me as much as she did, then I would have chosen Joanna. She's the prettier of the two. All I can do is pray that McGuire has learned his lesson and won't try to bid on this one.

My father gives the same speech about the girl again. This one is again highly educated and enjoys reading. She's also an avid motor car fan. I picture her laid out over my Ferrari. It would be a damn good sight.

"What shall we start at?"

"Two hundred." Earl Winters puts his hand up again.

"Three hundred," Laird McGuire replies, and I groan.

"Four." Viscount Mayfield steps through the crowd. Victoria gasps when she sees her father.

"Five," McGuire offers.

"Six," Winters adds.

Victoria is shaking her head. She has tears in her eyes, now. Mayfield bidding isn't something I'd expected. I know his wife came from my father's 'not chosen' girls. I wonder if he's continuing the tradition.

"Seven." He stands in the center of the room with his arms folded.

"Wit that frizzy hair I'm no paying any more. Ye can have her." McGuire gets up and stomps from the room.

"Eight." Earl Winters comes forward to stand next to my father.

I'm on edge as to where this is going.

"One million," Mayfield responds.

Earl Winter's shakes his head in defeat.

"Sold to Viscount Mayfield," my father shouts out.

Victoria gets to her feet and is running toward her father before the guards can stop her. She pulls her fist back and punches him square in the jaw.

Joanna, who has been standing quietly until this moment, screams and falls to her knees. She fears the worse.

I jump down from the stage and pull Victoria off her father. She's swearing and shouting at him still.

"You bastard, how could you? I hate you. I want you fucking dead. If you hurt Theo, I'll hunt you down and kill you myself." She's struggling in my arms. She doesn't even realize I'm holding her. All she wants to do is scratch her father's eyes out. She makes some ground when my dress shoes slip on the floor. I regain my footing just as she goes to pull another punch.

"Stop it," my father shouts, but she doesn't listen. Two other guards pull her away from me and flatten her to the ground. She's trying to kick out, but they use their weight to keep her in place.

"Viscount Mayfield, take your purchase and go," my father orders.

Victoria's father looks down at where she's being manhandled on the floor. I don't know about his daughter wanting to punch his lights out, but I'm struggling to keep the lid on my composure. My fists are balled, but I'm not moving. I can't.

He shakes his head.

"I thought she was brought up better than this, Your Grace. I'm embarrassed. Punish her as you see fit." I'm walking closer to Mayfield when he speaks. I have my hands on the collar of his shirt, and I'm dragging him away.

"The Duke said leave," I order with spit flying into his face.

"Theo," Victoria screams from the floor.

"When she regains her composure, tell her that I'll never

hurt my son. Lady Joanna is to be his wife. It's a family tradition — for the procreation of the next generation."

"Get out!" I'm inches from the Viscount's face. I have no further words for this man. He disgusts me. Violence is the only way that I can express what I feel.

"Nicholas," my father commands me, and I step away. The Viscount and his purchase leave. The other members of the society who attended the sale also start to file out. I go to the side of the room and calm myself. I can still hear Victoria's small whimpers for her brother.

"Well, after all that excitement, I think we need a rest before tonight," my father addresses the two girls who are still seated. "Ladies, during your stay you have free rein of the house, except for the second floor. Those are private quarters for myself and my son. If you are caught there, you'll be punished. Please make yourself at home. We have a society meeting tonight, and you'll be expected to join us. I'll have garments and instructions sent to you later. In the meantime, enjoy your day. Cooks are available for your particular diets. We have a pool in which you can swim. However, the gardens are off limits, at present. Please go." The two ladies get to their feet and shuffle out.

"What do we do with her?" one of my father's guards asks and points to Victoria.

"Put her in her room. She gets the same treatment as the other's, unless Nicholas decides she needs punishment."

I spin on my heels to face him.

"Punishment?" I question.

"If she's to be your wife, then she should show more decorum. I'm beginning to think she doesn't know the meaning of the word with her outbursts."

My father's testing me. He's never thought me strong enough to be his heir. I'm the only option, though. He would never choose… I shake that thought from my head.

"Place her in her room and lock the door until this evening. No food."

"Yes, Sir," the guard replies and pulls Victoria to her feet. She purses her lips at me, and I can see the curses flashing through her brain. She's imagining me boiling in a vat of oil. She's imagining bringing down the whole society.

"Wait." I stop them as they begin to pull her away.

"Make sure you remove all the books from her room. She's to think on her behavior."

"You bastard," she spits at me.

"Learn your lesson, little girl."

I turn and walk away as she continues to call me names.

CHAPTER NINE

VICTORIA

I've spent most of the day pacing my bedroom. I've searched again, four times to be precise, for an exit from this house. Everyone here's completely insane. My father bought a girl for my brother — my mother was paid for, by him, and I was bred purposely to go through this fucking charade. My head is a mess, and I just want to sleep, but I know that it'll never come. I'm in an endless nightmare, but not the sort where there are monsters under your bed. No, I'm in the type of horror where the monsters are real and controlling my future like I am a puppet on strings. Future — do I even have one? My stomach lurches. What happens if I'm not chosen? God, do I want to be selected? At least I know the devil I'll be with. I think back to the Scottish oaf who was trying to buy the girls. The thought of being sold to him would kill me. Literally, I imagine, after he's used my body in ways that no woman should have to suffer. I need to try and get my head together. I'm hungry. Nicholas banned me from having food today, and for the last hour, my stomach has protested his decision. I'm not going to let him beat me though. No fucking way. I'd rather die...I stop that line of thought again because, here, it's too real a possibility. Maybe, I should just keep quiet tonight. Do whatever it is they have planned and come back to bed and sleep. Sleep will make my head clearer, and if I can explore the house tomorrow, I might find a way out or, at least, get my books back.

I dress in the white gown they've left out for me. This one is silky and not like the white dress that was provided for my arrival. A maid comes into the room and ties my hair back in what seems like the requisite French pleat. I ask her if she's able to tell me what's happening tonight, but she doesn't reply. I guess they're allowed to make us look pretty but not actually talk to us. How can they let us go through this? Clearly money speaks louder than kidnapping and rape.

At precisely eight in the evening, I'm led into a banqueting hall with the other two girls. Amelia looked awful this morning but seems much calmer now. Elizabeth looks her usual stuck-up bitch self. I don't like her in the slightest. We're brought to stand at the head of the table where the Duke sits. Nicholas sits to his left-hand side in a formal dinner suit. It looks good on him. I chastise myself for even thinking that.

"Welcome, ladies." I look over the table. There must be at least forty men sitting around it. I recognize a lot of faces from functions my father has had in previous years. I look for him, but he isn't here, thankfully. I'm not sure I'd be able to behave, as I promised myself, if I had to watch him continue to act like a man who deserves to have his balls chopped off with a machete. The men range from their early thirties to late eighties, in age. I guess they're the men of title within each family. When one dies, another inherits and takes his place in this society of freaks. I memorize each face. One day, I'll get my revenge on them.

"As you can see, we have a meal here tonight to celebrate my son's birthday, and the start of his journey into his succession. You are joining us as his prospective brides. Our society needs a strong woman to stand at Nicholas' side. He will become the greatest leader we've ever had — I'm sure of that. I've taught him everything he knows, after all." The Duke laughs at his joke, and everyone joins in. Eventually, he holds his hand up to silence them. "Over the next few weeks, to help Nicholas choose between you, you'll be given tasks to complete. Tonight is the first of those."

He gestures to where three marble plinths stand at the other end of the table. I hadn't noticed them before, but they suddenly feel rather ominous and are the only things I can focus on. Our guard ushers us down to the marble stones. I'm naked under my dress, and I can foresee what's going to happen. No fucking way am I going to stand here, while they eat, in just a dressing gown, or, as I suspect, without it!

"Ladies, remove your dressing gowns and stand on the plinths. We're getting hungry for our dinner and can't start until you are in place."

Elizabeth eagerly removes her cloak and jumps up. She juts her hip out to emphasize the curves of her body. Amelia, like me, stands with the gown pulled closely to her chest.

"Nicholas!" The Duke's voice booms from the other end of the room. The Earl stands and comes over to us.

"Ladies, remove your gowns, or I'll do it for you?" His

deep voice is commanding in an 'I want to punch him in the head' way.

Neither of us moves. He takes a step closer to Amelia, and she instantly panics and drops the gown. She's up on the plinth, in a matter of seconds. She stands with an arm over her chest and a hand covering her lady parts.

"Hands at your side."

She shakes her head

"Please," she whispers.

"Sides," he demands again. I want to tell him to leave her alone, but I have to behave. I don't want to be naked, but I do want to be allowed out of the room, relatively unscathed. She reluctantly drops her arms.

"You have nothing to be ashamed of. You have pretty breasts, but I think I'll send someone in to wax your pussy tomorrow. I prefer a little less hair on my women."

I can't help but look and see she has a bit of a bush thing going on down there.

"Sorry, my father wouldn't let me cut it," she stammers.

"Not a problem," he responds and turns to me. "I'm not even going to ask you again to remove your gown because I know the answer will be 'no'." He steps forward, and before I know what's happening, the material lays in tatters on the floor.

Any thought of behaving goes out of the window when I spit in his face. He wipes it away with a smirk.

"If you want to swap saliva, I have a much better way of doing it. Now, get up there and behave." He looks me up and down with a lick of his lips. My skin heats in a good way. What the hell? I jump up on the plinth and put my hands at my side in the hope that he'll go away.

"Good girl."

I stick my tongue out at him when he walks away. It's childish but the only retort I can give.

"I have better uses for your tongue as well," he shouts over his shoulder. How did he know?

"Go to hell," I shout after him.

He turns and faces me. The playfulness, which was on his features moments ago, is gone. His eyebrows gather in, and he closes his eyes,

"I'm already there. Haven't you recognized it yet?"

His eyes flash open, and there's pain written in the blue hues of his irises. I don't respond — I'm too shocked. He returns to his seat, and to the congratulations of the men.

"Ladies, as my son's property, only he is allowed to touch you intimately. You have no say in the matter, and it'll serve you to learn that lesson quickly. The courtesy is also extended to me as the ruler of the society. The others at the table are allowed to touch you but not between your thighs, unless expressly given permission."

I snort quietly. If any of them try to touch me, I'll break their bloody hands.

"Miss Hamilton, do you have something to say?"

Shit!

"No, Your Grace."

"Oh, come on," he chuckles. "I'm sure the entire table would love to hear your feelings on what's wrong with the world."

"The world's fine. It's the people in this asylum that have lost the plot." Me and my stupid mouth. Why won't it be quiet? Shush, I tell it. We want to escape so we need to behave.

"You feel my household is suffering from some kind of insanity." He pushes his chair back and comes toward me. Keep your goddamn mouth shut, I tell myself. Of course, it doesn't work.

"Well, I'm pretty certain normal people don't buy and sell girls."

The Duke stands in front of me now.

"I think you'll find that it was your household that did the buying and the giving away. What am I supposed to do with five pretty girls? I'm just following the natural law of things."

"You're a freak who will get his comeuppance one of these days."

The Duke reaches out and grips me tightly around the throat. The plinths are low, so I'm at the perfect height for him to grab. I can barely breathe as I feel his strong fingers squeeze tighter around my slender neck and lift me off my feet.

"Your Grace." Nicholas pushes his chair back with a loud scrape on the tiled floor.

"Sit down, boy."

"She's mine to punish, not yours."

The Duke drops me, and I tumble back down onto the plinth, gasping for breath. He turns to his son. I can't see the look on his face, but I can feel the tension in the air.

"Sorry, I got ahead of myself for a moment." The Duke faces me again and holds his hand out. I reluctantly accept it and allow myself to be pulled to my feet. Big mistake. The Duke pulls me toward him with a caress to my breast. I want to tell him to get off me, but the look on Nicholas' face distracts me. The pain is back, and there is jealously intermixing with it. He wants to stop his father, but he knows, on this, he can't. This is all a game between him and the Duke. I'm just a pawn in the middle. Can I use that to my advantage?

I step quietly back onto the display stand. I hold my body straight. Years of deportment lessons come in handy. The Duke goes back to his seat at the table, and the entrée is brought in. Elizabeth, Amelia, and I stand there while the food and wine flows at the table. The chatter of the men fills the room. I can here talk of conquests with ladies, discussions about business deals, and I take it all in, learning everything possible, so that I can prepare my fight. I'll not submit to these people without starting a war between them all, if necessary.

The main course is cleared away, and several of the men, now a few glasses of the finest claret down, turn their attention to us ladies. I want to cut their eyes out with the cheese knives that are being placed in front of them, cn the table.

"Gentlemen, you may inspect my son's accuisitions if you wish. It's in the rules that you can touch them. Just remember between the legs is off limits." The last words the Duke speaks are said with a snide smirk at his son.

I brace myself as the men slide back their chairs, causing as eerie scraping sound from the floor. Stay calm, I tell myself — you can get through this. Hell, who am I kidding? I've never been naked before a man in my life, and now, I'm in front of forty plus men looking at me as if I'm a popsicle on a stick.

One of them, a man in his fifties with a comb over and greasy appearance, steps forward toward my plinth.

"Her tits are far too small. Nothing to play with." He

flicks his hand over my breast and pinches the nipple. I ball my fists at my side, knowing I can't move. If I do, I'll hit him, and I'm actually too scared to find out what the punishment for that would be. Someone runs their hand over my backside.

"This is pretty good though." He pinches a cheek. "Nicholas, I bet she takes it great up the ass." He calls over to the Duke's son, who's sitting forward in his chair. His whole body is rigid with tension, and, it appears, he can't bear to look our way. Prick!

The man runs his hand around the lower half of my body. I feel sick, sitting at the back of my throat, but I'm pretty certain that if I hurl on him, it's going to cause problems. He stops his hand just inches from the 'v' between my legs. All of a sudden, he's pulled aside.

"Too close," Nicholas snarls at him.

"I wasn't going to break the rules, My Lord."

The bell rings to signal the next course. The man who had his hands all over me returns to his seat. Nicholas looks up at me.

"Turn around," he snarls.

I go to open my mouth but think better of it and spin on the plinth.

"You two as well," he orders Elizabeth and Amelia. He stomps back to his seat, and the cheese course is served. I don't know if not facing the men is better, or not. I can feel my body shake. What kind of hell is this? Will I survive it?

CHAPTER TEN

NICHOLAS

"Can I get you anything else, Sir?" Reggie pours my second cup of coffee while I finish off the bacon with a poached egg that I always have for my breakfast.

"No, thank you — I'm full." We have the same exchange every morning. I sometimes think I should ask him for an apple just to alter the monotony of the conversation. "Are any of the girls awake?"

"I believe Miss Sandford has called for breakfast in her room today. She's apparently suffering from that 'time of her month' and needs to rest. Miss Amelia has been for a swim and is eating a croissant in the ladies' dining room."

"What about Miss Hamilton?"

"Miss Hamilton has been confined to her room."

"On whose orders?" I place my knife and fork down and look up at him.

"Mine, Sir. She was up early and looking for ways to leave Oakfield Hall. I'm afraid the guards found it rather tiresome after the third escape attempt, so I ordered her to be taken back to her room."

I shake my head and laugh.

"That woman will be the death of me."

"I have a feeling she may be the death of a lot of people before you make your decision," Reggie replies with a shake of his own head.

"Does she have any reading material left in her room?" I ask.

"You've not given me orders to have it returned yet."

"No, I haven't. I tell you what. Have one of the guards escort her to the pool. In her manifesto, it said that she likes to swim one hundred lengths a day. Have them tell her that if she swims that amount, then she'll be rewarded with the return of her books. If she defies, or tries to escape again, then all the furniture will be removed from her room. Hopefully doing something energetic will tire her out a little and placate her."

Reggie motions to look out the window.

"What?"

"I thought that I saw a flying pig, Sir."

"She does provoke that reaction." I push my chair back and go to stand, but I am interrupted by my father's gruff voice from the doorway.

"Who does?"

Reggie looks at me.

"Miss Hamilton." I reluctantly concede, knowing that there's no point in lying to him.

"What has she done now?" He stomps over to his seat at the head of our small family dining table and sits down.

Reggie steps forward and pours him coffee. My father doesn't say thank you.

"Nothing of concern, Your Grace. It's been dealt with." I finally get to my feet and bow to my father with the intention of taking my leave. He doesn't let me go, though.

"Why you had to choose her to continue on, I'll never know."

"She is different from the other girls. I don't know what I want in a wife, yet. I chose the girls that all offer me something unique in the hopes that I make the right decision for the society," I offer in reply.

"She deserves to be tied to a bed and fucked raw."

"If I choose her to be my wife, then I'll make sure I do that."

My father takes a long sip of his coffee.

"She spoiled my fun last night. Having one of the girls was my right, and you left me with one who just lay there and took it. She didn't even scream once."

"Daphne Knight?" I enquire with a hint of frustration in my voice.

"Don't get all high and mighty with me. You knew full well what would happen to her and the other one, when you didn't choose them." Reggie steps forward as my father speaks and places a napkin over his lap. "Full English breakfast, Mr. Hane."

"Of course, Your Grace."

Reggie disappears into the kitchen as fast as his tired legs can carry him.

"Is she still alive?" I ask.

"I don't always kill them." My father purses his lips in disgust.

"No, just leave them completely broken." I want nothing more to do with this conversation. A woman is a precious thing and not there to be beaten to a pulp while you get off in her pussy.

"She was fine when West took her."

"Did he fuck her as well?" I'm fuming.

"She has more than one hole — so of course he did," my father chuckles. I want to rip his head off. "Don't start having morals now. Everything that's happening here is for you and your future. Grow a pair of balls and man up." My father turns his evil eyes on me. They bore into my soul and deny me any hope I have of being innocent. Daphne Knight was brutally raped and beaten last night. She's probably lying dead in a gutter somewhere because of me. I can't change what's happening, but I can try to soften the blow for the three girls left. Once I make my choice, two more will be sold. I can only save one girl and bring her in to the hell I live. At least there, as my wife, I can protect her.

"You and that piece of paper may govern the tasks the girls have to perform, but it doesn't tell me everything that I should do. I'm going to spend time with each of the girls today — a date around the property."

My father lets out a rambunctious laugh.

"What's the point? You just need to marry her, fuck her, and stick a male heir in her belly. Then, once she has given birth, she can go up in the rafters of the house and descend into the kind of obscurity that is only found at the sharp end of a heroin needle — just like your mother."

I step back because I'm on the verge of punching my own father. I can feel my blood boiling with fury, and my hands shaking. I take hold of the back of a chair to ensure that my hands are gripped tightly around something, other than my father's neck.

"Actually, Father" –I stress the alien word with venom– "I would like a loving Mother for any children I have, not a drugged up waste of space like my own was. You always tell me that I'm a disappointment to you. Maybe, if I'd had a caring mother, I might actually have ended up as much of a bastard as you are."

I don't wait for his reply. I don't want to hear it. I'll take the girls out and get to know them better. I'm bound by the document that prescribes my future, but I don't have to do everything the way my father wants. If I'm going to have to marry, I'm going to make sure that it's with a woman who won't be a mess by the time she pushes out my first child. And fuck, I need to look into ways to make sure that any children we have are girls, so, hopefully, I can end this whole sordid charade.

CHAPTER ELEVEN

VICTORIA

A date? The freak wants me to join him for one on one time. What? Is this where he takes our virginity and sees which he likes best? If he thinks that he's getting into the panties, they've finally provided me with, then he has another think coming. I'd sooner chop his bloody dick right off. I bet it's microscopically small and riddled with infections. Covered in warts from all the whores he, no doubt, has shoved it in. I bet the 'virgin' and 'hidden away' clauses haven't been applied to him. All these men are chauvinist and think they can get away with rape and murder. Well I am going to be the one to change all that. I throw the book on 'decorum for a lady' down on the table. I swam a hundred lengths this morning with the promise of books, and I get etiquette ones. Bastard, and a few other choice words, that a lady isn't supposed to know, start to spill from my mouth, but I'm interrupted by a knock on the door. I don't bother to tell whoever it is to go away. They'd probably just remove the door and leave me exposed to everyone if I did that.

"Come in."

One of the guards assigned to me comes in.

"Earl Lullington requests your company in the sitting room."

"Tell him I'm busy studying his etiquette books," I reply without even looking up.

"Maybe I should rephrase my instruction. Earl Lullington wants you in the sitting room. If you refuse, I have orders to drag you there" –he licks his lips when I scowl at him– "by the hair, if needed."

"Well, why didn't you say so?" I reply sarcastically. Getting to my feet, I slip on a pair of ballet pumps. "We must go immediately. I wouldn't want to keep the Earl waiting for a moment. He's just such the gentlemen and his manners..." I roll my eyes.

"I hope he doesn't choose you," the guard replies, and I stop in my tracks.

"What? Scared I might actually be the one bossing you around when I become his wife?"

"No, not at all. I've heard we get time with the leftovers, if you know what I mean." He pushes me against the wall. "I want to hear you screaming in agony while I'm coming inside you,"

I push him away.

"Try it, and I'll have your balls as a necklace," I snarl.

He just laughs and pushes me into the sitting room.

"Jerk," I call back after him.

"Great, I have the rebel, Victoria, and here I was thinking

that you might have learned something from the books I gave you."

Nicholas is sitting in the corner of the room, rubbing his forehead. He looks tired and in his hand is a glass of brandy. He lifts it to his lips and takes a long drink.

"Doesn't that burn your mouth?" I ask.

"No."

"Oh yeah. I forgot you're the devil so it probably seems cold to you."

"Can we cut the crap? You're the third woman I've spent time with today. Amelia gave me one-word answers to my questions, and Elizabeth spent most of it trying to suck my dick. Just be your natural self and not the argumentative bitch you portray. This is happening whether any of us like it or not, so let's make the best of it." He motions to the chair opposite him. "Please sit."

"You're not going to rape me?"

He laughs.

"That's what you thought would happen here?"

"Well, every time I've seen you so far, I've been manhandled and naked. It doesn't set a very high expectation." I raise an eyebrow at him while taking a seat. He slides me a glass of brandy across the table. I catch it, pick it up, and sniff it.

"It hasn't got drugs in it."

I take a little sip and am satisfied that I'm not being plied with Rohypnol.

"You'll have to forgive me for being skeptical."

"I'm not the monster you think I am."

"Am I free to go home then?"

"No." He takes a drink, and I copy. I lick my lips to take away the residue brandy on them.

"Then, I'm afraid, you're a monster and always will be. Real men don't need to kidnap and imprison women to choose a bride. They go out on dates, like normal people." I cross one of my legs over the other. He watches my thighs rub together in the tight fabric of the skinny jeans that I'm wearing.

"Which is why I asked you here."

"You think this counts as a date?" I snort a contemptuous laugh.

"It's the best I can offer. This isn't prescribed in the governing document. It's something I want to do, though."

"Impress us with your witty repertoire in the hope that one of us falls in love with your good looks and humor and agrees to marry you. I don't think that's going to happen. Not unless they're as insane as every man in this place."

He sits forward in his chair and brushes his hand through his hair. It's longer on the top than at the sides and ruffles down to leave him with a sexy bed head.

"You know, I thought the bravado was all an act, but I'm beginning to see that you really are a bitch."

"I'm not a bitch. The situation has just made me a little angry," I interrupt and get to my feet ready to storm away.

"No, you're a spoiled little rich girl. I bet Daddy has always given you what you wanted all your life?" He gets to his feet and grabs my arm and turns me around to face him. I try to pull away, but he holds my arm tightly. "At least you've had twenty-one years of a normal life. I've known about having to force a woman to marry me almost since I was born. It was the first thing I learned, pretty much, before

I could even talk. That kind of messes with a kid's head, knowing his life is mapped out for him, and there's nothing he can do about it."

I try to pull away again but can feel his strong grip tighten and dig into my slender arm.

"You think my life has been normal? It's been far from it. Maybe knowing about my future would have made my childhood more understandable," I respond and give up struggling. I lean further into him, so our faces are inches away from each other. I am so angry. "My childhood was spent in the company of a governess. I watched my brother and my only friend, a maid's daughter, go off to school and come home talking about all the friends they made. They would go to parties, the park, concerts. Every single time I asked to go, I was told 'no'. If I left the house, it was under my father's supervision. I dreamed of going to university, of getting away, having a life, and learning more about art. But my father's answer was always the same - that I didn't need to work, so what would be the point in me learning things like that? I spent day after day alone. I had no idea why, until I was brought here. You think that's a normal life? Then, you're a bigger fool than you look. You may have known you would become a monster, but I had no idea I would become your victim."

He winces at my words. He lets me go and stumbles back into his chair. I should run away while I can, but my feet won't take me. Instead, I stay still, my chest heaving as I try to calm myself, after my fiery explosion.

"I went to university and studied Art. It was fun. What would your specialty have been?"

"My what?" My voice is quiet now.

"What would you have focused on? Fine arts? History of Art? Digital Arts?"

"History."

"I did digital. Art on computers. Why history?"

I look back at the chair, and he nods for me to sit.

"I like learning about paintings, the history behind them, and the artist who painted them. I like learning why they made certain strokes the way they did, and what it reflects about them in the painting."

"I've seen you looking at all the paintings around the house." He relaxes back into his chair and crosses his left ankle over his right leg. I sit forward in mine. I'm still anxious being here and want to be ready to run, should I need to.

"You have some good examples. Do they come from the Duke's work with the London galleries?"

"He's well connected when it comes to purchasing artwork. It helps him get the ones he wants."

I laugh — it's a sweet and genuine chuckle, which catches me by surprise. I've no idea where the sound comes from.

"What?" he asks curiously. He is intrigued to know what has triggered me to let my guard down around him.

"I was just thinking. I hope that those contacts didn't advise him to spend a lot of money on Van Gogh's Poppies. I doubt that's the original since it was stolen eight years ago in Egypt."

It's his turn to laugh, this time. I feel as though it's a private joke he's not ready to share with me.

"I don't know the price my father paid. It would serve him right if he had indeed been tricked. He's too pretentious when it comes to art. He likes the finest and will often over-look pieces by more modern artists."

"Modern artists are just as good as the Old Masters, in my mind. Is that why you chose digital to specialize in?" I'm slightly scared of the accord we have formed. I know my facts when it comes to art. For someone with no formal quali-fications, I'm well read. Discussing masterpieces with someone is enjoyable.

"I learned a lot about fine arts and history from my father. I guess choosing digital art was my way of fighting against what he expected."

"You and your father seem to do that a lot."

"Can we get off the conversation of my father, please. It leaves a bitter taste in my mouth." He shuts down the conversation with no room for me to continue it, in any way.

"Sorry." I pick up my glass and drink the last mouthful of brandy. He holds the bottle up to offer more.

"No, thank you. My father never allowed me to drink a lot. It's probably best I don't have too much."

"Did your father allow you to do anything?" he enquires with genuine interest.

"Not really. I had my friend, Tamara, my maid's daughter. I was allowed out once to a restaurant with her. But I had to have a bodyguard with me, and even then, my father called us home before dessert when he found out that several male friends of Tamara's had arrived at the place we were eating." I pause and go silent. I'm trying to find a good memory of my father. Currently, they're all tainted with the hate I now feel toward him. "He once allowed me to go to an art sale. He brought a Van Gogh picture there. It was a wonderful experience, even if I did almost go into shock when he offered twenty million for the picture."

"Twenty million? That's a lot."

"Yes, you would think that he'd have it locked away never to see the light of day, but he displays in our dining room, sometimes." I laugh again, and he smiles at me. The conversation we're having is natural and not strained, but I still feel nervous because of the situation I'm in.

"I'll have all your art books returned, so you can read more about the history of paintings."

My good mood is sullied. He's just reminded me that I'm a slave here. I can do nothing that he, himself, doesn't allow. I sit a little more upright in my chair, and my manicured nails grip the seat.

"I'm to be here a long time, then?"

"A while longer."

"And then?"

"Depends on my choice."

"So my fate, my life, rests in your hands?" I purse my lips together, and I can feel the anger rising in me again.

"It does."

I shake my head.

"I don't get it. You tell me you don't want to marry, but yet you continue with this," –I hold my hands out– "whatever it is. Put a stop to it. Let us go."

He sighs heavily.

"I can't do that."

"Why not?"

"Because it's my fate, just as it's yours. It's my birthright, nothing will ever change that. Please, Victoria, just accept what's happening, and it'll all be much easier for you." He gets to his feet while speaking and holds his hand out to me. I look down at his hand as though it's severely infected with all manner of diseases. He actually expected me just to accept this.

"I see it, now. You're a coward. That's why you go along with this. You may be resigned to the legacy of your succession." –I get to my feet and push past him with surprising strength and head to the door– "I never will be, though. You and your father have started a war. One you won't win."

CHAPTER TWELVE

NICHOLAS

I shake the three-quarters empty decanter of brandy. I think I should stop drinking. Since Victoria left me alone with her stinging words, I've drunk another three glasses. I'm not inebriated, but I'm on the way. I need to keep my wits about me while my father's on his mission to have me married off and not in a way I care to.

It is getting late. I get to my feet and stretch my legs out. I must've been seated in the same chair for a couple of hours. I'm an energetic person, most of the time. I love to go to the gym, swim, play tennis, horse ride, and drive cars really fast. Sitting down reflecting on life isn't something that I do all that often, but I'm feeling lethargic and have no desire to exercise. Maybe reading for a bit will quieten my mind and send me to sleep. I stumble in the dark to the library. The great-grandfather clock strikes eleven at night. Damn, I really was sitting there for a long time. I run a finger over the shelves searching for something that captures my attention enough to read. Nothing. Most of these books I've read, at some point in time — the remainder are just too old and boring. I turn around to look at the other side of the room, and my gaze goes instantly to the antique chest of drawers that sits proudly by the heavily carved door at the entrance to the room. My chest tightens — I know it's time as I take slow steps closer, toward the unit. I pull open the drawer, containing my mother's diary, which she wrote after she was brought to Oakfield Hall for the first time. My father's arrogant enough to just leave it lying around. The information it contains, I've been told, is potentially destructive. But then, I'm sure my father would just claim madness as the reason for my mother's words. I pull the diary out and stroke the embroidered cover. It's covered in the most elegant silk and etched with a monochrome of her name, Katherine. I was five when she died. She was only a year older than I am now. I barely even remember her. I open the cover and turn to the first page.

"My life changed today. I don't know if it'll be for the better or worse yet. All I know is that it has changed.

I was brought to Oakfield Hall to be entered into a contest to become the wife of Henry Cavendish. My father had told me it would happen when I turned twenty-one, but that doesn't make it any easier, leaving everything I know behind. This place is full of men. I don't see any women except for six other terrified girls like myself. The current Duchess of Oakfield keeps to herself and looks so sad.

There's something malevolent lurking beneath the surface here as well. I was branded. That doesn't seem normal, but in this place I don't know what is right or wrong anymore."

I wince at the thought of my mother being permanently scarred in the same way as the girls. She was my mother and shouldn't have been treated that way. Now, I'm just being ridiculous. I come from a long line of women who were chosen in the same way. I flick through a few pages.

"We had a horrible task today. I can't even write about it. It broke me. I'm not that person. I don't do these things. Why have I been put in this position?"

I turn more pages, unable to read about the tasks my mother had to endure.

"Henry Cavendish made his decision today. He chose me. The other girls were taken away, and I heard their screams most of the night as the other men in the society took turns with them. I feel so guilty. Why did he decide on me? I'm nothing special. We're to be married tomorrow. I don't think I've ever been so scared in my life. Henry isn't a nice man. He takes delight in what he's done to us. He isn't a man with humanity or kindness in his heart. God, give me strength. I never thought that this would be the life of a Duchess."

I slam the book shut and heave. My hands are shaking. Is this the type of man I am? Is this what Victoria, Elizabeth, and Amelia think of me? I turn and walk away from the diary. I can't read anymore. I have to do this — I don't have a choice. A few more weeks and this part will be over. I force an exasperated breath from my lips. One more passage, I tell myself. One more passage. Going back to my mother's journal, I open a page toward the end.

"They took my son from me today. My husband blames me for him not being perfect, but in my eyes he's everything. I have nothing left. This will be my last entry. I can't do it anymore. He'll come to me tonight and beat me black and blue. He'll force himself on me, and my body will die just as my mind did all those years ago. Goodbye, Katherine Cavendish, Duchess of Oakfield."

There are no further entries in the diary. I look at the date written at the top of the page, but I already know in my heart what it will be. It's the date of my mother's death. I close the book again and put it back in the drawer. One day, when this is all over, I'll read it again, but now her words will weaken me, and I can't allow that to happen. I need to be strong to be the man that my father wants me to be. Maybe, when I'm Duke, I can work on changing the rules, but for the time being, there's nothing that can be done. Victoria Hamilton may think that I'm a coward, but she doesn't understand anything. She's lived in a bubble, not the real world. It's do or die out there, and I have no plans on dying just yet.

My mother's words haunt me though,

"They took my son from me."

I wish she were talking about me in that statement, but she isn't. No, I have a brother. I've never understood why people call him *wrong*. He's just William to me. I think he's just what I need. I stumble down the corridor, again in the dark, toward his room. It's as far away from my father's as possible. The Duke has nothing to do with William, unless it's vital. I unlock the door and enter without knocking. I know he'll be awake. He likes to watch the stars.

"Hi, Bro." I swagger in and hold my arms open.

"Out!" he shouts back from his vantage point next to his telescope at the window.

"Why?" I ask in confusion.

"You didn't knock." He frowns.

"Do I really need to do that?"

He flicks his hand across his head, around his nose, and taps his foot twice. I can see he's getting agitated. William was diagnosed as being on the autism spectrum at a young age. In fact, the day my mother died. Most people think of a person with autism as having social inadequacies and learning disabilities, but William's nothing like that. He's incredibly intelligent, far superior to me. He has his quirks — like the fact, he's looking at me as though I've grown three heads because I didn't knock on his door before entering. But other than that, he's perfectly normal. Any social inadequacies are more likely to come from the fact that, since his diagnosis, my father has hidden him away in this room with only a governess for company most of the time. I think that would make it hard for anyone to interact the way that society decrees.

"I'm sorry." I hold my hands up and step back toward the door. "I'll come in again."

"Three knocks." His brows furrow together in anguish.

"Three knocks. I promise."

I leave the room again and shut the door. This time before entering I knock three times and open. William's smiling this time, and the anxiety of before is gone. Such a simple thing can agitate him so much. I feel guilty for upsetting him.

"Sorry," I offer.

"It's ok. His Grace came here earlier, and he always refuses to knock. I was scared it was him again."

"What did he want?" I hate the thought of my father upsetting William. He's two years younger than me, and I care a great deal for him.

"To tell me to make sure I'm quiet while we have guests. He doesn't want them finding out about me. I embarrass him." William sits down on a sofa. "I think Bertha told him I was playing my guitar earlier."

I sit next to him and place my arm around him.

"If you want to play your guitar, then play it. You're good at it. You could be in a band. Ignore Bertha and the Duke. They've got no taste." Bertha is my brother's governess. He doesn't need her — he's twenty-six for god's sake, but my father insists. She's William's jailer. The first thing I'll do when I'm Duke is get rid of her and allow William to see the world. He's been cooped up in this house since he was three. I hate it.

"I shouldn't. The girls may hear me."

"They're my girls, not father's. I'm not ashamed of you like he is."

William looks down at his hands. He taps one, his left on his leg three times and then the right three times. His autism is focused very much around routine. It comforts him.

"I'm not, William, I promise. When I'm Duke, everything will change. Father will leave for the country, and we can rule together. Brothers side by side."

"What about your wife?" he asks.

I go quiet.

"This doesn't have to be your legacy, you know." William

offers with optimism in his voice. "Your succession could be different."

"Not you as well. It can't — I have to go through with this."

"Not necessarily."

"To try to end this madness would assign far too many people to death. You and the girls downstairs included.

I kick my shoes off and push back on his sofa, my head resting on the duck down cushion.

"I may not be seen, Nicholas, but I do a lot of seeing. She's strong enough."

What?" I rub my hands over my eyes. Now that I've laid my head down, my eyes are tired. The alcohol and the emotions are draining the strength from me.

"I may not remember Mother, but she was weak. Victoria isn't"

"What has Victoria got to do with this?" My eyes drift shut. I'm trying to listen to him, but it's becoming a struggle. William has always been a comfort blanket to me. We've snuck into each other's room since we were little. Thankfully, Bertha and our father only caught us a few times.

"You have goodness in you. You aren't the devil Father wants you to portray."

I yawn.

"I think you're deliberately trying to confuse me. With all that 'seeing' you're doing, you must know I've drunk a lot of brandy."

I fall asleep to William laughing at me.

CHAPTER THIRTEEN

VICTORIA

"**T**ell me what you want me to do to you, Victoria?" Nicholas stands before me. He's naked, but I can't make out the lower half of his body. It's hazy. That seems so strange.

"I can't," I whisper back.

"Do you want me to touch you here?"

He touches my breasts, and I let out a moan

"Maybe here."

He dips his finger into my mouth, and I wrap my tongue around it.

"No. Definitely here." I feel my pussy start to throb.

"Please," I whimper. "More."

"You like that." That arrogant grin crosses his lips. I want to smack him in his face, but he touches me down there again, and I buck off the bed.

"Fuck!" I squirm under his touch. "Take me. Make me yours."

"Who am I to disappoint, my little Duchess?"

. . . .

CRASH!

I sit bolt upright in my bed. My breathing is fast, and the ache between my legs has my hand fly there to touch myself in the hope of relief. It's then I notice the human-shaped shadow moving in my room.

"Nicholas?" I pray it's no one else. The person's physique is the same stature as my captor. "Is that you?"

"Sorry." A deep voice rumbles. Then the intruder pulls at something by the wall, which reveals a secret door through which he disappears. I rub my eyes. Was I dreaming *that* as well as Nicholas about to take my virginity? My hand is still between my thighs, and I'm wet there. That part was a dream. I think I'm going to suppress the dream because otherwise it will freak me out. The more pressing matter is the man who was in my room and where he's gone? I turn my bedside lamp on and swing my legs out of the bed. I put on slippers and pull a lightweight robe over my shoulders. It's summer, but there's a little chill in the air tonight. There always seems to be in these big houses. Nothing looks out of the norm in my bedroom. Well, except for the mirror that I stare into daily, wondering how this has become my life. It's slightly ajar from the wall. I pull it, and a doorway opens. A secret passageway. My heart flutters with excitement. Maybe, this is a way out. The person, whoever he was, was showing me how to escape. I look around for anything I can use to light my way. I'd do anything to be back in my bedroom at home, right now. I have a love of candles. Then again, I wouldn't need this secret tunnel if I were at home. I can't waste any more time and decide that I'll just have to enter it in the dark. I pick a couple of books up and wedge them against the door, to keep it open and offer a little light. Especially when I turn on the overhead light in my room to add illumination. I peek inside the doorway. Spider webs are everywhere. My stomach churns. I'm such a wimp when it comes to those little creatures with eight legs. Big girl pants time, spiders can do a lot less damage to me now than the other occupants of Oakfield Hall. I step inside the dark stone corridor. Oakfield Hall is a brick mansion, and this hidden chamber must have been built within the walls. I chuckle as I imagine the clandestine liaisons that they may have been used for in the past. I look to my left, and it's boarded up, so I can't go that way. Right it is. My heart is beating so fast I'm sure that I can hear it vibrating off the walls. I hear a noise up ahead and quicken my pace a little. There is no light. I'm terrified, especially when I bump into some stairs and only just manage to keep my footing. I bend low to the floor and trace them up in a crouching position. I have no idea what I'm touching, and I really don't want to know. I get to the top of the steps and look around. It's still pitch black. Surely, to get out of this place I would need to go down, not up. I'm not going to take any chances with my footing again, for fear of tumbling downstairs, I keep low and crawl along the floor. Up ahead, I see a flicker of light. Is this where the person who was in my room has gone? Maybe they're waiting to free me? I scamper forward quickly, on all fours, then stop and listen at the doorway where the light is.

"Silly, silly. You shouldn't have left the room." I hear from the other side.

I push the door slowly. It creaks open and sitting there is a man. I recognize his features, instantly. They're the same as the ones I was just dreaming of, but younger and paler. Nicholas must have a brother.

The man swipes his hand across his head, around his nose, and taps the floor twice with his foot.

"Hello," I say quietly.

He looks up at me with fear in his eyes.

"You can't be here."

"You were in my room?"

"Yes." He does his strange movement again. It seems to be some sort of tic.

"Why? Who are you?"

"You must go back." He scrambles a little farther away.

"I won't hurt you. I just want to know who you are?"

I slide my body out of the secret passageway and step into the room. It's opulently decorated like a sitting room. A television sits in the corner with a games console attached to it, and a table is laid ready for breakfast. I went upstairs in the tunnel — I must've come to the second floor. There's a door to the other end of the room, and I wonder where that leads.

"You have to knock before you come in."

"Knock?" I enquire in confusion.

"Please, do it four times."

The man's strange behavior is getting worse. The agitation in his stance flooding the room with more fear than I have. I don't know why, but I go back to the doorway and knock four times.

"Come in," he calls quietly. "Thank you." He places both his hands down on his thighs and starts to tap a two beat on each leg alternately.

"Hello, I'm Victoria."

"I know. I've read your file." He leans over to the side and picks up a wrapped gift. "I was bringing you this, but you moved the chair. I crashed into it and knocked the vase over. You shouldn't move furniture. It makes it more difficult to understand."

"I'm sorry." I find myself apologizing again. "I'll put it all back. Can I ask who you are?"

"I'm William, Nicholas' brother." He doesn't meet my gaze but hands me the present. "Open it."

"I…" I'm lost for words. "You didn't have to get me this."

"I want you to like me — when you become Duchess."

His blunt verbiage is surprising in this house of lies.

"I don't think I'll become Duchess but thank you anyway."

"You should have more faith in yourself." He waves the gift insistently in front of me. I take it and unwrap it. It's a book on art.

"You didn't have to get me this." I reach forward and try to touch his hand in thanks, but he pulls it away.

"I've seen you read all the other books. This is the third one in the collection about Rembrandt. You spent a lot of time on those books."

"You've been watching me?" I shuffle farther away from him. I don't like the fact that he's been invading my private space.

"We can watch all the girls via the screens." He nods toward his TV. I must pale or look like I'm going to throw up, which I certainly feel could happen, because he gasps. "That's one of those things that I'm not supposed to say out loud, isn't it?"

"It's a little scary to know that people are watching me." I raise my eyebrows. "Why aren't you supposed to say it out loud?"

"I have autism. I often say things I shouldn't. I can't help it. When I first saw you on the screen, I told Nicholas that you had the best tits I've ever seen."

I must blush because he groans.

"See. I really can't help it."

"That's ok — it's nice to be appreciated." I laugh and this seems to relax William, a little, as he settles down. "Why haven't you been with your brother and father when they've been...um?"

"Torturing you?" he offers.

"Pretty much."

"My father doesn't allow me out with his society. He's embarrassed by me. I'm the reason my mother died, because I was wrong. It's better if I just hide out up here."

"That isn't right. I'm sorry."

"It's alright. I'm used to it. Safer to be in these four walls than out there." He looks toward the door — a means of escape. I take a sharp inhalation of breath. This could be my chance.

"You don't want to go through there." He taps my leg.

"Why?"

As if by magic, the door opens and a sleepy looking Nicholas stands in the opening.

"What the fuck!" He exclaims and stomps toward me. "What the hell are you doing in here?" He grabs me and pulls me to my feet like I'm a rag doll.

"Get off me," I shout and attempt to kick out. I just miss his leg.

"Nick, it was my fault. Please don't hurt her."

Nicholas looks toward the door that I entered the room through.

"You're an idiot. Damn it." Nicholas' grip on me becomes even tighter and drags me back to the hole in the wall. "Get to bed, William. If our father asks about this, you haven't left your room all evening. You hear me?"

"Yes." William holds the book up for me. "I just wanted to give this to her."

"Not now. I'll come back and get it later." Nicholas pushes me back through the door and starts to shove me through the dark corridor. I remember there are stairs somewhere around here, and just as I'm about to tumble down them, Nicholas grabs me. He slams me against the wall. I can't see him, but I can feel the anger emanating from him.

"If anything happens to William because you were in that room, then I'll kill you with my bare hands."

CHAPTER FOURTEEN

NICHOLAS

The need to protect herself must suddenly occur to Victoria because before I realize what she intends to do, she raises her leg and thrusts it hard into my shin. I step back and grab my aching leg.

"Bitch," I growl, but she doesn't hear me because she's taken off fast down the corridor. She manages the steps down without any trouble, and I listen to her rapid breathing in the darkness. I chase after her with murderous intent. William is my flesh and blood — he's my closest ally in this house, and I won't see any harm come to him from anyone. Especially a stuck up girl who thinks that she's better than her allotted place in life. She thinks I'm a coward. I'll show her just what I can do. She reaches her room and kicks at a pile of books holding the door open and tries to shut it. She's too late and too weak against my superior strength. I push the door open and stalk into her room. The lights are already on, and I can see that she's like a frightened little rabbit, cowering backward into a corner.

"Big mistake," I sneer.

"He came to me first," she pleads.

"William doesn't understand what he's doing. He thinks he's nice, but he doesn't understand the trouble it'll get him into with my father. You should have sent him away and certainly shouldn't have followed him." I prowl closer to her, closing the distance between us like a cheetah ready to pounce.

"You forget something. I'm not the monster in this house. I'm just as much of a victim as it seems your brother is. Both of us not allowed to leave and kept hidden away against our free will. If you want to look at who might hurt your brother, go look in a mirror," she hisses back at me. "Your brother was just being nice and bringing me a present."

I groan. Setting William up with an Amazon Prime account was the worst thing I'd ever done. I thought it would help alleviate the boredom he felt, but after he spent five thousand pounds on games consoles, books, and a massive television in the first month alone, I decided to limit his spending. He's obviously been on it again and buying presents for people that he really shouldn't.

"You have to promise me you won't tell anyone you saw him." She's in the corner, and I place both my hands on the wall either side of her. She's trapped. The only way out is to kick me again, but I'm anticipating that.

"Why?" she asks with utter contempt for me.

"Please?"

"Let me go, and I won't say a word. Let me walk out of this house, right now."

"You know I can't do that," I reply, sick of the same argument. Doesn't she realize that I could squash her like a fly?

"Why not?"

"For god's sake, Victoria. Just accept that this is happening. You aren't getting out of here anytime soon," I snap.

"Tell me something — I know what happens if you choose me. I get to be the Duchess of Oakfield and put my own children through the heartbreak I'm experiencing. What happens if you don't choose me?"

"I'm not talking about this. Just answer me. Will you keep quiet about William?"

"No, you answer me." She stamps her foot. I brace myself just in case she's about to kick out again.

"God, you're the most infuriating woman I've ever known. Fine, you want to know what happens. If you survive the task, *if* being the poignant factor, and you lose, then you'll be taken by the other men and raped. You'll then be executed —since you'll know far too much. Face it. One way or another, your life's over. Accept it. Save my brother in the process. Don't drag him down with you."

She gasps, and her legs give way. She sinks to the floor at my feet.

"How can you do this to me? You don't even know me. How can you be so cruel?" Tears pool in her eyes, but they don't fall. Despite her moment of weakness, she won't allow me the indignity of seeing her cry.

"It's not personal. If I could change things, then I would. I want this as much as you do." The anger of moments ago dissipates between us. I crouch down on the balls of my feet in front of her. "I've told you I have no choice. It's the only way to get rid of him."

"Your father?"

I nod an affirmative.

"I don't want to die."

"I don't want you to die. I don't want Elizabeth and Amelia to die either, but I have to get rid of him. Once I'm Duke, William can be seen. I'll be in charge. I'll make the rules."

"Will you change the rules of the society so that this doesn't happen to other people?"

I swallow deeply.

"I'll do what I can."

"You mean no." She pushes to her feet and walks past me to the bed. I follow her and wrap my arms around her. I don't know why. It just seems the right thing to do. She's distressed. She's been told she could die within the year.

"I don't know if that's a battle too far for me. I won't ever stop trying, though." I lay my head on her shoulder and whisper my words into her ear.

"William's safe. I won't mention I've seen him. He told me about the cameras you have on us. You might want to get rid of any video that's been recorded." She sounds defeated.

"Thank you. I'll choose you in return if I can. I'll make you the Duchess."

She spins in my arms and faces me. The tears she's been holding in begin to fall. Her stunning emerald eyes meet mine, and there's sadness and defeat in them.

"No, don't make a promise you can't keep. I'm not protecting William so I can gain favor with you. I'm doing it because he's as much a victim of this house as I am." She looks down at the ground. "I think it would be better if you go." With a wriggle, she attempts to pull out of my arms. I grip tighter. I don't want to go. She looks back up at me. "Earl Lullington, please."

I bow my head and bring my lips down on hers. She's soft and tastes of strawberries. At first, she doesn't respond. I pull back and see that tears still fall. She opens and closes her mouth like she wants to tell me off, to shout, scream, and rant at me, but nothing comes out. I let go of her waist with one hand and use my fingers to wipe away her tears. She turns her head and kisses the tears from my digits. My breath hitches, and I lean back in to kiss her again. This time, she responds, and before I know it, we're bumping into the bed and falling on top of it.

She breaks the kiss and stares at me intently.

"Make me feel. If I'm to die, allow me this one thing."

I slide down her body. She's wearing the silk dressing gown and set of pajamas that I bought for all the girls. Tradition dictates that they should wear these horrendous Victorian nightdress things, but I'm afraid they did nothing for me. If I can't see a woman naked, then I prefer her to look casual in low slung trousers and a tight t-shirt. I pull her pajama bottoms down and throw them on the floor. My face is inches from her pussy, and I can smell her arousal. It leaves a glistening coat on her neatly trimmed cleft. I shove my face in between her legs and start to sample her delights — like a man on death row consuming his last meal. I've eaten enough pussy to know a good one when I taste it, and this is the best ever. She's succulent, sweet and wet, just for me.

"That feels amazing." She squirms with pleasure under my exploration of her folds.

I pull my head up. "Has anyone ever given you oral sex before?"

She lifts her head up and raises an annoyed eyebrow at me.

"Err. You're the only man I've ever been alone with, except my father and brother. I don't know what other freaky things your family gets up to, but mine doesn't go for incest."

I chuckle and let it reverberate around her inner thighs. Even with my head in between her legs, she's still lippy. I like it.

"Believe me, neither my father or brother have attributes akin to yours, which entertain me in the slightest. I like the fact that I'm the first man to go down on you. I know once you've had me you won't want anyone else."

"Arrogant or what?" she snorts.

"It's my middle name."

I flex my index finger and tenderly sink it inside her. She clenches down on the intrusion — fuck, this is only a finger. I imagine sticking my cock inside her. She would grip me like a vice and milk the cum from my body in a violent explosion. But I mustn't get ahead of myself. First, I'm going to give her, her first orgasm from being licked out.

I push another finger inside her, and she groans even louder.

"So full."

"Wait until it's my cock."

I feel her entire body shiver under me. Dipping my head again, I devour her. It isn't long before she starts to writhe and jerk on the bed in a climatic orgasm. She moans my name in a raspy breath.

"Nicholas."

The way she says my name catches my breath and halts me in my exploits to send her high again. Fuck, what am I doing? I can't do this. I can't take her in this way. I can't develop feelings for her. It'll ruin everything. I jump from the bed. She sits up, her hair crazy with that 'just come' look.

"What's wrong?" she asks with disappointment on her face. "Did I do something wrong?"

"I'm not the man who should make you feel. I'm the devil. You've called me that yourself." I readjust my trousers, my cock is rock hard, and go to the door.

"What?" She slides from the bed on wobbly feet. Thankfully, her dressing gown covers her nakedness from me.

"Thank you for agreeing not to out William for his indiscretion. I'll see to it that he doesn't bother you again. You should get some sleep. We have a task tomorrow, and, as you've asked me not to, I won't go easy on you."

Her lips purse together, and her brow furrows. I know that she's about to hit me with another outburst, but I don't wait to hear it. I leave the room and take the steps to mine, two at a time. I can't get to it fast enough. The house is still dark apart from a small slither of moonlight cascading through the windows not covered by curtains. On entering my room, I slam and lock the door behind me. I need to relieve the ache in my pants. Fuck, I would have taken her there and then if my brain hadn't kicked in. I'm not here to fall in love with these girls. They're a means to an end: stick a child in them, raise the next generation, and free William from the confines of his seclusion imposed by my father. I drop my trousers and pump hard at my cock. I fist it so fast that I come in an instant. My essence spills onto the floor, but I don't care. I needed this release. I need to prove to her that I'm the devil who takes for himself. She's a lamb to the slaughter — a means to an end. I won't rest until I'm the next Duke of Oakfield.

CHAPTER FIFTEEN

VICTORIA

I'm naked underneath a gown again. I've learned enough to know, that doesn't end well. Elizabeth, Amelia, and I stand in front of the members of the society. The Duke and Nicholas are at the head of the group. They both wear tailored dark suits, white shirts, and matching ties. Nicholas fiddles with his ever-present cufflinks. He hasn't looked at me once since he entered the room. It's like he's brought a shutter down on what happened between us last night. I should step forward and shout at the Duke that William came into my room last night. I'm angry enough to do it because Nicholas is so damn stubborn. If only he would end what's going on, then we could all leave. He won't, though. His father controls him like a puppet on a string, and that's the reason why I won't tell on William. Feeling an intensity wash over me, I look toward Nicholas, his eyes are every-where except on me. William, I look up at a balcony toward the top of the high ceiling. I can't see him although I know that he's there. He hides in the shadows. I can't help but envy him. I wish I were up there hiding with him. I look back down and toward Nicholas, and he's scowling at me. It's a warning — he must've seen me looking up. I shut my eyes and let out a long breath before mouthing,

"I promise."

I don't look at him again, for the Duke starts his speech that will lead to today's torture.

"Welcome again, gentlemen. I trust you all slept well. It's been a few days since we conducted the last trial, and I'm sure you're all as excited as I am to continue with choosing a wife for my son." A few of the men murmur their eagerness to continue. I want to scream that they're all freaks, but I know it's better to hold my tongue. I shuffle my bare feet against the cold of the stone floor and wait to hear my fate.

"As the wife of a Duke, the chosen woman will need to take discipline and thank her husband for it. She'll be expected to be impeccably behaved and subservient to his needs at all times, but by nature, they're women and thus prone to faults. This task looks at how well the women before us will take the discipline that Nicholas will give to them, and it will probably set a precedent for the future of their marriage." The Duke laughs. I find myself beyond caring at this point. I thought I was getting somewhere with Nicholas, last night, but when he pulled away, it all crumbled, and I was the one who realized that my fate and his are intertwined forever. Until he understands the hold that his father has over him and stops lying to himself, there's nothing I can do to save either of us.

"Ladies. Would you remove your cloaks and form a line in front of Nicholas? He'll ask you a question, and you should answer it as you feel he would want you to."

I can't help but think that sounds a little too simple for a task. Where's the humiliation? I suddenly fear the question he'll ask. I remove my gown, as do Elizabeth and Amelia, and we stand as ordered. Nicholas walks the line. He stops in front of each of us and looks us up and down. I notice no interest on his face with Elizabeth and Amelia, but when it comes to me, the way he looks between my legs has me rub them together at the memory of his head in between my thighs. His nostrils flare as though he's aware of the arousal pooling between my legs. Fuck. I can't get horny for this monster. I'll become the freak then. I look down at the floor, and he walks back to Elizabeth.

"Miss Sandford, if we're out at a social function, and I ask you to get on your hands and knees, bark like a dog, and crawl around the room, would you?" Some of the assembled crowd laugh at his question, but it just confirms to me how insane this is.

Elizabeth pulls on a strand of her jet black hair and pouts at the question. She's pretending to mull it over? I can see the look on her face. I really haven't warmed to this girl. She seems to actually be enjoying what's going on. I, on the other hand, want to just gag. When she gets to her knees and barks like a dog, I'm pretty confident that I'm going to be sick.

"I'll do whatever you ask of me. As my husband, you'll be my master, and I'll obey your every command because you need to be satisfied in all things."

Yep, definitely feeling queasy.

"Thank you, Elizabeth." Nicholas smiles at her and offers his hand to allow her to get back on her feet. He kisses it and moves onto Amelia. The blonde haired girl seems to be stronger today. She's been dealing with the situation the worst of all of us. I've been desperate to get to know her better — I might be able to help support her, but we haven't had the opportunity to talk amongst ourselves. She turns her head to look at me and smiles with reassurance.

"Keep your eyes on me, Miss Rushbrooke, not Miss Hamilton."

"Apologies, Lord Lullington," she whispers, and I see her hands start to shake. Even though he isn't looking at me, I frown at Nicholas with utter scorn. He doesn't need to be such an obnoxious bully.

"The same question. What's your answer?"

"Yes, I would, My Lord." She doesn't hesitate in her answer, but there's no feeling in the words. They're said only because she needs to give an answer, and that's the one she thinks Nicholas wants to hear.

"Thank you, Amelia," Nicholas replies and comes to stand in front of me. He keeps his stare focused on my face, and I'm glad for that. The last thing I need is to have my thoughts muddled by lust.

"Miss Hamilton, what's your answer to the same question?" My survival instincts tell me to say yes and be done with it. Move on to the next task without torture, but the passion that burns inside me screams for me to tell him to go to hell. I find my own hands shaking. My legs feel like jelly. I just want to run and hide from the question. Why is it so difficult to answer? I swallow deeply and press my hands to my side to calm the tremor in them.

"Yes..." – I pause. Nicholas smiles– "should be my answer, but my father raised me not to tell lies. If I said yes and forego any punishment you are about to give me, then it would be deceitful to the *truth* of this situation." My last point's a sarcastic dig at what happened between Nicholas and me last night. He knows this is wrong but won't do anything about it. "My answer is, no, Earl Lullington. I wouldn't get to my knees and be a dog if you asked me to. Because you keep me here against my free will, you don't deserve my respect enough to do what you ask of me."

Nicholas' face reddens, and a vein in the side of his neck pulses furiously. Its beat matches that of the thundering tempo of my heart. He doesn't speak, though. He turns away from me and faces his father.

"Elizabeth Sandford was the most honest. She won't be punished as she doesn't need it. Amelia Rushbrooke, though she answered 'yes', I feel would be hesitant in obeying the order. Therefore, she'll be locked in her room for twenty-four hours with no food." He pauses, and my heart leaps into my mouth. "Victoria Hamilton was insolent and rude. She wouldn't obey my order and will get a harsh correction. She'll be whipped, here and now, twenty times. That would be my right as her husband."

I can barely take in his words. I expected a punishment but this? Whipping? It's cruel and degrading, not to mention will leave me scarred for life and in so much pain. Is this the sort of man Nicholas truly is? I was a fool to believe he might have kindness in him. He's lost — lost to the devil that is his father. I'm going to die. I'm twenty-one years old, a baby, and my life's over.

CHAPTER SIXTEEN

NICHOLAS

My shoulders slump in defeat, but the anger in me bubbles below the surface. I don't want to do this to Victoria, but she's forcing my hand. Why does she have to be so stubborn? I've told her just to comply with the rules, and I'll choose her as my wife. I'll save her life. What happens now is her fault, not mine. I have to do these punishments — they're prescribed in the founding documentation. She could be going to her room to rest and read her books, like Elizabeth and Amelia are, but no, she had to open her mouth again and spout a load of abuse. I'm not a liar. This is my right, to have a wife chosen for me this way. She should obey me.

I hold my right hand out, and a birch is placed in it. The bunch of thick twigs is the weapon of choice of the upper classes. In eighteenth-century schools, it was used to punish naughty boys. Girls didn't attend schools. Their duty was to learn how to be a wife. I remember when I was eight years old my father took a birch to me. This particular one is handed down through the generations of our family. I can't remember exactly what I'd done, but it was something silly–like refusing to eat my dinner of brussel sprouts. Needless to say after getting hit a few times, I have eaten the rotten vegetable ever since. I've experienced what Victoria's about to receive. I was only hit a few times, though. She'll be left broken and bruised, after twenty hard hits. I can't temper my aim or strength with everyone watching. My father will know that I've gone easy on her and use it against me. He'll demand blood, and he'll want to hear screaming. Blood, sweat, and tears, a misinterpretation of the saying, are the things he likes to witness coming from a woman the most.

Two of my father's assistants step forward and grab both of Victoria's arms. She's shocked and tries to struggle against them, but they're too strong for her. She's ushered, reluctantly, forward on the tips of her toes and bent over a table. The position leaves her pussy exposed for everyone to see. I step in front of her to block the view from the rest of the assembled society members. I don't want anyone else seeing her that way.

"I'd keep as still as you can. I can't guarantee my aim if you're moving around." I offer her advice in a helpful whisper.

"Fuck you," is her response. It angers me even more, and I bring the birch up and strike down on her pert bottom. She screams, and the flesh reddens.

"One." I count and raise my arm ready to strike her again.

"Stop." My father's voice fills the cavernous room.

"Your Grace." I turn and face him.

"I've just remembered something." The malevolent grin, which fills his face, has me shudder in anticipation. I'm glad that Victoria can't see him. "There aren't three punishments on the binding documentation. There are four." He strides confidently over to a box in the corner of the room. "The fourth has only been used once before on my grandmother. She was insolent and rude up until that point, but after this punishment, she became the perfect broken wife."

The men either side of Victoria let go of her — she stands up and rubs her bottom where I've just hit her with the birch. She turns and scowls at me. I return the look of contempt with all the anger still boiling inside of me and re-focus my attention on my father. He opens the box and pulls out an iron mask.

"Fuck," I exclaim, when I realize what he holds, and drop the birch. Victoria presses closer to me.

"What is it?" she asks with a tremble in her voice.

"A scold's bridle." I gulp the same time as my stomach clenches in disbelief.

"My grandmother was placed in this and humiliated in front of the society. She was beaten and berated with no method of response that wouldn't cut her tongue." My father steps forward holding the bridle. He's deliberately malicious.

"I've already chosen her punishment." I push Victoria aside and stand up to him.

"It's too tame for this heathen." My father grits his teeth together as he speaks. He shoves the bridle into my hands. It's heavy and the ironwork rusted from its age. "Put it on her."

"No. I chose the twenty lashes."

"The Duchess of Oakfield needs to be subservient. Twenty lashes won't cure Victoria Hamilton of her tongue — only humiliation will. You put her in this position, do it, or are you too weak to warrant the title of the Duke of Oakfield?" he sneers, and I want to punch him on his self-righteous chin. He knows full well that I'll submit to what he orders of me. I want the position to get rid of him, to provide a better life for William. I'm changing, and the man I was a few days ago is dying.

The bridle weighs heavy in my hands. I look down at it. The hinged iron framework encloses the head, and a bit fits into the mouth to suppress the tongue. Many have a smooth bit, but this one has a metal spike on it. If Victoria tries to speak while wearing it, the spike will rip into her tongue.

"Put. It. On. Her." My father's words are slow and menacing.

I'm wavering and want to run.

I feel the warmth of another hand over mine. It's Victoria's. She steps in front of me and takes the bridle. She places it over her own head and takes the bit into her mouth. She gags and whimpers when the spike must hit her tongue. She bows her head, so that I can fasten the contraption up.

"Excellent." My father steps forward clapping. "Maybe, the little bitch finally realizes that the word of man is law."

"The word of man is all lies," I comment quietly, and Victoria's eyes flash up to mine in understanding.

A clinking of metal has me flick my head around quickly. My father holds a chain.

"Time to walk your dog, my son."

He hands me the chain, and without looking at Victoria again, I attach it to her collar. This torture's all about humiliation for the victim. In olden times, the woman was walked around the village and abuse was actively encouraged, sexual and physical. She was called a variety of degrading names and left without food or water for hours. She was humiliated in every way, shape, or form for gossiping or talking back. Men sometimes suffered the same fate, but this was primarily a punishment for women.

"Gentlemen. In the box, there are horse whips. All marks must be confined to her back. You aren't to touch her sexually. Call her as many names as you wish, while Earl Lullington walks her in front of you. This woman has too much spirit, and, as you're all married, I'm sure you'll understand how harmful that can be to a man. It needs to be broken. Nicholas, proceed."

My feet feel like lead weights as I take the chain in my hand and step one foot in front of the other. I can't turn around and look at the pain being inflicted on Victoria. I'm a coward and not ashamed to admit it. The taunts she's receiving are enough for me.

"Whore."

"Bitch."

"Cock tease."

"Cunt."

"Slut."

"Virago."

I wince at every word, and the comments are even worse.

"Learn your place."

"On your knees and worship my feet."

"Cut her tongue out if she doesn't stop."

"Only good for fucking."

"Stick your dick in her mouth to shut her up."

"Women need to learn silence."

I make three passes. My father tells me to go for a fourth, but I feel the chain go taut over my shoulder. I turn around, and Victoria has slumped down onto the floor. I let it go and check on her. She's unconscious — her back bleeding and raw. One of the men steps forward with his whip held high.

"Enough," I snap.

He inclines his head in a bow and returns to the line.

"You, and you." I point to two of the guards. "Get this thing off her and return her to her room. Touch her intimately, while she's naked, and I'll use that sword" –I point to a massive metal blade hanging ominously on the wall– "to personally remove your hands."

They scramble to attention, and Victoria's limp body is removed from the room. I make a mental note that, as soon as I leave here, I'll have my personal doctor called to tend to her wounds, not the horrendous Dr. Fredrick Fallen. The other members of the society head to the bar to pour themselves a congratulatory round of brandies.

"Happy?" I face down my father who's picked up the bridle and is running his finger over the bit. Blood coats his digit where it must've dug into Victoria's tongue.

"Indeed. Although, it's yet to be seen whether she's actually learned her lesson or not. If you make her Duchess the way she currently is, it'll be the downfall of this family."

I laugh. I can't help it. I don't know where it comes from. It's probably the most natural reaction that I've ever had in my life.

"Or she might just be the savior of it."

I don't wait to hear his answer because my feet are propelling me toward the door and the woman I fear I've just destroyed.

CHAPTER SEVENTEEN

VICTORIA

I don't want to open my eyes. Am I dead? No, surely I wouldn't be in this much pain if I were. I try to shift on the bed from my front to my back but freeze the second that I experience a ricochet of agony so blinding, it shoots through my body. I cry out. I can't help it, which aggravates the wound on my tongue. The metallic taste of blood fills my mouth — I've opened a laceration.

"Wait, I'll help you" —a gentle feminine voice offers — "you're still very bruised."

"Amelia?" I recognize her soft tones at once.

"Yes," she replies, and I feel the covers being shifted from my back. "Do you want to sit up?"

"Please," I respond, and she helps me to turn over and sit. She places a soft cushion under my bottom despite the fact that I'm on my bed. I feel sick from the pain, and it makes my head spin. "What happened?" My mind feels foggy. I have a vague recollection of a mask and name calling.

I retch. The names were so cruel. Amelia puts a small

bowl in front of me, and I dry heave over it. Every jolt of my body sends aches through me. I have nothing to bring up as I haven't eaten or drunk for what seems like ages. I look down at my hand and see a cannula in it. I look up at Amelia and try to speak, but I'm breaking down.

"Breathe. It's alright. You're safe." She touches my hand. "Do you remember the punishment they gave you?"

I look into the haze that is my brain and remember the scold's bridle and the horsewhips. I blank the name calling. I'm not going to remember that again.

"Yes, they whipped me."

She nods.

"You were in bad shape. We thought you may die. The Earl called for his doctor. You have some deep wounds, which were stitched up. They gave you morphine to help with the pain and fluid to keep you hydrated. That's why you have this." She looks at the device in my hand. "It was thought best to let you sleep for a few days to allow your body to start healing. They stopped all the drugs this morning. I have some extra strength painkillers here if you need them." This time, she holds up a bottle.

"Yes, please." I don't hesitate. Give me all the drugs you can to numb the agony in my body. The morphine drip sounds good. Maybe I could get hooked back up on that.

Amelia hands me two pills and helps me sit forward to drink some water. My throat is raw, and the water mixes with the blood in my mouth. It's not a pleasant experience.

"They've advised you not to talk too much. The bridle had a spike on it, and when you passed out, it cut your tongue. It was rusty due to its age, and they feared you may lose your tongue to infection, but it seems alright. You need to rest it to let it heal." I take her advice and nod my response rather than speak it.

I collapse my head back against the headboard of the bed, I'm grateful for the plethora of cushions that cocoon me. I already feel tired from moving just a few times.

"How long?" I ask, keeping my words to a minimum, trying not to move my tongue. I think Amelia understands me, even if I do sound stupid.

"You've been asleep for three days. They've allowed me to look after you. Well, Nicholas said I could. The Duke, he said to leave you in your own filth. I don't like that man." She slaps her hand over her mouth. "Sorry," she whispers.

"I agree with you. Don't be sorry."

"I shouldn't say it, though." She looks up and around the room.

"Cameras," I say.

"Yes. The other brother told me to be careful."

"Other brother?" I'm confused.

She leans forward and whispers into my ear,

"William."

"You've seen him." I'm still trying not to move my tongue when I speak.

"He's been helping me look after you. He keeps to the side, so he can't be seen. He seems nice. A little inappropriate, the first thing he told me was that I had a bottom like a Kardashian. I'm assuming that's a nice compliment. He was smiling politely when he said it."

I try to stifle the laugh I feel, but when a little escapes, I regret it instantly. Damn, this pain's terrible.

"I don't think he's that good with social etiquette. He's nice, though." I give up on the no talking. The more I do it, the looser my mouth's feeling, and the taste of blood has gone. Of course, it could be that the painkillers have kicked in because my bottom suddenly seems to be less painful as well. "I can assure you that a Kardashian's bottom is a good one. Don't you know who they are?"

"Not really. I'm guessing they're celebrities, but I didn't really have a chance to follow all *that* growing up. My father made sure I was prepared for being Nicholas' wife."

"You knew this would happen?" I ask.

"Yes. Didn't you?" I shake my head. "It must've been such a shock."

"Just a little. I've always been kept hidden away, but I didn't know why, until I came here. Makes perfect sense now."

She rolls her eyes.

"Yes, evidently, as women we're sexually wanton. Even allowing us to go to the library on our own will risk our virginity because of all the orgies we are likely to have on the way."

I laugh again — it hurts.

"Oh don't make me laugh."

"Sorry. The tasks are all prescribed in the documentation of this society — my father made me practice them, all my life. I went through every alternative." She goes quiet and looks at the striped rug on my bedroom floor.

"You've had this done to you." It hits me. "Every alternative. No punishment, locked in your room without food and water" –I gulp– "hit twenty times with a birch and the bridle?"

"He didn't use a birch. We didn't have one. He had a

cane, though. It's only one stick instead of a few." She holds my hand.

"Still doesn't stop it from hurting any less or make it any more right. It angers me that these men think they can get away with doing this." I want to jump up from the bed and rant and rage. I want to storm to the nearest man with a horse whip, whack him across the back hundreds of times, and see how he likes it.

"Stay calm," Amelia pleads.

"We'll get through this. They won't always win." I move my hand so that it wraps around hers.

"I appreciate the sentiment, but I know what comes next. You don't."

Shit, I hadn't thought of that.

"Amelia?"

"We're lucky because we only have to do one task, but the original wife had to do all three. Fire, sex, death."

"Fire, sex, death," I repeat.

She looks up to where the camera is and shuts her eyes. I shuffle forward, ignoring the pain. If I can get some insight into what happens next, then I might be able to plan for it.

"You'll be fine. He won't give the one to you that'll destroy you. He loves you too much."

"What?" I'm baffled by her comment. "Amelia, what do you mean?"

She doesn't have a chance to answer me as the secret door in my room opens, and William appears from the shadows. His face is flushed red, and he is carrying a torch.

"You have to come now." He makes a grab for Amelia's hand.

"William?" She shakes him off.

"There's no time for arguments," he commands. "He knows she's awake."

Both of them look at me.

"What? Who knows I'm awake?"

"Good luck." Amelia allows William to lead her into the secret corridor.

"Good luck? With what? With whom?" I shout at them and wish I wasn't trapped in this bed, but my battered body won't allow me to move.

My bedroom door bursts open, and there's Nicholas. His brows are furrowed, and he looks like he's about to explode with anger.

"Cowards," I whisper to myself about William and Amelia and say a little pray to the pain gods to let me pass out again. I curse them in the next breath when I'm still awake. Oh well.

"Earl Lullington. What can I do for you?

CHAPTER EIGHTEEN

NICHOLAS

"You're awake." I storm into her room without waiting for admittance. She's sitting up in the bed, wearing pajamas over her bandages. Last time I saw her, she was naked and bleeding all over her sheets. Despite looking withdrawn from no food for a few days, she seems fine.

"I am. I woke not more than half an hour ago." She shuffles on the bed to get comfortable, and I can see that she's still in pain.

"Did Amelia give you the pills?" I ask.

"She did. I think they're starting to work as my body is more rested than when I first woke."

"You're to take them every four hours. I'll set a reminder on my phone to come and check that you've taken them." I pull my phone out of my pocket and pull up an alarm.

"There's no need. I'm sure I can manage to remember." She looks around the room for a clock — her face falling when she remembers that she doesn't have one. "Maybe I'll need that reminder."

My father decided when we were preparing the rooms for the girls that they wouldn't need clocks. He stated it would be better if they had no idea what time of day it was, other than by the rising and setting of the sun. It all sounded a bit more like adding additional torture into their stay to me.

"I'll have a clock put in here so you can keep an eye on the time yourself."

"Thank you, My Lord."

I grind my teeth at the form of address she uses for me.

"So, how are you feeling?" I'm still standing in the doorway. I can't bring myself to walk any farther into the room, yet. I want to strangle her for not saying 'yes' and thus preventing her body from being put through this. But at the same time, I want to kiss every inch of her body in the hope that it will stop the pain she's in. Argh. Women! Why do they have to be so complicated? Men are simple creatures, far more pliable. Particularly if you have a voracious dick like mine. Food, sleep, shower, shit, sex, not necessarily in that order, and several of those more than once a day.

"Just fine and dandy," she responds, and her own face darkens with anger.

"Why didn't you just say yes?" I can no longer temper my fury.

"Why should I? I'm not a liar, Nicholas."

"Because, if you did, then this would have been much easier, and I wouldn't have had to see you covered in blood and humiliated." I put my head in my hands and pull the strands of my hair through to the end. "I wouldn't have to worry that, because of what happened, you're broken."

She laughs at me. I see it hurts her, when she flinches, but she continues.

"You think this would break me? No, no chance. It's made me even more determined to make you see that what's happening here is wrong. You marry for love and with freedom of choice, Nicholas. If your wife misbehaves, you don't lead her around in some elaborate parade designed to humiliate her."

"You hate me." Her words hit me hard, and I want to go to her and hold her. I want to stroke her and make all the pain go away.

"No. I don't blame you for this. As I've said before, you're weak. What happened to me is because of the society, and your father's macabre nature. What happens now is down to you, though."

I finally dare to move closer to her and sit on the edge of the bed. While she's speaking, she reaches out and takes my hand. I look at the cannula embedded in her delicate flesh.

"What do you mean?"

"Stop this. Go to your father and tell him you won't go through with it anymore. Tell him that you're letting Amelia, Elizabeth, and I go, and when you marry, it'll be for love. You're the only one who can do that. Does the title of Duke mean that much to you? Would you rather money and prestige over your soul?"

"I lost my soul years ago. There's still much that you don't know about this society and what it does."

"Then, tell me," she interrupts me.

"I'm too entwined in this. Bringing it down will destroy everything. William also. I can't risk his future."

"But you can mine?"

"It's not like that."

"Then what's it like?" She lets go of my hand and moves away to the other side of the bed.

"Victoria, please. Let's just finish the trials, let me get the title, and then, I can change things from there." I'm begging her. I lean forward and press a kiss to her lips. She doesn't respond, but she doesn't push me away, either. She sits there without moving.

"Are you in pain?" I go for her hand again, but she pulls it away. "Victoria."

"I want you to leave." She turns her head away, looking out of the barred window.

"Don't be like this. I'm not saying that I won't change things when I'm Duke. I'm just saying, for now, it has to be like this."

She doesn't reply.

"Talk to me," I demand.

"Leave." Her eyes are dead. I've seen affection for me in them before, despite the monster I am, but there's nothing there now. "You think after this there can ever be anything between us. If you put a stop to this now, then maybe, I could work on forgiving you, but you've seen me humiliated, beaten, almost killed, and still, you won't fight for me. You could've had my love Nicholas, but you've lost that. Just leave."

"Are you serious?" I jump off the bed, and she whimpers when the ripples from the force shake the mattress. "I don't have a choice. I have to do it this way. It's the only way to make sure everyone gets the future that will be best for them."

"You're deluded. If I carry on like this, then I'll have no future. I'll be dead."

"Then, just do the tasks — I'll give you the easy ones." Why does she have to be so complicated? I'm frustrated and fuming at the same time.

"And let Amelia and Elizabeth get beaten or worse instead."

"Don't ask this of me. Just accept what I say."

"I shouldn't need to ask you." She turns away. It's the final nail in our conversation. She won't acknowledge me anymore. I see that when she shuts her eyes.

"Fine, have it your way. Just don't come running back to me when this is over, and the society's gone." I go back to the door and slam it shut behind me, leaving her alone to wallow in her self-pity. Doesn't she realize this is hard for both of us? Damn frustrating, annoying women. Doesn't she understand how much it broke me to see her savagely beaten? I wanted to stop it the entire time, and it could've been prevented if she'd just said 'yes'.

I go straight back to my room. I'm shaking and sweating — I'm irate, and I'm worried. I don't know what to do with myself. I want to shut this thing down, now, but the pressure on me is incredible. I can't let my brother down. I can't let other girls go through what's happening to Victoria. I want it finished and done with. I want to go out and fuck an entire catalogue of lingerie models. Who the fuck am I kidding, no I don't? Sex is actually the furthest thing from my mind. In fact, I don't actually know what's going on in my mind. It's a muddle of confusion and suffering. I'm the devil — I must be. I have to be as bad as my father in order to beat him. I've done wrong things in my life. I've killed, maimed, and stolen, all in the name of this fucking society. This fucking society. I pick up a wooden framed chair next to me and throw it hard into a wall. It hits a mirror, which smashes into a thousand pieces on the floor. Next up, I swipe everything off my chest of drawers onto the floor. I stop short of the brandy, sitting temptingly in the decanter at the end. Reggie must've known that it would be something that I need. I pick it up, pull the stop out, and take in long gulps, which burn my throat. I drink half of the bottle. My head swims with the instant hit of the alcohol. Fuck. Argh. I pick up some priceless ornaments and throw them at the artwork adorning the walls. They may be worth millions, but I don't care. I want to get paralytically drunk and destroy. It's all I'm fit to do. It's all I'll ever do in this life. My father has told me enough times that I'll never beat him, and I'm starting to believe it. It is now that I need to go to the dark side of my brain, if that is even possible. Fuck everyone but William. I'll destroy this society. I down another load of the brandy, and its high alcohol content instantly mixes with my blood, which is already compromised from not eating since breakfast. I look at my clock. Dinner time. Maybe I can make myself pass out before anyone comes looking for me. I'm pretty confident that I'm halfway there.

The door to my room creaks. I spin around, and Elizabeth Sandford is standing there. She bites her lip and allows the sleeve of the dressing gown that she's wearing to fall from her shoulder.

"I heard a noise. I think my room must be underneath yours. I know we're not allowed up here, but I was worried."

She sashays up to me and places her hand on my chest.

"What's wrong, My Lord? Is it something I can help you with? You seem upset."

I look straight at her. She's swaying a bit, or is it the fact that I've downed pretty much a whole decanter of brandy in ten minutes?

"This must be hard for you as well. To see us women hurt in a manner than your sensitive nature dislikes. I've seen the true man you are underneath. You want to do this about as much as we want to be married off in this way. You want to love and have affection. Something your father took away from you with your mother. He killed her."

I grab her hand and pull it off my chest. I push her back but don't let go. "Don't talk about my mother. You know nothing about her."

"I know she left you all alone with the man who tortures you night and day. He wants to mold you into his likeness, but you have a heart. He'll never win." I don't know if she's deliberate or not in her words, but her voice is seductive. The gown slips a little farther revealing the gossamer silk of a bra covering the curve of her breast. My eyes flit to it and back to her face.

"You want to sleep with me?" I ask.

She purses her lips together.

"Who wouldn't? You're a handsome man."

"I won't have sex with you, no matter how much you try to flatter me with your false praise of my character, contrasting it with my father's. He's the devil, but he taught me everything he knows."

I let her hand go and bring my other hand to my mouth. It still contains the brandy bottle. I need more to numb everything. Tomorrow, I'll gather my strength and try to fight again. But tonight, I've nothing left. Two weeks ago, I was carefree, and I didn't have to think about this stupid society. Now, it's all my brain can focus on.

"There's another way." Elizabeth's voice permeates my thoughts.

She drops to her knees. "You want to lose your mind for a while. I can help you with that." Her hand is placed on my dick through my trousers, and before I have a chance to say no, she's undoing my zipper and removing me. I'm not hard. I don't know if it's the alcohol, or my lack of lust for the woman on her knees in front of me. But the second she brings my cock into her mouth, I lengthen and lose myself in the moment. Victoria was right — I have no soul.

CHAPTER NINETEEN

VICTORIA

Two weeks have passed since the day I was savagely beaten. I move a little better, but I know that I'll always bear the scars of my attack. Not just physically in the silver streaks that mar my perfect skin but also in the nightmares that haunt me. The names — I want to forget them, but no matter how much I try to fill my head with positive synonyms for women, the negative always seems to invade my consciousness. I see, now, despite the advent of feminism and the burning of bras, women are still second-class citizens within the nobility of England. I wonder how many others have been sold into a world of slavery as I have been.

"Victoria?" Amelia's voice drags me from my reflection. "Do you want anything else to eat?"

"Err. No, thank you. I'm good." I push half an American pancake to the side of my plate. I enjoyed the fruit, but I am still finding it hard to eat a lot. I've always prided myself on being toned and curvy, but with not eating and no swimming, I'm a shadow of my former self.

"Maybe we should ask Nicholas' doctor to retake a look at your tongue. He said you should be eating well by now. You didn't eat much dinner last night and not much breakfast."

"I'm fine. Honestly. Just not hungry. I ate all my fruit. I'm being healthy." I laugh, but she still frowns at me.

"Dear God, stop fussing over her all the time. If she'd said yes, then she wouldn't be in the state she is." Elizabeth pipes into our conversation while shoving the last piece of her venison sausage into her mouth.

I haven't warmed to Elizabeth as I have Amelia. In fact, you could say I think she's a total bitch. She wants to marry Nicholas for the title and the money. That's completely obvious. I also question her morals — she doesn't seem to ask about anything that's going on here. Amelia doesn't make a show of hating her fate, but at least you can see she thinks it's wrong. With Elizabeth Sandford, you get the feeling she's enjoying what's happening. I shudder at that thought. Nobody could enjoy this.

"No one deserves what happened to Victoria," Amelia responds and wipes her mouth with a napkin.

"It's the rules — if she breaks them or doesn't answer in the way the Duke, or the Earl, demands of a wife, then she should be punished." Elizabeth picks up her coffee and takes a mouthful to wash down her breakfast.

"Were you aware of the tasks before coming here?" I ignore her misguided views and question her instead.

"Of course." She pouts.

"And you don't think that it's wrong?" I ask.

"Why should I? I'm a realist, not a dreamer like you."

"What's that supposed to mean?" Her words make no sense.

"We live in a male orientated world. If we want to succeed in it, we need to learn to be subservient."

"Why?" Amelia interjects.

"Because if we don't, then we'll end up with nothing."

"You do know that a woman can have a career of her own that doesn't involve opening her legs for a living, don't you?" I've had enough of this bitch.

"But it's a lot easier if you use what God gave you," she smirks. "Men are weak. They have one brain, and it isn't in their heads." She wiggles her index finger to illustrate a dick.

"Seriously, aren't you supposed to be a virgin?" Amelia snorts.

"You can still be a virgin and know how to give a man pleasure." She leans forward on her elbows. "Nicholas found that out two weeks ago."

I have my coffee cup halfway to my mouth while she's talking, but it never makes it there — I put it down with a thump.

"And what's that supposed to mean?"

"I sucked him off." She looks smug with her declaration I want to smack it off her face. I keep my calm, though. Mainly because moving fast still hurts. "He needed a release after all the stress that you're putting him through with your ridiculous acting out. I gave it to him. He's big — I gagged on him more than once. His cum is the sweetest I've ever tasted as well."

"Shut up," Amelia shouts at Elizabeth. I sit there dumbfounded. I know she isn't lying. I can see it in her eyes.

"I told him that he's welcome to come to me anytime he wants. It's one dick I won't ever say no to." Elizabeth carries on, and Amelia covers her ears, so she doesn't have to hear the conversation anymore. "If you don't want to end up dead, maybe, you should start showing him a few more favors of that kind," she sneers at me.

"I can't listen to this anymore. You're sick." Amelia stomps out of the kitchen. I push my chair back to go after her. I like the blonde, and I know talk of this will impact on her fragile emotions.

"You thought you had him wrapped round your little finger, didn't you?" Elizabeth stops my progress, and I swing back around to face her. "He called my name as he came. I've sucked enough men to know that, when they come, the name of the one they truly want is on their lips."

"I feel sorry for you." I step into her space. She instantly gets to her feet ready to fight me if needed. "You're the daughter of a Bishop and should have better morals. They seem to have disappeared down the drain with any compassion and kindness you might have. If you think that what's happening here is right and good for women, then you're as insane as the Duke and Earl. This is pure and simple kidnapping, murder, and then rape when he chooses a partner. When, not if, I get out of here, I'll see them all go to hell for this. Mark my words. If you want to get on your knees and suck Nicholas', no doubt, disease ridden dick, then go ahead. Open your legs and let him fuck you. I don't care. I hate him. If he chooses you as his wife, then I wish you the best of luck.

In fact, congratulations, have him. I'd rather die than have him ever touch me again." Elizabeth's eyes go past me toward the doorway. I spin around and come face to face with Nicholas — his jaw ticking with anger.

CHAPTER TWENTY

NICHOLAS

"Elizabeth, leave," I order the smug woman out of my sight. Two weeks, two fucking weeks, I haven't seen Victoria. I thought that she might've grown a brain during that time, but it appears not.

"My apologies, My Lord, for you having to witness that appalling attack on your character." The jet-haired woman, who pleasured me the night of my drunken rampage, sways her hips seductively as she leaves the room where the girls were eating their breakfast. She runs a hand across my chest. I don't move. I allow the show of dominance from her because I see the look of jealousy that flits over Victoria's face. She quickly suppressed it, but I saw it. Too late — I have her. "If you need me, I'll be in my room. Try not to get beaten again, Victoria, I'd hate to delay the trials any further. I want to get on with my life and obtain my rightful position." Elizabeth sashays off down the corridor.

"Trailer trash bitch." Victoria coughs under her breath. I

can't help the smirk that touches my lips because she's right. Elizabeth Sandford is a slut. She would make a terrible wife — she would fuck my entire retinue. I could never be sure that any children we had were mine. It isn't her fault, though. With a Bishop for a father, she was sexually repressed for years and has finally discovered her calling.

"Come here," I order Victoria — now that we're alone.

"Hell no." She takes a step farther away.

"Come here," I order again. This time with a little bit more force.

"Are you trying it on with all of us? I bet I was a big disappointment, seeing that you had to give to me rather than receive."

My lip lifts into a smirk again.

"You really are a freak. My god, you're actually enjoying this." She steps forward, this time, at a rapid pace and makes to go around me. I stand fully in the doorway, filling it with my muscular frame.

"You aren't going anywhere."

"I'm getting the hell away from you, and when I get out of here, I'm getting tested for STDs. You're probably a walking infection. Now, let me pass."

"You'd rather die than have me touch you again?"

"Yes." She makes a charge for me to try and get me to move out of the way. As she bounces off my taut body, I can see that she hurts herself more than she hurts me. "Get out of my fucking way."

"I didn't call her name, when I came."

She throws her hands up in the air.

"I don't want to hear this. Who you stick your dick into

isn't my concern. As long as you keep that thing away from me, I'm happy."

"I mouthed yours because I was drunk — completely pissed off that you still weren't listening to me, and what I want you to do so that we can get through this together."

"Great, you were pissed at me, so you stuck your dick down another woman's throat. That really makes you a good candidate to be a husband. You say that you want to marry me, but what happens the first time we have an argument? You find the nearest willing hole and stick yourself in it." She tries again to get past me. "Will you get out of my fucking way?" She balls her fist and punches me in the jaw. It hurts — it actually causes me pain. Damn, she's strong for such a little thing.

"Argh," she cries. "God damn it." She grips her shoulder where, I know, the deepest of her wounds is. It must still be healing and was jolted when she hit me. "Please, just move."

"You know, for hitting me, I'm within my rights to put you back in the bridle."

Her eyes fill with worry, but her cheeks turn pink with fury.

"You have no rights over me. I'm a woman with my own thoughts and mind."

"You're my property — your father gave you to me," I snarl back.

"I'm a human being. I'm no one's property."

"Wrong. Until this is over, you're mine."

"Jerk." She tries one final time to get past me. I move out of the way at the last minute, and she goes flying by. I grab her arm and start to drag her down the hallway.

"Get off me."

"No."

"Nicholas, you're hurting me."

"I don't care. For once, you're going to listen to me."

"What's the point? You have nothing to say that would remotely interest me."

I pull her up the stairs toward my room. She digs her heels in.

"I can't go up there."

"My father's out. What I want to show you is up there."

"Thank God, you didn't say it was in your pants."

"You back on my dick again? I can show you that as well, if you want," I chuckle.

"Drop dead," she snarls.

I tug hard, and she has no choice but to follow me. Reggie appears from one of the rooms.

"Help me," Victoria screams.

I glare at him. He holds his hands up and steps back into the room.

"Jesus, all the men in this place are insane," Victoria huffs.

We get to my room, and I pull her inside, shutting the door and locking it, to give us privacy, I put the key into my pocket.

"I'm not going to sleep with you or suck you if that's why you've brought me up here. I mean it. You're holding me hostage and should be in prison."

"I know."

"What?"

"I should be in prison. I know you aren't going to sleep with me, but that doesn't stop me from wanting to touch you whenever you're in the same room as me. It doesn't stop me from wanting to seek you out to talk to you. In fact, you being my possession makes it even harder because I know that I can't have you." Both of us are breathing rapidly. Our gasps for air fill the sudden silence in the room

"Don't, please." Victoria's sweet tones finally break the tranquility.

"You're at an unfair disadvantage to the others. They seem to all know what happens next. You don't. They've already learned, from their fathers, what is required to become my wife. I want you to learn what's involved from a Duchess."

"Nicholas, there's no Duchess? Your mother, she's dead because of this." The word dead is stressed with such poignant emotion that I have a momentary regret that I'm about to share a part of my life with someone. I've hidden it away for so long, but this is Victoria. I've known since the moment I first saw her, staring intently at Van Gogh's Poppies, that there was something different about her. I've known that she'd be the one to break this curse, hanging over our families. I step up to a chest of drawers in my room and remove my mother's diary from it. I brought it up here a few days ago and have read the whole thing since.

"Here."

"What's this?"

She looks down at the silk cover as I push the book into her shaking hands.

"Open it and read a page."

"I don't think I should."

I roll my eyes.

"For once, in the short time we've known each other, accept that I'm trying to do something to help you. Please read the damn diary," I snap and plonk my weight down into a Queen Anne armchair. It's my favorite and, thankfully, survived the attack I made on my room. I place my head in my hands. I can feel a migraine simmering at the edges of my temples. This isn't how I thought my day would go. I hear the pages turn and look up. Victoria's flicking through the diary.

"Is this…?" she hesitates, so I answer for her.

"My mother's."

"Nicholas, I can't read this. It's personal to you and William."

"If it helps you in any way with what's to come next, then it's more pertinent to you. William and I have read it. We've mourned our mother, and what she was forced to do."

Victoria flicks through another few pages then gasps. I don't know what has elicited such a reaction because the whole diary's full of such moments.

She opens her mouth to speak and shuts it again.

"Read it."

"Fire, sex, death. That's what they called today. A death that's what I had. I'll never forget it, the pale face, the blood, the pain. Freedom, he was lucky. I wished for it. I pray for it nightly, but it never comes. I'm in hell and became one of them today. There's no hope for me. I know he'll choose me. I see it in the way he looks at me. I'll have the last laugh, though. I'll end this — I'll conceive his son against my consent. The compassion that dies within me will be born into him. He'll rule and rid the world of the society of Oakfield."

When she finishes reading, Victoria closes the book and sits in her own chair.

"I don't know if I can read anymore."

"Take it with you. You need to prepare for tomorrow."

"Death? Nicholas, please tell me it isn't what I think it is?" she asks.

"I'm afraid toward the end my mother's words get a little jumbled. She wasn't in her right frame of mind."

"You've read this but still want me to go through with the trials?" I try to sense whether she's angry at that fact or sad, but I can't get a read on her.

"You should go." I pull the key out of my pocket and throw it toward her.

"Talk to me." She slides off the chair and picks the key up like it's a security blanket, but she's still hesitant and doesn't make a run for the door.

"I have to go through with this, Victoria. It's the only way. I can't let my mother die in vain. I can't risk William. I know I sound like I'm completely selfish, but please, read that and understand my point of view."

She looks down at the diary again.

"Thank you."

I shut my eyes and listen to her put the key into the lock, turn it, and leave the room. I'm no good at verbalizing what I'm feeling, but hopefully my mother can, in some way, show Victoria why I need to finish this properly. I need to take the title from my father and make everything right for William, for my mother, and for all the other girls who've been harmed over two hundred years of the Oakfield society. Even if it's to the detriment of the woman I'm falling in love with.

"You know — I can look after myself — I'm not that incapable. I could walk out of this place tomorrow if I wanted to." The hidden doorway behind me creaks, and William's voice comes through it.

"Your sense of direction's awful. You'll get lost before you get to the end of the driveway," I retort with a weary laugh.

"I'm not that bad. Better than you are. You got lost going out for Chinese once."

"They'd changed premises."

"No excuse."

He slaps me on the shoulder, and I sit up.

"What are you doing here?"

"Keeping hidden but seeing things again. You gave her mum's diary?" He pulls up a chair and sits next to me.

"I thought it might help her understand why I need to do things this way."

He snorts, and his tics appear. He strokes the side of his face, nose, and taps twice on the arm of the chair.

"William?"

"Listen. I meant what I said. If I chose to walk out of here, I would be alright. You should fight for Victoria over me. I know she frustrates the hell out of you, but I'm not a fool. I see the growing feelings between you both, despite the situation."

"Stop it," I command and take his hand to stop him from tapping on the chair. He taps on my fingers instead. "This is stressing you. I made a promise to you and Mum. I'll always be there to help you and protect you from our father."

"You were five years old. I don't even remember the promise. I was three."

"But I still made it," I interrupt.

"What if you don't succeed?"

"Then, I'll die for the cause. I won't allow another woman to go through this. Any children I may be lucky enough to have will choose their wives the conventional way. They'll go on dates and have their hearts' broken."

"Not heartbreak. Isn't that what women have and demand ice cream for all the time?"

"It is, but I'd never say that to them."

"Maybe I should ask Victoria if she want's ice cream while she's reading the diary?"

"William?" Because of his autism, my brother isn't always aware of the social norms. "That's not a good idea. You should probably stay away from her for a while. I'm not sure how she'll react to the diary."

"Joke, brother. I miss you smiling at me. I know that she needs time alone. I don't always understand everything, and I think that gazing at the stars is a lot easier than interacting with society. But, somehow, I have this built-in instinct when it comes to understanding women."

"You need to share that with me, then."

"You're doing well. The diary was the right decision."

There's a knock on my door. William freezes.

"Who is it?"

"Mr. Hane, My Lord."

My butler, thank god. "Come in."

He enters and bows to us.

"Hello, Lord William."

"Reggie." My brother gets to his feet and, without an understanding of personal space, embraces my butler with warm affection.

"William put the man down." I also get to my feet and pull my brother off.

"Sorry to disturb you. I've just had word from His Grace. He's to return home within the hour. He's sent the call out to the society members. No more waiting. You're all to be in the banqueting room for his return. The next trials will be happening then and there."

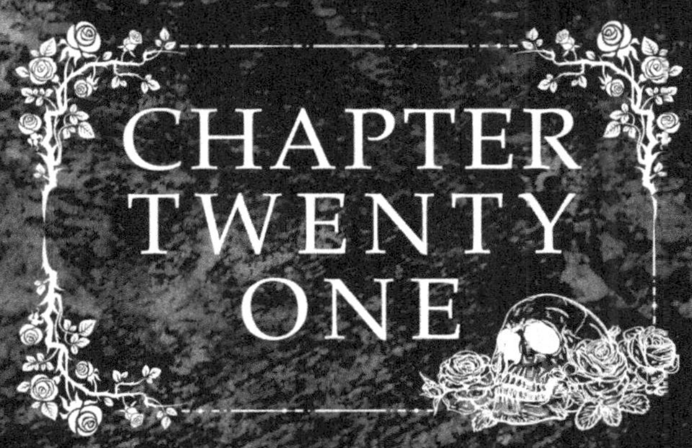

VICTORIA

I can barely read the pages before me for the tears that stream down my face. This is a diary written by someone who'd been through what I'm going through, and that someone was Nicholas' Mother. My heart breaks, but I'm still confused. If he's read this, then why didn't he put a stop to it? Is he that conflicted and controlled by his father that he can't see what's right and wrong. I want to go back to him and tell him that it'll all be okay if he stops this now. The world won't fall apart — he and William will be safe, but something sits uneasily in my stomach. I don't know everything that's going on here. I must read more. Firstly, though, I need to make a preference for the next trial, 'fire, sex, death'. I read a small passage about it earlier but didn't finish it when I came to my room. I wanted to start the diary from the beginning, so I got the whole picture. I flip to where I know it begins.

'Fire, sex, and death is the hardest task of them all. It's designed to break the weakest of the women who haven't already been destroyed by the punishment task. I was whipped, as you know dear diary, but nothing can prepare you for what you become when these tasks are handed out.'

My bedroom door flies open before I can read any further. I shove the diary under my pillow and glare at the Duke's guards.

"I thought our rooms were sacred."

"Maybe the others are, but yours is a whole different state of affairs. Get up, now."

"Go to hell." I ignore the twerp in the Duke's livery. They don't command me.

"Get up, or I'll drag you by the hair to complete the next task." He menacingly steps forward.

"The next task?" Shit, I think. I haven't had a chance to read all about it yet.

"Yes, it's time. Get up."

My legs suddenly feel as though they're ten ton weights. The words, 'fire, sex, death' are resonating through my head in a loop that sounds more imposing with every repeat. I manage to stand. I'm not sure how.

"I'm up."

"Follow me, then," the guard sneers and leads off. I want to run away into the hidden passages in the house and hope I can find a way out, but I know it will be futile. I'll be dragged out and probably put in the bridle. I have solid plans to never go in there again, so I follow him. Halfway down the corridor, Amelia leaves her room. She looks like a ghost. She's deathly pale and shaking like a leaf. Over the last few days, she's had an air of calm about her, but not now.

"Amelia?" I grab her hand to check that she's alright.

"No talking!" the guard shouts at me.

"Fuck you," I respond, not caring about punishment.

"Are you alright?"

She opens her mouth to speak, but the guard grabs me by the hair, before she has a chance. He pulls me into the room where the Duke's waiting and throws me to the floor in front of him.

"The bridle didn't work. She's disobeying the orders."

"I'm checking my friend is alright," I shout back at him and go to get up. I'm pushed back down.

"I like her at my feet. It's a good position for someone with a mouth like hers. Actually, no, on her knees sucking my dick would be better." The Duke laughs at his own comment. Nicholas comes into view, and he's not smiling. He looks tired and angry.

"The girls are mine. You can't touch them without my permission." He ignores me and vents his anger on his father instead.

"I shared your mother with my father and brother — why change tradition?" the Duke snarls back. I see Nicholas' fist form into a ball, ready to lash out, and my stomach turns with overwhelming nausea, at the statement.

"It's one tradition I can change without the society's consent, and I'm changing it now. None of these girls are to be touched without my permission. If I find out that they have, then you'll be tried by the society for corrupting the succession process. Something I know you take seriously because of the consequences." Nicholas is fuming, but it's the first time I've seen him stand up to his father, and the Duke actually backs down. The older Cavendish huffs and steps away to the side.

"Let the next trial begin." The Duke holds his hand up and thumps it down on a table.

"Ladies, my son has already determined the level of discipline that will be required to correct you, as his wife. Some needing more than others." He looks at me, and I can't help it — I sneer while getting to my feet. "As the Duchess of Oakfield, you'll have to set an example. You'll be called upon to accompany the Duke to social functions, which will contain a variety of people, including royalty. You'll be expected to act with the highest decorum at all times. That's not all that will be demanded of you, though. The society's a business — we undertake certain deals on behalf of the members to further our ambitions. You'll be required to take part in this as much as necessary. This is the purpose of these three trials." The Duke walks over to a sunken area in the hall. I'd noticed it before but never thought much of it. Four guards line up around the corners of the area, and the Duke nods. A cover's pulled back, and a pit of burning coal is revealed.

"To join the society, one of the tasks is to walk over hot coals. It's supposed to signify the age old tradition of being willing to do anything for advancement. One of you ladies will be given that task by Earl Lullington." The Duke looks at his son and motions for him to step forward and take the stage. I notice for the first time how tired Nicholas seems. He has dark circles under his eyes, and the stubble lining his chiseled jaw is longer than usual. A few more days of growth, and he'll have a somewhat unkempt beard. He still wears a suit, which is immaculately pressed, but somehow it doesn't hang on his shoulders with the arrogant confidence that it would have done a few weeks ago. I want to go to him, embrace him, tell him it'll be alright, and that the world isn't really falling apart. But I know that it is, and I've already promised him that I wouldn't lie. The sound of my name on Nicholas' deep tones draws me from my reflection.

"Victoria will walk the coals," he says.

"I'll do what?" I exclaim loudly in shock.

He glares at me. It's a look that tells me to keep my mouth shut. 'Fire, Sex, Death' pops into my head. Ok, maybe I'll be silent as this is apparently the fire, and I like the sound of the other two a lot less than walking over hot coals.

"How very disappointing," the Duke moans. "I was hoping that you would choose her for sex. I was looking forward to it." He laughs this time, and I look to Amelia. Seeing that she's close to tears, I reach out and take her hand. She grips mine back tightly, saying nothing as the Duke starts up with his annoying sermons again.

"In all ways, the wife of a Duke must be completely faithful to her husband, unless, for reasons known only to the Duke, he commands her to personally commit carnal acts with another person. I did this with my wife. I wanted to work with a particular client, so I gave him a night with my wife to seal the deal." He chuckles, and my blood freezes. "She didn't come back *too* bruised." I look at Nicholas as he stumbles back, grabbing a nearby chair to support himself. I'm sure his father enjoys teasing him. I look up to the hidden alcoves and wonder if William is listening to this as well. It must be hard on them both to know that their mother was brutally treated and chose death over being with them in life.

That she couldn't try to save them from the fate they faced. I will Nicholas to walk out and tell his father that he'll not do this, but I know it won't happen because this is the only way he can see to put an end to everything.

"For the purpose of this task, I get to have a little fun." The Duke stands proudly, and I have a horrible sinking feeling I know what's coming. "The chosen lady will be given to me by my son to complete fellatio. If you, in anyway, attempt to bite my penis, then I'll have your teeth pulled out of your mouth, one by one, without anesthetic. A good wife needs to obey her husband no matter what. Your body's his property, and he can command how you use it."

I can't help but be over the moon at not having to complete that task. I like my teeth in my mouth, and I would definitely lose them because I wouldn't be able to prevent myself from trying to gnaw off the Duke's gross dick. It would be the safest way of ensuring I didn't get any nasty diseases.

"Nicholas, who do you choose for this task?" the Duke asks, and I send up a silent prayer that he doesn't choose Amelia. It's already been proven that Elizabeth's a whore, so give her that task. I'm sure she'll enjoy it. She can compare father and son. Yuck! What a disgusting thought.

"Elizabeth. I happen to know that she has talents that you'll rather appreciate."

The assembled crowd murmur amongst themselves, but my attention's distracted when Amelia grips my hand even tighter and whispers,

"Thank you for being my friend. You've a strength I've never seen before. I know that you'll be the last Duchess of Oakfield to be chosen this way."

"What?" I ask, but the Duke interrupts us again. This time, I'm pulled away to the coals by the guards. Amelia's taken up to the front of the stage, and Elizabeth's pushed to her knees at the Duke's feet.

"The final task, which Amelia will complete, is the ultimate sin for both husband and wife. The society is brutal — as many of you know from the punishments you've received for misdemeanors. If you betray us, then the punishment is death. Public execution. No second chances. As wife to my son, you'll be expected to uphold this. You'll be expected to kill."

The bottom falls out of my world when I see a gun is placed in front of Amelia. No. No. Her words suddenly start to make sense. The only task she couldn't complete. I'm being held by the two guards, but I get free from them with unimaginable strength and throw myself at Nicholas' feet. He looks down in shock, and with an almost silent voice, I whisper,

"Swap Amelia and I — I want to do the killing."

CHAPTER TWENTY TWO

NICHOLAS

"What are you doing? Get up." I stare down dumbstruck at Victoria. "Have you gone insane? I gave you the easiest task." I bend down and, with gritted teeth, tell her to stop this madness.

"No. I want to kill the person." All the time she speaks, her eyes are flicking over to Amelia.

"I'm not going to give you the gun. Go back to the coals."

"What's going on?" My father shouts from the other side of the room. He's already undoing his trousers and pulling himself out. It's not something I enjoy seeing, but sadly it's something I've witnessed far too often. The society's members are infamous for their orgy nights. The one and only thing that I used to quite enjoy.

"Nothing," I reply.

"Can the bitch not even do the easiest of the tasks without causing a problem? George" —he waves his hand in the air toward one of the guards— "bring the scold's bridle. I don't have time for messing around." My father shoves his dick into Elizabeth's mouth, and she gags around the surprise intrusion. "I hope you're going to be better at swallowing me than that."

"It's fine. I'll deal with it. We don't need the bridle." I pull Victoria up toward me. "Stop this now. I thought giving you the diary would have knocked some sense into you."

"Please swap us," she pleads. I can see the desperation in her eyes.

"Tell me why? Give me one good reason. You know what's about to happen. I don't want that on your conscience."

"Amelia." She opens her mouth to tell me, but there's a commotion at the door. A man's brought in and thrown onto his knees in the center of the room. He's one of the 'workers', as we call them here in the society, who do the mundane work for us. They aren't paid well, for they're the lowest of the low. Pulled from the streets and offered a better life only to be thrown to the lion, that is my father, and forced to risk everything, so we don't have to.

"This man has stolen from us. He took money to perform a task, and he spent it on getting high instead. The work was not done to the highest standard, and I now have to get another loyal man out of prison in Egypt, as a result." My father's bucking his hips into Elizabeth's mouth while he speaks. He's using her like a rag doll with a hole to get himself off. There's no finesse about the act. It's raw fucking of a willing hole. Then again, that's pretty much all Elizabeth Sandford is: willing with three holes to stick a dick in. "The punishment for stealing from us is death. Sometimes, as the leader, we don't like to get our hands dirty, and that's where our wives come into the equation. Amelia, your task is to kill this man."

Victoria whimpers and grabs hold of my ankle. "Please, don't make her do this."

"You know I have to follow the rules," I respond.

"Let the games begin," my father shouts.

"Nicholas, please."

"Enough," I shout and grab Victoria by the arm. I drag her to her feet and, with the red mists descending, pull her across the room back to the coals. Behind me, I can hear one of the guards explaining to Amelia how to use the gun. To the side of me is my father's carnal grunts, and Elizabeth's wet suction. All the time, Victoria is squirming in my hands.

"No!" she screams, but I slam my hand over her mouth to muffle the sound.

"Damn it, please stop this. Just do what I ask. I can't handle this with every task. Why are you so bloody defiant all the time?"

"Kill him." My father's voice echoes around the room. "His punishment is death."

"Please don't," the man whimpers. The gun cocks.

Victoria's wriggling so much in my arms that I can barely hold her. She's like a piece of Jell-O. She bites on the hand I have clamped over her mouth, and I curse.

"Fuck."

I've had enough and push her onto the coals, so she has no choice but to walk on them. She's still defiant, though, as she stumbles back across them toward and then past me. I spin on my heels. The world turns slowly like those old-fash-ioned movies where the film breaks, and the world turns like it would go on forever. Victoria falls to her feet and screams.

At the same time Amelia puts the gun in her mouth and pulls the trigger, ending her life as her head explodes.

"No!" Victoria cries out, again and again, bringing the world rapidly back up to speed. I can barely catch my breath as Amelia's body falls to the floor next to the drugged up thief that she was supposed to kill. Suddenly, I'm running. I'm next to Victoria, scooping her up into my arms. My father's sexual grunts come back into my consciousness as he comes down Elizabeth's throat. I feel sick — I'm going to be sick. The stench of death fills the room. Blood is flowing all over the floor — parts of the dead girl's brain and skull are splattered everywhere. And still, my father comes and comes. I can't do this. I need to leave. My legs are carrying me, and I hold a still hysterical Victoria in my arms. We're going — we're getting out of here.

"Leaving so soon, son?" my father calls out. A gun goes off again. I turn back to see Elizabeth Sandford holding the smoking weapon, this time, and the condemned man lying dead beside Amelia.

"At least, the tasks were completed, and we're one girl down. Makes the choice a whole lot easier, don't you think?"

I don't wait to hear any more. I just get the hell out of there.

VICTORIA

Nicholas carries me out of the house and races toward a car. I'm still shaking. The only task that she could never complete. Her father had asked her to commit murder before, and she'd naturally refused. I dread to think the punishment she must've received from him. Whatever it was broke her enough that I just watched her commit suicide. I bury my head into Nicholas' chest as he shouts instructions to a liveried man.

"Give me the keys."

"My Lord, this is your father's car. If you wait a moment, I'll get one of yours."

"Just give me the fucking keys." Nicholas gently places me down against the midnight blue Land Rover. "Wait there," he orders. I don't think I could move if I tried. My legs are like jelly, and I use the car to hold me up. Nicholas spins around and stomps over to the guards. He pulls his hand back and floors the surprised man with one punch. He picks the keys out of the livery man's hand and clicks open the car. "Get in." I obey. He goes to the driver's side and gets in. He puts his seatbelt on, and I do the same before he takes off, speeding down the long driveway.

"Nicholas." I reach out and touch his leg, but he doesn't respond. He just focuses on the massive gateway in front of us. It starts to open — alerted, no doubt, by a sensor in the car. He's going to take me away from here. I squeeze his leg a little harder. His breathing's getting quicker and quicker. "Nicholas," I reassure again as the gate finishes opening. The path to freedom is laid bare before us, but at the last minute, he slams his foot down on the break. The car skids sideways over a manicured lawn and halts just before a garish statue of a little girl entwined with a snake. He bangs his hands on the steering wheel and gets out of the car and starts to beat the crap out of it. The thumping of the metal makes me shudder. He's falling apart before me. I undo my seat belt and slide across and out his side. He's going mad — the strength of his fury is so great that dents are appearing on the Land Rover. Without thinking, I step closer to him and wrap my hands around his waist. I'm standing behind him, and he stills. I can hear his heavy gasping breaths. I lay my head against his back and hear the anguished cries wracking his body.

"I killed her," he laments.

"No,"

"I didn't listen to you. I killed her. I want to take you away from here, but I can't. I should be able to drive through that gateway, but I can't. I'm going to kill you as well." He turns around, and I can see the tears falling down his face. I step up on the balls of my feet and use my thumb to wipe them away.

"You didn't kill her. The society did. She never had any

hope. She told me that her father had been preparing her for the trials since she was young. He was abusing her and hiding behind what this society is. She was broken. You didn't kill her. The murder was the one task that she could never complete. She'd rather go to heaven with her conscience clear."

"I should have seen how broken she was. I knew she wasn't right, but I thought it was the stress of the situation."

I shake my head.

"She was a dead woman walking. I don't think anyone could have saved her, no matter how much we wanted to." I feel sick. Amelia was only twenty-one and had known nothing but abuse all her life. "Her father is a vile man, and I won't rest until he's punished for this."

"Neither of us will."

I look over to the gateway. I could push off Nicholas and make a break for my freedom, but I'm pulled closer to him by the situation we're in. Somewhere, in all of this, I've developed feelings for my captor.

"William," Nicholas speaks.

"I won't risk him. We're going to finish this together." I step back and slide my hand down to his, so he can lead me back to the car.

"Victoria." He doesn't move. "Marry me?"

"What?"

"Marry me?"

I can't find the answer I want to give — my throat goes dry. Most people would think that I'm insane for even considering this, but I am. I'm in love with him and all that he wants to do. He's been in the worst position just as I have. We've both been oppressed and forced against our wills to conduct acts that have left us confused and hurting, but together, we've discovered we can beat our devils. Together we'll win.

"Make me your woman first."

"What?"

I step up on the balls of my feet again and press a soft kiss to his lips.

"Stop the pain in my chest — stop my heart from breaking at all the death and hate around us. Show me what love is."

He crushes his lips to mine, apparently not needing to be asked twice, to show me what pleasure feels like. Before long, I'm lifted up into his arms, and we're moving. Our lips part.

"Where are we going?"

"There's a summer house a short walk away. I want you privately, not in the middle of the driveway with the rest of the society leaving."

"Good idea." I join our lips again, and we stumble, well Nicholas stumbles, through the gardens to the summer house. The smell of roses hits me, and I pull back. Nicholas puts me down on my feet and opens the door. The summer house is filled with highly fragrant blooms. I pick a vibrant red rose and twirl it around in my fingers.

"They're my favorite flowers. The garden where I grew up had loads of them." Memories of my father being the one to put me in this position surface, and a tear escapes my eye.

"Wait here," Nicholas orders and disappears back outside. I take a look around. It's small and secluded — a place for bringing a book and lounging on the daybed in the center of the room. White blinds are at all the windows, but this place is private, and they don't need to be drawn. The daybed is covered in a white blanket. Oakfield Hall is masculine to the extreme, but this place is feminine. Nicholas returns with a few more roses in his hands. He pulls the petals off and strews them over the bed.

"This place isn't like the rest of Oakfield Hall."

"No, my mother had it built. She wanted a place to escape when my father had his mistresses over. He at least did one nice thing for her."

He pats the bed for me to go to him. I do and stand between his legs.

"Are you sure you want to do this?" he asks.

"Am I sure I want you to strip me naked and make love to me, or fuck me? However, it is you roll." I chuckle to diffuse the sudden tension that pools in my stomach.

"This is your first time. I'm going to be gentle. The fucking can come later."

"Sounds good to me."

He reaches up and strokes my face.

"Things will change."

"I know."

"She won't have died in vain."

"We'll always honor her."

I lean forward, and we kiss slowly. He pulls me onto the bed and lays me down.

We part lips, and he pulls the t-shirt that I'm wearing over my head. I sit up a little, so he can remove my bra. I'm not big breasted, but that doesn't seem to bother Nicholas as he instantly buries his head between them.

"Delicious." He flicks my nipple, and I moan low in my throat. I've always had a sensitive body, but around Nicholas, everything seems to double in sensation. I'm vibrating underneath him with the need for more. He flips me over and places the same kisses on my back. I feel him tense when he sees some of the bruising and deeper wounds, which haven't fully healed, yet. He pays particular attention to them as if apologizing for being a part of their infliction. I've long since forgiven him.

My jeans are next to be removed and then my knickers. He steps back and drops his suit jacket to the floor. I've never seen him without it and lick my lips at the sight. He pulls the left sleeve of his shirt toward him and unhooks the cufflink. He places it on a table, next to the daybed, and does the same with the other one.

"Do you always wear suits?" I ask while he removes his shirt and places that on the table as well. I take in his chest. It's defined with chiseled muscles and tapers down to a place of hidden promises in his trousers.

"I feel like I have, lately. I prefer jeans and a t-shirt, but unfortunately the position often requires a certain dress code."

"I want to see you in jeans," I blurt out, and he smiles. "Are you liking what you see, Victoria?"

"Maybe," I tease.

"Well, how about this?" He undoes his belt and then the zipper of his trousers, which he then lowers. Between my thighs starts to throb just at the sight of him in tight boxers. He kicks off his shoes and removes his trousers and socks. Next thing I know, he's back on top of me, kissing down my body.

"Isn't the underwear coming off?" I ask.

"Soon. If I take them off right now, I won't be able to take this slowly. I'm not going to risk hurting you *anymore*." The 'anymore' is said with poignant emotion. I need to reassure him that I'm not going to fall apart.

"I'm not broken. You've made me stronger, if anything."

"I'm still not prepared to risk that fact when it comes to carnal activities. Now shush and let me be the master here. I want to make you feel good."

I lay back and shut my eyes as Nicholas puts his head between my thighs. Before long, I'm coming on his face in a much-needed release. I know I'm mourning the loss of my friend, but she's been the catalyst to bring about change. No more women will be harmed as a result of the sacrifices that she's made in her life.

Nicholas slides up my body and kisses my lips. He tastes of me, and it's decadent and totally wicked. I forget, for a second, who I am and why I'm here.

"Last chance to say no." His eyes flicker with fear, a concern that he'll hurt me or worse.

"I'm beginning to think you don't want me as much as you say," I taunt.

He raises a playful eyebrow while grabbing the waistband of his boxers and pulling them down his legs. Holy fuck! My eyes almost bug out of my head at the sight of him naked. It's like one of the Greek gods in the paintings that adorn the walls of Oakfield Hall, except he's so much better endowed. His cock struts out from his torso, covered in clear liquid at the tip. He's ready for me already.

"I'm going to hurt you, at first. It's unavoidable. I was blessed with girth."

I chuckle at his formal use of words.

"It's a pretty big dick."

He shakes his head and positions himself at my entrance.

I lay back and allow my hands to entwine in the sheets when he pushes in. He wasn't joking when he said he had girth. I breathe through the discomfort until the pleasure takes over again, and I relax around his intrusion.

"Move, please," I pant, and he obeys. In a slow, tantalizing movement, he withdraws from me and pushes straight back in.

"Move." I shut my eyes and allow my head to fall back. I'm no longer a virgin. I've broken the rules: joined with the man I was given to, and I don't care. All I want is for him to move faster. To fuck me. I rotate my hips to encourage him, and he grunts out a strained response.

"Victoria, don't tempt me. I'm struggling to be gentle."

"Haven't you learned, yet. I don't break easily. Fuck me."

He moans deeper, and his pupils dilate to the pitch of the darkest night. The devil is released, and I'm pleased. He pulls his hips back and slams into me. The force sends me up the bed and an explosion rocks through my body. I'm coming again, already. Nicholas continues his thrusts as I reach my precipice and fall over. I'm flying in his arms as he fucks me like a wild animal. I'm raw and loving every moment. My lover buries himself, deeply, inside me and stills. He comes with a loud raspy call of my name. I feel the jets of seed flood my womb. Fuck, he's bare. No condom. He must see the moment that I worry, for he bends and kisses my lips.

"I'm clean, and you're protected. You have my word on this."

I relax again. Nicholas withdraws from me, and we entwine our limbs on the daybed. He pulls a blanket over us.

"Are you alright?" he asks.

"I feel different," I respond.

"Is that a good or bad different?" He looks worried and sits up a bit.

"Good. I made a decision for myself. It's probably the first time ever."

His face softens, again, and he lays back down. "Do you want to make another one? I asked you a question before."

"You did."

"Will you help me end this for good? Will you be my wife?"

"Yes," I answer — confident that I'm doing the right thing.

CHAPTER TWENTY FOUR

NICHOLAS

I watch Victoria sleeping — she looks peaceful. It's nice to watch her in person and not via a monitor. She opens her mouth and mumbles something about an oat and raisin cookie and then wiggles her perfect nose. I smile because I'm relaxed and happy. I've never enjoyed watching a woman this way before. It's been sex and goodbye, but with Victoria, it's different. After we made love twice more, we laid in each other's arms and talked about our childhood for a few hours. She fell asleep, but I wasn't tired. I've got far too much on my mind and none of it good. No matter what Victoria says, I'm responsible for Amelia's death. All this has been for my succession. I could have said no and walked away, but I didn't because of William and my fears for myself. I was selfish but no more. Together, Victoria and I will finish this. I slide from the bed and fumble around for my boxers. I eventually find them slung over a vase of fake roses. The flowers are everywhere. It's as if my mother knew that the girl I would fall for would pick them as her favorite.

Tiptoeing quietly, I grab the rest of my clothes and go outside. I need some air to think about what happens next. I pull my phone out of my pocket and dial Reggie's number. He may be my butler, but he's also a confidant.

"My Lord, where are you?" he answers after the first ring.

"My mother's summer house."

I can hear him exhale a sigh of relief.

"You didn't leave. What about Victoria?"

"She's with me."

"You have spent time together?"

"If you're asking if we've slept together, then yes. I've made my decision — I'm going to marry her. It may not have been a traditional courtship, but she's everything that I want in a wife. Together, we'll disband the society and see that no more girls are hurt by its rules."

He goes silent on the other end of the phone.

"Reggie."

"I'll help you in any way I can. It won't be easy. Your father is already putting things in place. He'll check Miss Victoria, the moment you return, to confirm that her virginity is still intact. You and I are both aware of the consequences when he finds out that it isn't."

"He won't touch her."

"You have to think carefully, My Lord."

"Is he at home?"

"No. He left after Miss Amelia's body was removed to her father." I wince at the mention of Victoria's dead friend.

"Did he take it?"

"No, she's caused shame on her family, and he refused her back. Your father has had her placed in the cellar until something can be done."

"I want you to make arrangements for her to be buried in the local church. They'll not ask any questions. They're used to random bodies suddenly appearing."

"I'll sort it at once, My Lord."

"Thank you, Reggie. Where's my father?"

"He went to his flat." I don't need to ask what my butler means by his flat. It's the place where he goes when he wants time to fuck in peace, away from Oakfield, even if it's still on the grounds.

"I need to go check on Victoria. I don't want to leave her for long. Can you send some food and clean clothing down here for her? I'm going to go and see my father. I want a guard as well, make that two. One for William and one for her. I know you have contacts."

"I do, Sir. I'll sort it at once."

"Thank you."

I hang up, and the summer house door opens. Victoria stands there, rubbing her eyes. She has the sheet wrapped around her body.

"I wondered where you'd gone?"

"I was just talking to my butler. My father has left Oakfield, but that doesn't mean you're safe. I don't know his next move, but I do know that the second he gets hold of you he'll have you before his doctor, again. That's not happening. I need to go and speak to him. Tell him I've made my decision. I want you to stay here. My butler has contacts. He's going to get someone to guard you and someone for William, also."

"Nicholas." She places her hand on my chest. "I've been thinking. We should run away — go to Scotland and marry. He can't do anything about it once we're man and wife.

You'll be married, and he'll need to step aside. Then, we can start changing the rules."

"I wish it were that easy." I pull her closely to me and press a kiss to her sex tangled hair.

"Your father and the rules."

"The last task."

"What is it?"

"The one that's essential to the society's business. It's the one that defines us."

"I don't understand?"

I take a deep breath and lead Victoria back into the summer house. We take a seat on the daybed.

"You know you asked me about the Van Gogh picture in the main hall." I run a hand through my hair with the nerves I feel.

"Yes. The obvious fake."

"It's not a fake. It's the real one."

"But that can't be possible. It was stolen eight years ago." She screws her nose up in confusion.

"I know. I was the one who stole it."

"What?" She pulls back from me like I've just told her that her favorite puppy has died, or something. She's in shock and confused. "You stole it? The real 'Poppies', you have the real painting in your hall."

"Yes." I nod guiltily.

"How?" she exclaims.

"I've been trained as a thief since almost the day I was born. Most of the members of the society are. Nobody suspects us because of who we are. We have a lot more pictures in our collection than are on show. Most of the stolen

Nazi pictures are hidden in special storage under Oakfield Hall. We're worth billions in collectable art."

Victoria slides from the bed and puts distance between us.

"And that's why the society was set up. To collect art. We needed money to maintain our positions. It was the one-way way to do it that the founders all agreed on. Over the years, to keep us going, we've allowed others who possess the appropriate skills to join. The majority of work is still the acquisition of paintings, but we also collect sculptures, architecture when we can steal it, and famous photographs and videos."

"I can't believe what I'm hearing."

"Are you angry?"

"I'm confused. You steal paintings and think it gives you the right to treat women the way you do?" She looks at me, eyes narrowed, and the expression on her face is harsh.

"When the society was set up, my ancestors were the highest ranked. They took on the most risk. In those days, losing their head would've been the least of their problems if they were caught. My four times great grandfather demanded something in exchange. He wanted a choice of brides for his son. The rules and trials were documented and have been in place ever since. My great, great grandfather tried to repeal them during the Victorian times, but the industry was exploding, and the artworks collected were being used for expanding the society's interests during the Industrial Revolution. New rules were put in place stating that should we try to stop the legacy of our succession, we'd forfeit everything, including our lives. The Dukedom of Oakfield would become extinct because all heirs would be executed. That's why I've fought so hard against this. Not only would I die but also William. He's an innocent in this. His only crime is having the father that he does."

Victoria squeezes me a little harder when I finish my mini-speech.

"The decisions of our ancestors have put us in the position we're in. We'll work together to try and put a stop to it. I'll trust your decisions. But, when we succeed, we must give the artwork back. It's not ours to keep." She sits down on the bed again. Her legs seeming too heavy to support her weary frame.

"Even 'The Poppies'? I'm quite fond of that one. I nearly got caught taking it."

She frowns.

"*Even* 'The Poppies'. When this is over, you can tell me about how you took it. I'm actually intrigued.

I bend down, kiss her and let go to search out the rest of my clothes.

I have to go and find my father. I need to tell him we're marrying."

"Is he going to make me do the last task?" she questions.

"I don't know, but if he does, I'll do all I can to help you. Trust your instincts."

"What is it?"

I nervously lick my lips.

"You'll have to steal a painting."

CHAPTER TWENTY FIVE

NICHOLAS

It doesn't take me long to get to my father's other residence. It's on the other side of the estate. It's the place he takes the whores, and judging by the noise coming from his bedroom, he's already at it with one. I swallow down the bile that comes from hearing the screams.

"Tell him I want to speak to him, now," I growl toward a guard who's conflicted about what he should do. It's a case of deciding which devil is worse between my father and me, at the moment. The fact that my fist is inches from breaking his nose forces his hand, and he scuttles up the stairs to interrupt my father's pleasures. I settle myself into a chair and wait impatiently

"Nicholas." My father saunters down the stairs in what I suspect is nothing more than a housecoat. "I was in the middle of something rather important. What's it you want? And what have you done with the girl?"

He walks straight past me and pours himself a glass of red wine from a decanter on the table.

"She's somewhere safe."

"You'll have her back at Oakfield Hall by dusk, and I'll have Doctor Fallen confirm that you've treated her honorably. I know your reputation."

"It's no different to yours," I snap back and jump to my feet.

"I think my satisfaction rates are much higher than yours."

"No, your hospitalization rates are more widely known than mine. There's a difference. Does the whore upstairs know what she's letting herself in for?"

He smirks.

"Oh, she's fully aware and looking forward to it."

"She's insane."

He laughs.

"Just say what you've come here to say and leave. I'm a busy man."

"I've made my decision. You can end the trials and start making arrangements for the wedding. I'll be marrying Victoria Hamilton."

At first, my father doesn't say anything. He just continues drinking his wine in a cold and calculating way.

"Do you know what I did last night after that stupid girl decided to decorate my hall with her brains? I went out and organized the final task. I want this over, and it won't be until the tasks are done. Elizabeth Sandford undertook hers a few hours ago and succeeded. We have a nice, new Picasso to hang up on the wall. A stupid private collector was insufficient with his security. She was good. I'll have to show you the video at some point." He places his glass down. I can feel the hairs on the back of my neck start to rise. I don't like this one bit. There's something not right.

"At the time, I couldn't find Miss Hamilton, no doubt, because she was sitting on your dick somewhere."

"She's pure," I lie through my teeth. I won't have him disregard her and seek to destroy her this way.

"Yes, about as pure Charles II favorite, Nell Gwynn, was." He waves his hand toward a stolen painting of the famed courtesan on the wall. "Anyway, it was fortunate that you chose to phone your butler this morning. I've had a trace on your phone since the day you got it."

The blood must drain from my face because my head starts to spin.

"What've you done?"

"At this very moment, I suspect that Miss Hamilton is being taken from your mother's summer house — it's a good place to go, by the way, and proves you're as weak as she was. Miss Hamilton will be put in location to steal her painting within the hour."

I don't wait to hear anything else from him. I'm out of the room, out of the house, and running across the grounds as fast as I can to the summer house. I leap over the formal gardens, filled with summer blooms and edged with boxed dark green yew. A water fountain has me skidding in a different direction, but, eventually, I burst in through the doors of the summer house.

"Victoria?" I call, but the only answer I get is Reggie, falling to the ground in front of me. "Reggie." I leap forward and pull him into my arms. He's holding a wound to his chest.

"I tried.," he splutters, and blood drips from his mouth.

"I'm sorry they took her."

"Shush," I urge him and press my hand against what looks like a knife wound in his chest. "I need to get you a doctor."

"No," he gurgles. "Too late."

"It can't be." I'm shaking my head. Reggie has been the father I've never had. He's looked after me for as long as I can remember. "Let me try?" I'm pleading with him. I can't lose him.

"I'm old. She's young. Help her." He coughs again, and his eyes roll back in his head.

"Reggie." I shake him, but there's nothing to be done. The room goes silent as he passes away. I lay him down on the floor. I can't breathe. This wasn't supposed to happen. I was supposed to go to my father and be marrying Victoria. Victoria, she's got to steal. I need to think. We have a list of works that we want. Which one would it be? Oh god, the ultimate prize. Would my father send her after that? The Mona Lisa. I have to hope that he has some sort of heart amongst the ego that dominates his body. I spin around, ready to finish this, but my father stands in the door, a tablet in hand, and a microphone headset on.

"One less expense on my budget, then." He looks over my shoulder to where my butler lays dead.

"I want the guard who killed him. I'm going to tear him apart, limb by limb."

"So dramatic." My father rolls his eyes

"Reggie wasn't just staff. He's been more of a father figure in my life than you've ever been"

"Well that explains the weakness in you, then. He always did pander to your whims when I thought you should be beaten black and blue, to instill some balls into you. I should've had someone stick a knife in his chest years ago."

"Give me the guard," I repeat.

You've more important things to worry about than the staff." He hands me the tablet.

"What's this?"

"I thought you would like to watch the woman you love."

I swipe the screen quickly, and it brings Victoria up. She's in a dimly lit room, but I can make out her silhouette.

"Miss Hamilton" –my father addresses her, and she jumps– "I trust you had a good evening with my son. I know you were expecting him to come back and whisk you away into a happy ever after, but I'm afraid I can't allow that to happen. I don't believe you'd be the best choice for Duchess of Oakfield. You're what I'd call 'a little too headstrong'. Alas, I have to go through the rules, and you must be given a chance."

"Fuck you," Victoria shouts out into the darkness, and I smirk at her bravery.

"I don't do sloppy seconds, Miss Hamilton. I'm afraid you are spoiled goods, now. When I prove it, I'll have you executed for your disregard of the rules, but, for now, this is much more fun."

"Let her go!" I snarl at my father.

"Nicholas?" Victoria must hear my voice.

"I'm here."

"Don't give into his demands. Remember, I'm stronger than I look."

I smile because I have a feeling that my father is the one who's doing the underestimating of the situation, when it comes to Victoria.

"I won't."

"Hush," my father snaps. "Miss Hamilton, you have half an hour to retrieve a painting from the vault you are in. If you fail to do it in that time, then you're at the mercy of the collector. I'd wish you good luck, but I'd be lying. Your time starts now."

My father takes the headset off his head and throws it on the floor. I stare down at the screen, and the lights come on. I don't recognize where she is but breathe a sigh of relief as I know it's not The Louvre, in Paris. The Mona Lisa isn't the picture she'll seek.

"Victoria isn't headstrong. She'll make a good Duchess of Oakfield."

"She'll destroy the rules, and the society will be left penniless."

"Is that such a bad thing?" I ask. "Haven't enough people died?"

My father yawns. "You've become such a bore. That's why I've had to do things this way. You gave me no choice. It's your mother's fault. She put weak genes in William, and they seem to have gone in you as well."

The door behind him creeks, and Elizabeth Sandford appears in the doorway.

"Your Grace, she drapes her arm around my father. He greets her with a kiss on the cheek and pats her stomach.

Oh, Fuck!

"There's only one way that this will end, Nicholas, and it won't be with you marrying Victoria. You'll marry Elizabeth and claim my son as your own. You'll then disappear, taking the bitch with you if she survives, and you still want her. I don't care. You'll leave me with the title until my, sorry, your son comes of age. I'll do this again. This time correctly and without your mother's weakness. Elizabeth Sandford is perfect for the mother of a Duke."

"Go to hell." I spit at them both. "Elizabeth Sandford is a title grabbing bitch. She'd just as soon stab me in the back as she would you."

Elizabeth smirks but doesn't deny the accusation.

"And that's why I trust her better than anyone. She's a devil, just like me. She's what you should be. We'll raise a boy together who'll make this society the greatest it's ever been. We'll eclipse the royal family for whom the society was originally designed, to provide them with our support. We'll become the royal family. Everyone will bow to us. Worship us. We'll be gods.

"You're delusional and will be thrown into a mental asylum."

My father laughs.

"Actually, maybe I should have you declared insane, instead of making you disappear. That would be fun."

"Please, stop now. This is no longer your decision to make," I plead with my father. I'm pretty sure I'm wasting my breath, though, especially when he stabs a pudgy finger at the screen of the tablet that I'm holding.

"You'll do this, Nicholas, or she'll die in that room. There'll be no way out with the picture that she's stealing."

"No."

Elizabeth kisses my father's cheek.

"I'm glad I chose the father over the son. He's a fool."

"He is, and one who's about to watch the woman he loves die."

VICTORIA

I squint as the artificial lights turn on and flood into my sensitive eyes. It takes me a few seconds to adjust to my surroundings, and what I have to do. The society, or rather the incumbent Duke of Oakfield, wants me to steal a painting, and he's talking to me through an earpiece. My heart beats fast. I can't do this. I'm not a thief and wouldn't have the first clue on how to steal a painting and get away with it. I could stand there and appreciate the brushstrokes for hours, but other than that, I'm probably screwed.

The world comes into focus and my breath hitches. I know exactly where I am. I'm back in my home, well, in the vaults underneath, which my father uses for a safe. It dawns on me what's going on, and just what picture I need to steal. When I first became interested in art, my father took me to a sale at Sotheby's in London. I fell in love with the place and the notion that decent paintings could be sold in this manner. Up until that point, all of the art that I'd researched was primarily on the walls of museums. We'd walked around for hours looking at the pictures, but every time I came back to the same one. A Van Gogh painting of roses. It wasn't a prestigious one in the art world, but I fell in love with it. When the auction started, I stood in shock and watched as my father bought it for me. I can't remember the exact price, but it was a lot of money. At the time, I thought I was a fortunate girl and had a father who worshipped me. I know better, now. My father doesn't have much other valuable artwork, mostly paintings of ancestors by obscure artists from the time, but the Van Gogh will be the one I'm here to steal. Oh, the irony, I have to take a painting that already belongs to me. I should call out for my father and demand he opens the safe, so I can walk out of here with it. But I suspect that's not the game the Duke of Oakfield wants to play.

I shut my eyes and try to think back about the security system my father has. I know it's state of the art because the vaults contain family jewels worth a lot more than the painting. Lasers are protecting the area around the safe, and there's a code to get into it. I know the code by heart. It's the date that he made his debut for the English polo team. He was a phenomenal player in his youth — he still is. Shame I'll never get to see it again, not that I want to. I grind my teeth together in anger. When I get out of this, I'm going to talk to Nicholas about confronting my father and making him pay. Hell hath no fury like a woman scorned, and my daddy will reap what he sowed. But for now, I need to figure out how I can get past these lasers, which, should I touch one, will lock down the room and call security guards to arrest me.

Thankfully, the Duke dressed me appropriately. I've got a black cat suit on. It's all very Catherine Zeta-Jones in the film where she tried to steal artwork. I'm pretty confident that to be a member of this society, which Nicholas will one day rule, you have to think with your dick, not your brain. It must be in the initiation process — if you can pass a math's test you are out, but if you can drool over a topless woman and masturbate in a room full of strangers, then you're a candidate for membership. My temper is rising. I want to damn them all to hell, but for now, I have to play the game. Thankfully, I've done Yoga and Pilates ever since I can remember — I'm flexible and have good balance. I get down on the floor. The first laser beam — I know it to be about hip height. I slide under it and over to the left, as the next beam dissects from a ninety-degree angle to the right. I get to my feet and step over the third, which is only ankle height but awkward because another beam comes straight down to it from the roof. I have to press myself against the wall to pass it.

I stop to get my breath. I don't know how, maybe it's because the Duke is twisted, but I know Nicholas is watching me. I can sense it in my body. I duck under a head height beam. My back still aches a little from the beating I received, and I'm a bit stiff from my exploits with Nicholas last night, but I'm determined to do this, to show the Duke he'll not win. I have three beams left. I shut my eyes and picture them. One on my left dissected by a waist height barrier and the last one coming down from the right. I can't help it — my hands start to shake. My father always said that his guards will ask questions, only, after they shoot whoever tries to steal from his vaults. I have to get this right, or I could gain yet more wounds, which might not heal as well as the physical and emotional ones that I already have. I take a deep breath and maneuver my body through the last three lasers. I make it. I want to jump and shout but decide on quiet being the better course of action. With shaking fingers, I enter the code into the safe door, and it opens. I'm so nervous that a fine layer of sweat has appeared on my body, and the sound of my teeth chattering together, fills the room. I inch into the room and past my family heirlooms. I'm tempted to take them with me to spite my father, but that would only hurt my brother in the long run. God, I hope that Theo doesn't know about the society. I don't think I could bear knowing that he's a part of it. I continue past the jewelry to where the picture is hung on the wall. I take both sides of it.

"Is this what you want, Your Grace? You going to put it in pride of place next to the stolen poppy picture? or with some of your other ill-gotten gains?"

Laughter echoes in my ear.

"I see my son is a talker during sex."

"No, not during. He's just got manners and talks to a lady after he's fucked her into oblivion. Mind you, I believe you just fucked a lady into a hospital." I'm finished with the politeness. "I've done what you've asked. I have the picture — now, get me out of here and let me see Nicholas. Your time as the Duke is over, retire quietly, and I'm sure we won't destroy everything you've worked for."

"You don't have the picture, yet," he retorts with a gravelly malevolence.

I pull the picture off the wall, and an alarm sounds.

Shit!

I've messed up badly. I forgot the hidden wire over the front of the picture. The vault door slams shut. I drop the picture to the floor and wait for my death.

CHAPTER TWENTY SEVEN

NICHOLAS

"Victoria," I call out at the screen when the piercing alarms start to sound. "What's happening?" I step closer to my father with my fists balled, but he stands there unaffected and continuing his eerie laughing.

"She was so close but allowed her temper to get the better of her and messed up. Now, she dies."

I lose it and grab him by the throat, pinning him against the wall.

"Put a stop to this now."

"Henry," Elizabeth screams and tries to pull me off, but she has no hope. I'll have blood on my hands in a minute, unless my father calls off the guards.

"You know my terms, Nicholas. You want me to put a stop to this then you marry Elizabeth and disappear never to be seen again," he spits into my face.

"I want William," I counter.

"He stays here. I'll not have him embarrassing my name with his weirdness."

"He's not weird — he's autistic."

"He's as crazy as his mother was. Now, make a decision. Tick-tock, tick-tock."

I push off the wall and stamp across the room and send my fist flying into the stone wall. I come off worse with what, I suspect, might be broken knuckles.

"Fuck!" I call.

"Tick-tock," my father repeats.

"Fine. Stop this. I'll marry Elizabeth." I turn back and slump down the wall. "Just save her."

My father presses a button on his tablet and struts across the room to throw it at me. I pick it up and see a figure, in the society's livery, flash across the screen. One minute, Victoria is there, and the next, she's gone. A few seconds later, a hail of bullets flood into the room and destroy the painting.

"She'll be kept in a safe place until you have upheld your part in this bargain. You'll prepare to leave at once. We travel to Scotland tonight. You'll be married by the morning. Say goodbye to Oakfield."

With those words, he leaves. I stare at the bullet-ridden painting. I wanted to save Victoria, marry her, and destroy the society, which has governed both our lives since the day we were born, but I've failed.

CHAPTER TWENTY EIGHT

VICTORIA

I'm thrown into a dimly lit room by the man who swept me off my feet from my father's vault. The door shuts, and a key turns in the lock. I scramble to my feet and try the handle, but to no avail, I'm locked in.

"Where's Nicholas?" I shout but get no response. "Let me out!"

Nothing.

I kick the door — however, given that it's solid oak, it hurts my foot more than it makes any damage, which could be used as a means of escape.

"Fuck, fuck, fuck." I jump around holding my sore toe. "Nicholas," I try again. What the hell is going on? I look around the room that I'm in and realize that it's my bedroom at Oakfield hall. The secret passages! I run across the room at a hobbling pace but don't make it to the door before it opens, and William appears. I fling myself into his arms.

"Oh, thank god. We have to go. You know these passages. We've got to get out of here. I need to find Nicholas."

I pull back and look up at him. He's pale, and he opens and shuts his mouth like a fish, looking for words.

"William. What is it?" My heart sinks.

"Words. They're funny. Normally, I have loads of them." He flicks his hand over his hair a few times. His other hand is against the wall and tapping repeatedly. "I can't find them."

"William. Is Nicholas alright?" He's scaring me. I'm fearing the worst, and my legs feel like they're sinking to the floor in defeat.

"He's gone."

"Dead?" I whisper, my voice breaking.

William shakes his head rapidly in the negative, and I suck in a breath of relief.

"Words, William, find them," he chastises himself.

"It's alright. I'm here." I hold the hand that isn't tapping.

"I wanted my brain to work properly, so I could be good enough to save him. He and you could run away. I'll be what the Duke wants, but I was made wrong. Miswired and a freak."

"Hush. There's nothing wrong with you. I need you to calm down, though, and tell me what's going on. Come sit on the bed." I lead the man who's almost the spitting image of his older brother, except for a bit paler, over to the bed. I settle him down, take hold of his hand, and allow him to tap his comforting rhythm onto my leg.

"Nicholas has gone." William won't make eye contact with me. It's a sign of his condition but also a result of his agitation.

"You said he's alive? Where's he gone?"

"Scotland."

"Scotland?" I question.

"To marry."

"Marry," I repeat with dumbfounded shock.

"He chose Elizabeth as his wife — she's pregnant."

The walls I've built around me, to stay sharp, tumble down. I stand up and pace. My head is suddenly all over the place, fearing the worst.

"Elizabeth's pregnant."

"The Duke wants them married as soon as possible." William still can't look at me. This time, though, I know it's because of the shame that he's feeling for his brother's actions.

"Elizabeth's pregnant," I repeat, and tears start to fall from my eyes. I've been played by the society again. Now, I see it was all a game. Nicholas is no different than his father. He warned me he was the devil, and I chose not to listen. I allowed myself to fall in love with him. I'm the biggest idiot on the planet. He was after whomever he could get pregnant first. He never had any intention of changing.

I look at William. He's tapping a rhythm on the bed. Is it all an act with him as well? The whole fucking family played me. They've no respect for women. It's all one big game to them.

"Get out!" I shout at him. He looks up and shakes his head.

"No."

"Get out." I step toward him and slap him hard on the face. "I hate you all. I'm sick of being a pawn in your twisted games. Go!"

"Victoria?" he stammers.

"Get out," I scream and cover my ears, so I can't hear any more of his lies. I screw my eyes shut, not wanting the reminder of my mistakes and foolishness in front of me, anymore. "I just want to go home. This is over. Nicholas has made his choice. Just let me go."

I open my eyes and see William is by the door to the secret passageway in my room. He shakes his head.

"William?" Something's wrong — I can sense it.

"I'm sorry. When you're told that 'you're nothing', you believe it. I wish I could help you, but I'm not strong enough. I don't know how to." He turns quickly and disappears into the passageway. The door closes behind him, and I hear it lock. No. That door is always open. Why is he locking it? I pull on the handle, but it doesn't budge.

"William," I call with trepidation but receive no response.

"Argh!" I pull on the door, once more, then turn and run back to the main bedroom door. I tug on that, but it's still locked. I ball my fists up and hammer hard against the oak. It hurts like hell, but I don't care. I want out of this room.

"I want to go home," I shout. "I've failed your stupid tasks. Nicholas has chosen his Duchess. Let me go. Let me fucking go!"

A laugh, I would recognize anywhere, comes from the other side of the door. I stop hammering and step back.

The door opens, and two guards flank either side of the Duke of Oakfield as he enters.

"Miss Hamilton, I see you've learned of my son's betrayal. Women are such weak creatures — easily convinced that they're in love, and so they drop their knickers. Whores! The lot of you." I step forward to slap him, but one of the guards grabs my wrist and pushes me against the wall. My face is slammed against the velvet lining of an ostentatious wallpaper that depicts the society's crest. The guard moves to one side and allows the Duke to press himself, and an erection, against the seam of my ass. I try to fight, but I'm not able to move.

"My son's made his decision. You're not under his protection anymore. If I want you strapped to the bed and to fuck you till you bleed all over my dick, then I can. But you're tainted, and I'm bored of your mouth."

"Fuck you." I spit behind me, and it hits him square in the jaw. He thrusts harder against me.

"Mind you, I can always change my mind." He lowers his hand over the clothed curves of my body until his fingers rest at the cleft between my thighs. I want to be sick. The cat suit is thin in texture, and I can feel his dirty nails digging into my sensitive flesh. He swirls a finger around my clit. I'm dry to his touch. I'll never feel pleasure from a man's touch again. "Alas," he continues his speech, "I have a wedding to get to. The future of the Oakfield line is assured. You thought Amelia would be the last to die for our name, but you were wrong. *Ultra Vires*, we're beyond their power. Nobody will ever stop us, and more will die for our pleasure. Women are nothing — they are weak and feeble. A womb to raise our sons. Not that, *that* will be your future." He rubs himself harder against me.

"Enjoy your last few hours of life, Victoria Hamilton, for by sunrise you'll be dead."

"Let me go," I whimper and plead on a sob.

"You know too much," he snarls.

"I'll never talk."

"Never leave a loose end."

He steps back and pulls me with him. I fly across the

room and smack into the wall on the other side. My ribs hit a brass hanging, and I collapse with the pain.

"You really thought you'd beat me. I'm the fucking Duke of Oakfield. I'm the ruler of this goddamn society. My word is law." The Duke stalks after me, shouting his diatribe. I'm on the verge of blacking out.

"One day, you'll be stopped. I might not have been strong enough, but there'll be more women like me. One day, whether it be thirty years or three hundred years, a woman will be strong enough to stop this. Your name and legacy will be destroyed.

The Duke kicks me right in my ribs, and I can't keep the shriek of agony inside me.

"I'll be dead and buried, by then. I really don't care. All I care about is now. Goodbye, Miss Hamilton. I wish I could say it's been a pleasure knowing you. Actually, no, it has. I've enjoyed defeating someone who thought they could match me. You've made this whole process much more interesting. I'll take that knowledge into my retirement and use it as fire when I fuck."

He strides to the door. I try to crawl after him, but I'm in too much pain.

"Until we meet again, in hell." He stops at the door and smiles. Then, he turns to one of his guards.

"Place the call to Laird McGuire — tell him I've got a pretty little toy for him to break."

My stomach lurches, and I vomit on the floor.

CHAPTER TWENTY NINE

NICHOLAS

As I stride through the corridors of my father's dominating castle in Scotland, Elizabeth Sandford tries to slide her arm into mine. I'm still covered in Reggie's blood, and his death hangs heavily on my shoulders. I wasn't able to arrange a burial for him, before I left. My father told me he'd deal with it, but I fear my beloved butler won't rest in peace until I can figure a way out of this.

"I'm feeling a little dizzy. Can we walk a little slower?" Elizabeth interjects into my thoughts. "It's been difficult to eat the last few days."

"Shouldn't have gotten pregnant with my father's spawn, then," I snap.

"Nicholas, this makes sense. Don't fight it. We all get what we want."

I grind to a halt and stare at her.

"Are you actually for real?"

"What?" she pouts.

"I've never met someone so greedy in all my life. This has

only ever been about the title for you. You'll let my father do anything to you, as long as you have the prestige of our position. You're sick."

"No." She stomps her foot. "I'm not the sick one. Victoria's right. Your society members are the insane ones. What makes you in charge of us? My father has worked hard and has nothing. He listens to all the crap you, and everyone else, spout. Just because he's a Bishop, you all think he's not worth your respect. Your father's the only one who's ever listened to him. Well, I'm going to show everyone you're all wrong. It's you, and your little boy scouts group, that's worthless."

"You're deluded." I shake my head. Elizabeth knows full well the reputation that her father has amongst the choir boys, and that's why he gets no respect from us.

"We'll see about that." She pats her stomach.

"Is it even my father's? You know he'll demand DNA testing."

She steps forward and slaps my face. I crack my jaw because it's one of those blows from a woman that ricochets right through you.

"You ever raise your hand to me again, and I'll become the devil everyone wants me to be. I feel absolutely nothing for you but contempt. I wouldn't normally hit a lady. But in your case, I'm willing to make an exception because, well, the term 'lady' only loosely applies." She goes to hit me again, but I grab her hand, swing her around, and dump her on the floor.

"Your father will hear about this."

"Tell him — I no longer care," I spit out at her before trudging off to my room and slamming the door like a petulant teenager. I need Victoria — I've not spoken to her since she was rescued from the failed painting theft. I don't trust my father, and the fact that he travelled after us leaves me suspicious. I pull out my phone and message William.

Nicholas: Hey, have you seen Victoria?

I look at the icon on the screen where the three dots appear. They flash for a few minutes then stop. I get impatient. Eventually, a reply comes through.

William: Yes. Not that you deserve to know.

Nicholas: What's that supposed to mean?

William: You married yet?

I'm getting the distinct impression that my brother's pissed off at me.

Nicholas: Still working on getting out of it.

William: Don't lie. The Duke told me everything.

I stare down at his message. What the hell does he mean?

Nicholas: I'm not marrying Elizabeth out of choice. I agreed to it under duress. I'm doing it because it's the only way to save Victoria's life. I saw the trial — she was about to die. Once the marriage is done, Victoria and I will disappear. The baby isn't mine, before you ask. I've never slept with Elizabeth, so it can't be. It's our father's.

I hesitate before sending that message. My father won't let me take William with me, but I'll never stop trying. I add a little bit on the end.

Nicholas: As soon as I can come back for you, I will. I'll never stop trying.

The dots appear again.

William: You love her?

Nicholas: With all my heart.

I wait a few minutes, but nothing comes back. I put my phone down on the dresser and head toward the bed. I need a shower — I've been in the same clothes for days. Removing my jacket, I place it into the linen basket for cleaning. My heart pangs for Reggie. This would have been his responsibility. I'm defeated and can take no more. I sit on the bed, place my head in my hands, and exhale deeply. I don't know how to win this game that I find myself in. I feel as though I'm drowning. I've been an arrogant sod most of my life: spoken down to people beneath me, fucked anything with a willing pussy, but Victoria Hamilton has floored me with her spirit. I'm not sure that I can continue with my life the way it is. I don't want to marry Elizabeth Sandford, nor do I trust my father that this will all end, now. I flop back onto the bed, allowing my eyes to shut. I need sleep. Hopefully, once I've had some, I'll be able to comprehend my situation better and deal with it. A rap at the door destroys my plans, though.

"Enter," I call and pray it isn't Elizabeth Sandford come

back for round two. I exhale a long sigh of relief when I see it's a uniformed servant.

"I'm sorry to disturb you, My Lord." He seems nervous, and his soft Scottish accent's tinged with trembles of worry.

"What is it?" I grumble.

"I have something for you. It's" –he stutters– "it's a letter."

"From whom?" I don't even bother to sit up on the bed. I lay my head back and close my eyes.

"Your mother." That brings me upright.

"What?" I demand. "If this is some kind of joke, I'll have you castrated."

"It isn't, My Lord. You have my word. I knew your mother well. I tried to help her and make her life easier, but I met her after it was too late. Her mind had already gone. She didn't deserve what happened to her…" He pauses. "It's not my place to say, but I don't believe she took her own life. Your father…" He stops. "I speak too freely. I'm sorry." He reaches into his pocket and pulls out a letter. "Shortly after you were born, she gave me this. It's always been the tradition to come here for the wedding, and she asked me to give it to you before yours."

I shuffle from the bed and stare at the man in front of me. I'm trying to size him up. He seems genuine, but I've been fooled already by my father, and I don't want to fall into his trap again.

"Why should I believe you?" I ask.

"You don't have to believe me. I'm just doing what I promised your mother." He drops the letter onto the dresser. "You have her eyes, and the sparkle behind them that I watched die. Read the letter, My Lord. Don't let your light die." With those words, he disappears from my room, not waiting to be granted permission to leave. I look down at the letter like it will bite me. My name is written on the front, and it seems like my mother's handwriting. I've seen it often enough in her diary. I reluctantly reach out and open it. There's a single sheet of paper inside, and what looks like a much older letter. I read the newer one first.

Dear Nicholas,

My handsome son,

If you're reading this, then I'm dead, and you're about to be married. I can pray until I'm blue in the face that it's to a woman you've fallen in love with, via conventional means, but I know your father too well. Your marriage will come as a result of the Society's rules placed upon you. Your bride will have gone through tasks, unimaginable to others, to finally be chosen. The girls who have failed will be lying in barely cold graves.

I've known, since the moment I looked into your blue eyes for the first time, that you'd be the one to end this nightmare. I saw more compassion and kindness in the eyes of a mere, few moments old, baby than I had seen my entire life. I knew then you were special, and I had to protect you as best I could. When William was born, I saw the same unique qualities in him. Despite the dark blood that runs through your father's sovereignty, you'd both inherited mine. My pure and gentle abilities. I spent all the time I could with you both — Firstly, in the hope I could keep it hidden from your father, and secondly, to stop him from beating it out of you. I took the blame for misdemeanors. I hid your brother's eccentricities. I prayed as hard as I could you would stay strong. Your father hated me for it. I don't like to speak evil of the man who's half of you, but I can't find a good word for him. He's the devil, my son. I've seen the things he's done to people, not just women. He's a tyrant and a dictator with delusions of grandeur. I'm sorry if this hurts you. I wish there were some other way. I know he's your father. The night I conceived you was shortly after our wedding. I'd been a virgin until that night, and I'll never forget how brutally my innocence was stolen. I'd not healed, physically or mentally. Your father became angry when the doctors stated I needed another week's rest before he could resume his activities with me. As always, he chose to ignore them. I was stripped by my guards and brought naked through the house to him. He was already in bed with another woman. I remember the fear in her eyes as I came in and was introduced as his wife. I don't know the story that he'd spun her about our relationship, but I could tell she wasn't willingly in his bed. She was chained, her lip was split, her eye black from bruising, and his rough marks had already left blemishes on her body. He started to penetrate her from behind, and she screamed so loudly. Then silence. An overwhelming and deafening silence. He had a knife hidden under his pillow and had slit her throat. She'd have seen her death coming but couldn't have prevented it. I mourn her every day, especially after what happened next. Your father withdrew from her and grabbed me around the neck. He shouted at me for being unready for him. He blamed it on me that he'd needed to treat the woman in that way. I had tears streaming down my eyes. He called me weak and useless and said that it wasn't the doctors' decision to make, regarding how he treated his wife. After that, he bent me over the bed, I looked at the dead girl, and we conceived you. I was bedridden for months after. They were terrified that I'd lose you due to the damage I had suffered. I'm sorry, my son, to tell you this. I've only ever wanted you to think that you were conceived from love, but I can't. I can't lie if it means that you remain ignorant of the truth *about what your father and this society are. They're evil men, and you aren't. You're the one who can put a stop to this.*

Contained within my letter is another. It's from the first Duchess of Oakfield who was submitted to the trials. There's a prophecy that one day a boy will be born who'll end this. He'll be pure of heart and able to cast off the evil of the legacy of his succession. The letter, it states, will only come to light when that boy is born. It's you, Nicholas...you're the child. I found it shortly after you were born. It proves you're better than this. It demonstrates that you can put an end to the suffering of the women who have followed my fate. Utilize the strength that I know is in you and stop the society. Don't let them win. If you truly love the woman you're due to marry, then go ahead with it and make her your wife, but if there's any doubt in your mind then end it here. Please, please my son, don't let another generation suffer. Have courage, I'm with you always in spirit and know that I'd never leave you unless it was through no choice of my own.

I love you,

Your mother.

The Duchess of Oakfield.

I take a stumbling step back onto the floor. My legs won't hold me. To read of her suffering, during a time which should have been romantic and filled with love, brings tears that tumble in rivulets down my cheeks. 'Grown men don't cry', my father would say to me. But I'm not weeping for myself, I'm mourning for the woman who nurtured me within her for nine months despite being broken and destroyed. I wipe away tears for a mother who fought hard to give me compassion and love when she was shown none for herself. She was an angel the day she was born into this society, and now she's an angel in heaven, giving me the strength I need to end this.

I take up the other letter and carefully open it — it must be over four hundred years old.

To whomever reads this,

My name is Alice, Duchess of Oakfield. I'm the first Duchess to be chosen under the rules of the Oakfield Society. But, I hereby declare that they are false and should have no future bearing on the generations to come. The rules are governed by men who were intent on the destruction of my husband. You see, you cannot choose to marry when you are already wed. The Duke and I were married before the trials began. I wasn't a virgin going into them, and I carried his child after the third trial. They were a sham, and the only reason I went through with them was to protect my husband's place in the society and to save his life. I loved him, and I couldn't lose him. The Oakfield's have a great name, an honest and trustworthy one, or so it was once, before the society's rules. Whichever future Duchess discovers this letter will be the mother of the son who is destined to return our name to greatness. We shall once again be the Oakfield's of my husband's previous gener-ations, and the legacy will finally be forgotten.

I'm sorry for my part in the terrible pain that others have experienced. I was weak and blinded by the love I felt. I hope one day I shall be forgiven.

Alice, Duchess of Oakfield

I can't believe what I'm reading. I've spent years thinking that this was forced upon women, but the first Duchess chose her fate, misguided through love or otherwise, and sealed it for future generations to come.

The anger grows within me. This letter was from a woman four hundred years ago — my fate, and the fate of the generations before me, has been determined because of her decision. It ends now, though. Enough!

I jump to my feet and am at my bedroom door in seconds. I pull it open and jump back when my father stands there with a gun. The man who delivered the letter to me lays at his feet — dead I assume.

"Your mother always did like to interfere where it wasn't needed. It's why I had to throw her off the roof of Oakfield Hall."

I growl my livid response and leap at him just as the gun goes off. Pain rips through my right shoulder, and I slump back against the wall.

"And this is why I've planned your succession the way I have. It's all been a game from day one. Elizabeth knew she would be Duchess from birth. I only needed you present for the wedding to take place. Thankfully, Elizabeth's father is a very helpful Bishop."

My father looms over me, as I slide down the doorway. I'm trying to focus on him, but the world's spinning and darkening.

"You were never destined to become the Duke of Oakfield. I was always going to be the one to take it on for another thirty years."

He kicks me in the shoulder, and I grunt in pain.

"Your destiny was to die."

CHAPTER THIRTY

VICTORIA

"**G**et off me, you bastard," I scream and thrash out as I'm dragged, unceremoniously, down the hallway by a guard. I don't want to die at the hands of Laird McGuire, and I'm going to do everything in my power to prevent it. I bite the hand of the guard, and he slaps me. It's a sad state of affairs — but, I'm so used to being a punching bag that I don't even react to it. We reach a closed door, and I can hear the Scottish Laird on the phone in his room. Even his voice sends shivers through me. Any pretense I had of trying to escape leaves me, and I sag into the guard's arms.

He knocks on the door and opens it when addressed to do so.

"I've got your present from the Duke, Laird McGuire."

I shudder when the brutish Scotsman looks me up and down then licks his lips. He's dressed in a plaid kilt with a white shirt and black waistcoat. He looks every inch the gentleman, but I know better.

"A very bonny lass indeed, ye must thank His Lordship for me."

"Where would you like her?" the guard asks.

"On the table, please. I've got cuffs for her hands 'n' feet. Ensure they're done up tight. Don't worry about removing her clothes. It's a part o' my fun." His face lights up in an evil grin, and as I'm taken across the room and laid out on the table, I watch him pull a bag from under his bed. The guard ensures that I'm securely fastened before standing back. He too looks smug and self-assured. At this very moment, I want to wipe the smirk off both their faces, but the fear has taken hold of me. Nicholas has broken me — the Duke has helped him. I thought myself in love. I gave my body to a man who played it like a musical instrument and wrote a symphony with my heart. Like many classical masterpieces, though, it will end in a violent crescendo of haunting melodies. An epitaph to the torture I'm about to experience.

"Ye can go," the Laird informs the guard, and the man sullenly leaves. "I'm going to do this in privacy."

I know he wants me to fight him, speak back, and enrage him into hurting me further, but I've lost my fight. I just want it over with and to be dead, hopefully in heaven.

"Let's get ye out of those clothes."

The ginger-bearded Scotsman pulls a large knife from his bag and comes to the table. I'm still wearing my catsuit. It's easy for him to cut away in seconds, leaving me in only my bra and panties.

"Such a bonny little thing. What to do first?" He brings the point of the knife down to my belly button and trails it up toward my breasts. A red line of blood follows behind it. He doesn't cut me open, but he marks the skin enough to cause me to bleed. He tucks the knife under my bra and pulls the blade up. It cuts the flimsy fabric in half and exposes my breasts to him.

"It's a shame they are na bigger. A like something, I can get my face lost in. A woman's tits are like honey to a man like me." He bends over and wraps his hair-lined lips around my nipple. I squirm away from his touch. Big mistake.

"Ye think ye can escape yer fate." He laughs and punches me straight in the stomach. I want to curl up, but I can't with my hands and feet tied. "I'm going to suck these tits until they're raw. Then I'm going to remove yer pants and stick my dick in that tight little cunt off yours for the next few hours. Don't get over excited about it, though, because I want ye dry as a bone. I'll rip ye apart — much better that way. Ye are going scream my name in so much pain that everyone in the place will know exactly what I'm doing to ye. Once I'm bored of yer pussy, I'll be going for yer asshole. A can be fuckin' all night, but if my dick gets tired, I have toys. Toys designed to tear ye so wide ye'll be begging for death. Once done with the fucking, the good part starts." He punches me again in the stomach and steps back toward his bag. He drops the knife into it and pulls a gun out instead. I will him to pull the trigger and end my suffering, but he's not done tormenting me...yet. No, he comes back over to me and trails the gun through the line of blood that he's left on my stomach. This time, he heads toward the lower half of my body. My legs are parted by the cuffs, and he places the gun at my entrance. I let out a small whimper...I can't help it. The smile of satisfaction on his face makes me sick. I shut my eyes. "The only way a whore like ye should die. Shot in the fuckin' cunt. Enjoy yer last few hours, Victoria Hamilton, because I'm going make them hell."

BANG!

The sound echoes in my head. Pain. I should feel pain. I must be dead. He shot me. A heavyweight lands on me, and a breath is forced out of me. I open my eyes, and the Laird is laying over me with a hole in the back of his head. I panic. I'm pulling the chains but can't get free.

"Stay still." William appears in my line of vision. A still smoking gun in his hand. He places it down and pushes the Laird off me before undoing the cuffs. I scramble up, off the table, and across the room away from the dead body. My stomach heaves, but I haven't eaten or drunk all day and nothing comes up.

"I need to get you out of this room." William comes up to me with a blanket. "Let me put this around you." I can't breathe. I should be dead. I don't want to be rescued. I want to go to heaven and find peace from this constant pain in my chest. I can't do this anymore. I want the torture to stop.

"Why did you stop him?" I push William away.

"It's ok. Let's go to a different room, and I'll explain."

I start crying, all the emotions flooding out of me. Over William's shoulder, I see the gun lying on the table. I can end this myself. I speed past him before he realizes what's going on. I pick the weapon up and hold it to my head.

"Goodbye." He turns to face me, and I pull the trigger, but nothing happens.

"I only had one bullet." He looks sheepish. "I didn't really think about what I'd do if I missed the Laird."

My situation is so utterly hopeless that I burst into laughter. Fate's conspiring against me, I can't even end my life or the suffering I'm under.

William dares to come closer to me. He places the blanket around my shoulders and brings me to his chest. He smells like Nicholas.

"We have to go to Scotland." He strokes my hair.

"Why?" I ask — my whole body is feeling weak and deflated.

"Nicholas was tricked by my father."

"I don't understand." I suddenly find firm feet and plant them securely enough to allow me to look up at the younger Cavendish brother.

"Nicholas doesn't want to marry Elizabeth. He's in love with you. The baby isn't his either. He's never slept with Elizabeth. It's our father's."

"I don't understand. Why's he marrying her then?"

"The Duke made him watch you, during your trial. When you went wrong, and your father's security were coming, he agreed to marry Elizabeth, so my father would save you."

I gasp and reach behind me to steady myself on the table that I was strapped to, moments ago. "He loves me."

"Yes."

"Your father's been playing games with us all along."

William nods.

"I think he still is. Nicholas said to me that once he's done what the Duke wants and married Elizabeth, then our father will allow you and him to disappear." My friend swipes at his worry spot on his face —it's something I've come to recognize as a part of him.

"But the fact that the Duke handed me to Laird McGuire

for sport and execution suggests otherwise. He's going to kill him."

William turns pale, but I spring into action. I push past him again and head for the door.

"Where are you going?" he asks.

I turn back to him.

"Well, firstly I'm going to get some clothes on. Then secondly, I'm going to Scotland. I'm going to rescue the man I love and, hopefully, kill the bad guy."

NICHOLAS

The murmur of voices wakes me, and the memory of being shot by my father floods back. I try to move, but I'm too weak — my shoulder hurts like a mother fucker.

"He's waking." A feminine voice enters my head, and I realize it's that bitch, Elizabeth Sandford.

"About fucking time," my father broods. "You, on your feet and get on with this wedding."

That brings me to my senses. Wedding! I open my eyes and see my father standing next to Elizabeth's father, Hubert Sandford, The Lord Bishop of Monchelsea, and is dressed in his full regalia. Hell no!

The Bishop starts to speak.

"In the presence of God, Father, Son and Holy Spirit, we have come together to witness the marriage of Nicholas Cavendish, Earl Lullington and The Honorable Elizabeth Sandford, to pray for God's blessing on them, to share their joy, and celebrate their love."

"Bullshit!" I interrupt.

"It's not. It's our wedding vows," Elizabeth counters. "Daddy, tell him."

"I…er," the Bishop stutters.

"I agree, it's bullshit," my father adds. "Just get to the part where he has to sign the register — then, I can end his miserable life.

"I thought you would at least make this special for me," Elizabeth whines.

"I'll make things special for you later." My father winks at her.

"I have to at least make some attempt at the vows," Hubert Sandford intervenes with a green color flushing around his gills.

My father snorts.

"I don't think you do. I've got a present for you outside, which suggests otherwise. One that I know you'll be very interested in."

The Bishop takes the register and signs his name on it. Elizabeth stomps forward and does the same, with a sullen expression on her face.

"You better do whatever I want tonight, my love." She kisses my father on the cheek and hands him the pen.

"You seem to forget who's in charge here, Elizabeth. You do whatever I want, or despite my feelings for you, once that baby is born, you might find yourself the unhappy victim of an accident. I did it to his insane mother. I'll do it to you as well — if you destroy my love for you with defiance."

"I can't believe you can say such hurtful things," she whimpers on the verge of tears.

I laugh.

"What?" She stamps her foot.

"My father loves himself, nobody else. I'm his flesh and blood, and he's going to kill me. You're nothing but a willing vagina to him. I did try to tell you. Shame you'll have to learn the hard way."

"Shut up, Nicholas," my father commands.

"Tell me that isn't true." Elizabeth throws herself at my father, and he glares at me over her shoulder.

"I'm just trying to make a better life for the two of us and our son. You knew I was a bastard when you fell in love with me. Don't expect me to change. I'll protect you with everything I have but defy me, in any way, and I'll cut you down."

Elizabeth sniffs back her tears. My head spins, and I'm not sure if it's the excruciating pain in my shoulder, or the sickening display in front of me. Part of me actually feels sorry for Elizabeth, only a tiny portion though. She's brought this on herself by being a bitch.

"I only meant that maybe I could go on top tonight. I like the way it feels."

My father pulls back and strokes her hair. "As long as I get to see those tits bounce, I don't care what position you're in, on my dick."

I make a gagging noise.

"Seriously, you're going to buy that? And you…" I look at Elizabeth's father. "You're going to let him speak to your daughter like that in front of us. I mean, have you no shame?"

"If your father has outside, what I think he does, then no, I have no shame. I'm giving my daughter to your father in exchange for rewards beyond your comprehension. He can have carnal relations with her in whatever way he wants," the Bishop retorts.

I shake my head.

"Victoria was right. Everyone in this god damn society is an imbecile." I've been sitting on the floor, against a wall, throughout this entire conversation. No doubt, this was where my father had his guards dump me. I push up to a standing position, but I'm dizzy due to blood loss from the gunshot wound. I rest against the table on which lies the register that requires my signature to seal the fake marriage.

"Sign the paper, Nicholas. Let's just get on with the inevitable. I'm bored of the conversations. I've got plans for this society, and I've had to wait far too long to implement them."

I stare him down with utter contempt.

"You've been in charge for almost thirty years. Why didn't you take on the world during that time? Why do you need my thirty?"

My father turns to the Bishop.

"If I just chop his hand off and sign his name with it, does that count? Does he really have to sign the register himself?"

"For it to be valid, yes. I can't in all conscience lie to God about marriage." The Bishop makes the sign of a cross on his chest and bows his head.

"Yet, you can rape a little boy," my father angrily replies.

"Some things can be overlooked." The Bishop pushes the papers toward me.

"You're sick." I snarl at him.

"Sign the papers, Nicholas." My father steps up behind me, and the next thing I know, I'm falling to the floor in the throes of torment. My father has his finger stuck into my wound. He's tearing the flesh farther away from the bone and rupturing more blood vessels to allow claret liquid to seep from the bullet hole. I should be stronger than him — under normal circumstances, I would be, but he's rendered me into a small boy again, begging at his feet for mercy from punishment. I thought I deserved it, then, but now I know what a demented bully my father is.

"Go to hell!" I scream.

He digs deeper, and my head swims with dizziness.

"You think you've got something to live for?" my father asks, and my mind goes to Victoria. No, what has he done to her?

"Where is she?" I ask.

"Right now?" he laughs.

"Probably flat on her back with Laird McGuire's dick in her cunt or ass."

I shriek in anguish and beads of sweat start forming all over my body.

"Seems I found a use for the Scots in the society, after all. I bet he's tearing her apart. I almost wish I could've stayed in London to hear the bitch scream. I bet it'll be loud. The very foundations of Oakfield Hall will be shaking with what he's doing to her."

"You bastard."

My father removes his finger from my wound. I breathe rapidly, trying to get through the pain and anguish that I'm feeling. Victoria will be dying in a torturous way, and there's nothing I can do to save her.

"I'll ask you one last time. Sign the papers." I roll onto my back, and my father places his foot on my chest.

I waiver. What have I got to live for? I've been an arrogant, rich brat all my life. The only good thing to ever happen to me was Victoria, and I'm the reason she's going to die. I shut my eyes again, waiting for the inevitable.

"You might as well kill me because I'm not going to sign them. I'll never make it easy for you to take over the society for another thirty years. I want to destroy it. Let's hope my death does that."

Silence. Nothing. I open my eyes again just as my father brings his boot down toward my face.

"I wouldn't do that if I were you." A dreamy feminine voice floods my senses, this time. It sounds like an angel. Victoria, my Victoria. I must've gone to heaven. But, no, I'm still on the floor of a room in a castle in Scotland. My father lowers his foot, and we all turn to the door. Victoria stands there next to William — both have guns pointed at us. They're dressed in jeans and sweatshirts, and both look ready for a fight. I'm not sure what I'm more shocked at: Victoria being alive, or the fact my brother has left Oakfield Hall, for the first time ever.

"I'm afraid Laird McGuire couldn't uphold his end of whatever bargain you made with him. He came down with an unfortunate case of a hole in the head. Couldn't happen to a nicer man, if you ask me," Victoria continues cockily.

"Did my other son finally grow a set of balls?" My father steps forward, but William cocks the gun.

"I wouldn't if I were you, Father." The last word is spat with venom. "I don't like the future you have planned for Nicholas and Victoria very much, and I've found that years of playing shooting games on consoles has left me with an excellent aim."

"You would kill your own father?" The Duke raises a

skeptical eyebrow, and I use his, momentarily, distracted gaze to shuffle to the side of the room. I need to regain my senses if I'm to help my brother and Victoria. Neither one is strong enough to survive the evil that could take place here.

"I've had enough of your games and self-righteous nature. You've no right to treat people the way you have. No bit of paper can decide my fate, only I can do that. The society ends here and now." Victoria meets my father halfway across the room. William remains at the door with his gun aimed at the un-moving Bishop and Elizabeth.

"So confident, yet I see the shaking in your hands. Tell me, how far did the Laird get before William saved you?"

Victoria smirks when she responds, "Not far enough to break me."

"Damn," the Duke replies unhappily.

"Why can't you just accept he doesn't want you and fuck off to hell." Elizabeth steps forward this time and wraps her arm round my father's.

"Are you talking about the Duke or the Earl, Elizabeth, because I'm pretty sure I would pass on the former."

"The Earl got me pregnant, you stupid bitch. He's a cheater and a liar."

"No." Victoria maintains her poise and calm so gracefully that, despite the situation, I can feel myself getting hard in my pants. "The Duke got you pregnant when you opened your legs for him for a title. I'm guessing that, as Nicholas is most definitely the better looking of the two, you slipped into a little fantasy world at some point and imagined it was the Earl. I know he wouldn't touch you with his dick even if it was on fire and needed a wet place to extinguish it." Victoria raises an eyebrow at the end of her retort, and I let out a little chuckle.

"Are you going to let her speak to me like that? Kill her," Elizabeth demands of my father.

"She's the one with the gun. I'm afraid there isn't much that I can do." My father edges closer to Victoria. I'm wary of the action.

"But you've got your own gun in your suit jacket," Elizabeth replies.

Everything happens in slow motion. My father growls and pulls his own weapon out. He fires at the same time as Victoria does. Thankfully, his shot skims past and into the wall behind. I turn to follow the path of Victoria's bullet just as I watch it slice through Elizabeth's chest. My father is behind her — he'd pulled her in front of him. Elizabeth gurgles blood from her mouth as the life drains from her. My father lets her slip to the floor. Victoria stands shocked at what she's done, and it's just the advantage my father needs. He grabs her and pulls the gun from her trembling hands and drops it to the floor. I'm on my feet as quickly as my blood loss allows me. William's rushing forward at the same time, but we're too late. My father has Victoria around the throat, and a gun pointed at her head. We both skid to a halt.

"My daughter." The Bishop falls to the floor and begins last rites.

"I've failed you, Father," Elizabeth speaks through struggled breaths

"No!" her father cries.

"I only wanted to make them see you're a good man. It's all you've ever taught me."

"I know, my child, I know."

Elizabeth tries to speak again, but only her final breath of life comes. She slumps lifelessly into her father's arms.

"You promised me that she wouldn't be hurt." Hubert Sandford's mask of piety slips. "I'll make you suffer for this."

Without even batting an eyelid, my father removes the gun from Victoria's head and shoots the grieving man between the eyes.

Victoria screams as he slumps forward in a heap on top of his daughter.

"Couldn't have happened to a nicer man," my father jests.

"How about you point the gun at yourself?" I counter and take a step closer.

"Uh, uh. No. You stay just where you are. I'm not a fool. Here's what happens. If you want Victoria alive, then I suggest you both move out of my way. I'm going to take her with me as collateral for a while. It seems that I need to think of another plan."

"Not going to happen. You're going to put the gun down. We still have a weapon trained on you."

"Yes, by the most stupid man in London."

"I'm not stupid — I'm autistic," William shouts.

"Same thing." My father rolls his eyes.

"You've no idea about either of your sons, do you? Who we actually are? Autism hasn't made me stupid. It's given me the ability to focus. I can do things with a computer nobody else can. If you'd actually bothered to be a father to me, then you could've used my skills to further your stealing of artwork. But no, I wasn't normal, so you disregarded me. And as for Nicholas, you've no idea what sort of man he is. You think he's the arrogant bastard you've made him, and in some ways he is, but he's a born leader with it. He'll take the society into the future and make it great. You'll just run it into the ground and have everyone, who doesn't agree with you, arrested or shot." William's foot taps the entire time he speaks. I can tell he's stressed beyond words, but he's maintaining his composure, thanks to his tics.

"I don't believe any of that for a moment. You're both weak and feeble, just like your mother. Her genes have spoiled you both."

"No." It's my turn to step up to the fight. "Her genes have made us the good men we are, despite the malevolence from you that runs through our veins. Enough games — you know that you won't get out of here with Victoria. Let her go."

Victoria's watching me get closer and closer. Her eyes flick to the wound in my shoulder and anguish fills them.

"I'm walking out of here," my father reiterates.

"And we'll let you — just not with Victoria."

"What do you see in her anyway? Elizabeth was the prettier of the two. She's got no discernible features as far as I can tell. How can you let her ruin what we could do for this society? Isn't there a part of you that wants more? We could rule the country together, you and me."

"Victoria has everything. She's beautiful, compassionate, and fiery. She's made me see that there's more to power than being a dictator. Plus, if you'd actually taken time to know her as a woman, not an object, you would've seen she probably knows as much about the art world as we do. Maybe even more." With every word I speak, I'm edging closer to where my father holds Victoria around the neck. He pulls the gun away and points it at me.

"Stay back."

It's the chance I need. With the gun pointed away from

Victoria, I'm close enough to leap at him. Despite the pain from my wound, I take him by surprise and punch him in the face. Reeling, he lets Victoria go, and she scrambles away. I need to disarm my father before he has a chance to fire off the gun again. I ignore the fiery spasms shooting through my body and wrestle him to the ground. I release his hold on the weapon, and I push it away. Now, we're even.

"Give up Father. I'll give you your life and a pension to live quietly somewhere, but this is over now."

"Never. You weren't born to lead." He punches me in the shoulder, and I cry out, swearing I see stars.

Then, we're on the floor and rolling over. I'm on my back when my father brings another blow down on my shoulder. If I have much more of this, I know I'll pass out. That's the last thing I want.

"William, do something." I hear Victoria say.

"I...I...I...," he stutters back.

I bring my good arm around and catch my father on the side of the jaw. He wavers a little but doesn't fall.

"Why couldn't you have just loved us?" I shout.

"Because he doesn't have a heart." I hear William shout — his voice filled with anguish.

A gunshot goes off, and my father's body goes lifeless on top of me. William appears and pulls my father off me. Then disappears to the side of the room to tap out a rhythm. I notice the back of my father's skull is missing, and my head swims with nausea. I don't have a chance to retch, though, as Victoria slams her body onto the floor next to me and brings her lips to mine.

"I thought I'd lost you."

"I love you. Everything he said was lies. I didn't want to marry her. I want you."

"I know. I know." She kisses me again through her tears, which fall freely. I reach up and touch one.

"No more tears." She's cradling me in her arms, and I can feel the dark clouds looming again. I look toward William, and she follows my gaze. "Look after him for me."

"What?" she stammers. "No, Nicholas."

I don't hear anything else for the world goes black.

EPILOGUE

VICTORIA

"How long is this thing supposed to take?" I look toward my best friend Tamara while she sits on the bed swinging her legs.

"It says five minutes."

"That's far too long." I pull on the ends of my vibrant red hair, due to nerves.

"You've got five minutes to spare. Remember the thing about having a whole life ahead of you." She tuts at me.

"That might be about to change."

It's been a month since the day the old Duke of Oakfield died, much has happened in the interim. I'm not sure that I've processed it all yet. Nicholas was rushed from the castle in Scotland to a hospital with barely even a faint pulse. William and I sat by his bedside for three long days before he woke. He'd lost so much blood that his body had started to shut down. The doctors had given him a transfusion and put him into an induced coma to recover. I don't know what happened with the Duke, the Bishop, and Elizabeth Sandford's bodies. William disappeared for a while and told me that he'd had someone deal with it all. There'd be no repercussions for anyone. I think it was at this point that I realized just how far above the law the Dukedom of Oakfield is. William had retreated into himself after that. It had taken so much courage for him to leave his home in London. I could tell that all the people who came and went from his brother's bedside disturbed him. I told him he could return home if he wanted to, but he refused. I didn't know what was going on in his head although I feared it wasn't good. He'd killed his own father to save his brother, in addition to his years of anguish and repression. None of that could be erased quickly or easily.

Eventually, Nicholas woke, and we rejoiced. The doctors said there should be no lasting issues with his shoulder, but it would take a while to heal. He'd need physical therapy to rebuild his strength. Nicholas, being the stubborn man he is, told them he'd be fine. Then he promptly spilled the cup of tea they'd given him everywhere, when he tried to lift it with the damaged arm. It was at that point I took control and told him he'd follow the doctor's orders, or I'd have him strapped to the bed until he agreed. He seemed to like that suggestion far too much because he then promptly called for a priest — we said our vows and consummated our marriage that same day. It wasn't how I pictured my wedding day, but when I told Tamara about it later, I was sobbing with the beauty of it all. That is what has led me to my current predicament — Tamara and I staring at a little stick I've just peed on. I'm unsure how I feel about the result.

I am the Duchess of Oakfield. I shouldn't worry about being pregnant as my future is secure. It's more Nicholas' reaction I'm scared off. This is all still so new for both of us, and the stigma of how we fell in love surrounds us daily. The former Duke's reaping his own type of torment, even from the grave. Why give us contraceptive injections at all if they were going to be fake? Yes, placebos apparently, another ploy by the Duke to mess with our heads. It was the one piece of information I was able to get out of Doctor Fallen before I told him that he'd better disappear because if Nicholas found him, he'd be dead.

A loud bang on the door makes me jump. The door handle rattles. Tamara gasps and shoves the pregnancy test under my pillow.

"Victoria, why is your door locked?" Nicholas shouts from the other side. "It's my right as your husband to get into this room whenever I want."

"He sounds furious," Tamara whispers.

"He's just being Nicholas," I reply and sweep off the bed toward the door. He bangs again before I can turn the key in the lock.

"Open up, now!"

I unlock the door as it almost comes flying off its hinges with the force of his entrance.

"Why was it locked?" he growls and stalks toward me. Nicholas will always be Nicholas. He has an arrogant and bossy side to him, but I love it because it's counteracted by the softer side he keeps hidden only for William and I. The younger Cavendish brother follows the elder into the room, and I wave at him.

"Me, focus on me," Nicholas moans.

"Yes, husband," I counter with a twist of my lips.

"Why was your door locked? Mrs. McDonald said you

didn't eat breakfast this morning. What's wrong? Who do I need to threaten to fix it?"

I look over at Tamara — William has come to sit next to her on my bed. They smile at each other, and I swear I see Tamara's cheeks blush. She refocuses her attention on my warring husband, and I shrug.

"Sit down before you hurt yourself," I direct Nicholas toward a chair. He reluctantly sits. He's still wearing his arm in a sling, to allow the wound to heal.

"Victoria, talk to me." His voice softens — I can see the worry in his eyes. I perch on the side of the chair.

"It would seem that the contraceptive injection Dr. Fallen gave me was a placebo."

"What?" his face whitens.

"You know that we've barely left the bedroom since you were discharged from the hospital. Well, it seems that every time we've had sex, we've been doing it without protection."

"You're pregnant?" he questions.

"I don't know for certain." I look to Tamara, and she pulls the stick out from under my pillow and waves it in the air. "The door was locked because we're doing a test."

"You haven't read the answer?" Nicholas asks.

"I have to wait five minutes."

"Have the five minutes finished?"

An alarm goes off on Tamara's phone. William quickly picks it up and silences it. He doesn't like loud noises.

"What does it say?" Nicholas demands of Tamara.

She gets up off the bed and comes over to us. William follows.

"I think this is something you two best do alone." She hands me the stick face down. "William, I've been hearing about all this great artwork that you have here and how it's going to be sent back. I'd like to see it before it goes. Would you show me?" She holds her hand out for William. He looks down at it.

"Is that the hand that just touched the pee stick?"

Tamara laughs, steps up behind him, and pushes him toward the door.

"Come on, I promise I'll wash my hands before we touch the pictures."

They both leave, and I'm left alone with my husband. Both of us looking at the stick in my hand like it's some kind of poisonous instrument of torture.

"Are you scared?" Nicholas asks me.

"No, I'm not, actually. If I'm pregnant, I know that you and I will be the best parents we can be to the baby."

"Even with my past?"

"Because of your past." I shuffle so that I'm straddling him on the seat. I feel his cock go hard underneath me.

"I love you," Nicholas offers me with genuine warmth and affection.

"I love you, too," I respond. "On the count of three."

He looks towards the stick.

"One, two, three."

I turn it over, and the words, 'You're pregnant' are on the little screen.

"Well, it looks like we're having a little Earl or Countess Lullington." He smiles up at me and brings his lips to meet mine.

"You're happy?" I ask.

"I couldn't be happier. A whole new start. I know we've still got a lot to sort out with the society. So many people, including your father and Lady Joanna Nethercutt, have gone to ground. We need to find them and prevent what happened to us from happening again. We've given our dead the burials they deserve, be they innocent or a villain of the peace." My mind flicks back to the day of Reggie's funeral. I thought he was just a butler to Nicholas, but I saw my husband break down that day. He was an emotional wreck and has still to employ another butler to replace his friend. Nicholas told me, the evening of the funeral, how Reggie had been like a father to him over the years. He'd been there for so many of his firsts in life. His father had never done that. Speaking of his father, that funeral couldn't have been more different. It was only Nicholas, William, and I in attendance, and I solely went with Nicholas to support him. There were no feelings of loss that day, only remorse that their father was so self-absorbed that he was unable to see them both for the great men that they'd become. I didn't cry. No one mourned the loss of the old Duke of Oakfield.

Nicholas' good hand has been on my backside supporting my weight on his lap, but he removes it and reaches into his jacket pocket. He pulls out papers. "I was going to give these to you later, but now seems a good time as any. The society and the title were all in my name, but I had my lawyer make everything fifty-fifty. All decisions on its future will be made jointly."

I take the papers from him. My heart falling even more in love with the man in front of me if that was possible.

"You didn't have to do that."

"It'll take me a long time to trust that I have a good nature. I've done bad things. I've been a bastard for so much of my life, but I know with your guiding voice I'll be alright.

This is my way of ensuring that, together, we rule. *Simul ut praeesset.* I'm changing the motto to reflect the way we're going to be working."

I drop the papers to the floor behind me and lean into my husband.

"I want you inside me."

"I want to be inside you." He gives me a lustful smirk, and we make short work of divesting only the clothes that are hindering our desire to be joined. I don't need foreplay, not today. I've been wet since Nicholas walked into the room. I always am around him. I slide myself down onto his erect length until he fills me. The sensation is overwhelming and captures my breath every time. Two people, as in love as we are, joining as one in this most intimate of ways. Nicholas places his hand on my hip and helps guide me up and down his cock. I'm breathless already with the fire burning brightly in my core. I've suffered. I'm not the precious little princess I was a few months ago. I've learned about life, discovered about love, and you know, I wouldn't change a thing that happened. Well, maybe I would have kept my mouth shut, so I didn't have to experience the scold's bridle.

Nicholas' thrusts get faster and faster. I meet him with every one. The urgency between us is frantic. I smash my lips against his and come with a call of passion while I shudder feverishly around his dick. His own climax hits him. I feel his cum flood my body and combine with my essence as it has done before when it formed the baby that now grows in my womb.

I slump down onto Nicholas' chest, and he uses his good arm to bring me closer to him. I know he has no plans on pulling out of me anytime soon. We will sit like this for as long as we can.

"I always thought the legacy of my succession would be the same as my forefathers," he speaks. "But no one counted on you being born into the society. The prophecy spoke of a boy to end the suffering, but in reality, a woman has been stronger. We are going to re-write all the rulebooks. A new legacy starts today."

THE END

William
& Tamara

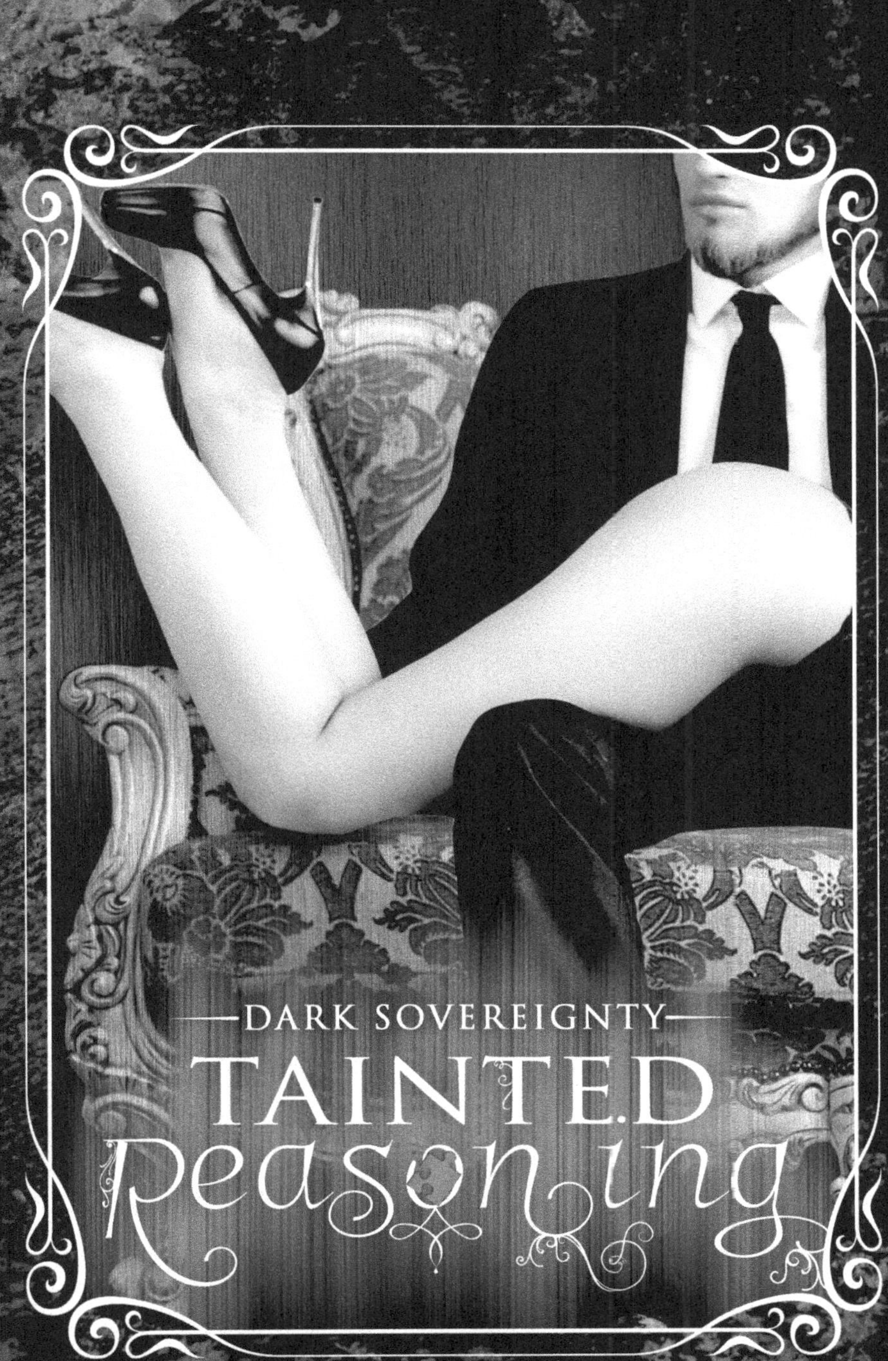

DARK SOVEREIGNTY
TAINTE.D
Reasoning

CHAPTER ONE

WILLIAM

I shut my eyes, allowing the stench of his fear, and his desperation for an end to the suffering, to wash over me. I can feel it surround every fiber of my being, and I revel in it. The man my brother, Nicholas, is currently torturing deserves everything that comes to him. He's a devil in the guise of a human being – landed gentry with a façade so convincing nobody knew for years he abused his daughter, Amelia. He raped her, beat her, and forced her to perform acts so degrading that in the end she placed a pistol against her sweet, innocent head and pulled the trigger. My sister-in-law, Victoria, still wakes in the night screaming from the memory. Nicholas doesn't know I can hear her way up in the attic area of the mansion we reside in. Her sobs are heart-breaking and make the man, whose fingers and toes are currently being removed, one by one, more than deserving of his punishment. Nicholas' hands are covered in blood. I know he doesn't like to do this. He would rather be home with his new wife, but this has to be done. The evil that exists within the society bearing our family name must be destroyed. It must be wiped from the surface of this planet as penance for the tortures inflicted on innocent girls since the society was founded by our four-times-great-grandfather.

"What you did to Amelia was sick. My name will no longer be associated with such crimes. We'll turn the society into one that honors the female of our species. Rejoicing in her beauty and worshiping her like the goddess she is. We'll not harm anyone, nor will we take any more property that's not ours without consent. Your membership is at an end, and that of your heirs unless they accept my authority and sign their agreement to the new charter I've put in place." My brother stands tall in front of Edgar Rushbrooke. His bloody hands now rest, folded across his chest. He wears a tailored suit that fits his body like a glove. It's an odd choice for the work we are doing, but somehow, it provides him with even more power. I'm in jeans and a t-shirt. I've never had the designer wardrobe my brother has. I've not had need of it, having been locked away since I was a toddler by my father, the previous Duke of Oakfield. Jeans are in fact an upgrade from the jogging bottoms I've previously worn. Green, my t-shirt is green. It always has to be. It's my favorite color, after all, and the only one I'll wear over my toned chest. The shade doesn't matter: forest, olive, mint, or even emerald– it just has to be green. I once borrowed one of Nicholas' t-shirts–he does have a few–it was burgundy, and I felt ill at ease all day. It wasn't right, and I was glad to get back to my comfort color the next day. My uniform.

My unruly brown hair is messily styled with my fingers brushed through it being the only nod to tidiness. Nicholas' is combed to perfection–no doubt by his new wife. I'm sure she's also given him a close shave this morning since his jaw is devoid of any hair. Mine is stubbled with two days' growth. I don't like shaving although I know I have to do it, but it feels strange. I can't explain why–it just seems wrong to me. I guess it's because of the autism I suffer from, wiring my brain in such a way that a natural grooming routine feels odd. My brain does that frequently, but thankfully, it also forces me to be a very clean person–I shower several times a day.

The tics start subtly: the swipe of my ear, a tap of my foot, the banging of the fingers of my left hand onto the right. My anxiety of the situation forces me into what I know will become my routine to cope with it.

"William?" Nicholas has turned to face me, and I look up at him. "You ok?"

"Yes," I reply, not wanting to worry him. This is me. The strange movements and oddities are who I am. Not everyone understands it, but I can't change them. They're a fundamental part of who I am and are with me for life.

"Good. Can you pass me the cutters? I want to remove his tongue."

"No!" Edgar shouts out. "Please. It was your father. I didn't want to do anything to Amelia. I loved her. She was my only daughter. The Duke forced me to prepare her. He said he would ostracize me if I didn't, and I couldn't risk that. My title is all our family have left–we've barely got any money left in our estate. I didn't want to do it. I even tried to smuggle Amelia away, but I failed." The once dignified gentleman is now a sniveling wreck. His eyes are blood shot, and snot drips from his nose. It's embarrassing to see how the men of the society respond to some of the tortures, which they would happily inflict on a woman, in other circumstances. Victoria took everything that happened to her with her head held high. This man is a coward, and in a few short moments, he will die like one. I don't hesitate any longer and picking up the cutters, I step forward. Nicholas holds his head straight, and I pull out Edgar's tongue and slice through the muscle. Gargled sounds of pain fill the room, and I shut my eyes, taking them all in. They excite me. The knowledge that this man is suffering gives me great joy. Is that normal?

I throw the bloody tongue onto the fire, which has been lit in the basement, and listen to it crackle as I watch it shrivel up to nothing. It's beautiful. Truthfully, is that reaction normal?

"Brother, the final say is all yours." I walk over to where a comfortable Queen Anne chair is placed in the corner of the room, its leather cover a deep green in shade. Nicholas placed it in here just for me. He understands my obsessions.

Nicholas pulls a gun from his pocket and points it directly at Edgar.

"The documentation you all seem to favor states at this point I should remove your head with the sword of my ancestry. I find that far too messy though. I'm going to deviate from the rules a little bit and try something new." The corner of his lip lifts into a devilish smile. He's the King of Oakfield, now, and he's cleaning out the trash. I shut my eyes, so I can allow my hearing senses to take over.

The gun fires as Edgar whimpers for his life. Well, at least, I think that's what he's doing because with no tongue, it's a little hard to understand him. I hear his skull crack and then silence. The smell of death invades my nostrils, and I open my eyes again. Edgar Rushbrooke is dead. Amelia can finally rest in peace. I've never felt so happy until the mess in the room hits me, and my need for cleanliness starts to itch at my skin.

Nicholas places his gun away and comes over to me. He picks up a towel to wipe his hands clean before tapping me on the shoulder.

"Don't worry. I've got a friend Matthew Carter who's ex MI-5. Since he found out what I've been doing, he's been more than happy to help with cleanups. We don't have to do it."

I laugh, looking back toward the dead man now slumped over in his chair.

I shift in my seat as the learning of my youth comes flooding back to me. Intricate details of the human body recollected in a photographic memory.

"Did you know the large intestine is bigger than the smaller one?" I ask Nicholas

"I remember something about that from my biology lessons at school. I preferred the sex education part, though. That stayed with me a good deal longer." He winks at me. "I enjoyed heading over to the nearby girl's school after lessons to show them just what I'd learned."

"How Victoria puts up with you, I'll never know?" I roll my eyes and look back at the body.

"We're still in the honeymoon stage. I'm sure it won't last. Then, I'll just have to keep fucking her, so she's too tired to care." Nicholas responds.

"Really don't need to know that." I push myself up from the seat and walk over to where Edgar is. The floor is covered in blood, and I can hear it squelch under the boots I'm wearing. The intestines always fascinated me as a child–the fact an organ that long could fit inside us. I place my hands over where they rest in my own body.

"William?" Nicholas is beside me. His voice full of concern. We've always been close, and he's protective of me–sometimes to the extreme. I'm the same with him, though. "What is it?"

"I want to see them." I tell him.

"See what?" he asks, his brows furrowing together.

"The intestines. This may be the only chance I get. I have to know if they really are as long as all the books say. Is that bad?"

His eyes flick over to Edgar. "It's not exactly normal, but I know you've always had an interest in the human body. My credit card knew it when you spent over five hundred pounds on books about the human body, as well as a massive skeleton and a muscle statue."

"I hope you're not bad-mouthing Indiana Bones and Macho Man."

"Never!" Nicholas chuckles and goes over to a table in the corner of the room. "Get him out of the chair and lay him down."

I look up at my brother and swipe my head, tap my foot, and bang my fingers.

"Are you sure?"

"I've got no interest in what happens to this man. You can cut him up into little pieces if you want. Examine his heart, lungs, and whatever else you want to look at. He can be turned into dog food for all I care. Edgar's in hell, now, and I'm not returning him to his family to bury. He doesn't deserve our respect." He hands me the knife. "You want to do it, or shall I?"

I look at the knife handle and then at the body. My stomach lurches a little before settling as my excitement builds at the thought of what goodies lie under the covering of skin and muscle.

"You can do it. I'll put some gloves on and help lay out the intestines. Do we have anything to measure them with?"

"Over in that drawer, there's a tape measure." He nods his head toward a modern IKEA unit. It looks out of place in comparison with the abundance of antique furniture we have all over our house, but I guess it was specially purchased for this purpose and can be easily disposed of. Not worth risking a thirty-thousand-pound sideboard when you can use one costing less than twenty pounds. I pull the drawer open and rummage through the contents until I find what I'm looking for. When I turn back, Nicholas is already pulling the intestines out through the massive hole he's cut into Edgar's abdomen. I breathe deeply, my body fizzing with excitement. I'm sure I should be worried about the perverse pleasure I'm getting from seeing a man cut open with his guts spilling out, but I need to see it. I've been told I've been wrong all my life, so why should I try to act any differently now. I've been presented with this opportunity, and I'm not going to waste it.

Nicholas finishes pulling the intestines out and cuts them off. The human waste from the body spills out on to the floor, and he curses when it splatters on his shoes.

"Fuck." He grabs a cloth and wipes the mess off before throwing the towel into a nearby sink. This basement is specifically designed for the work we're undertaking, but it wasn't Nicholas who set it up. It's a remnant from my father's time.

"Sorry," I tell him.

"Not a problem, really. I'll disinfect them later. Now, how do you want me to do this?"

"I think we need to lay it out flat around the floor." I take hold of the end that's attached to the small intestine. This is the large intestine or colon to give its proper title." I tell Nicholas.

"Paradoxically that's the shorter one, right?" He places some medical gloves on his hands and takes the other end, leading to the anus, and helps to stretch it out.

"Yes. It should only be around five feet."

We place it down, and I get the tape measure, which confirms it is about the correct length. I put my fingers around the organ and squeeze. It feels squidgy to the touch.

"This has never been my favorite choice of meat." Nicholas screws his nose up. "You remember when Nurse made us eat tripe because it would be good for us."

"I remember you trying not to gag and throwing it out of the window at every available opportunity."

We pick up the small intestine and start the more substantial task of laying that out.

"I don't think even the dogs or foxes would've wanted it." He laughs, and I join him. We finish laying out the small intestine, and I measure it.

"It's twenty-five foot long. That's about average. They can get up to thirty-four feet. I check the width of it and notice it's bigger than the standard of an inch. "It's dilated."

"What?" Nicholas is at the sink, washing his hands.

"The intestine. Its width is greater than it should be."

"You are going to have to speak in dumb people terms, little brother." Nicholas dries his hands and picking up his phone, he quickly types out a message. I know it's to call in the cleanup crew.

"When the small intestine is like this, it's a sign something is wrong. I think he might have been sick, even dying. It's not good like this. He would have been in pain."

"Damn," Nicholas exclaims. "I should have left him in pain. Mind you, I think we made sure he suffered enough. Amelia will be proud."

"She will." I smile as I think of the terrified girl I'd met. "It will give her peace."

"It will." Nicholas' face falls. I know the guilt of his part in Amelia's death weighs heavily on him. He suffers for it every day, and it's the reason he's trying to get rid of all the others who caused her torment.

"Come on," I say to him and wrap my arm around his shoulders. "Let's go shower and see that pretty wife of yours."

"A perfect plan."

As we leave the room, I turn back one final time and look at the intestines laid out neatly in a row, together. This is not normal. I know it. I can't help worrying about the effects of being confined away for so many years and what damage it may have inflicted on my soul.

CHAPTER TWO

TAMARA

My hands tap impatiently on the dividing screen of the black London taxi I'm traveling in. I swear this man could put his foot down if he wanted to, but he's deliberately driving slowly because he knows I need to be somewhere. I have to be at Oakfield Hall, but not today, not even yesterday. I needed to be there the day, all those months ago, when Nicholas Cavendish first set eyes on my best friend. I still can't believe she married the man. I swear he must have brainwashed her or something because I saw the state of her after she was handed over by her father to the Cavendish family. She had a brand burned into her skin by Nicholas himself, for fuck's sake. How can you fall in love with a man who does that? No, he's definitely brainwashed her.

I lean forward in my seat to speak to the driver, "Any chance we can go a little bit quicker. I really need to get to Oakfield Hall. It's very important."

"Sorry, Miss." The middle-aged cabbie, with grey flecks all over his hair,

waves his hand in the air. "The roads are icy after the 'eavy frost this morning. It's making 'em difficult to pass through because nobody salts 'em. Too many private lanes, you see. If you ask me, the Duke needs to look at gettin' some of his staff to make sure the roads are safe. It's dangerous. If you weren't a lass on 'er own, I'd 'ave made you walk the last bit. I don't know what's down the side of 'em ditches. One wrong turn of my wheel, and we'd be down one. You a friend of the Duke? You need to tell 'im. Make it safer for us all out 'ere."

"I know the Duke, well sort of. My best friend is married to him." I manage to get out from between gritted teeth. If we don't get to Oakfield Hall soon, then woman alone or not, I'm going to get out of this cab and walk. The roads are barely icy because the sun's been on them, and the frost melted ages ago.

"Lady Victoria?" The cabbie slows down even further, so he can continue our conversation.

I don't want to reply to him because I know he'll increase his speed if I don't engage in conversation, but I've been brought up to have good manners, and I know it's rude not to respond. "Yes." I keep my answer short, though, in the hope he'll go faster.

"Lovely lady she is. I live around these parts, so I've seen 'er a few times in the village. That 'usband of 'ers is never far behind, though. I'm not sure about the Cavendish family." The driver indicates left while speaking and turns off the lane up what appears to be a long driveway. I hold my breath, hoping we may have finally arrived. "The father dying so young then the other brother showing up out of nowhere like that. You 'ave to wonder where 'e's been all these years. It's a mystery. Your friend say anything to you about it?"

A massive mansion looms up ahead, and I've never been so grateful to see a place, even knowing what's happened behind its walls.

"I'm afraid not." I pull my wallet out as the driver pulls his cab to a halt. He presses the buttons to stop the clock and to give me the total for our ride. I can tell by the way he's huffing he's not happy and wanted some gossip from me to spread around the black cab network in London. Anything remotely associated with aristocracy is the '*bread and butter*' of his industry. I'm sure by the time the tale of my journey has been spun a few times, he will've had the Duke himself instead of me in the back of the cab.

"That'll be forty-five pounds and twenty pence," he tells me, and I try not to let my stomach turn at the exorbitant cost. I could have caught a train closer to Oakfield and then taken a taxi the last few miles, but it would've taken so much longer. I just want to see my friend and check she's alright. I bring out two twenty-pound notes and a ten and hand them to him.

"Keep the change." I smile, grabbing my small suitcase from the cab floor and jumping out of the vehicle.

"Thanks, love," the cabbie calls behind me, but I'm already making my way up the steps of the imposing mansion. Although I grew up with Victoria in a large house, there's something about this one that sends chills down my spine, and I can't help wondering if it's because of the horrifying historical events that have occurred behind its closed front door.

Using the ornate iron knocker, I bang loudly to gain entrance. A butler appears immediately and ushers me into a side room off the main entrance. He takes my name and tells me he will inform the Duke and Duchess of my arrival before leaving me alone. My hands are shaking so badly I have to clasp them together to stop. I need to see my friend I have to know she's ok. I hear a scream from somewhere in the house, and I know it's Victoria. I'm out of the room and following the sound when I hear my name called.

"Tamara." The shout comes as my friend flies down the grand staircase and straight into my arms. She's half dressed with her crisp white shirt ripped at the front. Then a man appears behind her, fumbling with the flies of his trousers clearly trying to fasten them as he descends the stairs. I see red. Was he raping my friend? Pushing Victoria aside, I go to meet him. I pull my fist back and slam it directly into his face.

"How dare you? You disgust me. You're a sick, sick pervert. If I had a knife, I would remove your balls and dick before feeding them to you." Bringing my knee up this time, I send it straight into his groin area, and he curls up in agony.

"Tamara, what the fuck are you doing?" Victoria screams out behind me and comes to the side of the man who's hunched over and rubbing his groin.

I grab her hand and pull her away, but she digs her feet into the carpeted flooring.

"We are leaving now," I snap, but my best friend tries to squirm from my hold.

"Tamara, have you gone insane?"

"No, but I'm beginning to think that whatever he's done to you has left you seriously in need of a doctor."

"He's not done anything to me."

"He forced you into a marriage. He branded you!" I hold my hand out as if to say, 'are you really that blind'.

"He did nothing of the sort," she replies in irritation.

I raise a knowing eyebrow at her.

"Alright, yes he branded me, but that was under his father's orders."

"Didn't he have a mind of his own?" I place my hands on my hips while Victoria goes back to her husband and starts to rub his groin area, but he pushes her hand away with a shake of his head. I secretly hope he gets himself hard, so that the bruised flesh stretches, and it hurts him even more. He looks up at me, and I glare at him with such a venomous look, I suspect it could kill if I possessed magical powers.

"It was different. Tamara, please. Listen to me. I love him."

I roll my eyes.

"Stockholm Syndrome," I tell her, but she shakes her head.

"No, true love. A 'til death do us part kind of love… because I couldn't survive without him kind of love."

A laugh comes from the top of the stairs, and we all turn our heads to look up. A handsome man stands there. My breath catches at the sharp cut of his jaw, which is littered with stubble. He's not dressed as formally as Nicholas but wears a forest green polo shirt and black jeans. His strong thighs are accentuated by the style of pants he's wearing. I lick my lips. He has a similar look to Nicholas, and I guess this must be his brother, William. He's the one who saved Victoria when the evil Scotsman tried to rape and murder her. I push past Nicholas and Victoria and run up the stairs to meet him. Throwing my arms around him, I pull him to me and give him a kiss on the cheek.

"Thank you, thank you," I tell him. "I can never repay you for saving my best friend. You're a good man."

Turning back around again, I scowl at Nicholas who in turn looks at Victoria as if to ask 'why do I get the crap kicked out of me, and my brother gets affection? Women are nuts'. He's the reason my friend suffered as she did, and it'll be a cold day in hell before I trust him.

"Enough, Tamara." Victoria takes her husband's arm and leads him into the side room I'd just come from. William links his arm through mine and assists me down the stairs, so we can follow them.

"He's really not that bad. My father was an evil man. It took Nicholas a little while to step out from under his control. He loves Victoria intensely and will do anything for her–he worships the ground she walks on. You really don't have to worry about her safety."

"Really?" I roll my eyes again. I was well known for doing it at university when people annoyed me. It's a habit I picked up from my mother–she was always doing it when I was younger. My mother is a placid person, most of the time, but get her onto a subject that irritates her, and her eyes start rolling around like a merry-go-round. "So why is her shirt all ripped?…and he was putting himself back in his trousers when I first saw him."

"Sex," William replies bluntly.

"I'm sorry?" I quiz in confusion.

"They were about to have sex. They do it most days… numerous times. I've bought a pair of headphones to escape the noise. They're like rabbits." Letting go of my arm as we walk into the room, he makes a circle with the index finger and thumb of his right hand and then sticks the index finger of his left hand through the middle of the circle. "All the time…like bunnies. Nicholas puts his dick in Victoria's pussy a lot."

My mouth falls open.

"William!" Nicholas and Victoria both chastise him at the same time.

"Inappropriate conversation in public," Nicholas reminds him.

William shrugs. "But it's true!"

Nicholas is sitting in an old leather arm chair while Victoria having collected ice out of a bucket in the corner of the room is now walking back toward her husband, clearly, he needs something to reduce the swelling I caused earlier with my knee.

"I know, but we don't say things like that in front of guests," Nicholas informs him.

"But she's not a guest. She's Victoria's best friend, and girls are always gossiping. I'm sure she knows all about the size of your dick, and what you can do with it."

"William, please!" My friend's shocked response comes as she unceremoniously drops the ice, now wrapped in a towel, into her husband's lap. When I look at her, a rosy tint spreads across her cheeks.

I suppress a little giggle at how embarrassed my best friend looks. We've not spoken a great deal since she was given by her father to the Cavendish family. It's one of the reasons I've been so worried. But now, taking the time to look at her, and the way she's interacting with Nicholas, it would be impossible not to see the love she has for him. Having removed the ice from her husband's lap, she's now tenderly stroking his face while he tries to get comfortable in the chair. My temper and worry for my friend got the better of me, and I didn't allow her to explain.

"I'm sorry," I admit with a wave of my hand toward Nicholas. I lower my head to look down guiltily at the ground. "Having been told by Victoria about everything that happened, I couldn't get past the bad stuff to see you two are happy together. I hope I've not permanently damaged anything…down there?"

I bite my lip and gesture toward his male parts. Nicholas stands and comes over to me, limping slightly, and formally holds his hand out to me, which I take and shake.

"Victoria wasn't always my first priority, and what you just did to me was a well-deserved punishment. But I can assure you Victoria's my world, now. I'll do anything to protect her." He shuffles from side to side as if to test out the discomfort he's still experiencing. "I think I'll be alright in a few hours. As William so eloquently commented earlier, my wife and I are in the honeymoon stage, and I can't disappoint her." He winks at me before pushing his brother along toward the door. "We'll go and arrange some food and drink. Leave you girls alone to catch up."

"Thank you." Victoria nods her head at him before coming up to me and pulling me into an embrace again.

"I really am sorry," I tell her.

"Like he said, he deserved it." She laughs. It's beautiful to hear and looking closely at her, for the first time, I can see how happy she truly is. She looks alive and free. I sniff and take in her rose scented perfume.

"Some things never change. Your favorite flower. I hope he buys you plenty."

"Everyday." She sniffs the air around me. "I see you haven't changed either… is that lily?"

"Of course."

Victoria leads me to take a seat on a chaise longue, overlooking the grounds of the house.

"Are you truly happy?" I ask her, just to confirm one final time.

"I've never been happier." Her reply blows away any lingering doubts I have, and we settle in for an afternoon of gossip and catching up on how very different her life has become.

CHAPTER THREE

WILLIAM

"Dinner is served," my brother's new butler, Alfred, announces, and I take Tamara's arm to escort her into the dining hall. We don't always eat like this. I normally sit in the kitchen with the chef and talk to him. He's lived an interesting life and cooked for a variety of people all over the world. Nicholas and Victoria usually eat at a smaller table in the cozy dining room, but Victoria wants to show her friend that she's truly happy, and so we're going all out with the grand gesture for our guest. Victoria is dressed in a flowing gown, and Nicholas is dressed in full evening attire. I've even dressed up, a bit, for the occasion. Instead of my usual green t-shirt, I've put on a formal shirt with a green tie and a black suit. It feels strange to wear something so restrictive. When my father was alive, I'd had to dress up for special occasions, but they were few and far between and never in polite society. I was too much of an embarrassment to him with my silly movements and inability to filter what I said. I swipe at my ear and then continue with my tapping routine. Tamara looks up at me.

"Are you alright?" she asks as a loose tendril of her long, jet-black hair falls out from the elaborate hairstyle she has pulled her locks into. I know Tamara's mother is of mixed heritage with African and Saxon ancestry, and these origins have combined in Tamara to give her an exotic beauty she shares with many a famous movie star or even a royal wife. She's dressed in a bright teal dress, stopping just above the knee, and black heels that make her legs seem like they go on forever.

"It feels a bit strange, wearing a formal outfit. I'm not used to it."

"I thought you would've been dressed like this for most of your life?"

"No. I didn't really eat dinner with my father and brother." I can feel my need to tic getting more urgent, and I swipe over my face and tap a few times. Tamara looks up at me, and then holds her hand out for me to take her arm. I do so and lead her into the dining room behind Nicholas and Victoria.

"I had a friend at university who struggled with formal occasions and preferred his own company. My university was a prestigious one, and we frequently had to dine in formal attire. He hated it, so I told him to imagine he was at home in his PJs and having a microwave meal. Those around him were doing just the same, and he didn't need to worry about the formality."

I can't stop the 'hmm' that escapes my mouth. It's the beginning of a thought I probably shouldn't voice, but one I know is going to spill from my lips anyway.

"I don't wear PJs."

Tamara laughs.

"Is this one of those pretend pair of PJs occasions?" I ask. My brain is wired differently to everyone else, and sometimes it takes throwaway comments far too literally.

"It is, but don't worry, I don't wear anything to bed either."

My thoughts go down a whole different route at that comment. Quickly pulling out her seat, I help Tamara to sit at the table before my dick manages to find its way out of my pants. I take my own place next to my brother who's at the head of the table with Victoria seated on his other side, and Tamara's next to her. The dining table is of carved, vintage oak and can seat many more people than just the four of us. We probably look a bit silly eating at this massive table when there are so few of us, but I can sense the anxiety emanating from Victoria with the need to please her friend and to reassure Tamara she has a happy life with Nicholas.

The butler and a maid appear and start to serve us the first course. It's a fiddly dish involving scallops and cauliflower purée. I'm aware of this because I was in the kitchen earlier when the chef was preparing everything, following Victoria's request for something fancy. I would've preferred baked beans on toast with a sprinkling of cheddar cheese, but that isn't considered the height of gastronomy, apparently.

Picking up my fork, I dig into the scallop and pop it in my mouth. It actually tastes good– I'm getting a little hint of curry flavor from it, but it doesn't overpower the taste of the mollusk. It's really tasty. I look over to Tamara and see her pushing it to the side of the plate.

"Don't you like it?" I ask, and Victoria looks over from her conversation with Nicholas to her friend.

"Tamara?" She frowns.

"I'm not the biggest scallop fan. We had some once, and they left me sick for a few days afterward. I've been put off eating them ever since."

Victoria lets out a heavy sigh.

"I knew it would go wrong"–tears pool in her eyes– "I told you." She turns back to my brother who's already getting out of his chair and coming to wrap his arms around his emotional wife.

"It's only the first course. It doesn't matter," Nicholas reassures Victoria and at the same time waves the butler over. "Can you ask chef for something different for Miss Bennett, please?"

"At once, sir." He picks up Tamara's plate, but she tries to stop him.

"Please, don't worry. Everyone has nearly finished. I'll just wait for the next course."

The butler hovers with the plate, waiting for Nicholas to instruct him on how to proceed.

"It's alright, Alfred. Take all the plates and bring the main course. It's lamb. Is that alright?" Nicholas smiles reassuringly at Tamara.

"My favorite," she responds, and the butler clears the table. "Victoria, please don't worry. I'm over my temper tantrum with Nicholas. I can see you love him, and he loves you. You don't have to impress me or get yourself stressed. I would've been just as happy with our childhood dinner of pizza and cupcakes in front of the TV."

"I'm sorry." Victoria leans over and brings her friend into

an embrace. "I do love Nicholas… I promise you. He's doing so much to correct the past wrongs of his family. Only today, he prevented a really nasty man from ever hurting anyone again."

Nicholas clears his throat with a deep cough. "Possibly not a conversation we should have at the dinner table."

I can't help but laugh. "I don't know…in some countries, the organs we played around with today are considered to be delicacies."

Tamara pales, and I realize instantly I've said too much.

"What…What do you mean?" she stutters.

"Nothing," both Nicholas and I reply at the same time. My brother gives me a scowl, which says I need to keep my mouth shut about other aspects of our afternoon excursion.

"No." Victoria, reaches out and takes her husband's hand in her own and squeezes it. "I want Tamara to know everything. It's the only way she can make an informed decision about whether she'll help us or not. She's a fantastic lawyer, Nicholas. She's still learning, but what we are trying to achieve will give her great experience in so many aspects."

"I'm not sure I like the sound of this, not when it's combined with the term organs." Tamara worries the edge of her lip with her teeth, and I can't help but think I'd like to sink my own teeth into that plump part of her flesh. What the hell is going on with me, at the moment? Every time I look at this woman, I start imagining her in a sexual way. I don't do this. Women are brought to me, I do what I need to, to get off, and then they're taken away again. I don't do feelings…they're too complicated, and heaven knows, the thoughts running through my head don't need any additional distractions. I look away from her and drain my elaborate wine glass, which had been full of the finest Chardonnay.

"I've told you a lot about what happened when my father handed me over to Nicholas. I also mentioned a girl called Amelia to you," Victoria says, turning her chair to face her friend. At this, Nicholas gets to his feet and walks over to take a protective stance at the door used by the staff. Our employees know of our exploits, but they don't need to be discussed openly in front of them.

"I remember. She died during one of the trials. You said that her father had abused her since she was born."

"Yes, he'd forced her to practice completing the trials that I had to endure. She didn't just do them once... he made her repeat them several times, so she would be prepared for whatever Nicholas threw at her. He raped, abused, and degraded his own daughter. I hadn't realized the full extent of the fragile state of Amelia's mind until her last moments. The only task she hadn't completed was to kill a man, and when confronted in the trials with having to commit murder, she simply couldn't. It was the one that broke her." Victoria pauses and wipes a tear from her eye as I look over to my brother. His head is bowed, and the guilt of Amelia's death causes his shoulders to slump. It's one of his biggest regrets that he couldn't save her. Her death will haunt him until the day he dies. I'd watched the girl numerous times during the trials, though, and I know she was beyond saving. Death gave her the peace she needed, allowing her to escape from the prison her mind had become. Putting a gun in her hand was the biggest favor Nicholas could have done for her.

"How can a father do that to his own daughter?" Tamara sits in her chair stunned. Her mouth has fallen slightly open, and confusion glistens in her eyes. "I just don't understand it."

"I don't think anyone does." Victoria dabs away another tear.

"Sometimes, people just have the devil in them. They remain completely unaffected by the damage their wicked actions cause other people. There is no good in them. Evil is a disease that riddles their entire being." I push my chair back and come to kneel between the girls. "My father had it, and Amelia's father was the same."

"And my father has it," Victoria adds.

Tamara lets out a long, slow breath. The realization of what has happened dawning on her. She looks at me.

"You killed your father when he tried to kill Nicholas and Victoria."

"Yes," I reply without regret.

Tamara looks over her shoulder at Nicholas.

"You killed Amelia's father."

Nicholas nods before replying.

"He died in agony, and his body was given no last rites or ceremony. His death was deserved for the abuses he inflicted on his daughter."

"But you had no right..." Tamara starts to lecture, but Nicholas puts his hand up to halt her.

"I may not have had the right to take his life, but he certainly lost the privilege of breathing with his actions toward his daughter. Too many people have been hurt, killed, or maimed by this society since its inception. I'm the ruler of it now, and I'll not rest until it's cleaned of all those who would seek to destroy a human life for power, monetary gain, or simply for sexual gratification. That is the world my father created. People who treated women like slaves. They abused them to the point they were unrecognizable as a human and then put a bullet in their heads. I couldn't save Amelia, but I will prevent this from happening again in my name. The Duke of Oakfield will no longer be synonymous with evil. He will be a loving husband, father, and ruler of a society helping to empower women."

"Why didn't you go to the police with the evidence of what Amelia's father had done?" Tamara asks, and I have to chuckle a little at her faith in the law. You can tell she is new to her profession and still believes in the honesty of all those working in it.

"Because the Commissioner of the Metropolitan Police was an active member of the society." Victoria says as she stands up from her seat at the dining room table.

"What!" Tamara exclaims, and her mouth opens and closes like a fish, trying to find sense in what she's hearing. "I can't…He can't…What?"

Nicholas comes to his wife's side and wraps an arm around her tiny waist.

"His wife suffered a stillbirth of a baby girl when Viscountess Hamilton was pregnant with my wife. If the child had been born alive, then she would have become my property on my thirtieth birthday. She would have suffered the same fate as the other girls I was given. I can only be thankful to god for not allowing another woman to experience the torment the others endured."

Tamara looks down at the floor, and I can see tears forming in her eyes. Reaching out, I take her hand in mine – it's warm to the touch, despite the chill in the air, resulting from her stark realization regarding the malevolence of some people in positions of respect and trust.

"How can they get away with this?" Tamara asks.

"They have the power," I respond. "It's the reason no one questioned the fact I disappeared after my autism diagnosis."

"I can't understand this. It's too much."

"It's a lot to take in," Victoria offers with sincerity and concern for her friend.

"What did you do to Amelia's father?" Tamara asks.

"No details," I tell her.

"Please. I need to know."

I look up to Nicholas, and he nods, affirming I can give her more details.

"I'm going to take Victoria to freshen up. I'll ask for dinner to be brought into the lounge. We can eat it in front of the TV." Nicholas places his hand on my shoulder before leaving with an arm wrapped around his wife to support her.

"William," Tamara pleads with me. "If I'm going to be here and get involved, I need full details of what you are doing. I want to help Victoria in any way I can. She's my life…my best friend, but everything is so scary, and I know nothing of this life. It's dark, horrifying, and alien to me."

"I know." I pull myself up and take a seat on Victoria's vacated chair. Scraping it along the wooden floor, I bring it nearer to Tamara, so I can still keep a hold of her hand while I talk to her.

"Nicholas and I captured Amelia's father and tortured him. We made him suffer by cutting off any distinguishing marks he had: moles that sort of thing. We removed his fingers, toes, and masculine parts before killing him. He needed to die that way to allow Amelia to rest in peace."

Tamara gasps and pulling away from me, she looks down at my hands in horror.

"You did it yourself? How can you do that to another human? Why not order someone else to do it?"

"I guess I have some of my father's darkness in me. I can't explain it. I wish I could. I understand if you want to leave here now and never come back. We won't stop you."

"Will he be the last one to die?" she asks with a quivering of her bottom lip

"I can't promise you that. I don't know what Nicholas wants to do with Viscount Hamilton."

"Victoria's father?" She gasps, bringing her hand to her mouth.

"Yes. He gave Victoria to Nicholas. Although he behaved better than the other fathers. At least he kept Victoria protected while she was growing up rather than abuse her. We will ensure he is ruined for his part in the society, but he's not as bad as some."

"These are people's lives you are playing with. Taking things into your own hands like God." I can see she's struggling to understand the motivation behind our actions. This evil world has only been revealed to her through tales of darkness. It's never been something she's experienced, felt, or thought about. She hasn't lived a life like the one Nicholas, Victoria, and I have endured.

"I wish I could explain it better to you. Victoria's father bought a girl during the trials. We've not seen or heard from her since that day. We don't know if she's alive or dead. He told us she was for Victoria's brother to marry, but as far as we are aware, he's still single. There is so much more going on, Tamara. These people are bad men. If they learn you are involved with us, they'll take, rape, and abuse you until the pain is so great that death is the only way out of the suffering. This is why we take the law into our own hands. Why we do what is necessary to put an end to the society we grew up in. It's the only way in our eyes. The people we are talking about are beyond the law in so many ways, but using what we know, we can restrict them and ruin them, so they can never rise again. The police chief is corrupt, so we'll find some incriminating evidence and use the law against him. Please, we don't want to kill anyone else unless they truly deserve it. That's why we need your help."

"I don't know. I'm still learning. I don't have the clout you think I do. I've not even completed the bar yet."

I shake my head.

"It doesn't matter," I reassure her. "Faith in your abilities is all you need. Just as Nicholas and I have in ours, even if our skills are a little different. This society's influence reaches everywhere… we need to destroy it!"

"I need to think about all this. Try to get my head around the truth that if I help you, then I'll have to look past the fact you and your brother kill people. It's not something I've been trained for or ever could be." When Tamara stands, I let go of her hand, and she walks toward the door.

"I understand." I remain seated. "Would you like food sent to your room?"

"No," she says as she turns to face me. "I want to talk to Victoria some more. I need to understand exactly what she went through. I've heard the pain in her voice as we've spoken about her experiences, but I need to also see it expressed in her face, visually, the way you and Nicholas have."

Pushing to my feet, I come to stand before her.

"I promise you, if there were any other way, I wouldn't do this either. The only reason it doesn't bother me more is because, I fear, I've been damaged due to the years of being in total seclusion."

"It hasn't damaged you, William. You showed the kindness within you by protecting and helping those girls as much as you could." She leans up and presses a chaste kiss to my cheek. "You helped save my best friend. I owe you silence and respect just for that, let alone for everything else you've told me today."

Bowing my head to her, I watch her turn to leave. Those familiar urges of sexual need rise within me again. I need to get this under control if we are to work together. Bad thoughts are what I need to focus on. My father... that should be enough to dampen any ardor.

Tamara gasps, drawing me out of my thoughts.

"What is it?" I step forward.

"My mother?"

It takes me a few moments to register who her mother is, and what she's asking.

"Nicholas has checked on her, and she's safe, as far as we're aware. She believes Victoria fell for Nicholas in the conventional way. Victoria has tried to get her to come and work here, but she refused out of loyalty to the Hamilton's."

"I have to see her." Tamara's eyebrows draw together. I can feel the fear rippling from her now. "Please, William. I have to make sure she's alright. If you say Lord Hamilton has a woman held captive and gave away Victoria in the manner he did, then she could be in danger. I need to check to make certain she's unaware of everything. She's all I have. I don't know who my father is. Please."

"Ok, you can go see her, but I'm going to come with you."

"What? You can't."

I take hold of Tamara's hand, probably a little too tightly, but the urge to protect her is surging through my body like a runaway freight train on steroids. I won't let anything happen to her.

"You want to see your mother, then I'm coming with you. No arguments."

The chauffeur opens the door for me while William comes around and offers me his hand to hold, so I can ease myself with ladylike dignity into the car. William's palms are clammy, and when he comes to sit beside me, I can see the trepidation etched on his handsome face. His jawline is square, dotted with the stubble of a day-old growth, and his dark brown hair is trimmed short at the sides and shaggy on top. His brother has the air of pristine grooming, but William is more natural. He's the type of person who can roll out of bed, have a quick wash, clean their teeth, and look catwalk ready. At the moment, though, he looks ready to climb out of his own skin. His left hand is flicking at his ear, then the top of his head while his legs bounce up and down in a rhythm known only to him.

"William,"–I reach out to take his right hand– "Is everything ok?"

He gives me a wry smile.

"You can talk to me," I offer a little more reassurance, but he won't look me in the eye.

"The world moves so fast in a car," he says, staring out of the window. Turning my own head to observe the lush green fields of the countryside change into the densely populated suburbs of west London, I hold my breath while we weave down the once familiar streets toward my childhood home. I guess it does move fast, changing so quickly. The calmness I've been feeling disintegrates into nerves.

"You're not used to traveling like this, are you?" I ask. Victoria has told me a great deal about William. For most of his twenty-eight years, he's been hidden away, rarely leaving his bedroom let alone his home. To suddenly have all this freedom must make him feel agoraphobic as the intensity of the different sights, sounds, and smells overwhelm him. I'm aware of his autism diagnosis and how that can heighten his senses in comparison to those not on the spectrum, leaving him with a fear of unknown danger in these sorts of situations.

"No. I've been in a car only a handful of times in my life, and I can't drive one." He looks toward the driver who is indicating to make a right turn. William's eyes narrow with the ticking of the indicator as if the noise is too loud for him even though it's barely audible to me. "The first time I left with Victoria to rescue Nicholas, I didn't really think about what I was doing other than getting to my brother. But the second time, they had to virtually tranquilize me to get me to our destination…there's too much stimulation. I don't think I want to drive a car. I'd prefer to have my driver do it. With all the noises and movement, it's a lot to concentrate on, and even though it's easing, I still feel nervous."

"I can understand that. I don't like driving in London anyway. The drivers are too unpredictable. They could turn left while indicating right…I've had that happen to me before. It's not something you should be scared of, though. Sometimes, car journeys can be beautiful, and at other times insightful. You see different things, which can help you learn and study the world we're living in. For example, take the fields we just drove by… at the moment they are green, but travel the same road in summer, and they will be scorched yellow with the heat of the sun."

I stretch out my arm and point to some buildings being constructed. They are halfway to completion, and workmen are sitting on the top of the scaffolding with steaming cups of tea or maybe coffee. "Look at those buildings as well. The last time I came down here there was an old run-down factory from the seventies. It wasn't really in keeping with the area, so they decided to replace it with luxury accommodation for London's elite. I remember the Viscount being up in arms about the houses, wanting me to find some legal bylaw or statute to try and stop them being built. He wanted to have the factory demolished and the land converted into green woodland to match the forest area at the back of his property. Unfortunately, the council had a target they had to meet, and this was a perfect opportunity for them." I chuckle at the thought of Victoria's father being outwitted for once. When I hear William also emit a soft laugh, I look up at him. He points out of the window at another factory close to the entrance of the long driveway, leading to our destination.

"Maybe I should get Nicholas to purchase that factory and turn it into accommodation for London's not so elite!"

"Yes!" I exclaim with an evil snigger. "I know everything

must be new and overstimulating to you, but truthfully, what you did for Nicholas and Victoria has already shown how strong you can be."

"Thank you." William replies and squeezes my hand in gratitude. "How do you want to play this with the Viscount, if we see him?"

My blood runs cold at the mention of the man who willingly sacrificed Victoria to hell on earth. I'm not entirely sure I'll be able to keep my calm around him. But for the sake of my mother, and a promise I made to Victoria in relation to keeping her brother, Theodore, in ignorance of all matters, I will bite my tongue. If I get time alone with him, though, he'll get a piece of my mind.

"I don't want Victoria to be upset, especially after her news this morning… she's too delicate." –William and I had left Victoria and Nicholas celebrating the news of a positive pregnancy test– "So I intend to be on my best behavior. I want to check on my mother and persuade her to leave with us. That is all."

"Good idea. I'll try to be on my best behavior as well. Though, my brain doesn't always listen to what I want."

I wink at him.

"I know. I've still not forgotten how you greeted me this morning."

"Hey, I brought you coffee." He smirks.

"Yes, and an appraisal of how beautiful my tits were looking."

"Well, they were."

We both laugh together, and the earlier tension in the car dissipates just as we pull up to Viscount Hamilton's home. Once I thought the sun shone out of this place. It was my childhood home. Despite being a single mother with an unwanted pregnancy, Victoria's father allowed my mother to keep her job and even helped to educate me. I wanted for nothing, and he treated me just like a daughter. In some ways more so than Victoria who he always sheltered, never allowing her to forge her own path in the world. Now we know why! He was part of a secret society who placed no value upon women except for their usefulness as a bargaining chip. It's a betrayal I feel deeply in my heart, despite not being directly involved. He was like a surrogate father to me, and now it hurts to know the evil lying beneath the surface.

Before I've even realized that William has got out of the car, he's come around to my door and opened it. He holds his hand out for me, and I take it… I could get used to being treated like a lady. I've walked on the wild side at university for the last few years, but this feels nice, to be respected and cared for.

"You ready?" he asks.

I nod 'yes' and pull toward the servants' entrance at the rear of the building.

William coughs and refuses to move.

"Where are you going?" he questions and looks toward the main front door.

"I don't use that entrance unless I'm with Victoria."

His brows furrow together.

"I've been hidden away and forced to use secret doors for most of my life. I'm free now. I won't skulk away and use a back door when a perfectly good front entrance is available."

"I thought we weren't going to antagonize the Viscount."

"We're not, but we're also not going to hide away as if we

are nobodies. Technically, until Victoria and Nicholas have a child, I'm the Earl of Lullington: Nicholas' old title."

I look at William, and I swear I can hear him chuckling with an evil laugh. I know it's all in my head because he's standing there with an expressionless face. The only evidence of his mischief is the glint in his eye and the ever so slight curl to his lip as he strides off toward the front door. He rings the bell and Viscount Hamilton's butler, Marcus, opens up with a wide-eyed expression.

"Earl Lullington and Miss Tamara Bennett to see Ms. Elsie Bennett." William doesn't wait to be welcomed into the house. He pushes past the butler and into the hall. "Where is the receiving room? This way?" He points to a closed door to the left, which I know is the Viscount's personal lounge and not one he would want William and myself entering. The butler tries to get an answer out but is so stunned at the intrusion into his day that he stands there with his mouth hanging wide open.

"Come on, man. Did you not understand what I said? Do I need to repeat myself more slowly for you?"

"The Viscount is in his study," the butler exclaims in shock, having nothing better to say.

"I didn't ask to see his lordship. I requested Ms. Bennett. Please have her brought to me at once. I think I'll have a whiskey as well. Its past midday isn't it, Tamara?"

I look down at my watch, stunned by the change in William. It's like he's suddenly turned into his brother, and it's intriguing to watch.

"Yes. It's almost one."

"I think possibly a spot of lunch is in order as well then. I'm sure Ms. Bennett is entitled to a lunch hour."

A figure appears at the top of the stairs, her head poking around the corner of a marbled pillar. I instantly recognize my mother who takes the stairs at a rapid pace to greet me as I race toward her.

"Tamara." She throws her arms around me. "I didn't know you were back. You should have called me. I would have asked permission to come to the station to get you. Where's all your luggage? In the taxi?"

The butler clears his throat with a loud cough and nods toward William. My mother's face instantly falls.

"Earl Lullington." She presents a small curtsy, but William waves his hand to tell her to stop. "The Duchess is she here?" my mother enquires and gulps…I wonder why?

"No, my sister-in-law is at home resting. She's had an eventful few months, and we discovered she's pregnant, this morning, so the Duke wants her to take it easy."

"You sure it's just resting." A new deep voice enters the conversation when Theodore, Victoria's brother, steps out of his father's lounge. The Viscount is behind him, and it takes all of my strength to stay rooted to the spot and not run forward and scratch his eyes out.

"Elsie, bring dear Tamara and the Earl in here. It will not do to keep them standing in the hallway like unwanted guests." The Viscount holds the door to his lounge open, and Theo steps out of the way to allow us through.

"Will you be alright, father?" I hear Theodore say with an icy tone.

"Yes, of course. Let me know what you find out."

"I will." Theodore disappears, and the Viscount follows us into the room.

"Was the purpose of your visit to bring us the joyful news

of Victoria's pregnancy? Or was there something else?" The Viscount's words are clipped, and we all stand around in the room on tenterhooks.

"Miss Bennett wanted to see her mother," William replies. He's like a totally different man from the person wracked with fear in the car. Now, he's confident and purposeful and stands up tall against his formidable foe. The Viscount shows no remorse for his actions. He must be aware I know the truth since I've seen Victoria and chosen to have William accompany me, but he wears the mask of a concerned father well.

"Of course, she does." The Viscount comes over to me and wraps his arms around me. He strokes my back and presses a kiss to my forehead. It has all the hallmarks of the tender fatherly display I would expect from him, but I can't help but feel cold and disgusted by it. "Tamara, I'm so proud of the results you achieved in your law exams. You put most of your class to shame, and the position you've secured at Wells and Partners is prestigious, to say the least. I'll have to see to it that all my legal affairs are transferred to the company in future."

William snorts and opens his mouth. He pauses, not saying anything before swiping at his ear and then his head. Viscount Hamilton steps away from me and looks toward William, warily.

"Is something wrong, Earl Lullington?"

"Nothing," William replies curtly and takes a seat, which allows everyone else in the room to also relax in comfort. The tension fills the room like helium trying to burst out of a balloon, but decorum is maintained at all times. This is how the upper classes do things. My mother remains standing. In this domain, she is staff and unless invited to sit, she'll not do so. Although I remain the daughter of a staff member, I'm finding it hard to behave in the manner my mother's position requires. All the respect I had for the man in front of me has gone.

"Mama, come sit with me," I tell her, and she widens her eyes toward the Viscount in concern.

"Elsie, join your daughter." The Viscount motions with a flick of his wrist, and that one action strengthens my resolve to take her back to Oakfield Hall with us.

My mother comes and sits beside me, and taking hold of her hand, I bring it into my lap. The room goes silent until the butler enters with a whiskey for William.

"Chef is preparing some sandwiches for our guests, my lord. Miss Bennett, may I get you a drink?"

"No thank you, Marcus." I reply, and we all fall back into quiet, again. William brings his whiskey to his mouth, takes a sip, and then places it down on the counter before standing and addressing the Viscount.

"Hamilton, I hear from Victoria that you have a beautiful winter rose garden. Maybe, you could show it to me, so I can pick one to take back to her. I'm afraid my parents were not as fond of the flower as your family. Our gardens are severely lacking in that particular bloom."

The Viscount reluctantly gets to his feet with a vicious glare toward William. The two leave the room, and I'm alone with my mother for the first time in almost a year.

"How is Victoria?" she asks.

"She's good. Very happy."

"Are you sure?" A line of worry mars her forehead. I take

a moment to properly look at her. She has aged during the last year and has lost weight.

"Yes. She and Nicholas are really in love. He worships her." I take in a deep breath. "Mama, Victoria told me she asked you to come and work for her, but you said no. Do you know what happened to her?"

My mother gulps and tears start to form in her eyes.

"You do. Then, why not leave?"

"I can't." She pulls away from me and stands. Her eyes keep flicking to the door. "It's complicated. I have to stay here."

"Mama, please. I'm worried for you here."

"I'm safe."

"How can you be? You know what he did to Victoria. Her own father! He gave her away like she was nothing but a tool to advance his name. How can you bear to be here any longer?" I'm really confused. My mother has always been a strong woman, and someone I look up to. She's terrified, though. Her hands are fidgeting. "He's forcing you to stay here, isn't he? That's it, we're going!"

I jump up from my chair and taking her hand, I start pulling her toward the door.

"Tamara, please stop. You don't understand." She digs her heels in, but I'm stronger, and we're out into the hall before she has a chance to stop me.

"I understand perfectly. He's an evil man. I'm not going to allow you to stay in this house for another moment longer."

William and the Viscount appear in front of me. William's brows are furrowed together, and anger radiates from him. The Viscount has a smug smile on his face.

"You sick, sick man." I let go of my mother and stomp toward him. My hand raises of its own volition and slaps him hard across the face. He grabs it and yanks me toward him, so my body is flattened against his.

"You think I'm sick? You know nothing, little girl. You're staying with the devil himself…a man who branded five girls to prove his ownership of them."

"Only because he had no choice, and one of them was the daughter you knowingly gave to him," I spit back in his face.

William seems to come to life and pulls me away from the Viscount.

"Don't you dare touch her," William snarls as he pushes me behind him.

"Why would I want to do that when I have Joanna?" The Viscount laughs, and I see William pull his own fist back. I remember Victoria mentioning a missing girl called Joanna who'd been bought at an auction by the Viscount. This must be the woman he's referring to.

"No! William. He's not worth the trouble. We are going." I return to my mother and grab her hand. "You are coming with us, no arguments. I'll have William drag you to the car if I need to."

"Tamara, please don't do this. Please stay, we can all discuss this together," my mother whimpers.

"I won't spend another minute under his roof."

It's uncouth, but I turn and spit at the Viscount's feet as William takes my mother's other hand, and we drag her toward the front door. At the same moment, the butler appears with a tray of sandwiches but instantly turns around when he sees the confrontation going on.

"Why don't you tell her why you don't want to leave,

Elsie? See if she wants you with her, then." The Viscount's evil laugh comes from behind us, and I feel a chill wash over my body.

"Tell her you knew all along what would happen to Victoria. That you were a part of my plan to keep her pure all those years. You watched her like a hawk. You helped dress her on the day I gave her to Nicholas, knowing full well what would happen to her. Tell her, Elsie. Tell her that if I'm evil, then so are you."

I'm vaguely aware of William letting go of my hand and heading back toward the Viscount. I don't look at what's happening, but the sounds of a fist meeting bone followed by a body crashing against the marble floor echo in the hallway. I should probably stop William, but all I can do is stare at my mother as she stands there repeating over and over again that she's sorry. I can't listen to it. I can't be hearing this.

"You knew," I cry.

"I'm sorry."

I try to say something else, but I have no words. My mother, the woman who I've always looked up to, knew what would happen to my best friend.

"Did he blackmail you to do it?" I ask as William appears at my side and wraps his hands around my waist. My mother looks to where the Viscount is lying flat out on the floor.

She shakes her head.

"It was my job."

My legs give way as my heart breaks, and William catches me. We leave my childhood home without a backward glance.

CHAPTER FIVE

WILLIAM

"Why, Mum? Why did you have to leave me?" I place my hand against the weathered head-stone of my mother's grave. This is my place of calm, and it's exactly where I need to be, following our meeting with Viscount Hamilton. I left Tamara sobbing in Victoria's arms after learning that her mother knew what would happen to her friend. I can't even begin to understand the betrayal they must both be feeling. But it's Viscount Hamilton's mention of Joanna that has left me feeling unable to control my oddities: my hand swipes every few seconds around my ear and then on top of my head. I can tell I'm particularly anxious because my tongue darts out as well, swiping around my lips. In the cold air, I can already feel the skin getting sore. I can't stop my body's natural reactions – they are a part of me, and until I can rid my mind of my concerns about Joanna, they will remain. Why can't we find her? Nicholas and I have been searching everywhere we know the Viscount is linked to but have discovered nothing.

It's as though she's vanished off the face of the Earth. Is she dead? No. Victoria insists her father told her Joanna was meant for her brother, but Theodore seems oblivious to the fact his father is hiding a poor girl somewhere. Maybe he's also involved? I'm sure Tamara never expected her mother to have been aware of Victoria's fate, let alone knowingly preparing her for it. The darkness we witnessed today is deep rooted and shows me Nicholas and I still have a long way to go to rid the world of the old Oakfield Society. There are still too many pockets hidden away, believing it's right to treat women as objects, fit only for their sickening desires. My ancestors including my father created a place for the monsters who dwell in the shadows to flourish. I just hope Nicholas and I can shed enough sunlight to destroy them all.

"It's so hard, Mama." I stroke her gravestone again and collapse down into the wet grass. "Everything is so different. Just being outside here in the fresh air. I never knew it could be so clean…no stale odors or dust. Why did he do this to me? Am I really that different?"

I shut my eyes and allow a memory from my youth to enter my head.

"Nicholas, don't be so stupid." My father stands with his arms folded across his chest, looking down at my fourteen-year-old brother with a stern expression.

"But, Your Grace, it's his birthday. Surely, he could join us for a little while. I'll look after him. He can sit next to me," Nicholas pleads.

"No."

"But…" Nicholas pleads again, and I look on from the shadows through a peephole into my brother's bedroom.

"If you ask me again, I will take him and lock him up in the

tower just to shut you up." My father pulls my brother toward him, using his superior weight and height to impose greater discipline. I wish Nicholas would stop asking for me to join them for dinner. I don't mind that it's my twelfth birthday. I'm perfectly happy up in my room. It's quiet up there, and my brother brought me some new books to read today about all the different countries in the world. I'm beyond excited to start. He bought me a book of flags last year, and he takes great delight in trying to trip me up in naming them, but I know them all, even the obscure countries that nobody has ever really heard of such as Nauru, Benin, and Suriname. He even tried to fool me once by showing me the old flag for Venezuela, but luckily the book had shown me that as well. The books on countries will be amazing because I'll be able to learn more about them, their populations, languages, and all those sorts of amazing facts and figures. My tutor thinks it's a waste of time, but then he thinks it's a waste of time for me to be taught anything when I don't leave my room. It's not as though I'll ever be able to take any exams and gain qualifications, which I could use for a job in the future. My father says my job is just to behave and not embarrass him with my weird hand movements and inability to keep my mouth shut. I try so very hard not to say silly things, but I can't help it. If a thought pops into my head, I tell myself to keep it to inside, but it's as though there is a wire in my brain that isn't correctly plugged in, and I can't control the opening of my mouth and the words that come out.

All of a sudden, I'm brought out of my reflection when the door to the hidden passage I'm in is pulled open, and my father's hand reaches in and hauls me out to stand next to my brother.

"You're so strange you can't even hide quietly because of all the stupid foot tapping and hitting of things you do." He throws his hands up in the air. "Damn it, William, why do you have to be such an imbecile? You're a freak of nature. A result of your mother's addiction to drugs. I should have done us all a favor and had you terminated when I could have. But no, I wanted a spare in case anything happened to Nicholas and look how I was punished. The most stupid child in the world."

"I'm sorry," I mumble and try desperately to keep my hands and feet still, but I just can't do it. My left foot lifts and taps three times in quick succession on the floor.

"Damn it, William. Stop it. You're an intolerable embarrassment," my father curses at me.

Nicholas drops to his knees and tries to hold my foot still. He looks up at me with so much worry on his face – no fourteen-year-old should ever have that expression.

"I'm trying, Your Grace. I really am." My words catch in my throat with the effort I'm exerting, trying to keep still.

"It's all your mother's fault. You're just like her. Why was I lumbered with her winning the trials? I could have had any of the other women, but no, I get the wife who gives me one belligerent son, and one son who's a monster."

My hand swipes around my head really quickly, and my father's face reddens with so much anger that I know I've broken the last vestiges of his control.

He balls his fist and pulling it back, I feel the punch as he lands it hard on my face. His hands move to his belt, and I know what is coming next. He's tried so many times to beat the 'wrong' out of me. It never works, though. I'm what he says I am – a freakish monster. Nicholas is quick to his feet and blocks my father's path to me.

"Your Grace, please. I'll take him to his room. We'll keep him secreted away for the night, so he doesn't make an embarrassment of himself in front of your distinguished guests."

"Out of the way, Nicholas," my father scolds, and I see my brother go flying across the room. Before I have a chance to draw a breath, the biting leather of his belt cracks against the skin on my back. Even through the t-shirt I'm wearing, I can feel it burning my flesh. Nothing will stop my father now, until he's satisfied there's a chance that he's beaten the 'freak' out of me. It never works, though. I'll be back with my tics tomorrow, and there is nothing he can do about it. It's who I am, and why would I ever try to fit in when I was born to stand out? This is my future, and with each lash of the belt, I accept it.

"William?" The voice of an angel breaks me out of my reflection, and I realize I'm curled up on the floor as I would have been all those years ago, protecting as much of my body from the beating as I could. "What's wrong? Are you hurt?" Tamara appears at my side and instantly checks my forehead to see if I've a temperature.

"I'm alright." I tell her and pull myself upright. "A memory..." Climbing up, I look down at the ground to try and calm my rapidly beating heart.

"Do you want to talk about it?"

"No...Honestly, it's fine. How are you?" I question with genuine concern. She still looks tired, and the rims of her eyes are red from all the tears she's shed. My heart's still beating too quickly, but for another reason now. This one is an overwhelming need to protect the woman in front of me.

"You can talk to me," she says, deflecting the question from herself and centering it back to me.

"I was remembering my father's anger toward my quirks when I was a child. He used to beat me, thinking that maybe he could get rid of them that way. I was an embarrassment to him. It's why he hid me away for so many years."

"Your father was wrong. You're not an embarrassment, but he was. He was a shameful example of a man, especially being in such a respected position, and Viscount Hamilton continues to remain so even now. The way they treat women and children is disgusting. Actually no, scrap that…the way they treat most other human beings is wrong. William, for you to be the man you are today, and to have saved Victoria and Nicholas the way you did, proves that you've survived your father. You're stronger than everything he did to you. You suffered but came out on the other side, stronger. The way you carried me out of the Viscount's house today is more evidence of that. Yes, you may be quirky at times, but that's a part of you, and it makes me laugh. Please don't try to hide it…I like it. Plus, it makes my best friend blush when you talk about her sex life." Tamara giggles, and I can't help but smile at the enthusiasm she's exuding for me. Nicholas and, now, Victoria always support me in everything I do and who I am. Especially when I relax and don't try to rigidly control everything to the point where I'm tying myself in knots and making myself sick in the process. Tamara sees the real me as well, which makes me happy and surprises me.

Pushing up onto my feet, I brush off a few leaves that have stuck to my trousers. The day has warmed up, and the grass, which was frosty this morning has dried, so my trousers are not soaked through, maybe a little damp but nothing uncomfortable.

"Thank you." Taking Tamara's hand, I offer her respect for the way she has spoken to me. I protected her earlier today, and she's cared for me now. It's strange – I may have only known her for a little over twenty-four hours, but I feel more relaxed around her than anyone else. Tucking her under the crook of my arm, we both look back to my mother's gravestone.

"I'm sorry for the way she died." Tamara bows her head in respect. "It was cruel to have her taken away from you."

"To have us both taken away from her, really. She was never allowed to be a mother to Nicholas. He was always supposed to be my father's shadow. I'm just glad he was able to step out from under it."

"I'm sure she's up in heaven looking down proudly on her two sons, for everything you are achieving, and the way you are trying to undo all the wrongs of the past."

We both lower our heads to my mother's grave before making our way back to the house while I reflect on my answer.

"It won't be easy to right all the wrongs. We will find obstacles at every turn, but we won't stop trying. I don't know if there will be a happily ever after, but I'm going to try my hardest to find one."

We stop just inside the patio doors to the lounge. Tamara inclines her body so it's facing me, and I feel a heated sensation cascade through my skin. She really is the most beautiful woman I've ever seen. Her eyes spark with intelligence, mischief, and a caring nature all combined.

"I think you'll find your happy ending. The one thing I've learned is that you have determination."

"Determination. I like that. Determination to have what I want." I can't help but push my body closer to Tamara, and she reacts with a hitch of breath as her eyes filled with lust stare up at me.

"When all this is over, what else are you determined to have?"

"A wife," I reply instantly.

"And?" she questions with a playful bite to her lip.

"Children."

"How many?"

"A whole army. I never want any of them to not have a playmate if they want one."

"That's a lot!"

"You up for it?" I ask her before lowering my head and pressing my lips against her plump ones.

CHAPTER SIX

TAMARA

William Cavendish is kissing me! I think the world is tilting on its axis, and everything is becoming slightly surreal. I've only known him for just over twenty-four hours, but I already know in my heart I'm his. I can fight it all I want, but our souls have already become entangled with the emotions of what has happened to us. He sees himself as the poor boy abused by his father, but I see the strong man he's become – the lover who will respect me and worship me. I need this just as much as he does. Damn to hell the consequences.

Opening my mouth slightly, I allow his tongue entry to ravage me with an urgency that seems to dominate his body. I'm pressed flat against the patio doors we entered through with the cold of the glass at my back, and his heat warming the front of my body. It's an assault on my senses, heightening the urgent need I have to feel his passion.

"William," I breathlessly utter into his mouth. He catches my words and responds by moaning out my name.

"Tamara."

He shifts his hips, and I feel the hardness at his groin as he strains to bring me to orgasm. If we don't find somewhere more private soon, I know he'll take me against this glass door for the world to see. I'm not sure Victoria and Nicholas will be impressed with having to clear a possible ass imprint off the glass panel.

"We need to go upstairs." I pull away but keep my gaze focused solely on him.

"You sure?" He brings his hand to my face and strokes the calloused pads of his fingers down my soft skin. "I'm different…I don't want to scare you."

"You are different in a beautiful way." My words are honest because he is. This isn't my first rodeo – I'll be the first to admit I was promiscuous at university. I'm pretty certain I nearly gave Victoria a heart attack when I told her about the orgy I participated in one night. As long as I was careful and set boundaries, then I was never one to think I needed to shy away from my sexual orientations. Yes, I've experimented: with men, women, both at the same time, and toys of different varieties. But William has seen the darker side of sex, and he's seen the pain and suffering it can bring. So when he says he's different, I'm not stupid – I know he's talking about his needs in bed and not his autism.

"If you want me to stop at any point, then you say, and I'll do so immediately," he offers me.

"Yes." Lowering my hand, I entwine it with his and lead him through the corridors of Oakfield Hall. My heart is thumping so loudly, and the need between my legs throbs with every step. As we walk, I can't help but hear the echoing screams of the many women who've been taken unwillingly to their fate in this place. The tables are finally turning.

On reaching my bedroom, I lead William in and go to sit on the bed. We're both silent as he remains stood at the doorway just staring at me. Finally, he turns and locks the door before striding over to me while at the same time removing his t-shirt. For someone who's been kept hidden away, he's clearly not been inactive over the years since his body is rippled with lines of taut muscles. His skin is slightly pale, especially against the dark tone of mine – ebony and ivory springs to mind when comparing us. I suck in a breath of lust at the sight of him.

"Stand up," he orders in a voice so deep and commanding it initially shocks me, and I jump straight to me feet. "I want to watch you undress."

William licks his lips while taking a seat in the plush Queen Anne chair in my room. He dwarfs the elegant chair with his size.

"Tamara, remove your clothes. Show me what I want to see."

With a shaking hand, I bring my fingers up to the top button of my teal blouse. My breaths are hitched while I slowly undo the fastenings and peel open the shirt to reveal a similar colored lace bra. William shifts in his seat, presumably to adjust the position of his hardness. I can't help but feel a little thrill of delight surge through my body that he likes what he sees.

"Tamara. The bra," he orders.

I drop my shirt to the floor and reach around my back to unclasp the fixings of my bra. I lower it carefully into my hands but keep the cups covering my breasts until the last second when I allow the gossamer material to fall and reveal myself to him.

"Fuck!" he exclaims. "Do you know how much I dreamed of them last night? I got off twice in the shower this morning just imagining my tongue wrapped around your flesh. They are even more beautiful, the nipples perter, and the shape more rounded than I even imagined."

"You played with yourself thinking of me?" I find myself shocked at the admission. I don't know why, because I found him instantly handsome from the first moment I saw him. I was just way too exhausted last night to contemplate using those visions to get myself off.

"You don't like me telling you that?" A line of worry creases William's forehead. "Tamara, I thought you'd have learned by now I say what I think, and that's both in and out of the bedroom. Around everyone else, I have to control it as much as I can, but here with you, I'm afraid, you're going to get everything." He rises to his feet and comes to stand directly in front of me. Grabbing the waistband of my jeans, he pulls me to him and grinds his hips into my waist. "Every dirty word…every commanding need. You will get it all from me. Say now if you want me to stop."

"No." The word spills from my lips before my brain has a second to even think about what he's just said to me. I need William between my thighs to relieve the urgent ache burning there.

"Good. Because I think we need to get these jeans off, now. I need to see that pussy I can smell getting ready to milk my big, hard cock."

Fuck! If he keeps up with the dirty talk, I'm going to come without any stimulation. In all my experiences, nobody has ever spoken to me like this before. It's intoxicating. His velvety tones, spilling filthy words about what he's going to do to me are almost like his fingers running directly over my clit.

William undoes the buttons of my jeans and pulls the fabric down over my thighs. He lowers his body, so he's kneeling in front of my pussy and takes a breath of air through his nose. I know he's sensing how much I want him.

"Please," I whimper… wanting…needing… something…anything.

"What do you want me to do, Tamara?" William looks up at me from under hooded eyelids, and when he hooks the tip of his finger in to my panties, I let out a groan of wanton desire.

"Please. Touch me."

"Touch you?" he says as he pulls my underwear down my thighs. I kick my shoes off to step out of my panties and my jeans. I'm naked before him, and every nerve ending in my body is tingling with desperation.

"Touch me." I repeat, and William presses his finger against my left arm.

"There you are…I touched you." He raises a playful eyebrow.

"No, not there."

He reaches up and swipes his finger over my shoulder.

"Please…" I cry, needing so much more.

"You have to tell me, Tamara. I need to know exactly what you want."

"Down there." I flick my eyes down between my thighs. Damn, what the hell is happening to me? I've taken the initiative before, but in front of William, it's like I've reverted back to an innocent virgin. He's messing with my brain, and it's making me so ready for him that I can feel wetness running down the inside of my thighs.

"You are going to have to elaborate, I'm afraid. I need full details. Remember, my brain's wired a little bit differently to others. They may know exactly what you want them to do to you, but I need to be told *explicitly*." The last word he says is so dark and demanding I groan and bring my own hand to my pussy. William stops it and lifts me effortlessly onto the bed.

"No," he snarls a warning that chills my blood but also sends electricity straight down to my clit. "You're with me. You don't touch yourself. I do all the touching." He looks around the room, and I wonder what for until I see him go for my dressing gown cord. Shit!

"William." My eyes go wide when he takes my left hand, and tying the cord around it, he threads the cord through the wire frame at the head of my bed before bringing it back down to secure my right hand with it. I'm trapped. "What are you doing?" I can sense the fear in my voice. The intensity of the situation is leaving me with little control. I'm not sure whether I'm willing to give up my say in the matter of our coupling. I don't have time to dwell on my worries, though, when once again William lowers himself down to my pussy and blows a long breath onto it. Fires ignite at the delicate current of warm air flowing over my heated flesh. He licks his lips and looks up at me. His eyes are dark, the pupils dilated so much he looks like the devil himself. Fuck! What am I getting myself into? With his dexterous tongue, William trails the length of my folds then flicks over the sensitive bundle of nerves at the peak. I'm writhing underneath him on the bed, wanting more. This is insane – I'm tied up beneath a man who's devouring my pussy and looks like Lucifer, and I want more. I want it all!

"William." I twist, thrusting my hips toward him, but he brings his hand up and pushes me down into the bed.

"No moving," he orders and goes back to eating me as if I was his last meal.

My body feels like it's on fire. I can barely make sense of anything but the throbbing between my thighs. I know I won't last long against this onslaught. His tongue is like a dangerous weapon, ridding me of all sense. I'm a wanton harlot, calling out for more, more, and even more.

The ricochet of an orgasm crashes into me when I least expect it. I thrash hard against the bindings on my restrained hands, but William is deft with a cord, and I can't pull them free. My body pulsates and jerks through every pleasurable sensation centered at my core. I've never had an orgasm like this before. It's taken over my whole body. My ears are ringing, my vision's blurry, and my limbs are shuddering of their own accord. Vaguely, I'm aware of William rising from the bed and divesting himself of the remainder of his clothes. I try to focus on his cock to prepare myself for what I know is about to come, but my head is still too cloudy with the aftermath of my orgasm. Something hard presses against my entrance, and I scream out with discomfort and overwhelming sensitivity as William pushes what feels like a massive dick into me.

"Oh God." I'm not religious, but at this very moment, if he can save me from this overload of pure, pleasurable sensation traveling through my body, I'm willing to attend church every Sunday for the rest of my life.

"Take me, Tamara." William says as he withdraws and then slams back into me with a thrust that seems to go on forever. How fucking long is he? I can barely breathe.

William pulls all the way out this time, and I'm given a few seconds to collect my thoughts as he releases one end of the cord before flipping me onto my front and lifting me up onto my knees. He slams hard back into me, and in the back of my mind, I briefly think of contraception, but then that thought is lost with his animalistic thrusts.

"I need it rough, Tamara. I need to dominate you. I have to know for the next few days you'll feel me in every part of your body. I'm not normal, not even here. This is what he made me." William uses my body as his toy to get off, and my mind worries at the implications of all of this, but my body is so overridden with pleasurable sensations it's beyond caring.

"Made you?" I question as he wraps his hand around my neck.

"He made me this monster."

"Monster?" I'm so confused I can barely understand what is being said. Who's made him a monster? I want to question him more, but another orgasm slams into me like a freight train racing down a hill. I scream out his name, and William thrusts into me one final time as his hand around my neck tightens, and I feel the airflow into my lungs being constricted. A mild panic sets in, but William's roar of ecstasy and the warm spurts of his essence coating my insides, tip me over the edge, again. The world stands still, and I'm floating, suspended in a ball of pleasure as wave after wave of orgasm crashes into me. Eventually, I come back to earth, and we collapse down onto the bed together. I'm gasping for air –

my neck hurts, and I need my hands freed. William pulls out of me, and I lament the loss despite the growing panic I'm experiencing.

"I...I...." William stutters. He unties my hands, and I turn around on the bed to face him. He's standing there covered in a fine sheen of sweat, his cock still half erect, and his chest heaving up and down at a rapid pace. He opens his mouth to say something but then slams it shut again. His hand comes up to his ear and swipes at it before going to his hair, and I listen for the foot taps, which quickly follow.

"William?" I move forward. My body jerks with after-shocks, feeling sore and overused from the exertion of our lovemaking.

His eyes flick to the full-length mirror, standing in the corner of the room. My gaze follows his and lands on the red ring forming around my neck from where he squeezed me during his orgasm. I look down to my wrists and see the burns on them, caused when I'd pulled hard on the fabric.

"I'm sorry." He flicks his ear again, and before I can respond, he's making his way butt naked out of the room, leaving me alone to stare at my well and truly fucked reflection in the mirror. I bring my hand up to my neck and touch the inflamed flesh there. He called himself a monster and said 'he' made him that way. It hits me what William meant – it was his father who taught him how to treat women. My stomach lurches, and I barely make it to my ensuite bathroom in time before I empty the contents into the toilet. If he's done this to me, what else has he done?

WILLIAM

Tap, Tap, stomp, stomp, swish, swish. I can do this – I can calm myself down before I do something even more stupid than I've just done by fucking Tamara. No, the fucking her wasn't wrong. It was beautiful – the best sex I've ever had. There was a connection between us until I went and spoiled it, allowing the monster within me to take over. My mind is a haze of confusion. Without showering or washing, I jump under the covers of my bed and pull the weighted blanket up to my neck. Instantly, I feel the plush fabric mold to my still naked form, enveloping me in its comforting embrace. I know it seems strange for a twenty-eight-year-old man to need a comfort blanket, but I really struggled trying to get to sleep until Nicholas read about these covers on the Autism UK website, recently. They're a new advancement in the fight against anxiety and the issues of ADHD and autism – specially designed to match the user's body weight, helping the user to feel grounded. I've slept so much better since he bought me the best one money can buy. When my mind is overstimulated, as it was before I climbed into my bed, it's the only thing that can prevent me from having a meltdown. And again, yes, I'm a twenty-eight-year-old man who has meltdowns and has been known to smash up his bedroom. It's part of my condition, but it isn't a daily occurrence. I need to fall asleep and try to forget everything that has happened today – chalk it up to a bad day and come back stronger tomorrow. Sometimes, that's all I can do when the world surrounding me borders on chaos in my mind.

A light knocking on my door draws me out of my reflection.

"William." Tamara's voice comes from the other side. Part of me doesn't want to let her in, but I know we need to discuss what happened between us. I sit up in the bed and pull the covers down to my chest. No point in being bashful, now. She's seen every part of me.

"Come in," I call back.

Opening the door slowly, Tamara peeps her head around the corner of it, and I instantly see she's been crying. I pat the bed, encouraging her to sit beside me. She looks at it, then me, and I can see the indecision on her face.

"I won't…I won't hurt you, again," I reassure her as she hesitantly comes to sit on the end of the bed. "I'm sorry," I offer.

She brings her hand to her neck. She's wearing a dressing gown, which shields her nakedness from me, but I can still imagine every curve of her body. The little mole she has on her left shoulder, and the heaviness of her breasts in my hands.

"Will you tell me about your past?" she asks, and I'm initially confused with her meaning.

"I don't understand? What do you want to know?"

"You've been locked away for most of your life, but I don't believe that was your first time. You had too much experience and knowledge of what you like in order to get off." Tamara doesn't look at me when she speaks. Instead, she seems to have found a space on my bedroom floor that's riveting.

"Oh!" I exclaim and find my own interesting spot to look at on the old-fashioned rug, covering the wooden floor. "No, that wasn't my first time. I know it wasn't yours." She quickly looks up at me with her eyes wide open. "I mean… I…Damn. I overhead you and Victoria talking on the phone once. I didn't mean anything bad by it."

"Just you knew I was a sure thing because I'm not a virgin."

I raise an eyebrow at her, and a small smile crosses her lips as if to say she's messing with me. It dispels some of the tension in the room, and leaning back, I settle into my pillow.

"My father decided when I turned sixteen that I needed to experience a woman. Nicholas wasn't exactly a saint at eighteen and was already renowned for his appreciation of the feminine form. I think he thought maybe it would make me less strange if I lost my virginity. You know, it might cure me type of thing."

Tamara rolls her eyes but doesn't say anything.

"He had this girl brought to the house. She came into my room, lowered her robe, and was naked underneath. It was really awkward because I hadn't been prepared, and suddenly I've got a naked woman in my bedroom. I was more interested in the differences in her form to mine than anything else. Needless to say, my father wasn't impressed. I suspect he was listening outside the door."

I go quiet and allow the memories of that day to return.

"He came into the room and showed me what to do."

"Showed you what to do?" Tamara screws her nose up in disgust at the meaning behind my statement.

"He led the girl to the bed. Explained what her breasts and pussy were before flipping her over and spreading her bum cheeks to show me her asshole. Then he lowered his trousers and proceeded to show me how to put a dick in each of those places, plus her mouth, in order to get myself off. I always remember her scream of pain when he pushed into her ass dry."

Tamara shifts closer to me on the bed. Her eyes are filled with watery tears.

"He did that? In front of you? Did the woman not protest?"

I shake my head. "She was paid to take whatever we gave to her. My father would have paid her a good amount, so she had no choice but to accept it. As for me, it was the way of the world I grew up in…silence for long periods, then my father would think of a magical way to cure his son, and I'd be thrown into some strange new situation."

"Strange new situation!" Tamara slams her fist into the bed. "This was abuse! It shouldn't have been allowed. Not just to the woman but to you as well. What type of father near enough rapes a woman in front of his sixteen-year-old son to teach him about sex?"

I can't help but let out a wry chuckle, seeing her anger at

the injustice of the situation I'd found myself in. To her, it's abhorrent, but to me, it was normal.

"What happened after your father had finished with the girl?"

"I don't think I should talk about this anymore." I can no longer look at the woman seated mere millimeters away from me on the bed.

"I have to know…please."

"Tamara."

"I have to hear it from you. I need to know why I have a bruise forming around my neck. It's the only way I can understand what happened in my bedroom. I know I agreed to everything, but there's a part of me that's scared, not only because of what you did to me but also because it resulted in the best orgasm I've ever had."

"What!" I exclaim and jerk her toward me. I pull the dressing gown away from where it's tightly wrapped around her neck. "It excited you? The monster I am?"

"It excited and scared me at the same time. Please, I need to know everything. I have to understand. At the moment, I'm terrified of what it means for both of us."

My breath catches at her words, and I get the overwhelming urge to put some distance between us. I slide from the bed, despite being still naked underneath the covers, and reach for a pair of jogging bottoms, which are neatly folded on a chair in the corner of the room. I hear Tamara gasp behind me when she sees my state of undress. At the last moment, I turn to face her, so she can see my dick standing at half-mast with the need for her body. She looks down at the bed as I pull my jogging bottoms all the way up.

"I have to understand," she repeats, and I take a seat on the chair.

"My father finished himself inside her ass. When he pulled out the girl screamed, again, and I remember seeing the blood mixed with my father's semen leaking from her. He'd been uncaring with her. She was nothing more than a set of holes to abuse. It felt wrong to me, but I knew nothing better. I'd never had a positive feminine role model in my life. My nanny was ordered about by my father and shown little respect. It wasn't until I had access to the internet and television that I realized men should respect women and not abuse them. Somehow though, the darkness has stayed within me from that first encounter."

Leaning back into the chair, I allow the story of my downfall to tumble from my lips. I'm unable to look at Tamara as I speak. That fascinating spot on the floor is back, occupying my ardent stare.

"My father put himself away and pushed me toward the woman. She lay back on the bed and parted her legs. I'd seen a pussy before because Nicholas had a thing for porn magazines, and he'd bought me some. I was more interested in the anatomy of that particular part of a woman than anything else. It was interesting to see a real-life vagina in front of me. She was shaven bare, so I was able to see everything. I stood in front of her and pulled her outer lips apart to see the sensitive flesh inside. It was glistening, and I knew in some way what my father had done to her, she found it enjoyable. She'd liked being taken roughly, despite the pain that must have surged through her body. She beckoned me with her finger, and I lowered my underwear. My dick was already hard, having been turned on by the situation. Pushing myself bare inside of her, I remember it feeling soft and wet. Welcoming. After a few tentative thrusts, my father came over to me and started screaming at me, accusing me of showing my innocence, telling me the woman wanted me to fuck her like the man I should be and not the imbecile my mother had spawned. Something inside me snapped, and I just remember my hips bucking wildly. I was only sixteen, but I was strong. I took from the woman without care while she accepted everything. I don't know why, but at the end I placed my hands around her neck and squeezed. She screamed out in orgasm, and it took me over the edge. When I came down, she wasn't breathing. I'd choked her so hard I'd completely cut off her breathing. Everything after that was such a blur. The woman was revived and paid off, but it was my father's laugh that haunts me to this day. It was evil, and it was the only time he addressed me as his son. 'Like father like son' were his exact words. I'd made him proud."

The room falls silent, neither Tamara or I speak again for a good few minutes. Both of us are trying to take in everything that has just been said. I'm sick, twisted, and freaky. She needs to run from me, right now, before I crush her under the weight of who and what I truly am.

CHAPTER EIGHT

TAMARA

I knew what had happened to him was dark, but I'd not expected something like this. His first sexual encounter had shaped him into the man I'd allowed between my thighs no more than an hour ago.

"Your father was a bad man." I finally speak, the words quivering on my lips.

"I know. I saw much more than anyone realizes." He looks toward his bedroom wall, indicating to where I already know passages reside, hidden behind the ornately decorated walls of the hall. "I kept to the shadows. I wanted to see if I really was a monster, or if what my father taught me to do was normal. One night, when I knew Nicholas had a woman with him, I watched them together, adding voyeur to my palette of skills when it comes to sexual matters. He had the woman tied up and was taking her hard. She screamed for more, so he pulled out and used a flogger to beat her. I thought it was normal. I didn't understand about BDSM and the experimental nature of my brother's encounter. I just presumed that in order to get off, I needed to stop the girl from breathing or beat her, and so it became my norm. I wanted to warn you properly, but I lost my mind. You intoxicated me with your beauty, and I'm sorry."

"William, please." I slide from the bed. I'm confused. I'm listening to a man tell me he's been programmed to beat a woman to enjoy sex. His father really did a number on him. The man hated his son so much, and knowing William's autistic tendencies would make him susceptible to the depravation, the former Duke rejoiced. I'd studied a case at university relating to a murderer who was on the autism spectrum. He'd been taught it was normal to kill, and his brain couldn't distinguish between right and wrong because of his learned behavior. He struggled with the concept that taking another life was wrong because it was routine to him. The victim had annoyed him, and murder was the automatic response he'd learned from his father. The man had been found not guilty, in the end, on the grounds of reduced capacity but was indefinitely detained for his and the public's safety. It's different from the sexual behaviors the Duke subjected William to, but fundamentally, the principle is the same. William was taught it was right to abuse women during sex. He only realized it was wrong when he became aware of how people from the outside world treated the opposite sex, but by then it was too late. There is a darkness in William, and I don't know if I'll ever be able to rid him of it, but he excites me, and I want to get to know him better even if I'm playing with fire.

"William." I kneel before him and place my hands on his thighs. He still can't look at me, but I know this is not simply about guilt, it is also related to his autism, so I don't push him. The stimulations he's experienced today must be leaving him in a whirlwind of emotions, and I don't want to heighten his senses further. I just need him to know I understand. "I need you to listen to me."

"Ok."

"Hold your hands out."

"What?" I'm watching him and see a line of confusion mark his forehead while he still keeps his eyes focused elsewhere.

"Hold your hands out for me."

Lifting them up slowly, his fists are tightly clenched, showing the white of his knuckles, which protrude from his shaking hands.

"Open your hands." I tell him. At first, he doesn't move, so I bring my hands up and rest them on the top of his. "Please."

Gradually, he opens them but continues to hold them rigid, guarding against the demons his brain is fighting at the moment.

"Shake your hands."

"Tamara..." he starts to protest, and I begin to shake my own hands floppily above his.

"Please," I almost whisper, pulling my hands back, so I can see his. They remain still for another minute before he gradually starts to shake them. I move my arms out to my side, shaking my hands again before I take the movement up to my arms and shoulders. "Now your arms."

He stops briefly and then starts to shake his arms around. I get to my feet.

"You know what's next?" I question.

He pushes up off his chair. "I'm guessing this." William shakes his legs, and I giggle.

"Feet, toes, arms, legs, hips, head." I shake every part of my body. "Loosen up everything. Take away the stress and the worry."

"And look like a complete dork while doing it."

"Not at all."

I take William's hands in mine, and he allows me to shake him while we dance all around the room. We must do our crazy little jig for a couple of minutes before I get short of breath and stop. William's eyes meet mine for the first time since our first kiss – I can see the sorrow and fear in them. They flick down to my chest, and when I look down, I realize my dressing gown has come loose, and the bra I'm wearing underneath is showing. Though his eyes lift back to mine with lust, the trepidation still remains. I go to speak, but nothing comes out at first until a melody I've not heard in a long time enters my head and flows out from my mouth.

"Hush, little baby, don't say a word,
Mama's going to buy you a mocking bird."

William gasps.

"My mother."

I stop singing, realizing instantly what he's trying to say.

"She sang it to me as a baby. It was the only song that calmed me." He brings his hand up to the bridge of my nose and allows the tip of his finger to run down it.

"And if that mockingbird don't sing,
Mama's going to buy you a diamond ring."

"My mother sang it to me when I couldn't sleep." I tell

him as the memory of my mother lying on the bed beside me, singing softly, comes to the forefront of my mind. We didn't have much when I was growing up, just a small room in the attic of the Viscount's house, but it was all I wanted. I had a mother who loved me, and there was no need for an absent father who never cared about me.

"I've not heard it since she sang it the day they took me from her. She was desperate to calm me down. Will you sing it to me when I need you to?"

"Always. You only have to ask."

William leans forward, and before I have a chance to think, his lips are pressed against mine. His warmth floods through my body, settling the nerves I was feeling, and dissipating the burning sensation of the raw skin on my wrists and neck. I forgive him because I know it's not his fault. The demons he's hiding within him will always surface, but there is a trust between us, which gives me hope. I push my body in closer to him and feel his hardness against my hip.

"Take me again." I say to him, pulling back from our kiss and breathing the words of my desperation into his mouth. He catches them with another kiss and leads us toward his bed. My dressing gown is pushed open, and his hands are on my breasts, cupping the flesh over my gossamer bra. I need rid of my clothes. My skin is sensitive – it feels like I need to climb out of it just to get relief.

"Please," I wantonly whimper, and William removes my dressing gown from me. Then lowering my bra, he pulls a nipple into his mouth and teases it. I'm writhing under him. Wanting…needing…hoping. Then our eyes meet, and I see terror there in William's – it damn near rips my heart in two.

I push him away when he goes to trail a path of kisses lower down my body.

"Stop," I tell him, and he regards me in confusion.

"What's wrong?"

I sit up on the bed and wrap my dressing gown around myself. William sits next to me.

"You believe you're a monster."

"Tamara, please."

"You have to believe it's not true. Tell me what was going on in your head. What made you look so scared?"

"I can't."

"Please. Trust me."

He goes silent, and I see a lone tear tumble down his cheek.

"I'll kill you," he finally says.

"What?"

"I'll forget one day how to be good and will kill you."

The words slam into my chest like a ton of bricks. I can barely breathe at his revelation because from his perspective, he believes it's the truth. He can't see the good man he truly is. This is no way to start a relationship, no matter the attraction between us.

"You can't do this, can you? Sex with me again?" I ask, and he shakes his head.

"I'm sorry. I thought I could. You were singing the song to me that my mother used to. It was beautiful, but I think I need you as a friend more than I do a lover. I've barely been free for more than a few months, and everything is alien to me. I've never been out to a fast food joint, or been to a club, a pub, or the cinema. Even cars scare the life out of me. All of my knowledge has been learned via television and books. I'm far from normal, and I fear I never will be. I need to find out what this world is about, first. I have to rid it of my father's evil, help Nicholas establish his place as the leader of the Oakfield Society, and bring the family name into the fresh, pure daylight of a new dawn. I have to repay my brother for all he's done to help me over the years, and I owe it to Victoria as well. She suffered because Nicholas was protecting me to the point he was torn in two directions, trying to save us both. I'm too consumed by these four walls and the horrors that have occurred within them, at the moment. Starting a relationship with me would only destroy you, and I don't know if I could have another person's suffering on my conscience. I'm sorry. As you can see, my dick wants you so badly I don't think he's ever going to go back down, but my brain, however fucking mis-wired it is, tells me I need to venture out and discover the world first.

I wipe away the tears that have started falling down my cheeks while William was speaking. They are not tears of remorse at being rejected by him but ones of pride for his bravery.

"Too much, too soon." I look around the room. "I can't begin to imagine what it was like being confined within this small space and the room next door for so long. I don't know what the future holds, but when this is over with the society if you still want me as a physical companion, just let me know. Until then, we are friends, and I'll help you, Nicholas, and Victoria in any way I can. You have demons you need to slay, and I'll be there to fight them with you, should you want me at your side. All you have to do is ask."

I slide from the bed and leaning forward, I press a chaste kiss to William's cheek.

"Just remember this William Cavendish, Earl of Lullington…you saved my best friend…you saved your brother… and you fought the devil who imprisoned and tortured you for most of your life…and you won. You beat the demon on the outside, now, all you have to do is slay the ones in your mind, and free yourself forever."

I pull my dressing gown all the way around me and leave William alone with his thoughts. Today has been emotional, to say the least. My body sags with exhaustion the second I get back to my room. Thoughts of my mother's betrayal, Victoria's pregnancy, Viscount Hamilton's continued denial of his part in his daughter's treatment, and the fight continuously raging inside William's head, all run through my mind. However, one thought lingers in my head as I shut my eyes to sleep – Father. Nicholas will be a father soon, William's father mistreated him badly, Victoria's nearly destroyed her, but I've never known my father and maybe it's time I tried to find out who he is…

CHAPTER NINE

WILLIAM

"**I** can't believe I'm returning a painting to an art gallery. This just feels so strange." Nicholas flicks a switch on a technical gadget he's holding, and all the alarms in the National Gallery in London are switched off. His little piece of wizardry was given to him by Matthew Carter and Ryan North, both MI5 alumni. I'm still amazed my brother was able to get them on side with his plan, but it seems righting wrongs is close to their hearts. We're both dressed head to toe in black with night vision goggles over our eyes. I'm liking the darkness – it's a big improvement on the flashing lights I saw, traveling into London. How anyone can sleep in this city when it's lit up like a Christmas tree almost twenty-four hours a day is beyond me.

"I think it just proves Victoria has you by the balls." I chuckle at my brother, which earns me a thump on the back. "Hey watch it! Precious cargo in hand. You don't want me to drop this fifty-million-dollar picture, now, do you?"

"Don't remind me of the value," Nicholas growls between

gritted teeth. "If I didn't love my wife so much, I'd be selling this picture on the black market and using the money to wipe out all our enemies. Instead, I'm giving back one of my favorite paintings."

I hold in my hands an original work of art called 'Poppies' by Van Gogh. Nicholas stole it from the Mohamed Mahmoud Kahlil Museum in Cairo eight years ago. It's small, little more than twenty-five inches by twenty-one inches, but it's hung in Oakfield's main hall since the night Nicholas brought it home. My father was proud of him that night. The irony isn't lost on me. He's proud of me when I almost kill a woman, and of Nicholas when he steals a famous painting. Why couldn't he have been like other fathers and been proud of us for cutting our first tooth or saying our first words? No, it could only be when we committed some despicable crime.

"At least she didn't make me take it back to Cairo. British museums are so much easier to get in and out of." Nicholas takes the painting from me and places it underneath Van Gogh's self-portrait.

"Why didn't she want it back in Cairo?" I question.

"As much as she hates the painting because of the reminder of what it represents, I think she secretly wants to be able to come and see it when she can." Nicholas strips off the protective film from the painting. He's wearing special gloves, which won't leave any traces of a fingerprint.

"Makes sense. You think Cairo will allow it to stay here?"

"Not up to me. That's for them to fight out amongst themselves. I think the UK might have a bit more sway when it comes to these things, so I'm hoping so." Nicholas steps back and looks at the picture in its temporary home. "Time 'til the guard comes around?" he asks me, and I look at my watch, which I'd synchronized with the guard's timings earlier. "Five minutes and twenty-six seconds."

"Good. Plenty of time. Flick the switch on your glasses and check for fingerprints or DNA."

I do as he asks, and using a special filter, I can see the picture is clean.

"All good."

"Ok, let's get out of here. I've got a wife waiting to reward me for being a good husband."

"Didn't need to know that, Brother."

Nicholas laughs, and we leave the museum the same way we entered, via the roof. Nicholas flicks another switch on his superhero gadget, and the alarms are reset.

"The guard is going to get a big shock in about three minutes and ten seconds," I chuckle. The tension of completing the feat disappears as we make our way back to the Lexus waiting for us with my brother's driver. Throwing all the equipment in the trunk, we get in the car and remove our black clothing to reveal full dress suits below. The driver pulls away, and we are finally home free. Nicholas straightens his tie and takes out a decanter of brandy from a compartment in the car.

"Drink?" he offers.

"A small one." I tug at the neck tie, hating the fact he chose this as a disguise. We were both at a function in nearby Kensington, tonight. I hated every minute of being the sociable Earl, but it was a necessary ruse as an essential part of our plan to return the picture. Providing us with an alibi should we be questioned. Nicholas made sure we were 'seen' even when we weren't there. I didn't ask because I'm reluctant to know the full extent of his abilities for subterfuge. My father trained him well.

I settle back in the car for the return journey to Oakfield Hall on the outskirts of the city. Shutting my eyes, I bring the amber nectar to my lips and allow it to burn down my throat with its velvety comfort.

I turn to face Nicholas who's checking his mobile with a look of worry on his face. I know instantly it's not because of our breaking and entering escapade. It's the look he gets when he's worried about his wife. "Is Victoria alright?"

"She's still feeling a little sick. Tamara prepared her a ginger tea earlier, which seemed to settle her stomach a bit."

"It must be hard seeing her feel so ill and knowing you not only caused it, but there's little you can do to help her until she's over the three-month mark."

"The consequences of not covering our dicks," my brother laments. "It's not us who suffer."

"I don't know. I think you're suffering as well. Well, you will when she gives birth. Victoria is strong, and she's going to give you hell." I can't help but laugh at my brother's impending doom. Victoria will curse him out like a sailor during labor, and if he doesn't end up with a broken hand, I'll be surprised. He's going to suffer, and then he gets to be a father and change stinky diapers. I can't help sniggering.

"I wouldn't laugh at me too much, little brother."

"Yeah, not going to happen to me." I sit back smugly and bring the brandy to my lips.

"So, the screaming I heard coming from Tamara's room had nothing to do with you?"

"What?" I spit my brandy out over the chair in front of

me. "You heard? Does Victoria know? Is she going to kill me?"

"Why would she kill you?" Nicholas frowns. "She's happy. She'd love having Tamara as her sister-in-law. She's seen the attraction between you both since the moment you first met. Wouldn't surprise me if she's overly sung your praises to Tamara for matchmaking purposes."

"It won't happen," I reply bluntly. Nicholas puts his brandy down and turns to face me. I won't look at him, though. If I need to, I'll shut my eyes, so I don't have to look directly into his. My fingers are itching to tap or swipe – to start their comforting routine. Nicholas reaches over and takes the brandy from my hand. I instantly bring my hand up to my ear and swipe across it then through my hair. One, two taps on the floor with my foot, and I'm already feeling calmer, but I know Nicholas isn't going to stop his questioning.

"William, you slept with Tamara?" he questions.

"Yes."

My brother pauses, and I know he's trying to find the right words for what he wants to say next.

"Did you hurt her?"

I want to say no – to tell him she enjoyed it as much as I did because her tight little pussy milked me so much I was seeing fucking stars.

"I think so." Is the only answer I can give. My hands do their routine again.

"How did you hurt her?"

"She's got a bruised neck and rope burns on her wrists."

"Shit!" my brother exclaims. "What did she say? After? During? Did she ask you to stop?"

I think back through the entire time we were together. She pleaded and pleaded with me for more. She never once asked me to stop.

"No. She says I'm not a monster."

"She liked it rough?" my brother questions with an element of shock in his voice. He knows what I like. He's seen the girls who've left my room after I've finished with them.

"I…don't know," I stammer. I want to hide away, now. I don't want to continue this conversation. It's too confusing for me. My mind hurts… my head hurts. Too much.

We pull up the long driveway to the house, and before the car stops, I'm out and running up to my rooms. Nicholas is after me, and I pass Victoria and Tamara on the stairs. They look at me in confusion, but I don't stop – I need to get to my safe place. My sanctuary. The only place I know I can be me and won't be judged. Behind me, I hear Victoria call to Nicholas.

"Nicholas what's wrong?"

"Give me a few minutes," he replies as his footsteps follow me up the stairs.

I enter my rooms and push the door shut, but I'm not quick enough to lock it before Nicholas uses his strength to force it open. I start to pace the room, and Nicholas tries to pull me to a halt and get me to look at him, but I shove him away.

"William, listen to me. It's alright. Tamara is fine. If she didn't tell you to stop, then you did nothing wrong."

"I strangled her."

"It can be a part of sex, not all the time, but some people do like it. It doesn't mean you're like him."

We both freeze. The truth of the matter hits us both hard. It's what we both fear. Have I been so damaged that I'm just the same as our father? Nicholas feared it about himself for so long until Victoria helped him to recognize he's his own man. But I can't see that. All I see when I look in the mirror is my father's reflection staring back out at me. He created the person I am. The freak who pointed a gun at his own father's head and pulled the trigger. I killed my father, and I don't have any regrets. No, if I had the chance, I'd do it again. Only next time, I'd make it more painful.

"William?" My brother tries to reach out to touch me, but I push him away.

"You need to leave, Nicholas. Go be with your wife. Protect her and love her. Keep the darkness from consuming you. She's the key to you staying on the right side."

"Tamara could be yours," my brother immediately fires back.

"Monsters don't fall in love. They exist only to destroy. Tamara's too innocent to be allowed on my path. I'll drag her down with me to hell."

"William, you have to listen to me."

My brother attempts to grab me for a final time, but I summon all the strength I have and send him flying across the room. My mind has descended into the dark recess where my anxieties mix with the rejection I faced for so many years. I no longer see what can be, only what is. I'm a freak who should continue to be hidden away for the world's protection.

Picking up a chair, I slam it into the wall beside me. It disintegrates into little pieces of splintered wood. Next comes a chest of drawers. With inhuman strength, I send them flying. Trinkets and pictures smash on the floor.

I'm vaguely aware of Victoria running into the room. She hands something to Nicholas – the only method of subduing the overstimulation and breakdown in me. I stop and stand still waiting for the sharp prick of the hypodermic in my neck, and when it comes, the numbing drugs flow into my body. Before the darkness of a sedated sleep claims me, I look up to see Tamara, standing at the doorway. Her eyes are full of the one thing I never wanted to see in them: sorrow. Despair for what I am, and what I can be.

CHAPTER TEN

TAMARA

"I'm never getting pregnant if this is what it does to you." I hold back Victoria's hair as she dry heaves into the toilet. She's been running back and forth to the bathroom for the last half an hour, but nothing has come up. It's early in the morning, a little after five am, and I spent last night sleeping in the same bed as her. She hates to sleep alone since her ordeal, and Nicholas wanted to stay with his brother to check on him when he woke. It wasn't exactly how I imagined I'd be waking up this morning, but at least it's giving me a distraction from worrying about William. I can see he's falling apart even further, and a feeling of guilt weighs heavy within me. A fear that I'm to blame because I pushed him into having sex with me, and it made him confront a side of himself he's hidden away and managed to control for so long. Rubbing Victoria's back and whispering words of encouragement to her as she fights her morning sickness, helps me to push the culpability aside, for now.

"You'll get pregnant one day, and I'll be there reminding you of this moment." She heaves again and then sits with her back against the clawfoot bath. "I feel like shit."

I can't help but laugh at the way her face screws up. She's not looking like the elegant Duchess she likes to portray in public, at the moment.

"Hate to say it, but you look it as well," I respond, handing her a glass of water with lemon in it.

"Some friend you are." She throws the towel she's been holding at me. "I want it to stop."

"Just remember it means that there's a healthy little baby in your tummy, taking all the good stuff from its mummy and leaving her exhausted."

She snorts.

"Sounds just like Nicholas after a mammoth sex session."

I put my fingers in my ears.

"La, la, la."

"I should've done that the other night." Victoria responds and raises an eyebrow at me.

Lowering my hands, I push up onto my feet from the crouching position I was in and reach out to help her to stand.

"I don't know what you mean." I play dumb as we go back into her room, and I pass her a dressing gown to cover her pajamas.

"Oh come on, the entire household heard you when you climaxed. Damn, Tammy, you're a screamer."

"Ria." I use my nickname for her and scold her with a scowl.

"It's not a problem. I'm happy about it. Are you a couple now?"

"I don't want to talk about this," I tell her and wrap my own dressing gown around my shoulders.

"It must have been hard seeing him have a meltdown last night. I've seen it a couple of times before. Nicholas hates using the sedative, but William has hurt himself previously, and he'll do anything to prevent that."

"Ria, not now!" I snap and walk out of the room and down the stairs toward the kitchen with Victoria following close behind me. In silence, I prepare myself an americano and a ginger tea for her to settle her stomach.

"I'm sorry," she says when I hand it to her.

"So am I," I respond as I add a little milk to my coffee and stir it. "It was hard to see him like that last night. I'm worried what happened between us has made him believe things, which aren't true."

"What do you mean?" Victoria asks, taking her tea and sitting down at a little table in the corner of the vast kitchen. It's normally a hive of activity with meals being prepared for the Cavendish family, but at this early hour, it's empty.

"The sex. It was good, really good, but a little rough." I join her at the table and swirl my coffee around in the cup, hoping for it to cool quicker, so I can get some caffeine goodness in me to calm my nerves.

"How rough?"

Last night when we slept together, I made sure I wore a high-necked top with extra-long sleeves to hide my bruises. I lower my dressing gown and roll up the sleeves of my top. Victoria's eyes go wide on seeing the red marks marring my arms. Biting my lip, I next bring my fingers up to the neck of my t-shirt and pull it down. This time she gasps.

"Tammy! What did he do?"

"I was tied to the bed, and when we orgasmed, he choked me."

"Shit!" she exclaims at the same moment the chef comes into the kitchen. I quickly let go of my t-shirt, covering the contusions around my neck once again.

"Sorry, my lady, I wasn't aware you were in here." The chef bows. "Is there something you need? Breakfast?"

"No, it's fine. We'll get out of your way. I'm sure you don't need me with my non-existent cooking skills in your kitchen."

"It's not a problem. If you and Miss Bennett need to talk, I can prepare ingredients in the pantry for now," the chef replies as he backs out toward the kitchen door.

"Thank you," Victoria tells him, and he disappears. She turns to me again, and it's all I can do to hold back the tears I've been wanting to let flow for the last twenty-four hours.

"Was it consensual? The sex…and the choking?"

"I pleaded with him to do whatever he needed to me."

"That doesn't mean it was right. Did you ask him to stop?"

"No, that's the thing," I say and finally take a sip of my coffee, which is now cool enough. "I enjoyed it. It scared the hell out of me, but it was the best orgasm I've ever had."

"Wow." Victoria stares at me with her mouth wide open.

"Can I ask you something?" I inquire hesitantly.

"You can. It's not a guarantee I'll answer, though."

"Is Nicholas rough?"

Victoria lets out a long exhale. "The thing you have to understand about the Cavendish boys is that virtually all the maternal figures in their life have been abused women. It's the norm to them. For a long time, Nicholas knew what he was doing was wrong, but the pressure he was under and the lack of maternal love meant he couldn't stop what was happening. That doesn't mean he's ever left me as bruised as William has you."

My eyes narrow at Victoria, knowing exactly what Nicholas did to her when they first met.

"Ok, yeah he branded me and led me around in a scold's bridle while his band of merry men whipped me. That's what I mean, though. No matter how much they care for a woman, it's hard for them after so many years of abuse to initially behave appropriately. Many people would say it should be instantaneous and they are monsters for not immediately protecting us, but their father's way of life is so ingrained into them they struggle to see past it. Unable to believe in a potential normality until they've worked through everything else. Their father skewed their moral compass and for all the brashness Nicholas, especially, likes to portray, underneath he's just a man trying to find his way in a fucked-up world."

"Their father really did a number on them both," I say woefully and finish my coffee while Victoria swallows the last mouthful of her tea.

"He did. Nicholas still struggles some days, but I've no worries about him being a good father despite his own father's influence. Of course, William has had to adjust to so much more. He's had to deal with his autism, and the fact he was locked away for so long, as well as coping with the violence he himself experienced and saw his father expend at every turn. His heart is good, though. He saved me when he could have so easily treated me like the others did. He had plenty of opportunities to rape me if he'd truly been the monster he now thinks he is, but he didn't. That shows the real truth of him. He just needs some time to come to terms with all the changes around him."

"So, I've not set him back by sleeping with him."

"No. You've given him food for thought."

"I hope so." I reach forward and squeeze her hand.

"Thanks, Ria."

"You're my best friend. I'm always going to help you."

Victoria winks at me and gets to her feet. "Speaking of food for thought, I had an idea in the night and wanted to run it by your legal brain. Come with me."

I follow my best friend as she meanders through the seemingly endless corridors of Oakfield Hall. It's lovely to see her in her element as the mistress of this place. It must be hard for her to love the building after all the history the four walls have seen, but somehow, she seems to soften the harsh exterior. She finally stops in front of a door marked as the 'Duke's Office'. She pushes it open, and I see two desks facing each other in the middle of the room. The one to the left of me has a pile of papers with a half-empty brandy glass placed on top. It's the more masculine of the two desks. The other one has a white folder covered in roses on it as well as a small vase with a single, fresh red rose. This is obviously Victoria's desk. Nobody else would have rose stationery. She's obsessed with the flower. Picking up the folder, she flicks through it.

"Nicholas has managed to get most of the members of the society to sign up to the new rules. Many of them were thankful for the change. Abusing women didn't sit well with them. However, a few have been a bit more hesitant.

Nicholas has barred them from all meetings, but he's been following their actions closely, and it looks like they are going to try to start causing trouble. We could have all the assets they want to use frozen by illegal means, but that gives them fuel against us. We want to try to do everything as legally as possible, and that is where you come in." Victoria pauses and hands me a piece of paper. "Can you figure out a legal way to suspend any funds these people have?"

I look down at the list. It consists of a few names, but two stand out to me, in particular. Lord West and Viscount Hamilton. I know Lord West from stories about one of the girls who disappeared, and Viscount Hamilton is Victoria's father, of course.

"You want me to go against your father?" I look up from the list to Victoria.

"I don't think we have a choice," she says matter of factly, but I can tell it's hurting her. He's still her father, no matter what he did to her. She does have some good memories of him being a caring parent toward her. In fact, we both do while growing up together.

"This could harm Theo in the end."

"I know. When Nicholas eventually allows me to visit my father's estate, I want to try and talk to my brother. See if I can explain to him everything that's happened."

"It might not be that easy."

"We have to do this, Tamara. We have to put a stop to what they are doing. Not just for the sake of the women involved, but for Nicholas and William too. They're out from under their father's shadow and can finally be their own men, but if my father has his way, he'll destroy them, so he can hold all the power and be able to do whatever he wants with women, again. I know his true colors now."

I look down at the names on the paper and back up to my friend. Ideas start to form in my head about what can be done to ruin the names and freeze the assets of these powerful, evil men.

"I'll do it."

CHAPTER ELEVEN

WILLIAM

"William. You awake?" The deep timbre of a masculine voice draws me from my slumber, and I open my eyes. Looking over to my alarm clock, it tells me it's the early hours of the morning.

"Nicholas?" I question.

"No, it's me," the voice replies, and in my sleep induced haze, I have to open my eyes to see who's in my room. When I open them, I see my friend Lord West, and he's accompanied by a vivacious blonde who's waving enthusiastically at me.

"Hello." I sit up, rubbing my eyes and yawning. "What's going on?"

"I've brought you a present." West leers at me and pushes the girl on his arm forward.

"It's not really the sort of present I want at three am. I'd rather another couple of hours sleep." I grunt and slide back down in the bed.

"Jesus, William. You really are strange. If I was to bring a *willing woman to most blokes, they'd get their dick out and say, 'which hole is mine?'. But you would rather sleep."*

"Fuck you, West," I retort. "If she wants my dick, she can get it out and bounce on it."

My friend laughs. "You heard him, love. Time to go all cowboy on his dick."

"That's not something you have to ask me to do twice, not if he's as good with it as you are," the woman sing-songs, and I try to ignore them even though I know it will be futile.

"He's not as good as me, babe, but he knows what to do with it. He's learned from the master after all. He's the Duke's son."

"Nicholas?" she exclaims.

"No, William," West replies, and I can hear them getting nearer to the bed.

"But I didn't think anyone ever saw him. There are rumors he's disfigured and can't speak because he's got the brain of a baby."

"Well, you've heard him speak, so I think that dispels that theory." Before I have a chance to grab the sheets, my friend pulls them off leaving me naked in front of him and the girl.

"Fucking hell, West!" I try to grab them back from him, but he's thrown them across the room, and the girl is crawling up the bed toward me before I have a chance to do anything about it.

"I don't see any disfigurements either. Why does the Duke hide him away?" She stares at me as she speaks, cocking her head from side to side as if she's examining me. I shut my eyes to try and block it all out while my hands go to my junk to cover it, so I'm not on display for them both.

"He's got something called autism. His brain is wired funny, or some shit like that. The Duke says he acts strange in polite society, and he's worried about him embarrassing him, so it's best to keep him hidden away."

"That's a shame," the girl laments woefully. "He's pretty hand-some. He'd be a catch in our circles."

"The Duke allows you in here to play, but William's not allowed out."

The girl giggles, sending an eerie shiver down my spine.

"As long as I get to play, that's all I want."

"You do realize I'm lying here, trying to sleep," I snap.

"Babe, suck his dick. We need to wake him up a bit more."

I hold on tighter to my junk, but it's to no avail. The woman slides herself over my body, tasting it as she works her way down to where my traitorous dick hardens. I let go of it, and she wraps her mouth around the length, causing it to stiffen further. By the time she finishes licking up the sides of my shaft and sucking on my balls, I'm hard enough to pound nails. I push her off before she makes me come because there's no point in wasting an orgasm if it's going to be unsatisfactory. No, I need more stimulation to persuade me to give up my cum. West comes behind her, and I can see him removing her clothes. He's giving me a display, knowing that this is the way we work best together. He lets me watch as he unwraps the present and takes her first before giving me what is left to fuck into complete oblivion. His clothes fall to the floor as he orders her to lie down on the bed, and I slide over to the side, so she has enough room to get on. Her hand reaches out for my dick, and she pumps it a few times before I grab her wrist and stop it. I don't need to tell her – the tight grip of my fingers around her delicate skin is enough. As she's one of West's girls, she'll be trained for what is about to happen to her. He wouldn't use her if she wasn't. I'm too dangerous to be left with a novice in our dark world. My father decreed, after the events surrounding the loss of my virginity, that he didn't want to have to deal with any dead bodies covered in my DNA. It would be too much of an inconvenience for him, especially when he's got better things to do like fuck his own slut into a hospital or worse.

"Here's what's going to happen," West tells the girl who's still holding my dick but no longer moving her hand. She turns her attention to the other man in the room. "I'm in the mood for something a little different tonight. Something daring. Something dark," West announces.

"Sounds exciting," the girl purrs, and I take a moment to examine her body. She's not what I'd call pretty although I'm sure most people would. She's too thin with not enough to grab hold of except for her chest, which is more than a handful, but I'm fairly certain they're not real. Her hair is a brilliant blonde, and with a face full of make-up there's nothing natural about her. Even her protruding ribs are fake – the result of her starving herself to give her appearance the catwalk look. I push her hand off my dick and shift so I'm standing. I take my own dick in hand, giving it a couple of hard pumps just to take the edge off the tension I feel building in my balls. I may not find this woman sexy, but what is about to happen will be all I need to get me off, when the time is right.

"It's very exciting." West says, drawing my attention back to him as he pulls a small knife from his pocket. "It's been a while since you've bled for me, beautiful. I think it's about time we painted the bed crimson, don't you?"

"Yes, please," the woman hisses with excitement, and I have to wonder about the mentality of someone who'd let a man do this to her. She must trust West implicitly not to harm her. I wouldn't trust him as far as I could throw him, but then I've seen some of the things this man has done to women. I'll never forget the night I heard pained screaming coming from my father's room. I used the secret passageway to investigate what was happening. My father and West were sharing a girl with one in her ass and the other in her pussy. She was covered in blood and bruises where they'd obviously beaten her. She was crying and pleading for them to stop, but neither did. They continued to assault her for the next few hours before West put a gun to her head and blew her brains out. I may lose myself during the moment, but I would never deliberately do that to a woman. She has to consent to what I do, and even though sending that poor girl to heaven may have been a blessing, it's not something I could ever do. Maybe that's why I'm the monster. I don't have the guts to finish the job properly and put them out of their misery after I've destroyed them.

"Hey, William. You going to concentrate on the job in hand, or are you just going to stand there and play with your dick like the pussy you are." West brings me out of my reflection with his harsh words, and I watch as he swirls his tongue around a line of blood on the girl's breast.

"So good," she moans, and he flicks the knife over her other tit. The crimson essence floods to the surface and trickles down over her nipple. "You want some?" the girl asks me, and I shake my head. Blood play is West's thing, not mine. I just need a hole to stick my dick in at the end.

"I'll watch, for now."

West takes his knife lower, making a few small cuts on the girl's stomach as he goes. When he gets to her pussy, he pulls the folds apart and swipes the knife over the delicate flesh. The girl screams in pain this time, not pleasure.

"Fuck, that hurt." She tries to shut her legs, but West pulls them apart and licks the length of her slit. He has blood round his mouth when he brings his head back up. "Don't do that again," the girl demands, but West doesn't listen to her. He cuts the other side *of her folds, and I know in that instant this has turned darker and into something the girl wasn't expecting.*

"My cunt. I'll treat it the way I want. William, stick your dick in her mouth to shut her up," West orders, but I'm going nowhere near the girl who's now trying to escape from the clutches of my friend.

"Fuck off. She'll bite it."

"Well, hold her down, so I can rip her pussy in two." He momentarily let's go of the struggling feminine form and gets a whack to the face from her fist. He retaliates with his own, and I hear the crunch of the girl's nose as it breaks. West flips her over and puts his whole weight on her. "Now, William, or do I need to tell your father you're being a freak again. He'll send you away this time – remember what he said about being sick of you showing him up. He'll make sure you never see Nicholas again."

Those final few words have me releasing my deflated cock and using my strength to hold the girl down, so she can't struggle anymore. West pulls her ass up and without warning slides hard into her pussy as she screams out in pain, and I switch off. My mind goes to its place of serenity, and I don't hear the cries or the pleas any longer. I'll suffer later for treating my brain this way. I know I'll meltdown, but for now I feel safe.

The gun going off brings me out of heaven. Blood splatters all over me, and the girl I'd been holding becomes a dead weight in my arms.

"Fucking cunt!" West exclaims, and I step backward. My hand goes to my nose and swipes across it, no doubt smearing blood and other matter across my face."Bitch got herself pregnant. I'm not going to have some piece of trash like her lauding that over me for the rest of my life. Shame, she had a fucking magical pussy. Why

don't you try it? I know you like them barely breathing. She'll still be nice and wet down there. I tore her up a bit. Lots of blood to ease the flow."

I look down to his dick and see it's covered in blood.

"Get out." I feel my fists forming into balls. West just laughs.

"Oh, come on, William. Stop being a freak. You losing your hard-on isn't my fault. It's all that wrong wiring in your brain." The laugh he expels is eerie, almost demonic in nature. People call me a freak, but the man in front of me has just fucked a woman and shot her in the head. In my fucking bed! "I best go tell your daddy about our little accident, hadn't I? Do us a favor, get your dick wet as well. Makes you look more culpable."

It's then I realize this has been a ruse all along. It's easier for my father to clear this mess up than it would be for West to do it himself. My father won't have our name dragged through the mud, so he'll get rid of the body without consequence for West or for me. Believing I'm the freak — the dangerous, dark monster who is capable of such atrocities. West leaves the room, and I'm alone with the dead girl. The way she's fallen, I can see her pussy on display covered in blood mixed with West's cum. I could do what they expect from me but I won't. I'm not that sort of person.

"William?" My brother's voice penetrates the foggy haze of my brain. "William, talk to me please?"

"Nicholas? What happened?"

"You had a meltdown. Victoria and I injected you with the sedative to calm you down. I didn't want to do it, but I was so afraid you'd hurt yourself."

I slowly open my eyes and allow my vision to acclimatize to where I am, which turns out to be my bedroom, and on my bed. I flinch, half expecting the bed to be covered in blood and with the body of a dead girl from what, I now realize. was a nightmare based on my memories.

"William?" Nicholas reaches out to touch me and ground me.

"I was back there."

"Back where?" he questions with confusion etched on his brow.

"The night West murdered the girl in my bed."

Nicholas exhales deeply and shuts his eyes.

"You did the right thing that night. You came and found me. Our father checked the DNA. There was none of yours inside her, only West's. It was all him. Not you."

"But…" I try to argue with him, but with an authoritative wave of his hand, he silences me.

"You've been too overstimulated the last few days. You need to rest. These memories are of a time in the past. Lord West will never have access to this house again, and you're nothing like the monster he is. When I can finally bring him down, then another piece of the corrupt society our father kept will fall. William, you're my brother. I love you dearly, and I will protect you always. Don't fear the world. Embrace it and allow it to give you the life you deserve."

My brother gets to his feet and straightens out his trousers. I can tell from the creases he's been sitting by my bed for several hours.

"I'm going to check on Victoria, but I'll be back up with some food. I'm the Duke, now, and I'm ordering you to rest for a few days. Away from that crazy outside world full of lights and sounds. God knows it drives me insane, most of the time. We'll spend time just the four of us, trying to figure out how to get rid of West and Viscount Hamilton, so we can live our lives freely."

My brother leaves the room, and I'm left alone in the silence, once again. I want to shut my eyes and sleep for longer, but I'm scared. I know I didn't touch that girl the night she died, but I'm terrified if I fall asleep, the conclusion to the nightmare might change.

The words on the computer screen in front of me are starting to go blurry, I've been staring at them for so long. Line after line of contract law. During my time training, I'd learned a bit about each division of the law: statute, criminal, common, and civil, but it would've blown my mind to delve too deeply into all of them. So, when it had been time to specialize, I'd gone down the criminal law route. Little did I know it would come in handy in the future because my best friend was going to marry into a notoriously criminal society. My head hurts, and my hands are jittery from all the coffee I've been drinking, but I need to continue reading to see if there is any legal way of dissolving the society as it was, and leaving those opposed to Nicholas' new rule financially ruined. Along with help from associates of Nicholas, I've applied for the assets to be frozen of two of the main culprits who refuse to toe the line: Lord West and Viscount Hamilton. I don't expect that to stick for long, though. The police must have thought me insane when I presented them with some bullshit about them funding terrorists.

After I read the same paragraph for what must be the sixth time, I know I need to take a break, and I stand up from the desk I'm using in Nicholas' office. The office was big enough for two extra desks, matching his and Victoria's, to be brought in, and there is still sufficient space to perform a 'jig' if you are so inclined– I'm not. But maybe just a stretch or two. I arch my back, and bringing my arms up above my head, I stretch them before lowering them and shaking out my legs. Yawning, I debate getting another coffee, but I know I'll never sleep if I have any more caffeine. I'll be dancing off the ceiling. No, the best thing I can do is to call it a night, but something is drawing me back to the computer.

A couple of months ago, I took one of those swab DNA tests for the ancestry website everyone raved about. A friend of mine had done it at university and found out an old family tale about her having Indian blood was true, and in fact a quarter of her DNA originated from that continent. She was thrilled to have it confirmed. I already know from my mother's side that my ancestry is African via my grandfather, who came to this country after World War One, and Anglo Saxon from my grandmother, whose family originated from Suffolk. By doing the test, I was really hoping to see if I could link into any relatives on my father's side, which might give me an idea of who he is. My mother has never told me the story of my birth. It's something I've always wondered about, but I can't force her to tell me. Something happened to her, and I'm scared to find out what it was, but I need to know where I come from, and this is my only means, at the moment, to try and discover more.

I shut my eyes and take a deep breath. I had notification a few weeks ago the results were back, but I've been too scared to look at them. Opening my eyes, I flick my mouse to bring up a new browser page and type in the website address. I log into my account and open up the tab labelled DNA, which instantly brings up my results. Twenty-five percent African, I expected that. I scroll further down, and my eyes flick over the rest of my genetic make-up.

"Tamara, what are you still doing up? It's past midnight." William strolls into the room. His eyes move to the computer screen and then up to me. I know I must have a guilty look on my face because his brows frown in the center. "What are you doing?"

"Nothing." I try to hide the tremble in my voice, but I know I fail.

"Tamara. Step away from the screen."

"It's nothing."

He raises an eyebrow at me, and then walking up to me, he lifts me up in the air. I bring the wireless mouse with me because my grip is so tight on it.

"DNA results, I did this once. I wanted to try and prove I wasn't linked to my father. It didn't work." He shrugs and looks down. "Mmm…let me see, totally British apart from your grandfather."

I nod, not able to form words. My heart is beating so fast. I've not even told Victoria I'm doing this. I know she wanted to do it at one time, but her father wouldn't let her. I think she got Theodore to do it, instead, but I'm not sure.

"You've got a lot of Scottish in there as well. Wonder where from? Probably your father."

William halts his train of thought.

"Shit. Sorry. I didn't mean…"

"It's ok."

I scramble back to the computer and close the browser page.

"Wait, did you check your matches? It could give you an idea about who your father is."

"No. William, please."

He reaches out, takes the mouse from my hand, and lays it down on the table. Then placing his hand on top of the laptop, he shuts it down.

"Come with me."

He holds out his hand. I look at it and back up at him, debating on whether to take it or not. I'm freaking out. I've just learned whoever my father is/was is most probably British. That's more than I've known all my life. I need comfort, but the last time I took William's hand, it led to him becoming so overstimulated that he broke down and near enough destroyed his room. I can't let that happen again.

"I'm ok." I keep my hands by my side.

"Ok." He looks defeated and lowers his head. "I wasn't going to…" Stopping, he turns away, and walks over to a cabinet in the corner of the room. He opens a drawer, pulls out a hip flask, and comes back over to me. "You had a shock. I was going to get you a drink. That's all. I understand completely that you want to know where you come from. They say autism is hereditary, normally down the male line. I would love to know if my past ancestors had it. Maybe find out more about what makes me who I am."

He unscrews the hip flask and gives it to me before turning and going back to the door.

"William," I call out, guilt washing over me because he

thinks I'm refusing to go with him in case he hurts me when in reality, I'm the one who's inflicting the pain.

"You should get some sleep, it's late. If you get too tired, you'll be no good at reading through all that law stuff," William replies.

He doesn't turn back to face me but leaves the room with his hand flicking around his head. I look back at the computer. The answers to everything lie within it somewhere, but right now, I just need to sleep.

CHAPTER THIRTEEN

WILLIAM

Turning over in my bed, I reach out for my phone, and through bleary eyes, I look at the time. Ten am. Urgh! I was supposed to help Nicholas in a meeting at nine. I guess he chose not to wake me. I should be grateful for small mercies since it was past two before I fell asleep. After speaking to Tamara, I needed something to clear my mind of the thoughts of failure, which I had running through it. It was then I remembered the app Nicholas had discovered and installed on my phone. A flag quiz. I spent the next two hours trying to beat my best scores from the previous times I'd played it, and needless to say, I did so with ease and fell asleep at two with a contented brain. Sadly, I've not woken with one though. Having still got the vision in my head of Tamara as she refused my hand, fearing I would hurt her again. All I wanted to do was comfort her with a stiff drink, but she thought I wanted more and was scared. Scared of me. I need to stay away from her. Give her time to realize…well, there is nothing to realize – I am a monster. She just needs to know I won't hurt her. I'll use the memory I have of her sweet velvety pussy for my needs, but I won't ever abuse the real thing again.

Sliding from my bed, I pull on a pair of jogging bottoms that had been lying, discarded from a previous day, on my bedroom floor. I fumble sleepily into the bathroom, take a piss, and splash some water on my face. If I'm hiding out all day, I don't need to be clean and presentable. Going back into my bedroom, I grab a t-shirt from a drawer and pull it on over my head.

I've got two choices now. Go in search of food, which is likely to be quicker, or order something to be brought up. My brother is currently running Oakfield Hall on skeleton staff while we sort out the issues with the society. Less chance of any underhand dealings being discovered that way. But I really don't want to risk seeing Tamara, so my stomach is going to have to wait. I pick up the intercom phone and call down to the kitchen.

"My Lord, William," the chef answers in a cheerful manner.

"Morning," I try to reply with the same happiness. "I'm going to take my breakfast in my rooms today. Can you send it up, please?"

"Of course, anything in particular you'd like?"

"No, just the usual."

I don't know why the chef bothers to ask. I've eaten the same thing, now, for twenty years. Two Weetabix with full fat milk and a teaspoon of sugar, followed by two slices of white bread toast with strawberry jam, which mustn't have any lumps in. I wash it all down with a glass of apple juice. No coffee, tea, fancy French pastries, or even sausage, bacon and eggs for me. Cereal, toast, and apple juice is all I need to start the day right.

"It could be a little while as the staff are busy with the Duke and his meeting. I'll see if I can bring it up myself." I can hear the chef start to juggle pans in the background. I know he's busy as well, and I appreciate the kind gesture.

"No hurry. I'll be in the playroom," I inform him and hang up.

Before I leave my bedroom, I push my feet into a pair of warm woolen slippers. Oakfield Hall has an abundance of wooden and marble floors, costing a small fortune to heat. It's often easier to wrap up warm in the colder months. I grab a sweater and slip it on over my head then leave my rooms and head down the corridor to the room Nicholas and I share. This place is our sanctuary, and only we're allowed in it. It's the place we came to as boys, whiling away the hours of boredom and monotony that came from being the sons of a Duke who wanted nothing to do with us until we were old enough to be useful. That happened at the age of ten for Nicholas, but it never happened for me. I was never of importance to my father. I was the spare, and a damaged one at that.

I push open the door to the room, and I'm immediately transported back to my childhood with visions of Nicholas and I running around playing cops and robbers. He was always the robber. Ironic really! When he became more involved in his duties as the future Duke, I discovered a love for Lego, and proudly displayed in the room, now, are many of the creations I made. I was obsessed with it and would sit for hours religiously following the instructions until I'd built what I was supposed to. I remember once there was a piece missing from a pack, and unable to cope with that, I started to have a meltdown. How could I complete what I was doing without that piece? I had to finish it. I'd started, and now it would remain forever incomplete. Nicholas found me sitting in a corner with my fists clenched tightly into little balls. He immediately broke apart a creation he'd made and found the piece I needed. The memory brings back happy thoughts for me, and I seek the model out in the row of my Star Wars builds. The Millennium Falcon sits proudly next to my Death Star and Sand Crawler. Like many boys, I went through a Star Wars phase. I guess, like most, I haven't really stopped. I still have regular binge-watching marathons.

Completing these three massive projects was my greatest feat in life. The instructions sit beside the Falcon, and I know instantly how my day of hiding will be spent. I pick up the Falcon and the instructions and bring them over to some cushions laid out on the floor. Placing them both down, I begin the painstaking process of pulling the Millennium Falcon apart, so I can rebuild it, once again.

After several hours and a half-eaten breakfast followed up by a half-eaten ham sandwich for lunch, I'm halfway through the rebuilding of Hans Solo's pride and joy. I'm just fixing one of the guns in place when I hear soft steps behind me. I wait a beat and turn my head around to see Tamara halfway across the room.

"Out!" I snap at her, and she flinches back but doesn't stop. "You can't be in here."

"Nicholas gave me a note to say I could come in to talk to you." Now standing in front of me, she bends down to place the note on the floor. "He said I'm forbidden to touch your Lego though."

My eyes skim over the note, and I see Nicholas has even written that exact phrase down. I can't help but snort out a laugh.

"He said something about girls not understanding the dynamics of what it takes to build these complex structures, and if I touch them, I'll break them."

I can't help but let another chuckle escape at her comment. I can picture Nicholas saying those exact words with his arms folded sternly across his chest, and his brows furrowed together. I can also picture Victoria behind him rolling her eyes in frustration at her chauvinist husband.

"I'm surprised he didn't tell you that we don't have pink and purple Lego, so you wouldn't be interested anyway.

"I think it was on the tip of his tongue, but Victoria purposely stood on his foot with her Louboutin's to shut him up before he dug an even bigger hole for himself."

"That's my brother for you!" I roll my eyes and pat the bean bag next to me for her to take a seat.

"Did you make all these?" Tamara asks as she gracefully lowers herself until she's sitting with her legs tucked under her bottom. She's wearing blue jeans and a maroon sweater today. It seems strange not to see her in the skirts and blouses she favors.

"I did...well, except for a few small bits. Nicholas was never good at following instructions."

"I can see him being that way."

"You've no idea." I crack another smile. Tamara goes quiet. "Is everything alright?" I ask her.

"Yes." She looks up at me, but I can't meet her eyes. I flick my ear then my nose. I know I'm doing it, but it's not something I can stop.

"I wanted to ask you something."

"Ok," I reply hesitantly.

"I've got this meeting in an hour, and I wondered if you would come with me? I volunteer at a daycare center whenever I can, and it'd be good for the children to meet a real-life Earl."

"I don't know." My initial thought is one of terror. Lots of people and noisy children.

"Please," Tamara almost whispers her plea, and I simply can't say no.

"Alright. I'll get ready to go."

CHAPTER FOURTEEN

TAMARA

The car pulls up outside the day care center, and I can't help but feel a little nervous. I've not told William the entire truth about this visit because I know he wouldn't have come. I just hope he's prepared to forgive me because I think he needs to see this place.

The driver opens my car door, and William comes around to my side to help me out of the car.

"If I end up with anything sticky on my clothes, you're washing it off. I don't like getting my hands dirty."

I click my tongue at him and walk off with a sway of my hips. "You forget. I've seen you eat. That's where anything sticky on you will come from."

"Hey!" he calls indignantly after me, but I can hear the amusement in his voice. He catches up with me, and I link my arm through his offered one. "When did you start coming here?"

"I was doing a certificate at school when I was sixteen – for part of it I needed to do some voluntary work for thirty hours. The Viscount helped me to find a place here. I stayed on afterward and help out whenever I can."

"Sounds good. So, is it just like a nursery? I don't really know the term day care," William asks, holding the door open for me to walk into the reception.

"Sort of," I reply, and before he has a chance to question me further, I'm speeding toward the receptionist, a short, grey haired lady called Eve. She's been working here since before I started, and I'm sure she told me she started back in the early nineties. She doesn't get paid for her job. She does it out of the kindness of her heart. They've tried to offer her a salary on numerous occasions, but each time, she's said no.

"Tamara, I heard you were coming in. Fantastic to see you." The spirited lady, who's age I'd guess is in the late fifties, jumps to her feet and comes around the reception desk to greet me with a big hug. "Congratulations. I hear you're qualified now. We're all so proud of you. You worked so hard. I bet you've already got a job lined up at one of those prestigious London firms."

I can't help but laugh at her excitement over the fact I'm now a qualified lawyer. "I've got a place at one, yes. I've still not decided if I'm going to take it up straight away or have a year's break to explore the world a bit. I need to juggle my finances a bit."

"You deserve a bit of a holiday after all that studying. Mind you, I remember you telling me about the night life as well, so it wasn't all hard work."

I laugh. "Well, I was at university. I needed to live a little."

"How's Victoria? I heard she's married now, and a Duchess as well."

"She is married. Nicholas is wonderful, and they're so

happy. It's not public knowledge, yet, but they have a baby on the way."

"Oh, that's fantastic. You'll have to tell her to come by and see us soon. We've missed her. I can't believe her father never let her come here after he found out about the two male nurses we have. They're both happily married and were unlikely to be a threat to her innocence. Mind you, if his over protectiveness landed her a Duke, then who are we to complain?"

"Yes." It's the only word I can form. I can't tell her the full story of what a bastard Victoria's father is, and how she was lucky it was Nicholas she met and not someone like the old Duke. "I almost forgot..." I bluster, trying to disguise the quick change in direction of my conversation. "This is Nicholas' brother, William Cavendish, Earl Lullington. I've brought him to see the children."

"Oh my god. Why didn't you say sooner? I've only just got here. I didn't know we were having guests." Eve presents a little curtsy in front of William. "Your Earlship, it's wonderful to meet you. I'm Eve Kitchener. It's fabulous to have you come visit our little place."

"Please call me William." He extends his hand and accepting it, she shakes it. I know this is hard for him to do, making pleasant conversation when he'd rather be hidden away. "Tamara has told me she's been helping here since she was sixteen. I'm intrigued to meet the children."

"I'm sure you'll love them. They have their quirks, but they're all fantastic little human beings."

"I'm sure I will," William replies, and I can't help but smile toward him. He may think he's destined for the shadows, but he's being the perfect gentleman, and I haven't seen him tic once.

"Tamara"–Eve turns back to me– "I'll get you both badges, but have you warned William about some of the children and their possible reactions to things?"

The moment of truth. I swallow deeply and turn to William.

"You were asking me if this was a regular nursery. It isn't – it's a place for parents to bring their autistic children for interaction, advice, and help."

"Autistic?" The word leaves William's mouth the same time as his hand goes to his ear and flicks it.

"Yes."

"I see why you wanted to bring me and not Nicholas, then," he states bluntly, and I instantly see the regret cross his face at allowing the comment to escape.

"It isn't like that. I promise you."

Eve bites her lip and steps back to allow us some privacy.

"I don't need to see others like me to know I'm wired wrong."

"That's not why I brought you here. This place has been helping children ever since the onset of better diagnosis and understanding of autism, in the early nineties. You and I both know of the intolerance to it in your world. I just wanted you to see that in the wider world it's more common than you think. If you speak to any of the doctors here, they will tell you that with advances in assessment, it will be more common to be on the spectrum than not in a few years.

"But you know what I'm like?" William lowers his voice and leans into me.

"You won't hurt anyone here. Please. Just five minutes. If it's too much, we'll leave."

"Five minutes," William states as Eve comes back to us with badges, and I exhale the breath I've been holding since he realized the nature of the center we're now in.

"Please go through, they're expecting you." Eve smiles at me, and I nod a little thanks to her. William takes hold of my arm as I lead him through the security doors.

"I'm sorry I didn't tell you sooner."

"I need to know things, Tamara. I was prepared to meet normal children. I can already feel my heart beating faster because a surprise has been sprung on me. I can't handle them. You have to be honest with me, or you risk a meltdown."

"I didn't think you'd come if I told you the real reason."

"I probably wouldn't have," William responds truthfully. "But you have to give me a chance, and a choice."

"I will, next time."

William goes silent as we stand in front of another door. It's closed, but behind it, I can hear the happy chatter and laughter of children. He flicks his ear and then his nose. I give him a minute to compose himself, but his movements are getting worse. His fists clench then unclench in between the tics. I know he's struggling. I open my mouth and softly sing.

> "Hush, little baby, don't say a word,
> Mama's going to buy you a mocking bird.
> And if that mockingbird don't sing,
> Mama's going to buy you a diamond ring."

His fists unclench, and his arms lower to his side. He takes a deep inhalation and then nods.

"I'm ready."

I push open the door, and we are greeted with lots of happy, smiling faces. Many are children, but some are adults. The staff wear black t-shirts with a little puzzle piece in the corner. Off to the left is a room, which I know to be the sensory room. It's furnished with small beds, and there are soft bricks of varying sizes in it. The lights are low intensity and multi-colored. It's been purposefully designed, so it won't overstimulate the younger children, but it will allow them to play and explore. At the back of the main area is a computer room for the older children, containing a PlayStation and X-Box, along with several high spec Mac computers. They are monitored by staff because we once had a child who was so high functioning he tried to hack into MI5. I've watched some of the children in there before, and I'm amazed by the skills they possess in relation to coding and computer programing. I'm not in the least surprised everything is monitored by our tech genius, Dave. Off to the right is a small kitchen with a few tables for people to sit at and eat if they want to. Cooked meals can't be prepared here, but people can make sandwiches and the like. This area of the building is specifically for the day care parents. It's a place for mums and dads to come and talk to other parents as well as to highly trained staff members who are available at all times, offering advice. This is not all the center provides, though. It also has respite and permanent housing facilities for those who need a break or can't live alone. In fact, this place has everything needed to help those with autism live life to the fullest.

"Hello." A little boy stands at William's legs. I've seen him before and know him as Cory. He reaches out and touches the material of William's formal trousers before quickly pulling his hand back. His little face creases up as though he's musing on something, and then he reaches out and touches the fabric again. "I like your trousers."

Shifting my gaze to William I see his hand start to lift toward his face, but he stops its progression and instead holds it out to Cory.

"Hello, I'm William," he informs the little boy and kneels down, so he's at his level. "Can I tell you a secret? I like your trousers better." Cory looks down at his jogging bottoms and then back at William. "I usually like to be comfortable, but I thought I should dress up today. If I'd known you'd be wearing jogging bottoms, I would've as well."

A woman pushes through the crowd of people starting to assemble around us. She's Cory's mum.

"I'm so sorry," she apologizes, grabbing the little boy and pulling him to her. "He's got a thing about different fabrics. I hope he hasn't made your trousers dirty."

"Please. It doesn't matter. I was just telling him I wish I'd worn my jogging bottoms like him. I feel overdressed."

"You're an important man. I'm sure nobody minds what you wear." The young mum blushes, and I try to stifle a laugh when I realize she thinks William is attractive. Certainly, with his broad shoulders, imposing height, and stunning good looks, he's the most desirable man I've ever met.

"Thank you." William immediately looks down to the ground, not being sure how to handle the compliment.

"Cory." A little girl approaches us. I scan my brain, struggling to recall her name, but when she places her hands on her hips, I see the supports on her wrists and remember straight away this is Lexie. As well as being on the spectrum, she also has hyper-mobility and dyspraxia. "You weren't supposed to touch the Earl. That's what they told us during the talk this morning. They said smile politely, don't touch him, and don't talk to him unless he speaks to you first. We have to follow the rules."

"I didn't mean to." Cory's little bottom lip quivers as though he's going to cry. "I couldn't help it. I needed to know what his trousers felt like."

Lexie keeps her hands on her hips, and for a minute I think she's going to tell the poor boy off again. She doesn't though, instead, she gives him a cuddle, and then pulls him off to play with his still blushing mother in tow.

"You ok?" I check with William.

"Yes. You know I did the same thing once. My father had a guest he was trying to con out of money, and the man had on these velvet looking trousers. I really wanted to know what they felt like. The only problem was I'd been painting with my nanny. When they entered the nursery, my hands were covered in bright green paint, and I smeared it all over his trousers when I touched him. My father didn't get the money he wanted, and I got a hiding and relegated to my room for a few days. We were never allowed paints in the house again." He looks down at his hands as though remembering the green paint that was once on them. "Maybe, I should ask Nicholas if we can get some?"

"Why ask? If you want something just get it."

William turns his head to look at me as though he can't quite understand what I'm saying.

"It's Nicholas' house. I have to obey his rules."

"Has he told you that?" I question.

"No, but it's just what happens."

I fall silent and make a mental note to tell Nicholas of this revelation when I return to the house. I'm pretty certain he'd prefer William to have whatever he wanted and not have to ask for it.

"Tamara…Earl Lullington." One of the doctor's steps forward and presents a little bow to William who shakes his hand. "My name is Dr. Brown. It's lovely to have you both here. The children have been very excited since Tamara's call earlier. Tamara is very popular with them, and I'm sure you will be loved as well, My Lord."

"Please. Call me William. 'My Lord' is for my slightly more formal and stubborn brother."

"Of course. Has Tamara told you details of our facilities?"

William looks toward me.

"I've given him a brief tour and overview," I offer by way of an explanation.

"Not a problem. Our facilities here are for children and adults with formal diagnosis on the spectrum. We don't turn anyone away, though. We simply help them liaise with the appropriate doctors to find a solution. We currently have ten long-term residents, varying in age and range of diagnosis." The doctor starts to walk through the rooms, showing every-thing to William as he goes. I stand back and observe him as he takes it all in. He asks many sensible questions, and I can see he's finally relaxing after the initial shock.

"I'm not sure if Tamara has told you, but I'm on the spec-trum myself." William tells the doctor.

"She hasn't, but I've seen in your mannerisms and lack of

eye contact that you might be. I've worked most of my life with children and adults, having all levels of diagnosis, so I recognize the traits straight away."

"I'm that obvious." William laughs nervously.

"Not at all. For someone with different social behaviors to the norm, you are doing extremely well."

"Thank you," William offers, and I gently take his hand. He allows me to do so and wraps his fingers around mine.

"Can I ask you something?" William says as he steps aside to let a little child go running past with headphones on to shield against the noise.

"Of course, please, if I can help in anyway?"

"How much does having autism shape who you are? Can it cause a darkness within you?"

The doctor opens and shuts his eyes rapidly, shocked at the question.

"That's a difficult question. There have been people who've committed crimes and have either had issues before or are subsequently diagnosed to be on the spectrum, but autism doesn't make someone inherently evil. It's just a question of different wiring. In relation to the nature versus nurture debate, I believe any darkness comes from the way someone is raised and their life experiences rather than innately from birth. I don't think you have to worry about an evil side though. I've found over the years that Tamara is an excellent judge of character, and so are some of these children. They've warmed to you already, which demonstrates to me the make-up of the person you are." The doctor smiles at William and I know inside his head his thoughts must be going a mile a minute. The doctor lowers his head in a bow again before returning to a nearby mum, trying to calm a distressed child whose jigsaw piece is missing.

"Do you want to go?" I look up at William. We are still holding hands.

He shakes his head.

"No. I like it here. It's calming."

"They do wonders. I'm so glad I found it."

William gazes out across the people in the room, and I see his stare focus in on a father and son. They are cuddling up together on a chair, reading a book about space together. His face goes blank, and I can no longer read his emotions.

"It was him all along. It was never me." He bends down and presses a kiss to my head. "I wasn't the one who was wrong."

Sitting at the breakfast table shoveling my Weetabix into my mouth, I keep staring down at the small piece of paper in front of me. It's a picture drawn by Cory from the center the other day. It's of me and him lying on the floor in the sensory room staring at the lights. We must've lain there together for at least half an hour just saying the color of the lights or a variation when they changed. He was really impressed with my knowledge of the color wheel and even more that I knew of a blue-green color called zomp. He'd always wanted to know if you could get a color for every letter of the alphabet. I was hesitant at first when I found out the center was for those on the autism spectrum, but the more time I've spent there, the more confident I've become. Although at the same time a sadness has developed within me when I see the interactions and the love between the children and their parents, reminding me of what I didn't have growing up. To be different is not the scandal or embarrassment my father led me to believe. It's something to be cherished, making the person unique. I need to try and keep that thought in my head.

My brother pops his head over my shoulder. "Good picture, little brother, but I'm not sure you are up to the standard of Van Gogh, just yet. I'm uncertain whether Victoria's critical eye will accept it as a replacement for the 'Poppies'." He laughs at his unfunny joke.

"It's not mine. It was drawn by one of the children at the day care center," I reply testily.

"I know." Nicholas chuckles. "If it was your drawing, it would be so much worse."

I snort my frustration and folding the picture up, I tuck it in my pocket. I think I'll get a frame for it and put it up on the wall in my room, later.

"Has Victoria got her head down the toilet again this morning?" I ask my brother with blunt honesty.

"You've such a delicate way with words, but you always speak the truth. I left her trying to eat a ginger biscuit to settle her poor stomach. I think I'll get a doctor out to her today. This has been going on far too long now," he says, shaking his head. The butler steps forward and pulls out a seat for my brother to take his position at the head of the table for breakfast. "I'll have two slices of toast with a piece of bacon, two poached eggs, and a large coffee please. The Duchess will also be down in a minute. She'll have a slice of toast and lemon water please." My brother turns to me, "What do you think Tamara will want?"

I shrug and push my finished bowl of cereal away.

"Food?"

"Helpful." He rolls his eyes. "Bring Miss Bennett the same as me, but with one egg."

"At once, Your Grace." The butler scurries away.

"I miss Reggie," Nicholas states flatly. "He would have known immediately what Tamara wanted.

"I know."

We both fall silent in memory of our previous butler and stand-in father figure who was killed during Victoria's trials.

"I don't give a fuck if he's taking his breakfast. I'll see him now, or I'll shove your head through this god damn door." I instantly recognize the not so dulcet tones of Lord West, coming from out in the hallway.

"He must have received the legal letters from Tamara." My brother pushes back his chair and prepares to greet our uninvited breakfast guest. I remain seated, continuing to eat my toast.

The dining room door bursts open and ricochets off the wall behind it. An antique vase on a nearby table wobbles but doesn't fall.

"I will ruin you, Oakfield." Lord West storms into the room. He's dressed in a navy blue, formal suit and brandishes an umbrella in his hand.

"I believe it is you who'll be ruined, West," my brother replies with a bored nonchalance. "In accordance with the letter, unless you comply with the new rules of the society, you will be ejected and will forfeit assets to pay the subsequent fines as a result."

"I'll do nothing of the fucking sort. Just because you're too much of a wimp to run the society as it should be and has always been, it doesn't mean we'll allow you to ruin all our hard work and fun."

"Fun!" my brother spits out. "Have you met my wife and seen all the trials she had to go through."

Lord West smirks. "Yes, I've met her, and I seem to remember how good her perky little tits felt in my hands. Shame I never got a chance to savor her pussy."

Nicholas steps forward, prepared to make Lord West pay for his statement, but I'm on my feet quickly and place myself between the two.

"No," I tell my brother. "He's baiting you."

"Yeah, Nicholas. Listen to your freak of a brother. Hit me and I'll have you arrested for assault. Another reason for me to gather a 'no confidence' vote in you as the leader." West waits a heartbeat before continuing to antagonize my brother. "I'm sure Viscount Hamilton would make a perfect new leader. After all he'll be able to keep his bitch of a daughter in control better than you can."

My brother struggles harder in my arms, and I'm on the verge of not being able to control him when I hear Tamara's authoritative voice. Seeing her so near to this man, and knowing what he's capable of, sends shivers down my spine.

"Lord West." Tamara steps into the room with her head held high while Victoria lingers in the doorway behind her, looking white as a sheet. Tamara's dressed in a tight skirt and blouse with a jacket over it. Her long black hair is pulled back in a bun at the nape of her neck, and she looks every inch the professional lawyer… fuck…she's hot as hell. "I must advise you that I've just recorded every word of slander you've made against my client, the Duchess of Oakfield." She holds up her phone, and I can't help but smirk at her genius. "In it, you've also admitted to touching the Duchess inappropriately. I'm sure if she were to give me a statement to that effect, then a court of law might find you guilty of sexual assault. Furthermore, should His Grace, the Duke of Oakfield, escape his brother's restricting arms and feel the need to administer a punch to your face – one, which given his strength and current demeanor, would be likely to damage your good looks via a broken nose, then I'm sure a court of law would also find he had due cause to protect his wife's good character and person. Especially having heard your previous admission of sexual assault upon her person." Tamara moves closer to Lord West as I let go of Nicholas who's stopped struggling in my arms. I step back into the shadows and can feel myself getting hard at Tamara's majestic display. I've thought her a weak woman before, but here in this room, she's commanding and authoritative. It's the biggest turn on ever. She could match me blow for blow in a duel of words. Maybe she is the woman for me and could handle the darkness within me.

"I suggest you leave this place immediately. At the very least, the recording I've made will be enough to have a restraining order put in place against you. I'm certain that would affect your ability to continue as an active member of the Oakfield Society despite its unlawful conception and activities." Standing directly in front of Lord West, Tamara places both of her hands on her hips and stares him down.

"Damn." West grabs his groin and re-arranges it in front of us all. "That made me so fucking hard. Do you talk like that in the bedroom?"

"I'm still recording, Lord West," Tamara counters while my fists clench ready to attack should West make any attempt to hurt the woman in front of him. My protective instincts are flooding through my body, but they are also joined by feelings of darkness, which shroud me in their shadows. Lord West finds her display a turn on, and so do I. He is evil incarnate, but I'm experiencing the same responses as him. Surely, this proves how dark and dangerous my soul is.

"You, my darling, will be fun to break," he sneers and turns his attention to Nicholas. "Oakfield, remove the sanctions against me and desist with your plans, or you'll regret it. I won't rest until I take everything from you. This house, your wife, your hot little lawyer, and even your brother. How would you like it if I get him locked up under the Mental Health Act for some of his past perverted deeds?" West's laugh sucks all the air out of the room, and I know he's referring to the incident with the girl in my bedroom. My heart is starting to beat rapidly, the air in my lungs feels cold and seems to lack oxygen. My head clouds with a foggy haze of emotions: anger, protectiveness, fear. The stimulation is too much. I know I'm rocking, and I know I'm tic'ing. "Are you videoing this one, Miss Bennett? There's all the proof needed to demonstrate that William Cavendish is not safe to be allowed free in society."

I can hear the words being spoken around me. More angry exchanges then doors slamming before silence. West has gone. His evil presence is no longer constricting the aura of the room. Now there's only mine, flowing and twisting around the edges of the royally decorated room like black plumes of smoke. It's as if the dementors from Harry Potter are pulling me under their spell.

"Victoria, get me a sedative, quickly," Nicholas calls out, and it permeates my bewildered brain.

"Wait." I hear Tamara say, and I can feel her getting closer to me.

"No!" I shout, bringing my hands up in front of my face. "That was beautiful. You were so majestic. But, I'm like him." I bring my hand down to my groin and can feel the hardness there.

"It's not wrong, William. I promise you. It excites me to know you liked my display." Tamara is speaking, and I know she's near, but she sounds so far away.

> "Hush, little baby, don't say a word,
> Mama's going to buy you a mocking bird.
> And if that mockingbird don't sing,
> Mama's going to buy you a diamond ring."

I feel a finger touch the top of my nose. It's soft and tender, and while Tamara continues to sing, it is stroked down to the tip and then back up.

"I'm here, William. Nothing's wrong...I promise you. Nicholas and Victoria are here as well. West has gone. You're *not* him."

I stop rocking and allow her words to sink in. *"I'm not him. I'm NOT him."* I shut my eyes and take a deep breath before opening them again. My mind has cleared, and my meltdown has been averted without the need for a sedative. I've responded to Tamara. She's talked me down when I needed her to. Reaching out, she takes my hand.

"How do you feel?" she asks, and I blink a few times to center myself further.

"Good. Thank you."

"You're not a bad man, William. Just because you liked

my little display of power doesn't make you anything like West."

Nicholas steps forward.

"Hell, little brother. I liked her display too. I might have to take Victoria upstairs and get her to talk all legal-like to me." Nicholas chuckles.

"That's probably a case of too much information." Tamara screws her face up.

"I'm sorry," I tell them both. "Everything is different from what I'm used to. The world is a crazy place and so vibrant. Sometimes, I can't fully handle everything around me."

Tamara leans into me, and I wrap my arms around her shoulders.

"That's what you have us for. Everyone has their mad moments. It's what you do after that counts."

She looks up at me, her eyes wide with both wonder and the affection she holds for me. For the first time ever, I don't see any fear. It's gone because I'm finally accepting my needs. It's then I realize that everything Tamara has been doing has been for a reason. She's been helping me to discover the life I can have outside the confines of my father's rules, giving me the chance to be myself, not a monster created by him. Leaning forward, I press a kiss to the top of her forehead just as Victoria comes running into the room with a hypodermic filled with sedative.

"Damn!" she exclaims. "I hate being pregnant. I spend all day throwing up and then get to miss all the good things."

We all laugh, and Nicholas strides confidently over to her.

"How about I take you upstairs and show you something good."

"If it's your dick, then I think I'll pass. It's got a lot to answer for at the moment!"

Tamara rests her head against my chest as we watch the comic interaction between husband and wife. With him trying to get laid, and his pregnant wife informing him she's never opening her legs for him again. For the first time in forever, I feel calm… natural…normal.

CHAPTER SIXTEEN

TAMARA

"Do you want another romantic comedy, or can we have something with a bit more action in it?" William flicks between the Netflix icon of *Fast and Furious* and *Crazy, Stupid Love.*

"You can put the car one on." I shake my head at him. "I'm done with romance for the day. Although I will have to tell you all the laws they're breaking in the film."

"Deal." William switches back to *Fast and Furious* and sets it up to play. He pauses the screen, though. "Do you want anything more to eat or drink?"

We've been watching films for the last few hours. Ever since the clash with Lord West this morning, nobody has felt like doing much. Nicholas arranged for a doctor to come and see Victoria about her morning sickness. She was prescribed some pills and, along with Nicholas, took to her rooms for some rest. I suspect she was also breaking her vow to never allow her husband near her again, especially when chocolate coated strawberries were sent to their room. I can't take my friend anywhere. Mind you, it's lovely to see her so happy. William and I took a walk around the estate to clear his head after his almost meltdown this morning. We sent the driver to fetch a traditional takeaway kebab for lunch because I'd discovered during the walk William had never had one before. The Oakfield's chef wasn't impressed, and I'm not sure William was either. I kept reassuring him it tasted better after a night out drinking at the pub. I don't think he believed me. The chef made us a platter of snacks, and we came into the cinema room to watch films for the afternoon. Following his kiss to my forehead this morning, we've not engaged in any other embraces but simply enjoyed being close to each other. It had been a perfect afternoon, and I didn't want it to end.

"Do you think the chef has any more of those chocolate cookies?" I rub my index finger through the crumbs on the plate and lick them off my digit.

William presses a button located in the arm of the comfortable sofa we're sitting on, and the voice of the chef fills the room.

"My Lord?"

"Do you happen to have any more chocolate cookies left?" William asks.

"I've just taken a fresh batch out of the oven." I can tell the chef is happy to be cooking, and I can imagine him sniffing the freshly baked smell into his nostrils.

"Can you send some for Miss Bennett, please?"

"Of course. Anything for you, sir?"

"I'll just have another coffee, thank you. Best make it decaffeinated, though, or I'll be awake all night."

"I'll bring them right through."

"Has Nicholas said whether he'll be taking dinner downstairs or in his rooms, yet?" William asks.

"I believe he's eating downstairs, but I've not been able to confirm that. He was called into an urgent meeting, according to the butler."

"Urgent meeting?" I see William's brows furrow together. I love the concern he has for his brother. The two of them are beyond close. I often wonder if it's what got them through their youth, making them the men they are today. The bond between them being strengthened with everything that was thrown at them.

"Yes, sir. I believe it was…" The chef goes quiet.

"Was who?"

"I can't say." The jovial nature of the chef has completely disappeared, and his voice is caged.

"Now," William orders, his voice terse and commanding. "I want details. Now!"

"I believe it was Miss Bennett's mother."

William turns his head to look at me, and my mouth must fall open in shock. Before I know it, I'm gasping like a fish out of water, trying to find words. William grabs my hand, and we are running through the corridors of Oakfield Hall toward the office we all share. Without knocking, William barges in. My mother is sitting in a chair with Victoria. My friend's arm is around her, and my mother's crying.

"Mum," I call, and I'm across the room in an instant and at her feet checking her for injuries. "What's wrong? What's happened?"

I look up at Nicholas and see the frown on his face. He looks over toward William and shakes his head.

"Tamara, why don't we wait outside? This could be nothing, but I'm sure Nicholas can handle it." William taps me on the shoulder and tries to assist me to my feet, but I jerk away from him.

"My mother is crying. I'm not going anywhere until someone tells me what's going on."

"She…came to apologize to me…for knowing about my father's plans and not helping me," Victoria stutters her answer quickly, too quickly, and I see it instantly for the lie it is. She's pale, shaking, and has also been crying.

"You told me she wouldn't know I've been here." My mother looks up at Nicholas while using a tissue in her hand to dab away the tears in her eyes.

"I'm sorry, Ms. Bennett. When William goes in the cinema room, he's usually in there for hours watching films. I truly didn't know they'd find out you were here."

"Will you stop talking like I'm not here and tell me what is going on? I have a right to know."

My mum lets out a long sob, and I squeeze her hand tightly.

"Whatever it is, Mummy, I can help you. Is it the Viscount? Has he done something to you after our last visit? If he's fired you, you're better off away from that place. Victoria wants you here. I want you here."

She shakes her head and inhales a whimper, trying to dampen it down, so it doesn't explode into a full-blown cry of anguish.

"I never wanted you to find out. I thought if Nicholas knew, he could protect you. It's the only reason I took the risk."

"Find out what? Mum, you're not making any sense?"

Victoria gets to her feet and going over to her husband, buries her head in his chest. I can hear her sobbing.

"Please, my darling daughter, you have to forgive me."

"Forgive you? If you mean, knowing about Victoria, then of course. I was mad at you the other day, but I know without your protection Victoria would have suffered even worse from her father. It turned out alright for her and Nicholas anyway. Mum, you're forgiven. Of course, you are." I get up and bring her into my arms, but she cries harder, and I can hear her whimpering, 'no'.

"Tamara. You need to let your mother speak," Nicholas orders, and I pull back from her in confusion before sitting next to her on the sofa. I search her face for answers, trying to read the lines of age on her weathered features. She looks so tired and old. To me, she's always been young, but in this moment, I see her for a woman who's had to deal with a lot in her life. I know instinctively what she has to tell me. William must as well for I feel his comforting warmth getting closer to me.

"My father?" I question not really wanting answers.

"Yes." Her voice is almost a whisper, but to me, it's as loud as a fog horn, sounding out a warning for ships to avoid the rocks that will shatter them and send them into the depths of tempestuous seas.

"You know who he is?"

She nods.

"I'll always remember the night you were conceived. I see it vividly in my dreams, every night. It's haunted me all these years. The day had started out perfectly. Having completed my work, I'd been given half a day off, and I went to the cinema. I'd always been a James Bond fan and was desperate to see the new one, *Golden Eye*. I loved it. He might be a little bit older than me, but Pierce Brosnan is a handsome man. I wandered back home in a bit of a daydream. I was working for the Viscount by then. Master Theodore had just been born and the Viscountess was resting after the birth. I went into the kitchen to get a drink. The Viscount was there."

My stomach sinks. In my heart, I know where this story is heading, but I don't want it to go there. Damn, I don't want it to be true. Please god, let me wake up and find this was a nightmare.

"We spoke for a while. Just general conversation. He asked me about the film, and I couldn't hide my crush on James Bond. The Viscount laughed at me and told me James Bond wasn't a real man because that wasn't how to treat a woman. He told me that if a real man took a woman as a lover, he'd make sure that they knew he'd been there. Breaking them forever. I joked that I thought Bond was renowned for that, and then he lurched forward and grabbed me, pinning me to the kitchen counter. I'll remember his words until the day I die.

'Not that sort of broken, but actually physically and mentally rip that pussy up, so no man can stick his dick in it again. Breaking her until she knows that all she is is a hole for a man to use and own.'

I'm vaguely aware of William sitting down behind me and placing his hands on my shoulders. I need his strength because I'm drowning in the revelations.

"The Viscount placed his hand under the denim skirt I was wearing and moved it up toward my private parts. I protested and tried to stop him, but his strength was too much for me. He pinned me down, ripped my underwear off, and did exactly what he said he would do. He broke me physically and mentally."

"And got you pregnant with me?" Tears start to stream down my cheeks. My heart is broken, and my head aches.

My mother nods.

"It's why when you and Victoria used to joke you were sisters from another mother, I would disappear to my room and cry for hours. You are sisters, half anyway, sharing the same father."

"Viscount Hamilton is my father?…He raped you?" I can barely get the words out. I'm still trying to will myself to wake up from this nightmare. It can't be true. It can't be. "William." I reach around, and as he pulls me to him, I start to cry. I cry for the years I fantasized about who my father could be. Maybe a soldier who died in battle, and my mother couldn't bear to tell me because she was so heartbroken at his loss, or a traveler with whom my mother had a brief fairytale romance. After he'd left, she'd discovered my existence and although she'd no way to contact him, it didn't matter because she had a part of him with her forever. No, the reality is horrible, disgusting, and sick. I'm the result of a brutal attack on my mother by a man so vile he needs to be sent to hell. He's ruined my mother's life, given his own daughter away, and he's bought a woman who's disappeared without trace. Even his own wife was purchased for him. I can only imagine what other atrocities he's committed in his life. I push away from William and get to my feet. I need air…I can't breathe. I open a window, and sticking my head out of it, I gulp the sweet oxygen into my lungs, but they don't seem to fill quickly enough. William comes up behind me and turning me to face him, he strokes his finger down the tip of his my nose.

"*Hush, little baby...*" He doesn't need to say the rest, I instantly succumb to his solace.

"How can I be his daughter?"

William wipes away my tears.

"I can't..." I start, but he hushes me with his finger against my lips.

"You can. You have to. I'm with you all the way."

I look around his colossal frame to where my mother sits, looking tiny on the sofa. Victoria is still crying into Nicholas' arms. She's my sister, something I've wanted all my life, and that wish just came true, but not in the way I'd hoped.

I nod at William, indicating I'm doing alright. I've collected myself and need to continue my conversation with my mother. He leads me back to the chair, and I take my mother's hands within mine when I sit. William sits behind me.

"I'm sorry, Tammy. I never wanted you to know this. I wanted to take it to my grave, so it wouldn't hurt you. I wanted you to think you had a father who loved me, and you were conceived out of love."

"You can't always protect me from the monsters, Mum. I need the truth. I'm going to go up against this man and destroy him for what he's done to Victoria and you." My calm outer voice disguises the quivering fear inside me at undertaking such a feat. "Why did you stay with him? Why not leave?"

"Where could I go? I had nobody else. Your grandparents weren't always around. My job was my life, and my color still a hindrance. The Viscount offered me a future despite what he'd done. A future, which included him paying for your education. I couldn't turn that down. It's one of the reasons I always made you study so hard because I wanted it to cost him as much as possible. To make him suffer financially even just in a small way. I was so proud of you for getting into Cambridge. I knew that one day you'd be able to put an end to the society and their old fashioned, evil ways. Use this news to spur you on, Tamara. Don't let it destroy the strength I know you have inside you."

"I won't, Mum. You have my word on that. We will both stand triumphant over the Viscount one day."

My mother and I embrace, again, but this time stay together and cry. The others in the room stand in silence, allowing us this moment to begin the healing process. Eventually, my mother pulls back.

"I've given Nicholas evidence from that night." Her eyes flick to a package rolled up on her desk. I realize it must be the clothes she was wearing. "I kept everything in case I needed it. There's a sworn statement and a couple of photos. It will remain as my word against his, and I know staying in his employment will count against me, but if it helps in anyway, it's there to use."

"We will keep it safe and use it against him." Nicholas says, tapping his hand on the desk next to the evidence. I immediately feel sick, knowing what will be contained within the package. I think I'll allow the men to deal with that as much as possible.

"What happens now? Nicholas, we need to get my mother somewhere safe?"

I can instantly tell from the Duke's expression that hiding her away is not part of his plan.

"No," I tell him in no uncertain terms. "There's no way I'm allowing her to go back to that house."

"It's not my decision, Tamara," Nicholas tells me, and I whip my head around to my mother.

"I have to. I believe the Viscount is planning something for Theodore, and I can't allow him to hurt that boy after what he did to Victoria. Theo doesn't know anything about the society. Viscount Hamilton has weaved a web of lies and deceit to trap the boy. I think whatever is happening may involve the missing girl from the sale, as well – the one the Viscount purchased. I've not seen her, but I know he has her. I have to try and find out what's happening."

"But it's too risky. What if he finds out you've been here? He was already suspicious when we visited the other day."

"Which was why I went along with his plans that day to upset you, making you think I'm a bad person. It was the only way."

"Mum, this is too dangerous," I plead.

"Nicholas is going to put protection in place for me. It may take a few days, but hopefully I'll be able to get the information I need by then and get out."

"I don't like it," I tell her like a petulant child, and she lets out a soft chuckle.

"I know." She strokes her hand over my head. "I don't either, but I don't have a choice. He may have broken me that night, but he also gave me a special gift. One that'll help protect me until my dying breath."

"Don't." I shake my head, not wanting to hear talk of her death.

Mum squeezes my hands one final time and gets up onto her feet.

"I'm so proud of you, of the woman you've become." She looks behind me to William and then back to me. "And the woman you'll become. You're in safe hands here at Oakfield Hall." Victoria comes over and embraces her. "You both are. I know you'll always be happy. That's all I've ever wanted."

CHAPTER SEVENTEEN

WILLIAM

I sit at my desk in the study, watching as Tamara flicks around the screen on her desk. It's been twenty-hours since her mother left, and she's barely spoken to anyone. I don't even think she slept last night because she's in the same clothes as yesterday. Before we'd watched the film, she'd changed from her business suit into jeans and a jumper, and she's still wearing them. Victoria and Nicholas huddle together over the other side of the room, reading through a document Nicholas drafted for the new constitution of the society.

I slide out of my plush leather chair, having done little more than play Roblox on my computer for the last hour, and pour a glass of water from the jug, which is resting on top of a seventeenth century sideboard. I take the glass over to Tamara and place it in front of her.

"You've not drunk anything for a while. It's bad for you. You'll get dehydrated, and then you'll get a heacache. If it gets really bad, you could end up in hospital on a drip. I know because I've read all about it." I want to slap myself in the face for having verbal diarrhea, but the smile crossing her face makes me feel less stupid. "Sorry."

"Don't be. I do need to drink." She looks back at her computer screen, then turns it to face me. I see it's on the ancestry page she was looking at the other day, and I notice her name and Theodore's on the screen. It says the probability of them being half brother and sister is high. "I guess we don't need to do an official DNA test. This proves it."

"I guess." I shrug, wanting to comfort her, but the words fail me. My social sensibilities are virtually non-existent at times like this. It's a curse but also a blessing. "Does that make you my half sister-in-law?"

"Possibly. I don't know how it works. I'll have to Google it." Tamara pulls up a fresh browser and starts to type while I hum a thought. "What is it?"

"Well. It doesn't make it illegal for me to fuck you does it?"

She can't help the laugh that escapes her lips. It's loud, refreshing, and much needed. Causing Victoria and Nicholas to look up from the document they are engrossed in.

"Thank you." She laughs again.

"What for?"

"Being you."

"I'm not always certain that's a good thing but alright."

"It's exactly what I needed."

"What's going on?" Victoria inquires with enthusiasm.

"William's being perfect," Tamara responds, getting to her feet and embracing me.

"Should I even ask what he said?" Nicholas wraps his arms around his wife.

"The right thing. He said the right thing."

"Cryptic. Definitely a lawyer." Nicholas rolls his eyes.

"Well can I?" I bring the conversation back to my question. I want to know the answer. It's important.

"Yes, William. If I say you can fuck me, you can. It's not illegal because we don't share any common blood."

"Hey, who are you saying has common blood? I've got the blood of Dukes, remember," Nicholas retorts with a chuckle. I like the fact the tension of the last twenty-four hours is starting to dissipate.

"I guess my blood's not as common as I thought it was either." Tamara sticks her tongue out at Victoria and my brother, her half brother-in-law. This is going to get so confusing and give me a headache. I'm going to have to develop a family tree to figure out how all the links work. It will bug me if not, and that only leads to trouble, or several hours spent distracting myself by trying to name as many facts as I can about space or the United States of America. My record is six hours discussing Florida with myself when I was trying to forget how Prince John was related to Marie Antoinette. Damn it. I'm going to get that thought in my head, again. I knew he was her fifth cousin seven times removed or something, and I drew a big diagram to prove it. Nicholas became frustrated because it took up too much space in the playroom, and in the end, he burned it.

Victoria bites her lip. "How do you feel? I mean…about us sharing blood? What my…our father did?"

"I can't lie and say I don't want to kill him with my bare hands for what he did to my mother. But, to be honest, I'm not surprised it was him. It makes sense being the type of man he is. He gave you up for financial gain to a society, which would've raped and killed you if it weren't for Nicholas being the man destined to inherit the title. I'm worried sick about my mother still being in the house, and everything that could happen to her, but I understand why she's gone back. Theodore is just as much an innocent in all of this as you and my mother were. He's being manipulated by the Viscount, and we need to put a stop to it. I'll never call him father but to know you're my sister is the best news I've ever had. It cements what we've known all along."

"I feel the same. I'm sad but happy at the same time. It's confusing." A smile breaks out across her face.

"Oh." Tamara claps her hands excitedly. "I just thought of something."

"What?" I ask at the same time as Victoria.

"The baby inside you. I know I was going to be its cool Auntie Tamara who let it get away with everything Mummy and Daddy won't, but I 'll really be this baby's aunt."

"You will." Victoria pats her still flat tummy.

"Oh my god. I hope it's a girl. I can take her shopping, and we can spend all Nicholas' money."

Nicholas puts his head in his hands and groans.

"William, help me here."

"Better a girl than a boy. If it's a boy, Uncle William will spend all Daddy's money on Lego to build with him."

"I'm doomed." Nicholas throws his hands up in the air and goes back over to his desk to resume reading the society's documentation. Tamara and Victoria continue giggling between them. I can hear something about first dates if the baby is a girl with Nicholas standing guard like a mafia hitman looking after the Don's daughter. I'm actually hoping for a little girl. After generations dominated by men, it'll be refreshing to take the family name in a different direction. Mind you, Uncle William will be standing right next to Nicholas, protecting his niece.

Tamara stretches, then yawns. I can see the tension has finally been dispelled from her body, and exhaustion is taking over.

"Why don't you go and have a nap?" I half question and half demand.

"I think I will. I could do with a shower as well." She lifts her arm and sniffs. "I'm surprised one of you hasn't already dumped me in a bath, because I smell so bad."

"I didn't think you'd appreciate it. I don't see you as a wet t-shirt competition type of lady," I tease, and she bats out at me playfully.

Victoria coughs. "Sorry to interrupt..." –She winks at us– "Tammy, can I sleep with you? I'm really tired, and I know Nicholas wants to finish looking at this document. I'm just... you know..."

"Of course..." –Tamara wraps her arm around her friend – "Sister." She tests the word on her lips, and I know from the smile reaching the corners of her eyes she enjoys it.

"See you later, ladies." I bow at them, and they leave the room. I look over to Nicholas who's got a frown on his face as he studies the documentation in front of him.

"Something wrong?" I ask and drag my chair over to his table.

"No. I just want to make sure everything is correct, and there are no possible loopholes."

"I'll read through it later. You know how pedantic I can be at times."

"Don't I just."

He tips his head toward the door.

"Bit of a shock for them both. Do you think they'll be ok?"

"We're living with two of the strongest women I know. They've been through shit and still come out the other side laughing and taking the piss out of us. They'll be absolutely fine. We need to get Elsie out of the Viscount's house as soon as possible, though. It's dangerous for her there."

"I know. I hated letting her go back. I wanted to put my foot down, but I think Tamara's stubborn streak definitely comes from her mother, and not her father."

"Oh, yes."

Nicholas opens the drawer to his desk and pulls out a bottle of whiskey and two glasses. Pouring out a glass for each of us, he hands me one, and I hold it up in a toast to his health. He does the same to me.

"I've not had a chance to ask you how you're coping with everything? There's a lot going on at the moment, and with you now having the freedom to be your own man, I wondered if you were managing ok? I've seen Tamara calm you down a few times, now." Nicholas takes a sip of his drink and then holds it to his nose, so he can inhale the honeyed scent.

"It's strange. Some days are better than others."

"I can understand that."

"The day care center was an eye opener. I realized autism is a lot more common than I originally believed. Our father often made me feel as though I was the only person with it in the world."

"I'm glad she took you."

"So am I." I place my glass down on the table. "I've been doing some research since I left. There are a number of places like that around the country. I spoke to the manager of one. He was really friendly." I pause, unsure of how to proceed with what I have to say. I don't need to worry though. My brother's always been able to read me like a book.

"You're leaving Oakfield, aren't you?" he asks – his face solemn.

"I think I need to. Maybe just for the short term It could be longer, I don't know. These four walls carry so many bad memories for me, and I need to figure out who I can be when I'm not surrounded by them."

He nods.

"You've applied for a place?"

"I have. I've been accepted as well. I can go whenever I want."

Nicholas places his own drink down on his desk.

"Whatever you need. You know I'll always support you. Just make sure it's somewhere I can visit whenever I need to get away from a pregnant wife."

"Of course."

We both stand up at the same time.

"You're my little brother, William. I'm always here for you. I know you need to discover yourself, but you'll always have a home here."

"Thank you."

Nicholas and I have never been touchy feely people, it's not how we were brought up, but the embrace complete with backslapping, which now passes between us feels right.

CHAPTER EIGHTEEN

TAMARA

"**F**or you." William puts a large wad of paper down in front of me.

"What's this?" I flip over the first few sheets and see they're bank statements. My eyes scan to the name at the top: Viscount Arthur Hamilton. "How on Earth did you get these? Actually, no, don't tell me. Everything about the code of ethics I operate under says I shouldn't even be looking at these."

"I'm sure if something has come from MI5, then it can't be deemed to be too illegal." William winks at me and sifts through the papers until he reaches a page on which he's stuck a Post-it-note. "I think it's probably a decoy, but the Viscount has been paying an amount once a week to this lady."

He produces another smaller wad of paper and puts it in front of me.

"Camilla Fentress. She's been interesting to research because she's not a real person."

"Not a real person?" I screw my nose up in confusion and scrutinize the information in front of me. Camilla's name is in bold at the top of the page. Underneath is a picture of a woman who can't be much older than twenty.

"Nope. It's a company. This is actually a photo of a woman named Lindsey Sharp, originally from Missouri. Three years ago, she traveled to Los Angeles to make her fortune, but I've discovered she never made it to LA. She disappeared and hasn't been seen or heard from since."

He flicks through the bank statements again and stops at another marked page. "This statement is from around the time when she disappeared."

I look down at the information in front of me and instantly see a cash withdrawal from an ATM in Missouri.

"The Viscount was there?"

"Yes. He was there and is now using a picture of her with a fake identity. If you ask me, something doesn't add up, and that's not just because I've got a mathematical brain."

"No. We need to research this Lindsay Sharp some more and see how she became a company called Camilla Fentress." I flick over the pages of the report William's given me on Camilla. There's nothing concrete in there to go on, yet.

"That's why I'm not just a pretty face. I've already got our contacts on it. This could be a lead on the missing girl Joanna, or it could be nothing. But I'm going to pursue it."

I reach out and take his hand.

"I think you're actually enjoying playing detective."

He shrugs.

"Maybe, a little."

A stray hair tumbles out of the small bun at the nape of my

neck. William reaches around and tucks it back in. His hand lingers at my chin, and I feel the heat of his body warm mine with desire. He leans into me and our lips meet in a quick kiss.

He pulls back. Neither of us speak – we just sit in silence, staring at each other. Sticking my tongue slightly out of my mouth, I lick what was left behind of his taste. He leans in again, but we're stopped by an abrupt knock at the door. William stands up and rearranges his trousers.

"Come in," he says as he looks wistfully over his shoulder at me.

The door opens, and the butler enters.

"My apologies, sir. The Duke and Duchess are still at their charity lunch, and there's a man here demanding to speak to either the Duke or you."

"Who is it?" William asks, and I turn back to the documentation in front of me, allowing him privacy to talk with the butler.

"It's the police, sir."

"Police?"

"Yes, sir." The butler lowers his head.

"I'll come at once."

William twists back around to face me. I can tell instantly that his anxiety is building.

"I'll come with you," I offer without hesitation.

"Thank you. You never know, I might need a lawyer."

"I'm sure it's nothing." I stand, and taking his hand, we follow the butler to the entrance of the house. I'm expecting plain clothes police officers, for some reason, but when I see they are in uniform, I can't help but feel even more uneasy.

"Hello," – William steps forward to greet the officers –

"I'm William Cavendish, Earl Lullington. How may I help you?"

"Good afternoon, My Lord. We have a um… a delicate matter we need to discuss with you." The two uniformed officers, one male and one female, look toward me. The policewoman barely looks older than eighteen.

"This happens to be my lawyer, Miss Bennett. Anything you have to say to me can be said in front of her."

"Miss Bennett…Tamara Bennett?" the female officer questions.

"Yes," William answers.

"In that case, is there somewhere more comfortable we can talk?" The male officer jerks his head toward the door to the lounge. It's as though he's trying to tell William something, but I can't quite understand what.

"Officers, if there is an issue, could you tell us please? We are very busy today," William responds and folds his arms across his chest to signify he's not moving.

"My lord, as you wish," the male officer replies and turning to his colleague, he nods at her.

"Miss Bennett. I'm sorry to inform you that we were called to an incident earlier today in Kensington Park. On arrival, we found the body of a woman. She'd been attacked, raped and murdered. I'm sorry, Miss Bennett, but from the records we have, we believe the woman was your mother, Elsie Bennett."

The sound of the officer's words rushes through my ears like the wind of a gale. I'm not quite able to take them in before I feel myself falling to the hard marble floor. I never land, though, for I'm scooped into William's arms and seated on a nearby chaise longue.

"Bring brandy!" William shouts, and I'm unable to tell him I don't need it because no words can come out. My mother is dead. Beaten and raped. I don't need to be told who the culprit was because I already know – it was Viscount Hamilton.

"Have you arrested someone for the attack?" I come back to my senses. "Viscount Hamilton, do you have him in custody?"

"I'm sorry?" the male officer questions with confusion. "Viscount Hamilton? Her employer?"

"Yes. Do you have him in custody?" I ask again through gritted teeth.

"Miss Bennett, the Viscount was the person who found her and identified the body. He's terribly distraught. From all accounts, your mother was one of his favorite employees."

"So favorite that he raped her twenty-three years ago to conceive me. I want him arrested. Now!" I shout, and William tucks me under his arm.

"My apologies. I'm afraid Miss Bennett is distraught at this news."

"I'm not distraught." I push William away. "Give them the clothes and the letter. It's my mother's proof."

"Earl Lullington?" the male officer queries, pulling out his notebook to start writing details down. Finally, they're taking me seriously. He doesn't write, though. He reads from something already entered.

"Miss Bennett. We've already taken samples of DNA from your mother. Nothing, so far, matches with that of Viscount Hamilton. He volunteered to be tested himself just in case it would help.

"No." I shake my head at them. "No. You've got it wrong. I want to see her, please."

The officer nods.

"We'll take you to the morgue, at once."

I try to stand up, but my legs are too weak. William picks me up in his arms and carries me to the police car. I'm barely thinking straight, in fact, I'm barely functioning as we speed through the streets to my mother. My mother is dead – raped and murdered. I didn't want her to go back, but she did, and now she's dead. It's my fault. I should have stopped her. Why did we have to get mixed up in this secret society in the first place? I want my mother – I want to hear her voice, and I want to know she's alright and not suffering. But it doesn't matter what I want because it can't change anything. She must have suffered so much at the end. She was hurting and in pain, and I didn't know. I couldn't stop it, and I couldn't save her. I'm crying – my tears soak through William's shirt as he holds me closer to his chest. I vaguely register us arriving at our destination and him helping me out of the car. My legs are walking, but I'm not controlling them. I'm relying on William for support because I know I'll crumble if I let go. Doors are opening, people are talking around me, but I'm not taking anything in. Nothing registers in my numb brain until I see her. She's so tiny, my mother, the only person who's ever loved me unconditionally. She's lying on a silver table with a white sheet pulled up to her neck. Her face is covered in bruises, and her lips are swollen. Her eyes are shut, and she's pale, so very pale, like a ghost, but then I suppose that's what she is now: a spirit in the ether. I can only hope she comes back to haunt Viscount Hamilton, tormenting him so much he jumps from the highest building.

"Mummy," I whisper. I want her to answer. I want her to open her eyes, but she doesn't. She's dead. She's really dead. Bringing my hand up to her cheek, I stroke it. There's still a little warmth to her flesh. "I'm sorry," I cry, the words coming out of me in ragged sobs. "I love you. I promise you I will end him."

I take one final look at my mother before returning to William who'd been waiting at the doorway to give me some time alone with her. His eyes are watery, and I know he's feeling the emotion of the situation. He wraps his arms around me, and I bury my head in his chest and allow the grief to come.

CHAPTER NINETEEN

WILLIAM

"How is she?" My brother pokes his head around the door to Tamara's bedroom and whispers quietly.

"Sleeping still. The doctor gave her a sedative," I reply and look down to where I still hold her hand, having done so for the last five hours. I helped her to change into her night-dress when we returned home from the morgue, and then I put her to bed where she's been ever since.

"He gave Victoria a mild one also. She was getting stressed, and it was affecting the baby's heartbeat. I've left her sleeping."

"It's going to be hard for them both to come to terms with this." My thumb strokes over Tamara's hand.

"I can't help but think I could have done something more to protect her. I should've had a team in place sooner." Nicholas looks tired, really tired. The guilt weighing heavily upon his shoulders. "I should've refused to allow her to go back in."

"It's not your fault. That's the one thing I've realized sitting here. Elsie was an amazing woman, and she's the reason both Tamara and Victoria have the strength they do. For her to have survived what she did that first time, and then to see her tormentor every day, knowing it's the best thing for her daughter and her daughter's half-sister, must've taken some considerable willpower. We could have banned her from returning to the Viscount, even locked her in a room, but she still would have found a way to go back. That's the sort of woman she is…was. She wanted to help Theodore." I look to where Tamara stirs and turns over in the bed to face the other way. "In her memory, we will make sure we do just that."

"Yes, we will," Nicholas responds as he pushes off from the door frame he's been leaning against. "Goodnight, Brother."

"Goodnight."

He disappears, and I'm left alone with my thoughts. They are sad and painful but defiant. I lean back in the chair, allowing my heavy eyelids to droop shut, and I fall asleep. I don't know for how long, but I'm woken by Tamara abruptly sitting up in the bed. She screams, and I know she's had a nightmare.

Bringing her into my arms, I hold her in silence while she cries. Eventually, the heartbroken sobs stop wracking her body, and she quietens in my embrace.

"William?" Her eyes flick up to mine.

"Yes?" I stroke her head as a gesture of comfort and strength.

Hi "I need to know what she felt." Tamara pulls away from me and sits on the bed with her knees tucked under her.

"What do you mean?"

"I want you to chase me...to make me run." She looks down at the bed and twists her hand in the crumpled sheets. "To take me against my will."

I leap off the bed in shock and disbelief.

"What?"

"Please."

"No." I turn my back to her, but she gets off the bed and presses her warm body to mine.

"Allow the monster out. Please, I need him."

"You don't know what you're asking of me. I could hurt you or worse." I shut my eyes, trying to block out what she's asking. I want to put my hands over my ears and shout out no until the madness goes away.

"I trust you."

"You shouldn't."

"But I do." Tamara rests her head against my back. I'm only wearing a t-shirt, and I can feel the tears she's still crying, soak into the cotton fabric. "You think your mind is dark. Well, my blood is jet black. If you're a monster, then I'm the devil's spawn. Give me what I need. You're the only person who can."

My entire body chills at her words. I know she's right. I know exactly what she needs because I feel every inch of it in my bones, and I want it as well.

Grabbing her hand tightly, I allow the walls I've built up, which hide my true nature to crumble. I stride quickly through the corridors of the house and out into the garden. Tamara follows behind me, her shorter legs running to keep up with my fast pace. We come to a halt at the edge of the patio area.

"Run," I order with an intonation so brutal she just stares at me open mouthed. "If you want this, then run. I *will* find you. If you don't, we go back up to the room and sleep until your grief no longer makes you insane."

"I don't think that will ever happen," she whimpers and looks out over the vast blackness that's beckoning to her.

"And I'll never change. This will always be in me. The tics and lack of filter are the autism. You showed me that my sexual needs are another part of who I am."

The moon appears from its hiding place behind a bank of thick clouds. It illuminates Tamara's eyes, and I see the need and desire within them. It takes my breath away.

"Just as mine are a part of me," she tells me before taking off across the lawn. I pause for a moment to wrap my head around what I'm about to do. I'm going to hunt down the woman fleeing into the shadows and take her brutally, without care for her wellbeing. I'm going to allow the monster I suppress to claw its way to the surface and take over my body, unleashing the side of me that made my father proud. The only difference is this is a game, not a way of life, and I have Tamara's consent. I might be a monster, but I'm not the monster my father was.

The realization slams into my chest, leaving me breathless, momentarily, but then I see a flash of the woman I need through the moonlight's glow. My legs carry me after her, and the thrill of the chase is exhilarating. I reach the body of trees that lead into a woodland on our property, and I know she's in here. It's somewhere we walked the other day, and she commented on how it felt like a sanctuary. She wants all her illusions of protection shattered.

"I know you're in here," I growl and step forward into the

darkness. I allow my hearing to take over in place of my sight. A twig cracks off to my left, and as I turn toward the sound, she's standing there with her eyes full of fear. I no longer have mercy running through my veins. She takes off running, but it doesn't take me long to catch up, and wrapping my arms around her, I lift her up into the air. She's so small and delicate in my hands. I could break her so easily. She's swinging her legs, trying to kick out at me, so I pin her up face first against a tree with her back toward me

"You wanted a monster. Well, now you've got one. Remember this. You asked for it, you cunt."

My erection is hard in my trousers, and I grind it against her bottom. She's pleading with me to stop but at the same time moaning her urgent need. I use my body weight to hold her in place and allow my rough hands to trace under the hem of her nightdress. I bunch it up around her hips, and she shivers when the cool air of the night hits her sensitive flesh. I don't give her any warning of my next movement and treat her just like the slut she's pretending to be. I kick her legs apart and propel three thick fingers into her core. She screams at the violent intrusion.

"No." Her skin pimples at the cold but also with the sensation of need tumbling through her body. She's an enigma of contradictions, at the moment. Need, desire, fear, and terror all combined into one yearning vessel.

"You are going to take everything I give you." I twist my fingers and thrust them in and out of her. She's dripping wet and coats me in her essence.

Reaching behind herself, she claws at my arm with her perfectly manicured nails.

"Bitch." I suck in a breath and add a fourth finger to

intensify the stretching she feels at her entrance. My movements become faster and faster as I fuck her with my hand. My dick strains against the zipper of my trousers, desperately wanting out. It needs to bury itself balls deep in her tight little pussy.

"Stop," she cries underneath me, but even I can tell it's halfhearted. The flush of heat over her skin, and the tightening of the walls of her pussy around my fingers, tell me she's on the verge of an orgasm. I pull my hand away, and she lets out a long wail at the loss.

Leaning into her, I trail my tongue up the side of her face.

"This isn't about you getting off. Sluts don't get to come unless I say so." I jerk my hips toward her, so my hard shaft pokes her. "Do you know what happens next?"

"Please…" The whimpers are coming thick and fast, now. "Please…please don't hurt me."

"Too late, this monster's never retreating now. It's all about claiming what's his. You're. Mine. Forever."

I bring the fingers I've just had inside her up to her mouth, and I dip one inside. I feel her start to test the power of her teeth against my digit, and in the darkness surrounding us, I give her an ultimatum.

"Bite it, and I'll take you in the ass."

Her teeth retract, and I pull my finger out of her mouth. Lowering my hands to my trousers, I unzip them and pull out my hard length. I stroke it a few times, smearing the precum at the head over the entire length. I don't think I've ever been as hard as I am right now.

"You know what girls like you get?" I ask.

"No," she cries.

"Hard and fast."

Before she has a chance to realize what I'm doing, I've thrust forward, bottoming out within her. My dick is now shrouded by her heat, and my mind flips completely as the dark mist clouding my brain, wraps around both of us, entwining us together. Two figures, in the dead of night, taking what they need from each other. My hips buck wildly as I withdraw and slam hard back into her. She'll feel me there constantly for the next few days.

"Please!" Tamara's screaming, her voice hoarse with the tears she's shed and the crying out she's been doing since I captured her. I know her last vestiges of control are hanging on a knife's edge. She needs one more thing to send her flying. With my nose, I nudge the material of her nightdress to the side, and as I bite down on her shoulder, her pussy clenches tighter around my dick, and she explodes in my arms. A powerful orgasm causing her body to shudder and shake under me as my own orgasm bursts from my balls and out of my dick to coat her insides.

Eventually, we are both still with me inside her, and my teeth embedded in her shoulder. My dick jerks, occasionally, but we remain silent in the shadows of the trees while far off in the distance, a church clock strikes midnight.

Tamara's legs give way, and I slip out of her and take her gently down onto the ground to protect her from a bad fall. She turns in my arms to face me. Speckles of moonlight through the branches of the trees illuminate her face.

"Thank you." She shuts her eyes. All her tears drying up. "This isn't wrong." Her eyes open, again, and I see honesty and happiness in them. They are tired and still edged with the grief she feels, but contentment is there. "We both consented, and that is the difference. The darkness is a part of us both, and it won't ever disappear. We just needed to find the right person to share it with."

Leaning forward, I press a soft, almost too tender kiss to her lips.

"Monsters together."

"Forever."

CHAPTER TWENTY

TAMARA

he sheets are twisted around my legs, and I kick out to free them. The friction between my thighs causes me to moan with the pain I feel down there, and I shift carefully, knowing I'm going to feel tender for a few days. The bed next to me dips, and I open my eyes to see William.

"Water and painkillers. You'll need them."

I groan and close my eyes again. Memories of the day before flood back: my mother's death, seeing her body in the morgue so broken and bruised, and being chased and caught by William in the forests of the Oakfield estate. My shoulder hurts from where he sunk his teeth into the flesh there, and I'm not looking forward to peeing because my lady parts are so sore, even the flats of my feet feel torn apart.

"Why do you have to have such a big dick?" I pout, needing to distract myself from my mother's death. If I let the grief overwhelm me, I won't be able to channel the anger I have into destroying Viscount Hamilton.

"I was born with it." William chuckles, and I hear him place the water and tablets down before wrapping his arms around my shoulders and pulling me up in the bed.

"Ouch, ouch, ouch." I squirm and open my eyes to glare at him.

"Stop being a baby." He opens my mouth, pops the tablets in, and hands me the water to help swallow.

"A baby!" I cough as one of them gets stuck in my throat. I hate taking medicine.

"Yes." He raises his eyebrow.

"You want me to tell Victoria you called me that?" I retort with a smug smirk on my face. "I swear she's going to go after your balls today. I can't believe she saw you carrying me back to my room!"

William grumbles and gets to his feet to take a sip from a cup of a coffee he must have brought for himself along with the water for me.

"I'll get Nicholas to give her stronger sedatives next time. I like my balls where they are."

I laugh and then realize the words he chose.

"There will be a next time?"

William stops drinking midway with his cup to his mouth. He places it down on my bedside table and climbs into the bed with me. He shifts me effortlessly, like a rag doll to his needs, so I'm sitting across his lap. Part of me likes it, but part of me wishes he wasn't all toned and muscular. I need a softer cushion similar to the memory foam mattress I've been sleeping on. He must sense my discomfort and tucks me into his side instead.

"Do you want another time?"

"Not right now, but yes."

"Ok, we'll do it again, but no sex for you until your fully healed. I'll just have to stick my dick in your mouth for now."

I must stare at him blankly because a mischievous smirk crosses his face.

"Only if we both agree and consent," I retort as he kisses the tip of my nose and says,

"Always."

I lean into his chest, listening to the beat of his heart.

"How are you feeling?" William questions and fresh tears prick in my eyes. I shouldn't be this happy when I have my mother's funeral to arrange.

"Numb, I think. I'm happy I'm here with you, but I still can't believe she's gone. My mother, my beautiful, wonderful, caring Mummy. I'll never get to speak to her again. Who will I ask for advice?"

"She'll still be there for you if you need her."

"How?"

"Something my brother told me when our mother died. I was upset because I needed her, having fallen over and scraped my knee. I cried for her to help me. My father got frustrated and stormed off, but Nicholas kneeled down next to me and told me that if I ever needed my mother, I just had to talk to her. She was an angel and although I'd never get to see her again, she was always there for me because angels were allowed to walk the Earth to help those they love. I stifled my tears and started talking out loud, asking her to take the pain away. It may have been the wind, but I'm almost certain I felt her blow on my knee, and it immediately stopped hurting."

"That's beautiful. I've always believed something similar. I'll miss her every day." My voice cracks, and William squeezes me a little tighter to him. "But I know she's here with me."

"Just not when we're having sex," William adds.

I can't help but let laughter engulf me. It's needed.

"What?" William huffs, not realizing the bluntness of his words. "That's just a no-no."

"I promise. My mother will shut her eyes when we're having sex."

I pull myself up from his chest, so I can bring my lips to his.

"Tamara."

Victoria's hammering on my bedroom door while at the same time she's shouting in a shrill voice.

"Are you decent? I'm coming in."

William jumps up off the bed and stands beside it with his hand cupped hard over his manhood.

"She's not getting my balls."

"Victoria, I said you're not going." Nicholas' stern tones come through the door next.

"Fuck you," Victoria responds and without waiting for me to invite her in, she opens the door and storms in. She grabs my discarded jeans and jumper from the previous day and throws them at me.

"Put them on."

"Victoria, I said no." Nicholas grabs her arm while trying to reason with her.

"And I told you to fuck off with the rules and regulations. I don't give a shit about them, right now. All I care about is seeing him arrested," Victoria adamantly spits words at her husband.

"She consented," William mutters from the other side of the bed to the warring husband and wife.

"What?" Victoria turns toward her brother-in-law and screws her tiny little nose up in confusion.

"Tamara consented. It was mutual between us. You can't have me arrested," William protests his case, and I open my mouth to agree with him.

Victoria shakes her head, though, "I'm not having you arrested, you great lummox. Whatever you did to Tamara left her with the same goofy look on her face Nicholas gets after I suck his dick. I knew she was happy and had consented. No, this is about my father. Our father."

I shuffle gingerly forward in the bed.

"What about him?"

"I don't know all the details, but the police are going to bring him in for questioning." Victoria makes a hurrying motion with her hands, and I pull my jumper on over the clean nightdress William put me in last night.

"On what charges? My mother's murder?"

"We don't know," Nicholas replies and quickly turns around to give me privacy when Victoria pulls the covers away from the lower half of my body. "All I know is that the police are on the way to bring him in for questioning on a matter of importance. The fact they are going to collect him and not allow him to surrender himself at a police station, suggests it's likely to be for a criminal offense of a serious nature."

"Yes, it will be." I hold my breath, not daring to believe that maybe the Viscount actually made a mistake when he killed my mother and will be charged with her murder.

"Do we have my mother's letter and DNA evidence? We might need to present it to strengthen the case."

"It's in safekeeping. If it comes to it, I'll make sure it finds its way into police hands," Nicholas confirms.

"Put some shoes on," Victoria interrupts. "We don't have much time, and I don't want to miss this."

"Miss what?" William asks the question also on my mind.

"Duh!" Victoria rolls her eyes and throws my trainers at me, narrowly missing my head. "Seeing my father get arrested. We're going to Hamilton Manor. I wouldn't miss this for the world."

"No, you aren't," Nicholas grinds out through clenched teeth.

"Again, husband dearest, fuck you." Victoria smiles at him, and Nicholas raises an eyebrow at her, daring her to test him further. "I'm not missing this. I deserve it for all the years he closeted me away like a hermit, then sacrificed me without a second thought."

"He gave you to me?" Nicholas reminds her of how they came to find love.

"No, he gave me away for his advancement in the society."

"I think we should go," William adds. He's already slipping his feet into a pair of socks and shoes. "If Viscount Hamilton's getting arrested, I want to see it as well."

"I want to go too." I say, pulling on my trainers.

Nicholas throws his hands up in the air.

"Am I the only one with any sanity?" He shakes his head and stomps back toward the door. "I'll call for the car."

The journey to Victoria's and my childhood home is completed in tense silence. All of us willing the car to go quicker, so we can witness Viscount Hamilton being arrested. When we pull up the driveway, there are several other cars already parked. Some are marked police cars, and the others, I suspect, are unmarked ones.

William helps me out of the car at the same time as Theodore descends the steps of the manor house with a smartly dressed older man.

"A lawyer, just what my father needs," Theodore addresses me while shooting daggers toward William and Nicholas.

"Will this be your father's defense barrister?" The smartly dressed man asks. "I'm Detective Inspector French."

"No," I reply instantly. "Prosecution, maybe, but it'll be a cold day in hell before I'll defend him on any charges."

"Have they taken him yet?" Victoria asks her brother. I know she's nervous to see the man who gave her away like a chattel, but she holds herself upright with all the decorum of her new position as the Duchess of Oakfield.

Theodore shakes his head. "I don't know what hold they have over you, Victoria, and you Tamara, but whatever it is has gone too far. False allegations against our father of tax avoidance. It's ludicrous."

"Tax avoidance?" Victoria and I both say at the same time.

"But what about murdering my mother?" I step forward, and the detective motions to some of the uniformed officers to be prepared in case things turn nasty.

"Murder?" Theodore exclaims with utter indignation.

"You want criminals, Detective? Then look no further than the Cavendish brothers. They are guilty of brainwashing, abuse, and god knows what else. They've turned perfectly intelligent women into lunatics. My father did not kill your mother. You want a culprit then, maybe, look closer to home."

"He raped her. I'm your sister," I spit at him.

"Detective, I want these people off my property."

"It's just as much my property as it is yours," Victoria counters.

"No it's not, Sister. Our father has more intelligence than the lot of you put together. He knew something like this would happen, so he signed everything over to me. Right before he disappeared."

"Disappeared?" I feel my legs wobble, and William is there behind me, holding me up.

"Yes. I've not seen him since the night your mother was murdered. He's been threatened by the Cavendish brothers for some time now. I know they killed their own father to take over the title, and I'll not stop until I see them rotting in jail for what they've done. Now, I want you off my property. All of you."

Theodore storms back up the steps of Hamilton Manor and slams the front door firmly shut behind him. The police officers give us funny looks and start to mill back toward their cars – all but the senior detective.

"Interesting," he says, rubbing his beard and resting a hand over his rotund stomach.

"I think I might have a new case to investigate besides the one against Viscount Hamilton." He bows his head, recognizing Nicholas' status as the Duke. "Your Grace, Earl Lullington, I'm sure this won't be the last you'll see me, assuming Lord Hamilton's accusations are true. If this young lady is a lawyer, you might want to start working with her on your defenses."

As the detective walks away, Victoria slides down onto the steps leading up to our hated former home. Defeat is written all over her face.

"He's got away with it," I announce– almost in a dream-like state.

William pulls me into him.

"Not yet. He may have won this round, but I'm not stopping now. That's one of the good things about autistic people. Once we get a hard-on for something, we don't give up on it easily."

CHAPTER TWENTY ONE

WILLIAM

"And now to him who is able to keep us from
    falling,
and lift us from the dark valley of despair
to the bright mountain of hope,
from the midnight of desperation
to the daybreak of joy;
to him be power and authority, for ever and
    ever.
Amen."

Tamara picks up a handful of soil from the ground and follows the priest by throwing it on top of her mother's coffin. She leans back into me as Victoria does the same with her little piece of earth. We say goodbye one final time and turn away, back to Oakfield Hall. There was, initially, some debate as to where Tamara's mother should be buried until Nicholas suggested she could have the vacant plot next to our mother – the one my father should've had his body buried in when he died. Instead, we'd had his body cremated, and we'd flushed the contents of the urn down the toilet. It seemed a really fitting tribute to the woman who was considered to be not only a surrogate mother to the current Duchess of Oakfield, but also the actual mother of the woman for whom my feelings are increasing in intensity the more time I spend in her company.

Tamara's fragile, at the moment, and we have good days and bad together. She's frustrated that Viscount Hamilton disappeared as are Nicholas, Victoria, and I. But we all know we can't let this set-back stop our ultimate goal, which is to destroy all that remains of the previous Oakfield Society. It will happen – along with the downfall of Viscount Hamilton. It's just going to take a while longer than we expected.

"Anyone want a drink?" Nicholas asks as we enter the lounge.

"Please," I reply and escort Tamara over to the sofa. Victoria takes a seat on the high-backed armchair she's taken a preference to, and Nicholas tucks a blanket over her lap to keep her warm before going to prepare three brandies. He calls down to the kitchen to request hot chocolate for Victoria.

"To Ms. Elsie Bennett" – he raises his cup when we all have drinks in hand – "a woman whose courage and fortitude knew no bounds. I'll be forever grateful to her for imparting some of that to my beautiful wife. Even if she uses it to bust my balls on occasion."

Victoria snorts a wry smile and holds her hot chocolate up.

"To my nanny and surrogate mother. I'll miss you every day, but I'll make sure this little one"–she runs her empty hand over her stomach– "knows all about you. Thank you."

I hold my glass up next. I don't have much to say, just a few words. "Thank you for giving me Tamara. She really is your greatest gift. I promise I'll protect her for you."

Tamara stares blankly into her brandy, and we all wait for her to find the words she wants to say.

She pushes up onto her feet.

"I could rant and rave and say I'll avenge your death. That I won't rest until the Viscount is rotting behind bars or better yet dismembered and rotting in the ground, but I'm not going to. I'm just going to share my first memory of you." She shuts her eyes and licks her lips to steady herself. As always, I'm close to her, ready to catch her should she fall. "My greatest time spent with you was always in the kitchens. I don't know how you stood to be in them after what happened to you there, but I guess I gave you new memories, ones to replace the horror. I always remember the day you tried to teach me how to prepare the meal your father had taught you. His mother's recipe for pineapple sandwiches. You took the bread and placed on to it a slice of ham and one of those round rings of pineapple from a can. We then smothered it in cheese and put it under the grill until all the cheese was melted. The chef was a stuck-up bastard, and he was horrified we were preparing such mundane food in his kitchen, but I loved it. My favorite meal in the world." She laughs, but it catches in her throat, turning into a sob. "Always. I'll always be your daughter, and he will die for what he did." Bringing the brandy glass up to her mouth, she drinks the burning nectar down in one long steady gulp before placing the empty glass back down onto the table in front of her. "William, I'm tired. Will you come sleep with me for a while?"

She looks straight at me, and I know we'll be doing anything but sleeping when we go to our bedroom. It's what she needs, though, and who am I to deny my woman? I've been doing a lot of thinking over the last few days. I've put a halt on my acceptance at the autistic home, mainly because Tamara can't join me there and the thought of being away from her breaks me out in a cold sweat. I've also come to realize it's not my autism causing the darkness within me – it's the result of my upbringing, and my father's influence. However, it's also something a part of me enjoys. The difference is now I can control it, and I know I won't murder or destroy a woman just because I can. I'll always have oddities because my brain is wired differently, but Tamara brings the best out in me. I was locked away for so many years, and although the world outside of Oakfield Hall is terrifying as hell, I want to see it. I want to go on a plane, a boat, even a train – experience things I never have before. I'm not sure about having to queue to do it, but I want to try. I want to be as normal as I can. That's what the children at the day care center had, and it showed me I could have it too. A warm feeling settles in my chest, but it's swiftly replaced by a swelling in my groin when Tamara winks at me.

"Of course." Taking her hand, I lead her to my bedroom.

"Is this wrong?" she asks as our lips meet, and I'm ripping her smart, black suit from her body.

"Do you want it?"

"Yes," she whispers breathlessly. "I need to feel. I want to lose myself in your taste and touch, so I don't have to think."

I step back from her. I've totally destroyed her clothes, and she's standing before me in a black bra and matching thong. Fuck, she's sexy as hell. Part of me feels it's wrong to be doing this so soon after burying her mother, but I know Tamara needs it. She needs to forget in order to start living and breathing again, and this is the only way. We've not done anything since the night in the forest – just spent our nights together in each other's arms.

I allow my monster to take over, and as I transition, I realize, for the first time, that even as a monster I'm still the same person because it's who I am. I like the wild side. I pick a cushion up off the chair beside me and drop it onto the floor at my feet.

"On your knees," I order, and Tamara licks her lips.

I unbuckle my suit trousers, pull down the zipper, and lower them along with my underpants to my feet. Tamara kneels in front of my dick as it springs out, ready for her succulent little mouth to wrap itself around it. As a couple, we are a contradiction in terms. Sometimes she's bossy and looks after me, and sometimes it's the other way around. But here in the bedroom, I'm always in control, and I couldn't give a fuck if anyone says I'm weak because I let her rule me elsewhere. They aren't about to get their dick sucked by the hottest woman in the world.

"Open," I demand, and she does so without question. "I've been on edge for a few days. My poor dick, spending its night lying next to that pussy of yours but not being able to get inside. I'm going to take your mouth. Claim it. I won't be gentle. I'll make you gag, but you'll take every inch of me."

Fuck, I nearly shoot my load, there and then, when she circles her tongue around her partially open lips in anticipation.

I stroke up and down my length a few times before pushing it in between her plump, pink lips. Her mouth is wet and warm with the still lingering effect of the brandy, caressing me with its heat. I push all the way in until I hit the back of her throat, and she gags. Damn, it's beautiful. Her eyes widen when she realizes I really won't take this easy on her. I pull my hips back and slam back in again.

"This is my hole to fuck. I'm going to do so while you swallow me deep until I come down your throat."

I allow the speed of my hips to increase and wrap her hair around my hand, so I can keep her head still. Saliva pools in Tamara's mouth as she remains helpless to the onslaught. I piston in and out of her mouth like a jackhammer. Her eyes water and tears fall from them, but they're not the same as the ones she shed earlier. These are tears of a woman being taken and worshipped by her man. I know I won't last long, because this feeling is just too good. Tamara tries to swirl her tongue around my dick as I push in and out, but I'm wide in girth, and there's too little room for her to do anything other than take what I give. Her hands come up and rest on my taut thighs, but she applies no pressure to stop me. It's merely to steady herself. My balls draw up, and I know the end is near for me. I want to stop time in this very moment and remember it forever. Once I've emptied myself, I plan on ensuring Tamara is pleasured and will be walking with a strange gait tomorrow. My orgasm races up through my shaft, and I bury myself deep inside Tamara's mouth and throat. I hold her head so tightly the roots of her hair must be burning with pain as I come with a loud moan of her name. Spurt after spurt of my cum shoots down her throat, which is working overtime to swallow everything, including my dick that's so far down it's constricting her breathing. After what feels like an eternity, probably for both of us, I pull out, and she collapses on the ground, breathing air into her parched lungs. My dick doesn't soften – it wants more.

"I'm not finished yet." I grab her and throw her onto the bed, and in one swift movement, I'm inside her pussy. "Not at all. I plan on spending the next few hours in my cunt. Reminding it that it's mine. You wanted the monster in me, Tamara, and now you've got him because he's fallen in love with you."

She gasps at my words, and I pause in my thrusts.

"Love?" she breathlessly utters.

"Love," I reply, not needing to hear it from her if she isn't ready to give me the actual words yet. The way her pussy is already clenching around my dick tells me all I need to know, for now.

CHAPTER TWENTY TWO

TAMARA

"I won't be long. I'm just going to drop these papers off at court, and then I'll be back. You stay in bed…keep it warm for when I return." I lean in to kiss a sleepy William's lips as he lies in the bed we've shared every night since my mother's funeral, almost two months ago. He was up late last night, returning another one of the art pieces the society had stolen. It's the last one to be returned, for now. The rest have been hidden away deep in the Oakfield vault and are likely to remain there for some time, yet. It's a shame the valuable pieces won't be seen, but the risk to Nicholas and William from their breaking and entering is becoming too much. Security is tighter, and if they are caught, it is highly unlikely I'd be able to get a custodial sentence of anything less than twenty to thirty years for them both. It's a life time, and one Victoria and I are not prepared to spend without them.

"Don't go alone," William murmurs as his eyes drift shut again.

"I won't. I've got one of Nicholas' bodyguards coming with me."

"Good." He turns over in the bed and before long is softly snoring again. I made a spur-of-the-moment decision to do this, last night, while I was finishing the documentation I needed, and I managed to get an appointment with a judge I admire. I haven't actually spoken to Nicholas, but I have spoken to his driver who'll sort it all out for me. I stop, for a few moments, and watch William – I've been so lucky to find him. We are both very different from each other, but that's what makes us so strong together. Sometimes he's the controlling one, and sometimes, maybe, I am. It allows us both to get exactly what we need from our relationship, and it's only going from strength to strength. Between my thigh's throbs at the thought of the heights of ecstasy he can bring me to. I think maybe later I'll ask him to chase me through the forest again – I want it rough and dirty tonight. I can't get enough.

I reach for my Mulberry briefcase, sitting ready on the top of the sideboard, and place it over my shoulder. I open the heavy oak door to the bedroom, quietly, hoping it doesn't squeak on its antique hinges and wake William again. I breathe a sigh of relief when I'm out of the room, and I take the stairs down to the front door at a skip. The driver's waiting in the hallway for me.

"Good morning, Miss Bennett." He bows his head at me out of courtesy.

"Good morning," I reply.

"I've had the car running to warm it up. It's below zero out there at the moment. I think we could get snow later."

"I bet the Oakfield grounds are pretty when it snows."

"They are. I remember the current Duke and Earl running around and building snowmen as boys. It was good to see."

"You've worked here a long time, then."

I place my bag on the ground, and he hands me a thick overcoat to put on while he collects my bag and then waits for me to finish doing up the buttons on the coat.

"Almost thirty years."

"You don't look old enough."

"I don't know. Days when the wind is this cold, I certainly feel it." The driver laughs as he opens the front door and escorts me to the waiting car where I slide into the back seat. It's lovely and warm when I get in, and I immediately start to undo my coat.

"That's the thing I hate about this weather. It's on and off with coats all the time."

"Tell me about it." He removes his thick jacket and places it on the passenger seat. The car pulls away before I have a chance to register that we don't have one of Nicholas' guards in the vehicle with us.

"Aren't we supposed to have a bodyguard with us?" I lean forward and query.

"In the vehicle behind." The driver looks in the mirror, and I turn my head to see a black Range Rover following us.

"Good."

I settle back into my car for the journey into London. I'm going straight to the highest authority with the papers I want signing, and then I'm meeting with a friend of mine at the criminal courts in the Old Bailey. Opening my bag, I pull out the sheets of paper to check them one final time. I become engrossed in the information, knowing the contents will help to freeze the assets of some of the key conspirators within the society who still want it to be run the old-fashioned way. It's not going to happen. Once these are filed, Nicholas and William will be fully in control of the new Oakfield Society and can start to run it the way they want. We spent the other night discussing ideas, and they have so many great ones. The Oakfield Society will become synonymous with helping people, especially woman. Not destroying them.

When I look up from my papers, I expect to see the sights of London around me, but I don't. It's still countryside.

"Are we going a different way?" I ask the driver, but he doesn't reply. He simply flicks a switch on the dashboard, and all the doors lock around me. The skin on the back of my neck pricks, and I know I'm in trouble. I reach into my bag and look for my phone but it's not there. I'm certain I put it in there this morning – I remember doing it. "Please, stop the car," I say to the driver, but he doesn't reply. He puts his foot down, and we go a little faster. I lean forward, again, and see my phone in a compartment between the two front seats. He must have taken it out of my bag. I make a grab for it, but he's quicker.

"Sit down, Miss Bennett," he orders.

"What are you doing?"

"Making sure you don't destroy what I spent most of my life working hard to help build."

I turn around in my seat and start to wave at the vehicle behind us, containing the bodyguard. The driver laughs, an eerie cackle, which brings bile to my throat.

"Wave all you want. They aren't Nicholas' bodyguards. They're helping me bring you in to him."

"Him?" I question but don't get a response. "Turn this car around and take me back to Oakfield Hall. I will see the brothers pay you handsomely to disappear. You won't get into any trouble from whoever is paying you to take me."

"Do you think I'm stupid? The brothers will kill me and drop my body parts around the country as a warning to others. No. It's going to be your parts delivered, not mine."

The car turns left, and we drive up what looks like a deserted road at the end of which is a small house. Trying to stay calm, I think of what I need to do and look for ways to escape, but my stomach is tied in knots. I'm struggling with the emotions flooding through me because all I can think is… Will I see my father when the doors to the house open? Is he the one who's come for me? I don't think I'm ready to face him, yet. I can't. I can't know what he did to my mother. I shut my eyes and whisper in my head for William. I know he can't hear me, but I want to believe he can.

The car comes to a halt, and the driver unlocks the doors. I make the split-second decision I need to run for it, and thrusting the door open, I'm out of the car and running as fast as my legs can take me. I wish it was William chasing me and this was a game, but I know it isn't. Men shout behind me, and footsteps thunder in pursuit. I don't know how I'm keeping in front of them. It's sheer determination. I can see the road, and I know there were houses as we pulled in. If I can make it to one of them, I'll be safe. I will my legs to propel me faster, and they do. I lost my smart shoes ages ago, and I'm now running bare foot. I can see a house – it's there in front of me, my sanctuary, my safety. I'm going to make it, but a hand wraps around my waist, and I'm hoisted back-ward. I go to scream, but another hand slams over my mouth. No. No! I'm dragged back toward where the car is parked as my sanctuary disappears into the horizon. My legs kick furiously, connecting with solid matter, and I sink my teeth into the hand over my mouth.

"Fucking bitch!" a man shouts, and he drops me to the ground. I'm pushing myself up ready to run again, but he kicks me in the stomach with his heavy snow boot so hard all the air is expelled from me. A fist meets my face, and the pain shatters through me. The fist connects again, and then the boot repeats its action only this time higher and in my ribs. I hear them crack.

"Enough," an authoritative voice orders.

"The bitch drew blood," the man who'd been hitting me protests.

"And I'll give you time with her to punish her, later. First, we have business to conduct, and I need her as conscious as possible for that."

My head is spinning from the assault, but I try to focus on where the commanding voice is coming from. Is it my father? I can't distinguish the inflections, because of the ringing in my ear.

"Get her inside. Remove her clothes and strap her up. It's time for me to have fun and destroy the Cavendish brothers, forever."

I'm lifted up, my head flopping uncontrollably as I try to maintain consciousness. Behind me, I see figures as I'm carried like a rag doll into the house, but everything is blurry. I can't see who gives the orders, a flash of blue swipes in front of my face and words flood into my ears.

"Don't worry, Tamara. I'll make this as painful for you as possible."

It's then I realize who holds me, and I know I won't make it out alive.

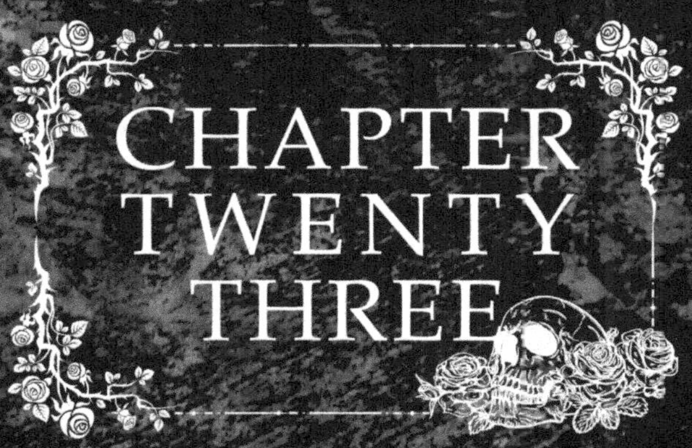

CHAPTER TWENTY THREE

WILLIAM

"Are you getting up today, you lazy ass?" My brother throws a pillow at my head, and I reach out, grab it, and hurl it back at him.

"Sleeping," I groan

"It's two o'clock in the afternoon!"

That wakes me up.

"What?"

"You sleep any longer, and you won't sleep tonight."

"Thanks, Mum!" I roll my eyes at my brother and sit up in the bed.

"Where's Tamara? She was supposed to wake me up when she got back from court."

"Court?" my brother asks, his brows crossed in confusion.

"Yeah. You gave her a bodyguard to take with her."

"No. I wasn't aware she was going anywhere. I've been with Victoria all morning. She's so bloody horny all the time I think my dick's getting chafed." Nicholas smiles smugly.

"She told me you gave her a bodyguard."

"Did you dream it? You do sometimes get confused." The tension in the room thickens as we both try to make sense of where Tamara is.

"No. She definitely told me that. I'm sure." I reach over to the night stand and pick up my mobile. Using the fingerprint reader, I open it and call Tamara. It rings and rings before going to voicemail. I try again, but there's still no answer.

"Get up, and we'll go search the house. I'm sure she's here, somewhere. Probably working away and paying no attention to the phone."

"Ok." Nicholas turns around to allow me to get out of the bed and put some clothes on. I throw on a pair of jogging bottoms and a t-shirt from yesterday. I'll worry about being clean later when I know where Tamara is. My mind is confused, and I can't fully understand what's happening. Tiredness and overstimulation are combining to make me forgetful. I'm trying to focus, but it's not possible at the moment.

"We'll find her." Nicholas must sense my worry, for he places his hand on my shoulder. "I'll check the house. You go down to her mother's grave and see if she's there."

The short walk to where Tamara's mother and my mother lie side by side, seems to take an eternity. I know instantly she's not there and hasn't been recently because a light covering of snow has fallen on the ground, and there are no footprints. I stand between the two graves and place my hands on top of them.

"Look after her, wherever she is."

I head back to the house, kick my boots off by the patio doors, and remain standing there when I see Victoria sitting on the sofa, chewing nervously at her nails.

"Was she there?"

I shake my head. Nicholas appears, and worry lines mar his face.

"Did you find her?"

"No, and my driver is also missing. The butler said Tamara left with him early this morning. He didn't know where they were going. If he did, he would have informed one of us immediately."

"Oh god." Victoria covers her mouth with her hand.

Nicholas takes his mobile from the table, next to where Victoria sits, and dials a number. He puts the phone on speaker while it rings, but it goes to the driver's voicemail.

"Try Tamara's again?" he suggests with trepidation lacing his normally calm tones.

I pull my phone from my pocket and call Tamara with bated breath. I will her to answer, but when it goes to voicemail, I gulp and try to moisten my rapidly drying throat. Something is wrong… seriously wrong.

"Would she have her phone turned off if she's in court?" Victoria asks, trying to find a reason for her not answering.

"Maybe, but my driver wouldn't. He's expected to always answer his phone. If he doesn't, he's fired. It's in the contract my father made him sign, and I've not renegotiated it yet." Nicholas' response burns down that theory. "I'm going to call in some people I know, see if we can get a track on her phone." He starts typing a short message into his phone while Victoria and I both watch him. My hand comes up to my head and swipes across my ear then my nose. I'm anxious, and that does nothing for the mis-wiring in my head. My other hand forms a fist then relaxes before forming a fist again.

"She's tough. We'll find her." Victoria appears beside me, leaning in to give me comfort, and I wrap my arm around her shoulders. Nicholas looks up from his phone, and his face immediately goes white as a sheet.

"Move!" he shouts, and he's running for us just as the wall and door behind us explode in a hail of glass and bricks. I can't believe what I'm seeing when a car comes speeding in. I grab Victoria and throw her out of the way toward Nicholas and dive sideways, managing to narrowly avoid being hit as the car slams to a halt in the center of our lounge.

"Nicholas." I'm on my feet and coughing due to the debris and dust in the room. I hear another masculine cough, and Nicholas gets to his feet. The butler and some of the other staff run into the room.

"Ok," Nicholas informs me.

"Victoria?"

"Safe," she replies, but I know from the blood dripping down the side of her head she's not uninjured. She places her hand on her stomach and groans.

"Get me a doctor," Nicholas shrieks, and people start running around like crazy.

"I'm ok." Victoria says as her legs give way. Nicholas sweeps her up, and we hurriedly leave the room. I think I pulled something in my left leg when I leaped out of the way of the moving car because I'm limping, and my calf muscle is painful.

Nicholas puts Victoria down in the hallway. He's examining her body.

"The baby?" he asks.

"Ok. It's kicking. I think it's angry," Victoria reassures him.

"Thank god."

He tilts her head back and scrutinizes the cut on her forehead. "It doesn't look too bad. I'll get the doctor to look at it."

He motions to one of the maids.

"Take the Duchess to her room, help her change, and then put her to bed."

"Nicholas, I'm not a child. We need to find Tamara."

"No arguments. You've got our child in there, and if it's kicking you because it's angry, you need to rest to placate it."

"Seriously?"

"Yes."

"Ok. Keep me informed of everything, though."

"I will." Victoria kisses her husband and disappears up the stairs with the maid who's supporting her on her unsteady legs.

"You ok?" Nicholas asks me and nods down to where I'm flexing my painful leg.

"Yes. I think I pulled something," I reply and perform a calf stretch.

"It didn't hit you?"

"No. Narrowly missed. What the fuck, though?" I look into the room where the dust still billows out.

"My thoughts exactly. I better call the police." Nicholas rubs his dusty hand over his head and hair, leaving it with a grey sheen.

The door to the lounge opens, and the butler comes out. We don't need him to speak to know something is seriously wrong and not just because there's a car sitting pride of place in the lounge where our sofa once was.

"Your Grace, I think you need to see this before you call the authorities."

Nicholas and I file into the room behind the butler. We make our way over the discarded bricks, being careful not to catch ourselves on shards of glass. The dust is starting to settle but is likely to linger in the air for a long time to come. My cough is triggered again.

We step nearer to the car, and I see instantly through the smashed glass of the windscreen why the butler was so worried. The body of our dead driver sits there with the word traitor carved into his forehead. Half of his skull is missing where it's obviously been shot away by a gun. I'm looking behind him for Tamara, but the back seat is empty except for her phone.

"Do you hear noise?" Nicholas questions, and I listen carefully. I can hear voices, and they're coming from Tamara's phone. I reach into the vehicle carefully and retrieve it.

"Hello?" I speak into it.

"About time." A deep toned voice I instantly recognize comes through, and the phone beeps. I pull it away from my ear and note a request for a FaceTime call. My finger trembles as I press it. Tamara's face appears on the screen. It's bruised and blood drips from her lip. The phone camera pulls away, and I see she's naked and tied to a bed. Her arms and legs are secured by chains.

"What have you done?" I ask with my voice quivering.

"Nothing yet. I hope you like my little gift. Your driver was so easy to manipulate, you need to watch your staff better. I gave him the send-off a traitor deserves though. Can't have him reporting this to the police, now, can we?" The phone swings away from Tamara and onto the face of my old companion. The man who I've shared women with, Lord West. "But you know exactly what I'm capable of. I warned you both. I told you to leave me alone. Now, I'll force you to."

He turns the phone back to Tamara, and I watch as a bucket of water is thrown over her to revive her. She screams out with wild eyes when she realizes what's happening. The caller hangs up before I'm able to speak to her.

Nicholas takes the phone from my hands.

"William?"

I don't hear him, though, as I allow the darkness in my mind free rein. Lord West wants the monster. He's going to get him!

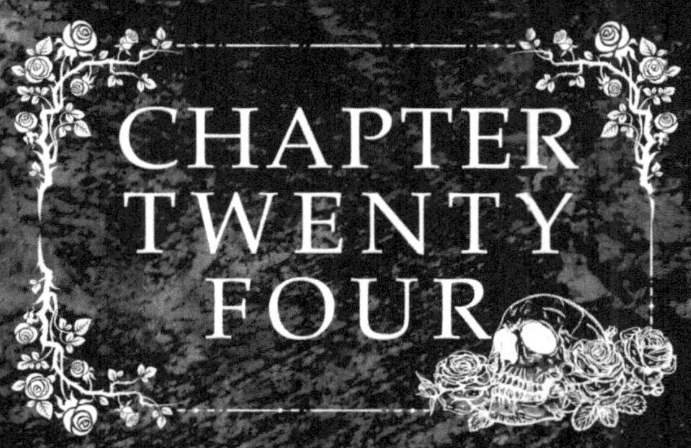

TAMARA

The water splashes into my face, and I'm brought completely back to my senses by the icy coldness of it. My ribs ache, and my face feels like I've gone ten rounds with Mike Tyson.

"Welcome, Tamara. You've just missed William. I gave him a call just to show him how lovely you look when tied to my bed. I'm sure he'll be busy trying to find out where you are at the moment. Shame nobody knows I have this place. It's my sanctuary from the outside world – the place I can be myself." Lord West runs his foul hand over my body while talking to me. I want to jerk away and stop him, but I'm tied down so tightly I can't move. I take a moment to scope out where I am. It appears to be a small room, sparsely decorated with rich red walls that have candle lamps hanging from them, giving a dim light. The place has a feeling of being old, a place of torment from a bygone time. There are two other men in the room. I recognize one as the guard who captured me when I ran, but the other is the face of a stranger. I half expected it to be the driver. I guess he doesn't get to see through his plan to destroy the Cavendish brother's now he's brought me here.

"You're a sick freak." I let the words escape from my mouth before my brain engages, and I know the instant they leave I'll regret them.

"Not a good thing to say to the man who now owns every part of you until I tire of it. That's the thing about the original Oakfield Society: it puts women in their rightful place, not like these modern feminist movements, trying to empower women and making men weak in the process. You should be home ready and willing, for when your master demands it. Women are made for sex. Why else would you have holes and us the staffs to punish you with? Women have become less humble and more stupid as the years have gone by. We need to return things to how they used to be by reinstalling discipline. This is what Nicholas doesn't understand. He allows his wife to wear his balls around her neck like a trophy, celebrating his downfall."

"Whereas, you just wear yours as a sign of how small your dick is?" I just couldn't stop myself saying it.

"You'll soon find *that* to be far from the truth. It's a shame you were still sleeping when I spoke to William. He could have confirmed the damage I can do with just one thrust. He's been there cheering me on before with his dick in hand because, let's face it, nobody wants a freak near them. Even if he's the Duke's brother."

Lord West is still trailing his hands over my body. I'm going to need a damn good shower with bleach after this.

"I always find those who are all talk have little going on

for them down there." I muse into the air. I know I should be frightened, but to be honest, I'm more pissed off because even if I get out of this alive, I'm going to be ruined for William. Maybe he was right, and we are freaks together. A situation that should leave me a quivering wreck is making me angry. Go figure!

"Whatever you're planning on doing can you just get on with it. No wonder William had to take matters into his own hands. You like to hog all the attention."

Lord West looks down at me.

"My god, it's not a disguise is it? You really aren't scared of what I can do to you."

"Nope." I roll my eyes.

"Wow. I've never had that happen before. There's always fear from the underlying threat of what I can do. It leaves a glimmer of doubt in a girl's eyes even when they try to disguise it. I don't know – it feels strange." He reaches into his trousers and re-arranges himself. "You have a pussy, though. Screaming or not. I can still rip it in two."

He takes his hand from his trousers. My legs are parted on the bed with my most intimate parts freshly shaven and bared to him. My pussy is William's property, but that doesn't stop Lord West from taking two of his filthy fingers and pushing them straight into me. I'm dry, and they rip at the sensitive flesh. There is no pleasure, just pain, and the promise of retribution. He thrusts hard, trying to illicit a scream from me, but I will not give it up. If he wants me begging for mercy, he's going to have to try harder.

"You do realize who I am don't you?" I sneer at him when he withdraws his fingers and licks them.

"A frigid little bitch?" he retorts with amusement at his choice of words.

"Hardly. I'm Viscount Hamilton's illegitimate daughter."

"What?" That piece of information stops him in his tracks. "You can't be."

"Why not? Isn't he the same sort of bastard as you are? A rapist and murderer? I always wondered why I didn't have a father, never realizing he was there all along. He just couldn't say because he knew I'd hate him for the way he treated my mother."

"More like he made a mistake. If you get them pregnant, you put a bullet in their brain before they have a chance to spawn a bastard. Nobody in our position needs that."

I gather as much salvia as I can in my dry mouth and spit it into his face.

"You're not a god. You don't get to make those decisions."

"Don't I? Let's see what happens with you, shall we?"

Lord West nods toward one of the other two men in the room, and the man holds out a machine to him. I instantly recognize it as one of those TENS machines, which are used to relax taut muscles. I'm pretty certain that whatever Lord West intends to use it for, it won't be for that. He places it down next to me on the bed and presses a few buttons, and the machine fires to life.

"This was an expensive purchase for me. It may look harmless and seem like you're about to get a nice work out, but it's got a bite to it."

My skin is still wet from where the bucket of water was thrown over it. Water and electrical current don't mix, as I find out to my cost when he puts the charged, pointed prong onto the skin of my stomach. It sizzles and crackles as excruciating pain jolts through my body. I bite down so hard on my lip, willing myself not to scream, that there's the metallic taste of blood on my tongue.

Lord West laughs.

"I don't smell burning. Obviously not high enough."

He turns a dial, and I clench my stomach muscles hard, preparing for another shock. But this time the tip is placed on my left nipple, and I'm unable to stifle my scream of torment. Sharp, shooting pains burn through my body, and the stench of singed flesh enters my nostrils. I close my eyes not wanting to see what he's done to my breast.

"That's better. So much nicer to hear a scream than misplaced defiance."

"Fuck you!" I scream, and he immediately reapplies the electrical current to my inflamed nipple. "Fuck you!" I scream again through a pain so intense my head is spinning, and I'm on the verge of passing out.

"You know, they used this torture in England around the time the society was first formed. They passed some act a while later, though, which called it inhumane. If you ask me, I think it's one of my favorites, and they need to use it on some of the low-life criminals out there."

"On rapists and murderers like yourself? Why don't you let me throw a bucket of water over your minuscule dick and then see if I can find anything to stick the prong onto. Actually, scrap that. Why don't I just stick it up your fucking ass?"

The two men watching what Lord West is doing take in a sharp breath, shocked at my outburst. The devil himself, though, laughs a malevolent chuckle, which fills the room and has me shutting my eyes and imagining him tied to the bed, writhing in pain.

I hear him flick a switch on the machine, and I brace every part of my body for what's coming next. I'm panting, and my eyes flicker open just in time to see him push the electrical prong between my legs. He runs it over the outer edge of my pussy lips, and I want to cry. I'm screaming so hard my throat feels like it's ripping apart, but I won't let him break me. I can't. I need to stay whole for when William comes, and then we can end this nightmare together.

"So pretty. So very pretty."

He places the prong down and switches the machine off. I desperately try to shut my legs when I feel his tongue trace a line over the burn he's just inflicted.

"There's nothing better than a dry pussy, waiting to be ripped and torn until it's beyond repair.

He licks me again, and I can feel despair starting to take over. I need this to end.

One of the two men in the shadows steps forward. I notice he has a pair of hair cutting scissors in his hands.

"May I, My Lord?" he asks and grabs the ends of my hair, which are tied together in a pony tail.

"Of course."

The snip ricochets through my body as he severs years and years of growth from my head. I'm not sure what's causing me the most pain, at the moment – the singed flesh of my nipple and pussy, or the loss of my hair.

"My associate likes to keep hair. He's got a pretty good collection now. I don't ask what he does with it. It's not my kink."

"No. Yours is just pain and humiliation."

"Finally, she realizes. Does this hurt?"

Lord West wraps his mouth around my nipple and bites down into the scorched flesh with his teeth. I can't stand the pain. My head swims – I know I'm being dragged into unconsciousness again, and I welcome the respite from the pain. It doesn't come, though, as another bucket of icy water is thrown over me, reviving me and returning me to a world of torment. Lord West takes his three fingers again and pushes them inside me. He scissors them, and I feel my flesh tearing. He nods his head toward the other man in the room while the one from before is now standing in the corner, sniffing my freshly severed hair.

"I don't think my fingers are big enough. Let's have something else to use."

The man turns to a wooden chest in the room and pulls out one of the drawers. Retrieving a massive phallic staff, he holds it up while I'm mentally trying to squeeze my legs together as tightly as possible. William has the biggest fucking dick I've ever seen, I'm talking hung like an elephant, but that thing is like twice the size.

"This one?"

"No. The pear." Lord West's lip curls up in a smile, which has me seriously questioning his sanity for about the hundredth time.

The man by the chest roots around in the drawers and eventually brings out a metallic object. It's shaped like a pear with a device at the bottom.

"Do you know what this is?"

Lord West waves it in front of my face. I turn away, refusing to give him an answer but also knowing where the device is going, and I don't want to think about what it does.

"In Tudor times, it was a way of getting answers from criminals. It went up the ass, and then they'd gradually turn the screw." The guard who'd been standing by the chest of drawers comes over and placing his hands on either side of my neck, he jerks my head around, so I have no choice other than to face Lord West. I shut my eyes, but he forces them open with his dirty fingers. Lord West is turning the handle on the device, and I can see it opening wider and wider. The part of me concerned with self-preservation wants to start pleading with him, now, and beg him to fuck me and get it over with. However, the angry part is still in control, and it spits at him, again. A hand whacks me across my face, closely followed by a twist of my damaged nipple by the guard who cut my hair. I scream so loudly I'm sure the very foundations of the building are rattling.

Lord West winds the pear device in so it's small again and without ceremony or preparation inserts it deeply into me. It's agony, especially when he instantly turns the screw, and it begins to widen. I bare down to try and expel it from my body, but it's no use. All three men step back, and I watch as they take their dicks out and start stroking their already hardened shafts.

"It's time to take the edge off. Decorate this beautiful body with our cum, and then the real fun can start."

The two guards furiously pump their dicks while Lord West takes it slower. He switches the electrical current machine back on, and with one hand stroking himself, he uses his other hand to dot the prong all over my body. One guard cums over my face, and the other on my sore breast. Lord West is the last to find his release, which he does over my previously broken ribs. He groans out a long breath as spurt after spurt of his disgusting essence covers my skin. His lip twists again, and he brings the prong down to rub it through the sticky fluid directly over where my ribs are broken and twisted inside me. I try to stay conscious to defy the weakness in me he wants to expose, but it's too much, and the darkness claims me once again.

CHAPTER TWENTY FIVE

WILLIAM

"When was the last time you drove?" I ask my brother who, despite being in a Lamborghini, is driving like an old grandad.

"William, I'm doing over a hundred miles an hour. If I go any faster, we'll attract the police, get pulled over, and we won't be able to get to her in time. Calm down."

"It feels slower," I protest and check the gun attached to my body for the millionth time since we got in the car.

The phone rings. I look down at the caller ID on the screen and it reads, 'Matthew Carter'. I know he's my brother's contact in all matters requiring a bit of additional help. He's ex-MI5 and still has connections there. He's also the current bodyguard for one of the richest men in the UK, a property tycoon named James North.

"Matthew?" Nicholas answers.

"Yes. We've identified the last known location of Miss Bennett's phone prior to it being, unceremoniously, returned to your house...my men are on the way there now."

"Our ETA is five minutes." Nicholas tells him.

"You'll probably be there before my men. You going in alone?"

"Yes," I reply before giving my brother a chance to say no. I'm not going to leave Tamara alone with Lord West for a minute longer than I have to. I know exactly what the bastard is capable of, and I refuse to let Tamara be subjected to that while I wait around outside for reinforcements.

The line remains silent while my brother neither confirms nor denies what we are going to do when we get to our location.

"I understand. I'd do the same for my woman," Matthew finally responds. "Do whatever you need to, to get her out safely. My men can handle the aftermath."

"Thank you," Nicholas replies. "So, what do I owe James this time?"

Matthew laughs down his end of the phone.

"I think he'd like to surprise his wife with a title of some sort for Christmas. Perhaps you could have a word in Prince John's ear. I know you and he have been close in the past."

"If you're suggesting I've fucked alongside him, then yes I have, but not since Victoria came into my life."

"He's too busy being ridden cowboy style by his pregnancy hormone flooded wife," I mutter without thinking. Damn. That's one of those filter things I'm supposed to remember. There is too much etiquette when it comes to society. Why can't we just say what we want and not have to mind our tongues.

"Good to hear it." Matthew chuckles at my faux pas.

"I'll see what I can do," Nicholas answers.

"Be careful. Call me when it's over."

"Will do." My brother ends the call, and we pull over in a densely forested area. Up ahead, I can see an opening, which appears to lead to a long driveway. There are one or two other houses scattered around but nothing that would cause major issues if we make a bit of a disturbance.

We're dressed all in black – our standard uniform for returning artwork seems to have transformed into the perfect outfit for rescuing damsels in distress and slaying the bad guys without a spot of blood showing.

It's dark out, the winter sun having set hours ago. Nicholas pulls down his night vision goggles, and I do the same.

"We go in the back way. You got your silencer?"

"Yes," I reply.

"Stay together. Follow my orders. We'll get her out."

"I know. You've got my word…no heroics. You've got a wife and baby to go back to, and I've got a woman to repair." I reply, reassuring my brother that I'm not going to go all commando on him and lose my head in there.

"She's stronger than you think. She'll give Lord West a run for his money."

"I hope so."

We go silent and switch on the intercoms in our ears. Like lions creeping slowly up on their prey, we make strides through the trees toward our target – a dimly lit house in front of us. It's old and a little run down. The perfect ghost house for Lord West's activities. I shudder as I think about the number of girls whose last view of the outside world was this building.

"Guard at eleven o'clock." Nicholas' voice comes through the intercom in my ear.

"Got him."

"Take him," my brother orders.

The guard is around the side of the building, having a crafty cigarette. He can't be seen by the other guards on lookout. I pull my knife from its holder on my trousers, and before he has a chance to notice, I'm next to him and have sliced through his throat.

"Shouldn't smoke. It's bad for your health in more ways than one," I tell him as he falls to the ground dead.

Dragging him, I deposit the body out of sight. Nicholas and I then press our bodies closely to the wall and shuffle around the building toward an entrance we'd examined earlier on Google maps. What a wonderful invention, but there's no privacy in the world any longer.

My feet shuffle, and I hit something heavy. I stop abruptly, and Nicholas knocks into the back of me. Looking down, I realize it's another body.

"What is it?" Nicholas asks.

"A body?" Not quite understanding. There's little light in the area, but through my goggles, I can make out a gunshot wound in his head.

"What?"

"Looks like a guard." I examine his clothing and see a knife attached to his trousers.

"Did you kill him?" Nicholas asks.

"No. You saw me deposit the guy I killed in the bushes over there."

"Someone must have pissed West off. Pretty messy clean up if you ask me."

"Maybe he's busy and will sort it out later?" The second the words leave my mouth, they turn my stomach because I don't want to think what he's doing to Tamara in the house. "Let's worry about it later. I want to get inside."

"Keep leading," Nicholas orders, and we peer around the side of the building.

"I've got two talking," I tell Nicholas.

He peaks over my shoulder.

"Confirmed."

"Shoot, or try to take them out in person?"

"Person. It's quieter and less chance of missing."

"Agreed."

On my count," Nicholas starts. "Three…two…"

"Fuck." I exclaim as a bright light illuminates the garden area, and our hiding place is discovered. We both rip off the night vision glasses and bring our guns up ready to shoot. It's no use, though, as I can't see a thing.

"Your Grace, Earl Lullington." A man steps forward, and I get ready to fire, but we're both quickly captured, and our weapons along with our earpieces are removed.

"If you'd follow me." The man indicates the path we are to take. I have a guard behind me and two on either side – Nicholas has the same. I'm not restrained, and I look to my brother for orders. His face is a mix of deep thought and concern. With a nod of his head, he signals we are to see where we are led, for now. I don't doubt it will be to see West, and where West is Tamara will be, so I'll happily oblige, for now.

I'm mentally bracing myself for the state I'll find Tamara in. I wear my emotions with no filter, but I can't show them to her. She'll need the strength the monster inside me imparts when I first see her. I can't show weakness. We enter through a small door into what I suspect is the lounge.

The building is incredibly run down – the ornate paintings and wall hangings are littered with spider webs, and there is enough dust covering the gothic sculptures on antique wooden furniture to write my name in. This place hasn't been inhabited in years. It's unloved – a place where the terrors are real. I control my emotions with a deep breath while we wait for the door to open. What I don't expect on the other side is Lord West on his hands and knees with two guards on either side of him. He has a gun pointed at his head, and two men lie already executed on the floor in the corner of the room with blood pooling around them. Tamara sits on a sofa wrapped in a blanket. There are newly forming bruises on her face, which is wet with a mixture of fresh tears and blood. Her beautiful, long hair has been cut short.

"William." She tries to get to her feet when she sees me, but her legs are wobbly, and she sinks back down. I look to the man who led us here. He motions for me to go to her. I do so and wrap my arms around her.

"What happened? Are you hurt?"

"There will be time for questions later, Earl Lullington. Our business here is concluded, now," the man speaks and steps forward with a note for my brother. He also hands my brother back his gun. "I suspect you have reinforcements on the way. I'll allow them to do the clean-up operation." The man whistles, and everyone leaves the room. Lord West suddenly realizes he's free and scrambles to get to his feet. Nicholas is quicker, though, and points the gun at him.

"Back down."

Lord West's eyes are filled with menace, and my brother's are laced with confusion but also determination. Lord West understands this and gets back down onto his knees in the center of the room.

"I think I want to see what's going on here."

My brother keeps his eyes and gun trained on West but comes over to me. He drops the note into my hands.

"If you would, Brother."

I open it and read it aloud.

"I'm afraid I couldn't wait for you to play heroes this time. There will be other opportunities, though. This isn't over yet. Take care of my daughters, both of them. They are not Lord West's to destroy. Viscount Hamilton."

"Viscount Hamilton," Nicholas repeats. "They were his men?"

Lord West snorts.

"Seems the old man got one up on you."

Nicholas strides forward and uses the barrel of the gun to smack him over the head. I turn my attention back to Tamara.

"What did he do to you? Apart from this." I stroke her tufted hair.

She lowers the sheet a little to bare her breast. It's inflamed and blackened. The skin burned on the tip.

"Lower?"

"Yes," she whimpers. I shut my eyes, trying to keep hold of my control. "Let the monster out," she pleads with me. My eyes flash open, and she turns her head toward the corner of the room. In the shadows under a table, I can just about make out a figure.

"He had her here. One of the missing girls."

"Joanna?" Nicholas asks.

"No," Tamara replies. "The one you believed your father killed, Daphne Knight."

"Shit!" Nicholas exclaims. "You're a sick fuck." He whacks West again, and the man slumps to the floor. Nicholas stomps over toward the girl and whimpered pleas can be heard coming from the shadows. They turn into song, and it sends shivers down my spine. Nicholas grabs a lamp from a nearby table and points it down, so he can see the girl. What we find there is not the Daphne Knight I saw sold that day at the auction. She's lost an eye, and the socket is infected and inflamed. Her hair is shaved short. She has scars, cuts, and bruises all over her body, and several of her fingers are missing. Her leg is at an odd angle, obviously, having been broken at some point and not allowed to heal properly.

"No, no, no, no," she sings. It's obvious that the young girl she once was has completely gone. I know in my heart there's no hope for her.

"Daphne." Nicholas motions for her to come to him. She shakes her head.

"I won't hurt you."

"It hurts already."

"I know it does." He keeps his voice even and low. I pull Tamara close to my chest. She doesn't need to see this.

"He said it would stop one day, and the angels would come and take me to heaven. Just like the baby he beat from me. Just like the parts of my body he took already. He won't kill me, though. He said that would be too easy. I'm one of the special girls. I can withstand anything for the society, but I don't want to anymore. I want to sleep, but I've forgotten how."

I can see how visibly shaken my brother is. He's always blamed himself for these girls. They were given to him, and Daphne was one of the one's he didn't choose.

"Come to me, Daphne. The angels are here. I can see them. Tamara starts to squirm in my arms. She realizes what Nicholas is about to do.

"He can't," she whimpers into my chest.

"It's the only way. That's not a human anymore. It's no life. Trust me, I know."

I don't look as the gun goes off behind us, but I know Daphne has finally found her peace. Tamara lets out a cry of loss.

"Do you want this, Brother?" Nicholas asks, indicating toward Lord West who remains semi-conscious on the floor.

"No. Just end him. I want to take Tamara home."

Nicholas strides purposefully over to West and kicks him until he starts to stir. He doesn't give him any last words, or prayers for redemption in heaven or hell. No, he fires the gun twice. The first shot destroys that piece of his anatomy he was so proud of. The second is straight between his eyes and ends his pitiful existence.

TAMARA

Three months later

"Why do those people have to queue when we get to walk straight through and onto the plane?" William asks me as he flashes his ticket toward the flight attendant.

"We're in first-class," I tell him and show the lady my ticket.

"Thank you, ma'am." The attendant gives me a little smirk, and we walk down the corridor toward the plane.

"It's not because you told them I have autism?"

"No. We've paid to board first."

"But if I didn't want to pay, could we tell them?"

"Yes, we could," I reply and wrap my hand around his.

"Then it does work the same way as it did at that theme park we went to, and you told them about me, so I didn't have to queue."

"It does, but you've got money, and I don't plan on flying economy when you can afford a first-class flight."

"Ok."

William strides confidently toward the next waiting attendant at the entrance to the plane.

"Welcome, sir." The lady bows her head to him. I show her our tickets. "You're seats one and two to the left. I believe you are the only people in first-class for the flight. You'll have a dedicated attendant. If you need anything, please just ask."

"Thank you."

William starts to stride off to our seats but then pauses, and I can only just suppress the laugh threatening to escape because I know what's coming next.

"How many years of flight practice has the captain had?"

"I'm sorry, sir?" the lady at the door responds.

"Flight hours?"

"A lot. He's one of the most decorated in the company."

She gives him her well-worn smile.

"And the co-pilot?" William continues, standing there next to me.

"I believe roughly two thousand. Miss Lewis is a fantastic pilot, as well."

"A woman?" William questions, and I know it's not a sexist remark. It's because all the information he's been frantically researching on the journey to Heathrow airport has been related to male pilots. "Do they have the same training?"

"Yes, sir."

The footsteps of the other passengers start to echo down the corridor as they approach.

"Right. It didn't say anything about that?"

"What didn't, sir?"

"Female pilots. The internet."

The attendant looks at me and I mouth, 'first time'. She nods with understanding.

"I can assure you women pilots are as safe as men. It's proven."

"But I didn't read that."

The other passengers arrive, and the attendant tries to turn away to greet them.

"One more thing."

"Yes, sir."

"The fuel. Has the pilot used the standard calculation for it? We need to make sure we've got enough to get to the Caribbean."

The eyes of a little boy waiting with the other passengers go wide, and he tugs on his mother's jacket with worry.

"I can assure you the pilot has had all her calculations checked, and the plane is full enough."

"Good, I know it's seventy thousand kilograms of fuel to get to New York, so she'll need more than that."

"William"–I tap his arm– "can we go start our honey-moon, now, please?"

He looks between me and the flight attendant.

"Of course. Thank you."

To a relieved exhale from both the flight staff and the passengers, my new husband finally decides to take his seat.

"You're suddenly very bossy," he tells me.

"You can talk!" I roll my eyes at him and put my bag down to pull out my Kindle for the flight. "Wasn't it little more than seven hours ago you picked me up out of bed, threw me over your shoulder, and carried me to the family church where you demanded—in front of Victoria, Nicholas, and a vicar—that we marry then and there."

"You didn't like my proposal?"

I laugh at him and pop my new Marc Jacobs bag into the overhead locker.

"It was a little unorthodox. Put it that way."

"I thought there was less chance of you saying no, doing it like that."

"That's true." I slide into the seat next to him.

"Are you happy?"

"To be Lady William Cavendish?"

"Yes." He turns to me with a look of worry in his eyes.

"I couldn't be happier."

"Good, because we're going to spend the next two weeks putting a baby in your belly."

I roll my eyes at him.

"You're not joking, are you?"

He shrugs his shoulders and then does his seat belt up.

"When have you known me to joke?"

"Never. It's one of the things I like about you along with the fact you find it impossible to lie."

"What else do you like about me?" he asks while he pulls a thick blanket out and places it over my lap. I'm wearing a summer dress, having left my thick coat with Nicholas and Victoria when they dropped us at the airport. Victoria was moaning she was the size of a house and wished she could go to the Caribbean. Nicholas promised it would be the first place they would go to as soon as the baby was old enough to be left with Auntie Tamara and Uncle William. William and I laughed at that because we both know Nicholas would never let his child out of his sight for more than a few minutes. Victoria and I have bodyguards with us constantly. The threats may have died down, for now, but Viscount Hamilton is out there somewhere, and there's also another missing girl still to be found.

"Do you think Joanna's still alive?" I change the conversation abruptly.

William sucks air into his mouth.

"After this much time, I doubt it. If she is, you saw the condition Daphne was in. I guess we have to hope that somewhere, deep down, Viscount Hamilton does have a heart. He saved you from West before I could, and I'll owe him forever for that. It took you long enough to heal from the injuries West inflicted on you, and he only had you for a short time."

I shift in my seat still thinking of the pain of that day, and the scarring to my left nipple. It will never heal properly, and it's unlikely I'll be able to use it to feed my babies (How many had William threatened to have with me?). But I'll deal with that when the time comes. My ribs still give me a bit of pain, but that's to be expected in England with the damp weather even in the summer. The main thing is Lord West didn't break me. William and I still have the same sex life we did before I was taken. We both have a passion for the darker side of things, and I trust William with how far he'll go.

Before we left Lord West's property to burn down, that night, I'll always remember his words as he removed the dead deviant's brain from his skull and threw it on the fire. *'People say my brain is wired wrong, but I think his was. Woman are not creatures to be destroyed. They are to be worshiped and loved. Treated with kindness and devotion. Lord West was the wrong one. Not me.'*

When all this is finally over, whether we are alive or dead, that will be William's epitaph forever because he's not wrong. He's unique, my husband, and I love him.

"I love you too," he whispers into my ear.

"Did I say that out loud?"

"No, I can just read the goofy look on your face."

"I did not have a goofy look."

"Oh, you did. It was something like this."

He pulls a funny face, and I can't help but pull him into a kiss.

"Do you think the monster wants to come out and play for a bit?"

"On the plane?" He raises an eyebrow.

"Maybe only a little bit of the monster until we reach our destination."

He licks his lips, and we both sit back in our seats. William slides his hand under my blanket as the plane starts to taxi down the runway. As we thunder into the air twisting and turning until we're level, he brings me to an orgasm with three of his fingers inside me. Reminding me just who owns my pussy.

EPILOGUE

JOANNA

"Is anyone there?" I sit up in my bed when I hear the bang of a heavy door in the darkness I've become so accustomed to. "Hello?" I shout again, but there's no answer. It's my mind playing tricks on me, again. It often does that. The worst times are when it imagines I'm no longer in this place. That I've been whisked away to a different life, in a different country with a new identity, and I'm a new person living somewhere where the Oakfield Society doesn't exist. A place where I can make decisions for myself. One where he doesn't come in the night and abuse me because he can't have *her*.

The door opens, and I jump from my bed to stand beside it as I've been taught. My hands clenched behind my back, my head bowed, and my legs slightly parted in the ill-fitting nightdress I wear. I don't look up. No, that would be wrong. I did once, and I couldn't get out of bed for a week because the bruising was so bad. I must wait…wait for him…my father.

"Good evening, Joanna," Viscount Hamilton addresses me.

"Good evening, Daddy," I reply in the only manner I know, now.

"I have a present for you."

"Thank you," I reply, still not raising my head. I've not been told I can, yet.

"I'll give it to you soon. I need to vent my anger first."

He shifts a chair and takes a seat in it. I stand painfully still. My leg muscles are weak, and my eyes are unable to adjust easily to the light in the room. I wonder how long I've been here? It feels like an eternity. It could be weeks, months or years – everything has blurred into one. Day and night merged into a perpetual darkness.

The door opens and closes again. I know it's Camilla, the lady who looks after me.

"Your drink." I hear her place the glass down on a table.

"Thank you," the Viscount replies. "Joanna. Come sit on my lap."

I do as I'm ordered. I don't even question it anymore.

"I hope she behaves for you tonight," Camilla tells the Viscount, but I know that's a warning for me. She doesn't need to worry, though. Her training has all been received and understood. I'm the perfect woman, now, and I'm ready for my future.

Camilla leaves, and I take my place on the Viscount's lap. He instantly bunches my skirt up and rubs his hand over my pussy. I used to protest and scream when he did this. I'd curse him and try to escape, but I'm so broken, now, I don't even flinch when he sticks a finger inside me.

"My daughter had her baby, today? A girl, which I knew

it would be. It's fitting that Oakfield finally has a female. All we need now is for you to marry Theodore and conceive a male, and our family can rule again."

He pushes another finger in, and my body tightens with the need to expel him.

"That's not behaving like the good wife I've taught you to be. He won't want that."

"Please." I let the little whimper fall from my lips with regret.

"Too late." He withdraws his hand and pushes me to the floor. "Tonight, will have to be our last time. I can't take any more risks with you. On the bed. Clothes off, and legs apart."

I know what comes next: the degradation, the pain, and the feelings of disgust. There is still a tiny part of me that wants to protest and tell him to go fuck himself in the ass with a sharp knife. Inform him I'm never opening my legs for him again. But I don't. I get to my feet. I strip out of my nightgown, and I lie back on the bed and part my legs to give him a view of what he will abuse shortly.

Viscount Hamilton removes his clothes. He's not a handsome man. His physique is aged and not well looked after. He strides to the bed, and I try to will my body to relax because it hurts less that way. It refuses to listen, though, knowing too well the suffering it's preparing for. He leans down over me then pops up again. I hope for a moment he's changed his mind.

"I almost forgot. Your present." He reaches for a box he must have placed on the table when he entered the room. He opens the lid and pulls out a black wig. "This is your special present to me."

He comes to the side of the bed and rearranges the wig

over my hair. The hair is long and styled just like *hers* is in all the pictures he's shown me of her.

"Perfect." He stands back. "And to think the man who took it from her head thought he would get to keep it. My men soon destroyed those illusions when they put a bullet in his brain."

The Viscount strokes himself a few times.

"First it's time to see whether Tamara lives up to her mother's standards. Then it's time for you to get married and for me to become the ruler of Oakfield. With you married to my son, I'll be able to manipulate him into working against the Cavendish brothers and my daughters. They will all be destroyed, and a new leader will be chosen for the society, and I'm next in line.

THE END

AFTERWORD

William's autism is not the cause of his darkness, however, throughout the book he's worried it is. He needs Tamara to show him he's been tainted by his father's treatment of him. For anyone to be locked away in a room alone for most of their life would leave them with issues, not only that but also William's father introduced him to sex, and his version of what it should be – abusive in the Duke's case. William has seen murder, he's seen violence, and it's all he's been taught until he meets Tamara and discovers a love different from the affection he holds for his brother, Nicholas. What he and Tamara engage in is consensual, and they are hopelessly devoted to each other. William and his brother are striving to rid the world of the evil of the Oakfield Society. They are the good guys, just having to do bad things to make everything right.

Autism DOES NOT make William a monster. He's a hot, alpha male with a taste for the dark side. My kind of guy!

Thank you for reading.
Anna xx

Theo &
Joanna

A FATHER'S
Insistence

CHAPTER ONE

THEODORE

"She looks just like you." I bring my newborn niece up into my arms and gently rock her while she coos quietly. "Thank you for allowing me to come and see her." Looking out of the corner of my eye, I can see Nicholas and William standing sentinel: one at the door to the lounge, and the other by the patio doors to the garden. These are the only exits to the newly rebuilt and decorated room I am currently sitting in, and they are being covered in case I should decide to make a run for it with baby Rose. Tamara sits opposite in a smart suit with her hand resting over the small swell to her stomach. I guess she's here in case of any potential litigation. Judging by the size of her, she can only be a few months pregnant, but when we entered the room, William was already playing the protective soon-to-be father. I'm not here to cause trouble, though. I just want to check on my sister and my niece, but that doesn't stop me from looking down my nose at Nicholas Cavendish for being my niece's father. He's not the man I would have chosen for my sister.

"I don't know," Victoria muses and strokes her daughter's head. "I think there's a lot of Nicholas in her. I've seen a couple of pictures of him when he was a baby, and they look so similar. You'll have to bring over a picture of me next time."

"You could come to our house?"

Victoria looks over to Nicholas, and I see him shake his head.

"I'm sorry. It's better that you come here."

The fury I carry around with me starts to burn a fire in my veins. Nicholas Cavendish is obviously controlling my sister. I want to see her free and happy away from him without the act she's putting on in front of me. It sickens me he's abusing his position of power to do god knows what to my sister. My father told me about the society and why he feels the need to change it. He told me of how the previous Duke was trying to steer it away from the abuses that were being inflicted upon women, but Nicholas and William killed their father, so they could take over. He told me he'd had no choice but to give my sister to Nicholas, because Nicholas would have ruined us all and taken Victoria and killed her, otherwise. I don't want to believe it's true, and I have to be honest with myself and say that Victoria seems happy, but I saw the sadness behind my father's eyes. He was a broken man the day he told me everything. He'd given his daughter away to a life of torture—it was enough to destroy any father. Something inside me snaps at Nicholas' refusal to allow Victoria to visit her childhood home, and before I can think about what I'm saying, my mouth opens in an uncontrollable outburst.

"And why can't she visit her childhood home? Are you scared that by being out of your presence for a few minutes she might actually see sense and report you to the police for your crimes against women?"

The room goes silent. Even little Rose seems to sense the tension and stops her cute baby noises. Nicholas breaks the impasse by pushing his tongue against his teeth and inhaling. The resulting hissing noise echoes in the large room.

"Theo please?" Victoria pleads and tries to take her daughter back from me.

"I should walk out of here now with Rose before you have a chance to sell her to the highest bidder."

Nicholas still doesn't say anything, but the edges of his face are flaming red, and I know he's trying to control his temper. William, who's standing by the door, swipes at his ear and then his head. His mouth is moving, and if I'm not mistaken, I'm sure he's reciting mathematical equations. I'll never understand these two brothers. They are both insane.

I want to test Nicholas' limits. Maybe I can walk out of here with my sister and her daughter? Pushing to my feet from where I've been sitting, I cradle Rose tighter to my chest, and she whimpers a little.

"Th-Theo..." Victoria stammers quietly.

"William, Tamara," Nicholas finally speaks. "I thought you had a doctor's appointment at twelve thirty. You don't want to be late. Hearing the heartbeat of your baby for the first time is a wonderful experience."

William pushes away from where he was casually lounging against the frame of the patio doors, and going over to Tamara, he assists her to her feet. Nobody says anything. I hold Rose tightly, waiting and watching to see what will happen next.

"It was good to see you again, Theodore." William bows his head at me and leads Tamara out of the room. She looks over her shoulder and takes a last sorrowful look toward me before leaving with her husband. We've never addressed the vicious lies she spouted at me the last time we met when she told me she was my half-sister, and that my father had raped her mother. It's something I can never forgive her for, but I don't doubt it's the Cavendish brother's influence that instigated them.

Nicholas strides over to Victoria and kisses her on the cheek.

"I need to make a phone-call to Prince John. I'll leave you and your brother to talk. You don't need me here." She reaches up to him with her hand, which he takes and gently squeezes before placing a kiss on it and letting go. He comes closer to me, and my hands involuntarily tighten on Rose. His eyes are focused squarely on his daughter, and I know he's going to take her with him, but he surprises me when he bends down and kisses her on the head.

"Enjoy you time with your uncle, my little button. Daddy will be back later." Rose replies to him with baby babble as if she understands him, which she doesn't, of course, since she's only a few weeks old and probably can't even see him properly yet. Then Nicholas turns his attention back to me.

"I'm sorry your views of me are tainted. I can assure you I have nothing but respect and love for my wife and daughter although I know you don't believe it. I need to protect my family, however. It's the only reason I won't allow them to visit you at your home. You're always welcome here though.

Victoria will always be your sister and Rose your niece. My brother and I will not stop you from seeing them. I shouldn't have been here today…it was wrong, and I'm sorry. Please, stay as long as you want." Nicholas then bows his head to me, which is something he doesn't have to do since he's a Duke, and I'm only the son of a Viscount. I have no title, yet, and should defer to him. I can't though. Despite his words, I know this is all merely a part of whatever game it is he's playing, so I don't show him the same respect back. He sighs heavily and leaves the room.

"Why do you have to be this way?" Victoria immediately chastises me. "Why can't you accept he's a good man?"

"Because I know differently," I reply and hand Rose back to her when my niece starts to fuss.

"You only know what our father has told you."

"Then you tell me the truth. Tell me what is really happening here," I demand as Victoria settles Rose against her breast to feed her while stroking her daughter's head underneath a strategically placed blanket.

"Are you even willing to listen to the truth?" Victoria questions.

"I just want to know you're safe, and while you're here, I don't think that is the case." I let out a long-frustrated sigh. "Tell me honestly, sister, two things: Do you have the society's crest burned into your thigh? And has Nicholas led you around naked in front of other members of the society?"

"That's what he told you?" Victoria's eyes fill with unshed tears.

"Our father? Yes, he told me how you were paraded like a dog and had your skin permanently branded. Did Nicholas do that? Did he hurt you in that way?"

"Yes…but…" she begins to protest to me. No doubt, she wants to tell me about how he's a good man, now, but her words will fall on deaf ears. Any man who could do that to the woman he's supposed to love will always be the devil to me, and my sister knows it. She stops all conversation and focuses on her daughter. There is little point in me staying here since it's obvious I can't save my sister today, and the guilt of that starts to twist in my stomach.

"If you ever need me, just call. You'll always be my sister, no matter what."

I leave Victoria in the room, and as I shut the door, I can hear her softly sobbing. Nicholas is standing in the hallway and on the phone as he told me he would be.

"I'll call you back in a minute, John." He hangs up. I'm done, though. I can't be in this place anymore. The burden of the suffering, which has taken place within these four walls, weighs heavily on me. Without saying another word, I turn heel and stride straight out the front door leaving it open behind me.

It's not until I'm home and getting ready for bed, later the same evening, that I feel remotely calm after the meeting. I want to be a part of my sister's and my niece's life, but while they're under the thumb of Nicholas Cavendish, I've got no hope—I can't have while imagining the cruel way he's treating them. I might never get Victoria away from him. She's too far under the evil Duke's spell, but I have to save Rose. I can't let her be raised in a household where her father treats women as sex slaves.

I wish my father was here. I've had some cryptic messages from him over the last few months, but I've not physically seen him since the day he went into hiding because he was going to be questioned for Elsie Bennett's murder. He didn't kill her. My father is a good man. Okay, my mother and him had an interesting relationship—they weren't overly affectionate, and I think that's why they live separately now. I barely see my mother. But that doesn't make him the man Victoria and Tamara claim him to be. He gave Elsie a home when she became a single mother with no family who could support her, and she'd nowhere else to go. He even paid for Tamara's education at Cambridge. If it wasn't for him, she wouldn't be a lawyer, now. Not that she seems to be rushing to go into practice. No, she's exploiting everything he helped pay for by using it against him in her position as the Cavendish brother's legal adviser. It's ungrateful and disloyal. He's never hurt Tamara, only helped her. Even more upsetting is the fact my father was always a loving and doting parent to Victoria. I remember them playing happily together in the gardens. I know he was strict with her and prevented her from going to university, which was sometimes a bone of contention between them, but it's not a reason for her to turn against him as she has. I guess she blames him for what she had to endure at Nicholas' hands.

"Ugh!" I exclaim and lash out at the wall closest to me. "Everything is a big mess."

I've drank half a bottle of brandy to try and ease my worries since returning from Oakfield Hall. I'm tired, frustrated, and just need to shower and sleep. Decision made, I undress and drop all my clothes in a pile on the floor. I've my own personal butler now my father's gone, and I know even though I should pick everything up he won't mind doing it for me when I'm so exhausted.

My father told me I could move into his rooms during his absence, but I've chosen to stay in mine, preferring them to the grandeur of his decoration. I've always been more of a simple man. After school, I went to Oxford University and studied business. I really enjoyed my time there and made many friends who I'm certain will be associates for life, but I've always known I'm destined for the title of Viscount, so I've not tried to branch out on my own. My father has drilled it into me since birth that I'm his heir, and he wants me ready to take over his title when I'm called upon to do so, eventually. I wouldn't be in a position to do that if I was knee-deep in running my own business. It's a little sad, because I had a fabulous idea for a company: assisting children with learning difficulties to get better exposure to the art of the world. Victoria had always been in love with art of any kind, and I'd seen first-hand on a work experience trip at university how it inspires children. Sadly, my future wasn't to travel down that path, though…maybe one day? Until then, I'm running the estate in my father's absence.

I step in the steaming shower and allow it to wash my worries away. I'm full of tension. Moving my hand down to my dick, I give it a few strokes to bring it to life. It's the easiest way to relieve my mood. It's completely at odds with the worries I have for my sister, but damn, I'm a man, and the way to my heart is through my dick. It's the only way to ensure I get some sleep tonight. I had a girlfriend for a short while at university, and I bring to mind the memory of her bouncing on my dick with her perfect tits rising and falling as she rode me like a cowgirl. My hand strokes faster and faster until my boys tighten, and my cum shoots off like a bullet into the shower wall. I feel all the tension ease from my taut body, and I yawn. Turning the water off, I reach for a towel and dry myself. I clean my teeth and do a final piss for the night before heading into my bedroom. Sliding between the luxurious sheets of my massive bed, my eyes instantly shut, and presumably I fall asleep because it feels like hours later when I'm awoken by a crash in the room.

"Theodore, it's just me," my father announces, and I rub my eyes still full of sleep.

"Father?"

He holds his finger to his lips while another man with him points a torch in my direction. Movement to my left captures my attention, and I look up just in time to see another man press a needle into my neck.

"What the fuck?" I exclaim. The world starts to spin as my head fogs with exhaustion again. "What's going on?" I slur, fighting to keep my eyes open.

"It's ok. It's the quickest way," my father reassures me, and before I can question him further…the world turns black.

CHAPTER TWO

JOANNA

The last few days have probably been the most peaceful of the year I've spent in captivity. I've not seen anyone apart from Camilla when she's dropped my food off. Today's meal was a bit more elaborate than the others. Most of the time, it's been a standard fair of brown toast for breakfast followed by a sandwich of some sort for lunch, and then fish or chicken with vegetables and potatoes for dinner. I've lost so much weight the clothes I was originally given now hang off my skeletal frame. I wasn't a big person a year ago, but I wasn't a skinny supermodel size either. I liked my food, especially steak, and I had a terrible weakness for chocolate. My favorite dessert was one of those chocolate cakes where the middle was still like molten lava. My mouth waters at the thought of it while my stomach cramps at the richness of the steak I've just eaten. Why after so long would they give me a steak? I can't help but think of myself as a prisoner on death row, and the meal I've just eaten is my last. If it is, I'm ready. I've got nothing left to live for. I don't know what living is anymore. I'm a girl whose father gave her away only to be sold to a monster. I've thought often about the other girls from that terrible night and wonder what has happened to them. I know the man who bought me is the father of one of them. I guess he exchanged one woman for another in effect. He told me once that she'd married Nicholas Cavendish. I can't help feeling sorry for her, wondering whether she or any of the other girls are still alive. No, if I'm to die tonight, I'll welcome it. I've been trained to within an inch of my life to obey Viscount Hamilton's rule, and should I fail, I'm fully aware of the disastrous consequences. I don't want to be raped by him anymore. I just want to go to sleep and never wake up.

I push aside the book I've been engrossed in for the last hour—reading provides the only form of sanity I've not been deprived of, yet—and getting to my feet, I stretch my legs and arms. The steak was far too rich for me, and my stomach still doesn't feel right. I'm rubbing it to relieve the discomfort when I hear my door being unlocked, and Camilla comes barging in. Without saying a word, she grabs me by the wrist and drags me from the room.

"No!" I try to force my feet into the ground, but she's too strong.

"Shut up," she shouts at me and whips her hand across my face. I reel back in shock. Although I'm used to beatings, I wasn't expecting that tonight. Camilla is joined by a man who lifts me off my feet and carries me down the hall. I initially panic before a calm sense of fate descends over me. This must be it…the moment I die. Why do I feel so happy? I surely shouldn't. After death, there is nothing: no coming back, no feelings, no pain. The. End.

I'm deposited into a room where the Viscount is already standing. It figures he would want to be the one to finish this. I kneel down before him as I've been taught.

"I warned you the time was approaching for you to fulfill your destiny, didn't I?" He informs me, patting the top of my head.

"Yes," I reply quietly. A speck of dust catches my eye on the floor, and as I let out a breath, the dust flutters along like an angel on a floating cloud. I wonder if I'll get wings? I must have earned them. Death can't be *it*...all there is left when life in this world ends. I've always believed in some sort of after-life. Men like Viscount Hamilton deserve it, so they can be punished for their atrocities in this life. They can't just end. I have to know that somewhere they'll suffer for what they've done. My breath catches at the thought of there being noth-ing. This being the end for me. My twenty-two years on this planet equating to little more than an abuse victim who dies at the hands of her tormentor. I'm too busy trying to remember how to breathe when the first punch comes. Any chance I had of getting air into my lungs is ruined when pain explodes into them, instead. Several more hits rain down on me, and I curl into a little ball, desperately trying to protect myself. It doesn't work, though, and I know I'll be bruised tomorrow...if I'm still alive. I'm pulled to my feet by my frizzy, blond hair. My father always hated my hair with its natural curl. He said it left me looking like a wild child who'd been dragged through a hedge backward—an image I most definitely resemble, currently.

"You remember what you've been taught. I'm going to have to trust you from this point on, but remember I'll always be watching. I'll be there should you falter, ready to bring down hell upon you if you ruin this. I'm your master, your ruler, your everything. Without me, you'd be dead," Viscount Hamilton spits into my face. "Get her dressed," he orders, and my clothes are ripped from my body. Red marks, precursors to bruising, litter my porcelain skin. I'm forced into a white linen dress like the one I wore the night I was given to Nicholas Cavendish. I've traveled full circle. I'm back there, waiting to discover what my future will be, and only too aware of the trials. I'd been taught about them as I'd grown up, but my part in the Oakfield Society was short-lived. I was not one of the chosen girls, and I was sold off instead. I sometimes think the trials would have been easier than this existence.

Camilla grabs my hair out of the hands of the man who's been holding it tightly and rips a brush through the dry and tangled ends. I have my own shower, so I am able to keep clean, but the products aren't really suitable for my type of hair. I need a good haircut and conditioning treatment. I suppose, if I'm to die, it doesn't really matter. From the little I know of God, I don't think he's the type of person to judge someone for the style of their hair as they enter through the pearly gates.

Viscount Hamilton looks down at his phone when it makes a sound.

"He'll be here soon."

Camilla finishes re-arranging my hair and pushes me back down to my knees in front of Viscount Hamilton. The man who's terrorized every moment of my last year, both awake and asleep, pulls my chin up, so he can bore his pene-trating gaze directly into me. I want to shut my eyes, but I know I can't, and even if I did, I couldn't block him out, because he's burned into my senses: I can see the little curl of his lip when he's enjoying what he does to me, I can hear the grunts of his exertions, and I can smell the foul stench of his breath as he kisses me all over my face. The steak sitting in my stomach bubbles, and I can't stop myself from heaving and then vomiting on the floor.

"What the fuck?" Viscount Hamilton steps back to avoid getting any on his designer leather shoes. "I was being nice to you and have provided you with a good meal, and this is what happens. You better not mess up your task, Joanna. You've been prepared. You've been trained, and you *will* lead us to untold power."

My head is spinning from the sickness and the beating. I've no idea what he's talking about.

"My son is nearly here. He'll be your husband within the hour, and you will take him straight to your room and make a child. You've been left in peace the last few days because your contraceptive injection ran out. He'll take you tonight, and together you'll make a boy capable of ruling over the Oakfield Society. One who will run it properly, not like the Cavendish brothers."

A bell sounds somewhere in the house.

"Get her up." I'm dragged to my feet, and a blanket is wrapped around me. Camilla brings me into her arms and buries my head into her chest. It's almost as if she's comforting me, but I know the things this woman is capable of, and it's nothing of the sort: it's an act. Everything happening here is designed for a purpose. The beating, the outfit, the fake show of sympathy are all part of a show. The game continues, and I'm still a pawn in it. I'm not going to die today, but something much worse is about to happen: I'm about to be married to a man who doesn't have a clue about the world he lives in.

I shift my head just in time to see two men enter the room, dragging a comatose body between them. A priest follows behind with his long garments flowing along the floor, and a bible in his hand. I would expect him to look shocked at the situation he's seeing, but he looks all too accepting and comfortable. He's clearly been hired specifically for his ability to turn a blind eye to the half-asleep groom and the battered bride.

"Theo," Viscount Hamilton addresses his son. I recognize him vaguely from society functions we both attended growing up. He was always one of the confident men in the background, surrounded by women but not particularly interested in anyone. It appeared to me his behavior was guided by his responsibilities to his family name. He was never one to use his future title to advance himself, though. Not like Nicholas Cavendish who used his on more than one occasion to get a girl into bed.

The men lower Theo into a wing-backed chair, and I can see he's trying his hardest to open his eyes.

"Father?" he groans and rubs his face. "What's going on?"

The Viscount brushes his hand against his son's shoulder, pretending to be the kind and caring father.

"I'm sorry for the subterfuge, my boy, but it's all necessary. I'll explain later. First, we need to make sure that this woman is safe, and there's only one way to do that. You need to marry her."

"Marry her?" Theo looks up confused. His eyes keep opening and closing. He's struggling to come out of whatever drug-addled state they've put him in. "I don't understand."

"I couldn't save your sister, Theo, please. We have to save Joanna."

I'm thrust forward nearer to the father and son who are currently engaged in a conversation, which will shape my future.

"Joanna?" Theo rubs his head again. "Can I get water?"

The Viscount nods at one of the other men in the room. Minutes ago, they were beating me, but now they look as though butter wouldn't melt in their mouths. They are devils in disguise. A glass of water is brought over to Theo, and he drinks it down before trying to focus more fully on me, standing before him. I look down at my hands, and I realize they are shaking. I try to control them, but my body acts like it's not attached to my brain.

"Theo, this is Joanna. My men have just rescued her. She's been held captive by the Cavendish brothers for over a year now."

I raise my eyes from the son to the father. Shock should probably register on my face, but my body is numb to anything by this point. This is the plan, and I must follow it.

"Is that true?" Theo asks, his words still slurred, and his eyes still closing every now and then as he fights to stay alert.

"Yes, sir," I reply like a programmed robot. Viscount Hamilton smiles at me from behind his son's back.

"We don't have much time, Theo. The Cavendish brothers will be searching for us. I need to send them a message."

"Can I just get my head straight? Why did you have to drug me?"

"I didn't want to. I didn't have time to explain. I had to get back here."

Theo pushes gingerly to his feet and sways. He keeps one hand on the chair but reaches out with the other to me.

"Do you understand what's happening?" he asks as his hand rests on my shoulder. I can feel weight behind it and know he's using me, as well as the chair, for support.

I flick my stare quickly to the Viscount, and his eyes darken with the promise of a fury so great it will eclipse anything that has occurred before should I not give the correct answer.

"I don't fully understand anything at the moment. All I know is I don't want to go back into that room. I don't want to be tortured the way I was. I want help, and if what everyone is telling me will give me that, then I'll do it." My voice breaks with the honesty of my words and the lies mixed in. A lone tear trickles from the corner of my eye and tumbles down my cheek, following a path of guilt and utter bewilderment at the situation.

"Do it," Theo instructs the priest without any further thought. He lets go of the chair, and testing how close I'll let him come to me, he brings me into his arms. We support each other as the priest carries out the ceremony to make us man and wife. Theo signs the marriage documentation with effortless ease, but my hands shake so much my signature is barely legible.

"You're safe, now," Theo reassures me. He is becoming more alert as time passes. I want to scream at him that he's being played for a fool by his father, but I know I can't. It's too late to stop what is already in process.

The priest proclaims us man and wife, and the ceremony

ends with subdued cheers from the gathered witnesses. It's not how I pictured my wedding when I was younger. There's no rejoicing crowds, beautiful bouquets, or a luxurious white silk dress. I don't love my husband, and I'm terrified of what comes next. Mind you, that's probably the same for any virgin bride, not that I'm a virgin anymore. I was when this all started, but that changed the day I was bought.

"You should take your wife up to your room to rest," Viscount Hamilton advises my new husband.

"What?" Theo blinks at his father.

"I'm not sure when she last slept properly."

"Of course."

"We'll talk more tomorrow. It's been a long day for all of us."

I look at the grandfather clock standing in a corner of the room when it starts to chime, and I notice it's just gone past midnight. Three hundred and sixty-six days in captivity, and yesterday wasn't my last day on this Earth.

Theo takes my hand and stumbles in a dream-like state from the room with me following, and Camilla leading the way. I turn my head back to take one last look at the Viscount before the door closes. He purses his lips together and mouths one word that sends shivers down my spine.

"Baby."

CHAPTER THREE

THEODORE

I'm not entirely certain whether I'm awake or still in a dreamlike state after being injected with that drug. This should be a dream because otherwise, fuck, I just married a stranger. However, the ice-like hand of the tiny woman who's following me into the grand bedroom of a house I've never seen before is all too real. I'm married. Shit! I don't understand any of this, but the instant I saw Joanna's hands shaking with fear, I knew I had to protect her. She's little more than a bag of bones with fading bruises that shadow her eyes, and I'm sure under the white linen dress she's wearing there'll be more. She's broken. I only need to see the distance in her eyes to know that. What she must have suffered is beyond comprehension to me. There is a part of me that wants to run from the room, find Nicholas Cavendish, and murder him with my bare hands. But the sane part, which is probably still a little worse for wear from the drugs, knows I can't do that. I have to stay here. I have to protect her. I have to give her life again...if that's even possible.

I let go of her hand, and she goes over to the bed. It's king-sized, covered in freshly laundered sheets. She looks at me and then at the bed. I watch her, still unsure of what is real and what is a dream. Slowly, she lifts the linen dress over her head and underneath, she's naked. I can see old and new bruising to her body. Scars from wounds mark her perfect skin, and I fight hard to tamper down the rage surging through me. She drops to her knees and bows her head.

"How would you like me, sir?" she offers in a voice so delicate it snaps my resolve.

"I don't!" I tell her and stomp forward. I grab her arm, and she whimpers. My head is screaming at me to calm down and be level-headed around her, but my heart is filled with fury, overruling any sensible thought. This girl has been through so much and has just offered herself to me.

"I'm your wife. We must do..." She tries her hardest to express what should happen next, but she can't. The words seem to stick in her throat—the mention of what normally comes after a wedding, silencing her. I throw her onto the bed, and as she parts her legs, ready for me, I turn away.

"Put the covers over you."

"*Please*," she pleads, and I can't hear any movement of her doing as I ordered.

"Joanna, cover yourself up." I swallow deeply. "Now!" The word leaves my mouth as an authoritative order, and I instantly hear her scrambling to do as instructed. I turn back to find her sitting in the bed with the sheets pulled up to her neck. "Thank you...stay here and get some sleep. Nobody except me will be allowed in here. I'll be back later."

"Where are you going?" She shifts to try and get out of the bed, but I put my hand up to halt her.

"Stay."

"I have to…"

She starts, but I cut her off.

"You don't have to do anything but sleep. Get some rest." I find myself at her side. I stroke my hand down her cheek, and she lets me without showing any fear of the possible consequences in her sorrow-filled eyes.

"Ok." She slides down into the bed. I flick a switch on the wall beside her, and the main lights in the room turn off. The only illumination in the room comes from a bedside lamp beside her. "You'll come back?"

"I'll be back in a little while. Sleep. You're safe in here. Nobody will hurt you."

She shuts her eyes, and I watch her for a few minutes. The feeling of protectiveness I have over her is strange—it's strong for someone I've only known for less than an hour. I need to make sure she's going to be all right, but the only way of doing that is to find out what is going on.

I quietly leave the room and go in search of my father. I find him sitting in the drawing room of the unfamiliar house with the lady who was comforting Joanna earlier.

"Theo?" my father asks quizzically when I enter the room. The woman jumps to her feet and bows toward me even though she doesn't have to. My father dismisses her with a wave of his hand. "I thought you would be resting."

"Not until I know what is going on here."

My father gestures for me to sit, and I do so in the chair vacated by the woman. He indicates to a brandy decanter, sitting on the table next to him.

"I think I'll pass. I've drunk my fair share this evening already, and mixed with whatever you drugged me with, I'll be asleep in a few minutes. I need to know what is going on. I'm married to a woman because it's the only way to save her, evidently. What is going on father? How much trouble are we in? What is happening with Victoria? Is she likely to end up as broken and bruised as Joanna is in a few months?"

"That's a lot of questions." Without lifting his head, my father talks into the half empty brandy glass he's holding.

"That's less than half of the ones I've got floating around in my head at the moment."

"Ok. I owe you an explanation. I had hoped to do it with a fresh head in the morning, but I guess it can't really wait. You remember how I told you I had to give Victoria to Nicholas Cavendish, or he would've destroyed our family name and killed me?"

"Yes." I say, sitting with the foot of one leg resting on the knee of the other.

"Joanna's father was forced to offer her up as well. Nicholas was given five women that night. His right, he insisted, based on years' old rules. I tried to argue they could no longer be valid in this day and age, but I was shot down by those who support his rule. Out of those five girls, only two are still alive: Joanna and your sister. Unlike Victoria, Joanna was not put forward to participate in the trials. Instead, she was sold to a mystery buyer and then disappeared. Victoria's story, you already know. She ended up married to Nicholas, and is now the mother of his daughter. A couple of days ago, my men got word of where Joanna was located. It's been exactly a year ago tonight since we started searching for her. We put together a plan and managed to rescue her."

My father goes silent, and his eyes fill with unshed tears. I know he must be reliving a horrible memory, which he wants to keep buried, so he doesn't have to experience it again.

"She was hidden away in what was little more than a dungeon. No clothes, nothing. The smell is the thing that will haunt me forever: feces, decaying human flesh. Another girl long since passed was left lying there in the darkened room with her."

"What?" I can't quite understand the words I'm hearing. They don't make sense to a brain, which is untuned to such horrors and has been laced with alcohol and drugs.

"It was horrible, Theo. I don't know how she survived. She's so thin. We gave her a steak when we got her back here to try and revive her, but as you saw on the floor when you married, she brought it straight back up. Her stomach is not used to it. We've had a doctor examine her. She's been repeatedly violated. She's not pregnant, thankfully, but…"

My father places his brandy down and slouches forward in his chair. His head's held in his hands, and he's shaking it.

"I'm sorry, son. I'm so sorry. I panicked when I saw her that way. All I could think about was what my own daughter will be going through. I needed to make Joanna safe, and this was the only way I could think it would work."

I slide from my chair and come to sit at my father's feet. It's a position my sister and I used to take when we were younger, and we wanted to offer him comfort.

"It's all right. I understand why. As my wife, Joanna is safe from the Cavendish brothers. You've told me they have eyes and ears in the police, so we can't go to them. Indeed, Nicholas and William are the reason why the police are investigating you for Elsie Bennett's murder. This was the only way of making sure they can't take Joanna away again. We're married, now, and she's safe."

My father shakes his head.

"She needs to be your wife in all ways. If you don't consummate the marriage, they'll figure out a way of annulling it. I know they will."

I hold my hand up to my father.

"I can't think about that yet. After what she's been through, I'm not going to force her into anything."

"You need to bear it in mind though, Theo. They have Tamara on their side with all her fancy education and knowledge. She'll do everything possible to get the girl back for them. William Cavendish has turned her against us. I fear Victoria will never trust us again, either. Nicholas has poisoned her brain, and she doesn't see what he's doing is wrong. I've lost my daughter and her best friend. I can't lose Joanna. She's the only one left to save."

"I know. I'll talk to her. Just not tonight."

My father nods—lines of worry are etched on his face. He's aged so much in the last few months with the stress of everything. I resolve then and there that from this moment on I'll no longer sit back and allow him to take the burden of his fight alone. I'll stand by his side in battle.

"I'm sorry about the drugging. The man who did it shocked me as well. He said it would be the quickest way to get you here, rather than having to take time out to explain it to you. I had to go along with him in the end. I pay him to know what's best in these situations."

"I understand." I've never had any reason to distrust my father, and I won't start now. I'm terrified for the future of our name and the society we operate in, but what I do know is I have a wife now, and it's time to step up and fulfill my destiny.

CHAPTER FOUR

JOANNA

A chill in the air wakes me from my sleep. I pull the blanket farther over my shoulders and nestle down into the comfortable mattress. The sheets feel softer than the ones I'm used to, and the bed's more comfortable, bigger even. Am I dreaming again? It feels so real though. If I had the courage, I would open my eyes and seek the truth, but I'm too scared of what I'll find. As I start to move, one hand brushes against the other, and I freeze when I feel the ring on my left hand. The memories from yesterday are real…they aren't a dream. I'm married to Theo Hamilton. I spring up into a sitting position in the bed and stare down at the antique wedding band on my ring finger. I'm married. Fuck! My head spins again. I didn't die yesterday, but I did fail. Theo didn't sleep with me. I'll be in big trouble.

Looking frantically around the room, I search for a place to hide. If I can't be found, then I can't be punished. No, he'll find me. I tried that once before and was beaten so badly my ribs were broken. But he can't beat me, now, can he? Surely Theo will notice new injuries on my flesh? My head whirls around so fast with all the thoughts running through it. It's like one of those roller coasters at the theme park where your stomach turns on every peak and fall.

Where is my husband? My brain stalls, rapidly braking to a standstill when the thought sparks alive. He should be here? Has he abandoned me already? I jump out of the bed and reach for a dressing gown that's been placed over the back of a chair. Quickly wrapping it around my naked form, I search the room for signs he slept here with me, but there's nothing. Not even discarded dirty laundry from the day before although I can't remember much about what he was wearing, possibly a pair of jogging bottoms and a t-shirt. He's left me already. The Viscount is going to be so angry with me. Maybe I didn't die yesterday, but it's likely I will today. Sorrow fills me up. I wish I could do something right —I'm forever making mistakes. I feel so tired again and crawling back into the bed, I pull the covers over my face. Hiding in plain sight. It's the only option I have left until he comes for me.

I must drift off to sleep, at some point, because I'm woken a little while later to a crashing sound in the room. I jump out of bed and drop to my knees on the floor with my head bowed.

"I'm sorry." Theo comes to stand before me. He offers me his hand, and I stare at it like it's diseased. "I won't hurt you. I just want to help you up. You don't have to kneel for me."

Tentatively, I reach out and taking his hand, he helps me to my feet.

"Did you sleep all right?" he asks, and I just stare at him blankly. This is far too normal. He should be beating me or forcing himself on me.

"Joanna? Is everything all right?"

"You didn't come to bed." I say, looking at the rumpled sheets where I've been lying, alone.

He points at a different door to the main one in the room. "This is an interconnecting room. I slept in there. I wanted to be near you should you need me, but I think you probably need space, for now."

"N-No," I stammer. "You should sleep with me. We are husband and wife. We need to make children."

He laughs at me, and I can't help but feel a little hurt.

"I'm sorry," he apologizes and guides me back to sit on the bed. "I went to speak to my father last night. He told me about your treatment at the hands of the Cavendish brothers. I'm not the sort of husband who would force himself upon you. You need to heal both in body and mind, first."

"But…" I start to interrupt him, and he places his finger over my lips to silence me. I don't flinch at his touch.

"No. We're going to return to London, in a few days. I don't want to leave the estate alone for long. We'll look into finding a psychiatrist and arranging further medical checks for you when we're there. Then, we can discuss the fact we're married. In the meantime, we'll focus on your healing."

I can't answer him. Medical examinations and talking to someone about what I've been through fills me with a terror so great I'm lost for words.

"I've got to head out for a couple of hours. Stay here and rest. Have a nice long bath. Camilla will feed you whatever you want. Don't have anything too rich. I think your stomach is still a little delicate. My father is downstairs if you are worried about anything."

Bile rises in my throat at the mention of his father. Keeping down food, at the moment, isn't going to happen. I just nod. Maybe the time alone will give me a chance to get everything straight in my head? Does Theo truly have no idea what's happening right beneath his nose? I'd like to believe he's foolish rather than compliant with his father's deviances. He's been nothing but kind to me, so far, and to have that illusion shattered would be the final straw to my sanity.

"Do you want me to run a bath for you before I go?" Theo asks as he picks up a set of keys from the dressing table. Is he going to lock me in the room? My eyes flash to the keys and back up to him. "For my car," he reassures and turns his head toward the bathroom.

"Please. A bath would be good," I tell him and slide from the bed. Following behind him as he walks confidently into the bathroom and turns the taps on, I can't help but notice the way his backside fills out the jeans he's wearing. It doesn't mean I want him sexually. It just means I like the look of him. I can look—it's normal. I can be normal.

"Joanna." I startle when he appears in front of me. "I put some bubble-bath in. Are you sure you'll be all right? I'll send Camilla up to check on you in ten minutes." He looks worried. He must be thinking I might drown myself in the bathtub. Little does he know, over the last year, I've had opportunities to kill myself, but I've not had the courage to carry it out. There's something buried deep down inside of me that's still fighting for life.

"I'll be fine. I've not had a bath in a year. Just a shower. I'll enjoy relaxing."

"All right. I'll be back as soon as I can. I'll fetch you some clothes as well." Theo leaves me alone in the bathroom, and the only noise is the gushing of the water from the tap. Padding across the marbled floor, I find a toothbrush and toothpaste laid out for me. I squeeze a little bit of the paste on the brush and clean my teeth. There is also mouthwash sitting on a shelf, and I gargle with that. For the first time in a year, I've had access to a decent toothbrush and paste, and my mouth feels clean and fresh. I stare at the girl in the mirror in front of me. She looks so very different to the one I remember staring back at me before. She looks older, a lot older, with dark shadows under her eyes, skin that's sallow and pale, and a wild mop of frizzy hair on her head. I was an innocent girl the last time I looked in a mirror. I'm a woman now, and a victim. I stand staring until the mirror steams up, and I can no longer see my reflection. Turning around, I catch the bath just before it overflows. I turn the taps off and place a foot towel ready beside the bath, so I don't slip when I get out. I lower my dressing gown to the floor and step into the almost scalding water. Sinking down into the bubbles, I shut my eyes and enjoy this moment of peace and normality. Who knew a bath could provide so much tranquility in a place of such chaos?

"I see you are already acting as lady of the manor." The rough voice of the Viscount sounds from the doorway, and I sit bolt upright. I try desperately to reach for a towel. One part of my brain is telling me I need to get out of the bath and kneel before him, but the other is telling me I'm naked, and he'll see everything. I'm conflicted. I preferred it when I didn't question my training. I choose instead to twist in the bath and kneel for him. Thankfully the bubbles cover my breasts. The Viscount laughs. "I guess I'll accept that."

I don't say anything back to him. You don't speak unless questioned.

"What happened last night? Did my son take you?"

Not the question I wanted him to ask. I can't lie to him. He'll know. He always knows.

"No, sir. I slept alone. He was in the adjoining room."

The Viscount tuts.

"That's not what I wanted to hear. You were supposed to make him want you, using whatever means necessary."

"I'm so sorry, sir. I tried, but he wanted to speak with you, and I fell asleep. He didn't return last night. This morning, I tried again, but he went out. I'll try as soon as he comes back. I'll plead with him." I'm babbling now. Terrified of the punishment, which follows swiftly when my head is grabbed and thrust under the water. I'm held in place as the water fills my nose and constricts my breathing. I try thrashing and pushing back, but I can't free myself. I'm pulled up just as the last of the air in my lungs leaves me. Coughing and spluttering, I try to bring more precious oxygen into my body as quickly as I can.

"I didn't ask you a question."

My head is thrust back under the water, but this time I don't have enough air in my lungs to prevent the dizziness from coming on immediately. When I'm yanked out again, I'm gasping and desperate to breathe.

"You failed me. That means punishment." The Viscount

has one hand wrapped tightly around my hair. His other hand goes to his trousers, and he removes his dick from its confines. I'm pulled closer to him, and he pushes himself into my mouth.

"Take it all." He bucks his hips, and there's nothing for me to do but allow him to violate my mouth. "You will do this to my son later. You will allow him to stretch that tight little pussy of yours and fill it full of his cum. You will make a baby boy, and I will mold him in my likeness. I'll make him the greatest heir to the Oakfield Society there's ever been. I'm next in line to becoming the leader of the society, and with William and Nicholas gone, I will get it all." He's thrusting wildly into my mouth—my cheeks hurt, and he's hitting the back of my throat as I gag around him. I can't help being thankful that I've not eaten anything yet. All I wanted was a relaxing bath, but instead, I'm back being terrorized and abused, again. Nothing will change. Ever! I'm to be a human sex toy for eternity. Maybe I should have drowned myself in the water when I had the chance? No! The part inside of me that still clings on to life screams repeatedly in my head, *we are stronger than this…we will survive.* The Viscount buries himself at the back of my throat and with a foul grunt, releases his semen. I work hard to swallow it all when what I really want to do is spit. I did that once and was left unconscious for a few days from the beating that followed.

Withdrawing from my mouth, the Viscount lets go of my hair, and I collapse down into the now cool water as he puts himself away. He then pulls the plug, and as the water starts to drain, he stomps over to the bathroom door.

"I've laid out clothes on the bed for you. Get dressed and

get downstairs. You'll be ready to greet your husband when he arrives back. Every time you fail in your task, you'd better be prepared for punishment. You're a whore to my needs… nothing more, nothing less. Don't get illusions of being anything else."

CHAPTER FIVE

THEODORE

I offer Joanna my arm, but she hesitates before taking it. I'd hoped her new found freedom would have helped her find some inner strength and confidence, however, over the last few days she seems to have withdrawn even deeper into her shell. She refuses to sleep alone. She wraps her body around mine, and I've had to tell her more than once our relationship is not sexual. It's as though she's had the need for such things ingrained in her and can't cope without them. We've spent very little time together while I've been busy preparing for our return to London as husband and wife. I made sure a message was sent directly to the Cavendish brothers, informing them I'm back in town, but I haven't mentioned Joanna or even the fact that I'm now married. I didn't hear anything back from them, of course, only a request from Victoria to meet up soon. Although given she's not allowed to visit my home, and I'll be dead before Joanna goes back to Oakfield Hall, I doubt that will happen until after the Cavendish brothers have met their just desserts.

I've spent many hours watching Joanna, wondering what goes through her head. She's panicky, especially when other people like Camilla and my father are in the room. I guess she's not used to being with people after a year hidden away. But she does seem relaxed when she's around me, which I'm pleased about. I'm glad I can make her feel safe.

"Where is your house again?" Joanna asks as the car pulls away from our temporary home. My father has to stay behind in his sanctuary. He's still a wanted man, at the moment, and returning with us would lead to his arrest. I wish he didn't have to stay here and could join us. I feel the weight of responsibility on my shoulders, having to run the estate and look after Joanna. But I know I'm ready for it, and even though it would be good to have him around should I need his advice, I'm certain it's only temporary. He'll be home as soon as we can deal with the Cavendish brothers. I'd been in favor of reporting them to the police, but as my father explained, they have spies everywhere, and it would only lead to more trouble for us than them. Furthermore, Joanna is reluctant to report her ordeal.

I rest back in my chair before I answer her question.

"Just on the outskirts of London. Surrey way."

"How old is it?"

Joanna is wearing a pair of skinny jeans and a t-shirt today. It's hot outside, the middle of July, and the weather is really heating up. The air conditioning is on in the car, and she's shivering. She's gained a little weight over the last few days, but she's still skin and bones. Reaching over, I hand her cardigan to her, and she smiles at me in thanks.

"It's late sixteen hundred. Nothing too fancy in the grand scheme of things, but it's home. I love the windows. They are massive. The Hamilton family has always been proud, so there was no bricking them up to avoid the window tax like a lot of our contemporaries did in the seventeenth century," I inform her.

"I remember my father telling me about that. We had a couple of the windows blocked up at my childhood home. I always found it strange until he explained."

"Some of the Old English laws are pretty funny, when you think about them?"

Joanna nods in agreement and says, "They are. I did some research after my father told me about the window tax. I'm...I was a bit of a geek for random facts. Did you know it's illegal to carry a ladder on a pavement in the London Metropolitan Police District?"

"Really!" I chuckle at the absurdity of the law.

"Truthfully, well as truthful as the Internet is, every time you see a workman carrying a ladder on a pavement in London, he's breaking the law." Joanna's face lights up, and for the first time since I've met her, I see her smile. It's beautiful. Underneath all the sorrow and fear is an amazing woman trying to get out. "I'm sorry...I'm talking too much." The smile instantly disappears when she catches me staring at her, and she cowers back in on herself as though preparing for punishment.

"No. I like it." I respond immediately, feeling the need to placate her worries. "Tell me another."

"I...I..." She hesitates, fighting within herself to determine what she should do. Then she flicks her head to the side and looks out of the car window at the surroundings. The house we were staying in is far behind us now, and we are speeding down the motorway in the direction of my family home.

"Is it just us going to the new house?" She turns back to face me.

I nod.

"Yes, my father's in trouble with the law. He's wanted on a murder charge. He didn't do it, but we can't prove that yet, unfortunately. Nicholas Cavendish has provided the police with information that somehow suggests my father is responsible. We'll eventually clear his name, and he'll be able to return home. Until then, it'll be just us and a few members of staff at Hamilton Manor."

"Nobody from where we've been staying?"

"Joanna is something wrong? Has someone upset you there? Camilla? One of the guards?"

"*No*," she replies instantly. "It's just everyone there knows what happened to me. What I was forced to do. I'd like to be somewhere people don't know… if that makes sense?"

"Of course." I tentatively reach out and take her hand. I've limited physical contact between us, not wanting to scare or give her the wrong impression, but this feels like the right thing to do. "I understand. No one except me will know what you've been through unless you choose to tell them. Should you need Camilla to visit for some female company, then I'll arrange it. I promise you, Joanna, in my home, you'll be safe. Nobody will force you to do anything against your will."

She turns back to look out the window, and we fall into an easy silence for a few moments.

"Salmon." Joanna suddenly announces.

"Salmon?" I query confused. "Would you like it for dinner?"

"No. It's one of those old laws. You can't handle salmon in suspicious circumstances."

I chuckle at the revelation.

"No dancing around the lounge with a dressed salmon at Christmas then?"

She shakes her head and proceeds to tell me for the remainder of the journey about how beached whales have to be offered to the Queen first.

When we pull up the driveway to my home, I'm relieved to finally be back. I hadn't exactly expected to leave, and a lot has changed since I was drugged and taken by my father. I help Joanna out of the car and show her around the house. I've put us in adjoining rooms again. I know the last few nights I've stayed with her as a comfort blanket, but I don't want to presume anything tonight.

"Do you like it?" I ask as she strokes her hand over an antique dressing table. The room she's in is painted a pale pink with a silk wallpaper hung on one wall. Everything in the room is a family heirloom, including a silver brush and comb my mother used to use, which rest on the dressing table. When she looks out the window, she'll be able to see all the beautiful roses in blossom that Victoria loves so much.

"It's beautiful. I love it."

"I'm glad."

She picks up the silver mirror and stares at herself in it.

"This looks old. You should put it away somewhere safe."

"It's Victorian. From my mother's family. We don't really have anything to do with them. Apparently, they didn't approve of her marriage to my father."

Joanna places the mirror down and comes over to stand by me.

"Where is your mother? Is she here?"

"No." I shake my head. "Her family were right…the marriage didn't work. She and my father are still married for appearance sake, but they live separately. I don't see her that often."

"I'm sorry. My parents are similar." A sadness crosses her face.

"It's a curse of society marriage, which we won't repeat." The words come out of my mouth before I have a chance to truly think about their implication.

"What do you mean?" Joanna asks, her brows knitting together in confusion.

"That's a matter for a later discussion. As I said, we need to ensure you are healed first."

She turns away from me and looks over at the bed. Her shoulders slump.

"Will you be joining me in here?"

"If you need me, yes. Again, my room is just next door."

"You promise me nobody here knows about me?"

I don't know what propels me toward her, but I suddenly find my arms wrapped around her waist, and her slight body pulled closer to mine. She doesn't flinch but melts into my embrace as though she welcomes the comfort I can offer. With all the abuse Joanna has suffered, alarm bells should be ringing in my head, alerting me to the fact she hasn't run screaming from my touch, but they don't. Instead, I enjoy her warmth against me.

"I promise you. You're safe here. If I'm not around, I will have a guard with you at all times, so the Cavendish brothers can't get to you. You're mine to protect now, and I will with my life. Trust me."

Joanna goes up onto her tiptoes and presses a soft kiss to my cheek.

"Thank you. You don't deserve any of this."

"Hush." Placing my finger over her mouth, I let it linger there, and she presses her lips against it. There is an undeniable sexual attraction growing between us. For the first time, I start to entertain the thought that this marriage could be more than just a means of offering her protection. I've seen glimpses today of the happy woman she can be. I want more of that. I let go of her and walk to the bookshelf in the corner of the room. Flicking through the titles, I snort out a laugh to myself when I see just the book for her, and pulling it out, I hand it to her.

"Here."

She looks down at it.

"The Guinness Book of Records?"

"I thought you might enjoy it. Considering your passion for random and obscure facts. I'm going to go and make a few calls. You can enlighten me with your new-found knowledge at dinner."

She clutches the book to her chest, a big smile blossoming over her face. I adore that smile. It lights up the room and warms my heart in the knowledge there is hope she can overcome her past.

"Thank you, Theo." She looks down at the book and back up to me. "I'm so glad to have met you."

"Me, too."

I head for the door, but as I reach for the handle I stop, remembering something I need to tell her. As I turn back, Joanna is settling herself in a comfortable seat ready for a few hours of reading.

"I almost forgot. I've arranged for your mother and father to join us at dinner in a week. They are desperate to see you again."

CHAPTER SIX

JOANNA

"It'll be ok." Theo reassures me with a squeeze of my hand. He's the only person I'll allow to touch me. Yesterday evening, we ate together at the large table in his dining room, and I sat next to Theo while he took his place at the head of the table. At one point, when leaning over to place a plate of grilled chicken, vegetables, and potatoes in front of me, the butler accidentally touched my arm— I immediately jumped up from my chair, sending the food flying across the table and straight into Theo's lap. I was mortified at my own stupidity, but Theo did his best to calm me down. I feel so lucky it's him I'm spending my time with and not his father. Maybe my stars have changed? It's been a week, and I've not been raped or forced into any sexual act. I feel sort of normal, or as close to normal as I'm ever likely to experience again in my life. I'm anxious, though. I'm so very nervous of meeting my father as I don't know how he'll react, and there's no way of telling. When I was a young girl, he was kind enough to inform me of my fate, which is something I'm aware Victoria's father never did for her. He was also different from Amelia's father because he didn't insist on training me for the trials. I was told what I would need to do but never forced to try them out beforehand. If I wanted to attempt something, it was my choice…but I didn't. I wanted to enjoy my childhood before the inevitable came. Will he be angry at me for not succeeding in becoming Nicholas' wife? He must know it was Viscount Hamilton who bought me, and not Nicholas? Will my father be able to end this charade once and for all? My mind has been filled with tumultuous thoughts all night, trying to envisage all the alternative ways today could go. But every possibility I considered descended into screams when I imagined it was Viscount Hamilton who came to see me instead of my father.

"I promise you," Theo reassures me again as a stray lock of hair falls from the neat French plait I have braided into my long blonde hair, to keep the frizz at bay. Reaching forward, Theo tucks the loose strand behind my ear. His touch is so different to others and sends warmth cascading through my body.

"What if he's angry at me?"

"Angry?" Theo shakes his head in confusion. We're sitting together on a sofa in his lounge. The room is formal in style but with a touch of modernity here and there.

"Because I didn't win? Because of what happened to me?"

I give Theo a couple of alternatives.

"He's your father. He's been worried about you. The second I spoke to him to tell him you were safe and under my protection, he was thrilled. He's been worried sick about your whereabouts over the last year. The Cavendish brothers prevented him from going to the police. He believed you were dead and became a defeated man. I've never heard so many screams of joy when I told them you were safe. It'll be all right. You'll see."

"I know," I reply and find myself leaning into Theo. Am I becoming too dependent on him? I pull away again, but he tugs me back to nestle under his arm.

The door-bell rings, and I almost jump out of my skin.

"I don't think I can..." Getting to my feet, I race for the door, which I know leads me away from the hallway and toward my bedroom. A strong arm wraps around my waist and pulls me into a solid mass of heat.

"You can," Theo whispers into my ear. "I'll be with you the whole time. I promise."

My breaths come out in ragged heaves, but I allow the warmth of Theo's body to bring me comfort.

"You'll stay next to me the entire time? I don't want them to touch me. Please. You have to promise they won't. I can't have them touch me, yet. Please, Theo."

"You have my word."

A knock comes at the door opposite to the one we're currently standing by, and I allow Theo to lead me back to my seat. He settles me down but remains standing.

"Ready?" he whispers again.

"Yes," I reply, knowing I need to face my parents at some point.

"Come in."

I can feel my heart almost beating through my chest as I watch the door open. It's unhurried and tormenting as if in slow motion like when an old fashioned film breaks. My mother and father enter the room, Edgar and Sarah Nethercutt, the Earl and Countess of Linton. They're still just as regal as I remember. My mother wears a skirt suit in a teal color, and my father is dressed in a formal suit with a monogrammed tie. They look like they are off for an afternoon tea, not meeting the daughter they haven't seen in a year. Theo is wearing a shirt and smart trousers, but I'm just in a long jumper and leggings because I've lost so much weight I don't really fill anything else out. It's easier to hide it this way.

"Lord and Lady Linton." Theo extends his hand out for my father to shake it. My mother lets out a whimpered gasp when she sees me. I can tell she's been crying from the red rims around her eyes—I hate the fact she's upset. She's my mother, and I don't want her to be distressed. She's not a part of this secret society. She's merely an obedient wife who's done as she's been told. Woman have no place as rulers in my world. We are toys to our men's whims.

"Theodore, a pleasure." My father shakes Theo's hand. "I can't thank you enough for what you've done for our daughter."

"Joanna." My mother steps forward and tries to bring me into an embrace, but I shuffle farther behind Theo. I can't let them touch me, and I wonder why? They are my parents— they wouldn't hurt me. Except, that's not true, because my father freely gave me to Nicholas for the sale. He's the reason I've suffered as I have. If he'd left England, taking me and my mother and hiding us away, then none of this would've happened. I drum my fists against my father's chest as the anger bubbling inside me explodes,

"This is all your fault!" I scream with tears streaming down my face. I bash his chest over and over again. All my tension and fear is being dispelled from my body through my fists into bruising punches. Nobody moves for a few moments. I vaguely hear my mother's weeping getting louder, but I'm too focused on the fury seeping from me. Eventually, Theodore wraps his arms around me and pulls me away.

"Enough," he orders, and I bury my head in his chest and allow the tears to soak through into his shirt.

"What did they do?" my father questions, his voice quivering with emotion.

"We don't know the full details, yet." Theo's deep voice rumbles through his chest, and I allow it to soothe me further. "I'm not sure we'll ever know, but the main thing is Joanna is safe."

"And married." my father adds in a poignant tone.

"In name only."—Theodore's voice is tense—"I'll not force her into anything she's not ready for."

"Good," my father answers.

Theodore turns me around, so we are able to sit down together. When I finally lift my head, I notice my father and mother are sitting opposite us. Both have lines of worry etched on their faces. My mother looks older...so much older than I remember her being a year ago. This has been hard on her. She wanted to run away, but it never happened. My head hurts, my body hurts, and I want to go back to sleep.

"Joanna." My father leans forward in his chair. His eyes are full of kindness and love. He's sorry for what happened. I can see it in that moment and let out a whimper. "If I could have changed anything about that night, I would have. You're my only daughter, my little princess, and I love you so much." He stops himself when his voice breaks and takes a deep breath. "I'll do anything it takes to put a stop to your hurt. You have my word. Theo is a great man. I couldn't wish for a better husband for you."

"Thank you." My response comes out like the squeak of a little mouse.

"How do you feel?" my mother asks.

"Good." I find my voice. "Theo has been feeding me well. It will take a while, but I'll be all right." I repeat the motto, which Theo used to calm me down before my parents entered the room.

"You will." Her mouth smiles at me, but it doesn't quite reach her eyes. I know she fears for my mental stability after just witnessing the attack on my father.

The butler re-enters, and Theo looks up at him.

"My apologies, sir, there is a phone-call for you. It's one you really need to take."

The butler taps his hand three times against his leg. It's like a code to convey a message to Theo. He immediately gets to his feet, but I grab his hand.

"I won't be long. I have to take this."

"But…"

"You'll be fine." He smiles at my parents and then looks back to me. "You've got this."

I reluctantly let him go, and he leaves the room. My mother, father, and I sit in silence.

"Theo's a nice man," my mother observes.

"He is. He's being very patient for a man who's suddenly found himself married," I reply and bring a finger up to my mouth and nibble on what's left of my tattered nails.

"Not the Duke but still a catch, I suppose," my father adds, and I open my eyes wide at him. "It'll have to do for now. At least I'll be second in line to the title when we get rid of the brothers. My deal with Viscount Hamilton has gone well." My father gets to his feet and comes to sit on the chair next to me. He brings his arm around my neck and pulls me closely to him. I don't like the touch—it suffocates me and doesn't give me any of the warmth that Theo's does. It freezes me with its icy intentions.

"I've got a message from Viscount Hamilton, my little Joanna. He might not be here with you, but he hopes you are still working hard at your task." He squeezes tighter around my neck. "Given Theo's declaration that he'll never make you do anything you don't want to, though, I think not."

"Edgar, please," my mother begs but is silenced instantly with a furious growl from my father.

"Get Theo's child inside you before the week is out, or there will be consequences, Joanna. Do you understand?" My father is cutting off my breathing now. I can't believe he's in league with the Viscount. I hoped for a father who'd be sorry for giving me away, but no, I have a devil who is still using my body and mind to get his own way. I try to speak, but I can't. I nod my head instead. I know the consequences he speaks of will involve me being returned to the Viscount, and I don't ever want to see him again.

"Good girl."

He lets go of me, and I gasp for air. My heart breaks all over again when I turn to my mother, and she immediately looks away and down to the ground. A true mother would fight for me, but she's too lost in her own tale of sorrow and despair.

"Sarah, it's time to go." My father gets to his feet just as Theo comes back into the room, and I manage with some difficulty to control my breathing in front of him.

"So soon?" A look of concern crosses Theo's face, and coming to my side, he draws me into his arms. I hope he doesn't feel the rapid beat of my heart. It might give away the fact I'm terrified, having finally realized I've no hope of ever escaping the impossible position I've found myself in.

"I fear little and often is going to be all Joanna can cope with for now. We don't want to overdo anything so soon." My father gives me the look of a caring and protective father, but I know differently, now. "I would like to come and see her again in a couple of days if that is all right?" my father asks.

Theo looks down at me. "It's up to Joanna."

I want to scream no. I'm desperate to tell him that I want my father to leave the house and never return.

"Yes, of course," I reply in robotic fashion.

My mother and father take their leave, and I remain alone in the lounge while Theo sees them out. I'm drowning under the pressure placed upon me. I'm breaking with no chance of a reprieve.

CHAPTER SEVEN

THEODORE

I can't help worrying that presenting Joanna as my wife at the society function we're about to walk into is too soon. It's only been a few weeks since my father rescued her, and in the formal halter neck evening gown she's wearing, it's still possible to see how painfully thin she is. Although the deep purple colored gown is designed to hide the scars that litter her back, she's conscious of her appearance and fidgets constantly, which is something society girls are schooled against at an early age. Common sense tells me to turn away from the ornately decorated doors welcoming us into the banqueting hall, but instead, I allow the inherent determination within me for revenge against the Cavendish brothers to take over.

"The Honorable Theodore Hamilton, son of Viscount Arthur Hamilton and his wife Lady Joanna, the daughter of the Earl of Linton," an announcer introduces us, and to an audible gasp, we enter the room with our heads held high. Well, my head is held high—Joanna is trying her best, but the sea of faces greeting her must be daunting. I can feel her body shaking under my touch as I guide her into the room. I take us straight over to an old school friend of mine whose wife I know will be happy to keep Joanna company for the evening.

"Sebastian, Emily," I greet them with a handshake for my friend and a kiss to the cheek for his wife.

"Did we just hear right?" Sebastian asks, a glass of Champagne poised at his lips.

"You did. Let me introduce you to my wife. Joanna, this is Sebastian, an old school friend of mine, and his wife, Emily."

Sebastian leans forward to greet Joanna, but she steps behind my back. My friend eyes me questioningly, and I shoot him a look to tell him not to ask here but to accept it. He does so with a mouthful of Champagne.

Emily waves at Joanna.

"I love the color of your dress. Who's the designer?" I knew my friend's wife would be able to put Joanna at ease. I turn around to bring her back to my side, and she looks up at me as if asking permission to answer the question.

"Freedom, remember," I tell her, and she strokes her hand down the purple silk of her gown.

"It's Stella McCartney. I love her clothes, and Theodore bought it especially for me to wear tonight."

"She's an amazing designer. I've got so many of her outfits in my wardrobe." Emily replies.

A waiter passes with a tray of Champagne, and I take two glasses. I hand one to Joanna, and she looks at it like it's poisoned.

"I've not had alcohol in a year," she whispers so quietly I can barely hear what she says.

"Would you prefer a soft drink?"

She shakes her head.

"I want to be normal. I like Champagne."

"Then drink as much as you want," I say, laughing to try and dispel her tension.

"I'll just have the one." She takes a sip and a big smile crosses her face. I'll need to watch how much she consumes as her body is still recovering and won't be used to the potency of the alcohol, but I'm glad she's trying it, at least for the time being. When I look up, I see the dark fury behind my friend's eyes. He's not stupid and is forming his own opinions as to what has happened to Joanna because it's well known she's been missing from society for a year. My conversation with him later is going to be a very interesting one indeed.

The conversation hushes again when the gong sounds to announce another guest.

"His Grace, Nicholas Cavendish, Duke of Oakfield. William Cavendish, Earl of Lullington, and his wife, Tamara, Countess of Lullington."

The silence is broken when a glass smashes on the floor. I look down at my feet to see Champagne splashed up my trousers and crystal at my feet. I don't need to look up to know it's Joanna who's dropped her glass at the introduction of the new guests. Emily reacts before I do as the crowd goes back to their gossip.

"Oh brilliant, another klutz just like me. I'm terrible. The first time I met Sebastian's mother, I bumped into a table and knocked a family heirloom on to the floor. Ever since then, whenever I go to visit them, they hide anything valuable away." Emily laughs and offers Joanna her hand. "Why don't we go and powder our noses and allow the men to sort this out. Is that all right, Theo?"

Joanna's eyes go wide. She looks between me and Emily, and then across to where Nicholas and William are being greeted by other guests at the party. My nostrils flare with anger. How these two deviant monsters can still be freely walking around when the woman next to me was broken by them is unbelievable? They will get theirs, though, I'll see to that. But not just yet. For now I need to be the strong man I've been taught to be, and pushing all feelings of retribution aside, I need to look after my wife.

"Of course," I tell Emily. "I'll clean my trousers as well."

"I'll join you," Sebastian immediately adds, placing his empty glass on a passing waiter's tray before taking his wife's arm. I bend my arm to allow Joanna to place her hand through mine, and we lead them to the bathrooms as waiters scamper behind us to clean up the broken glass.

"I'll wait here for you," I inform Joanna before Emily takes her a little reluctantly into the ladies' bathroom. Sebastian follows me into the gentlemen's bathroom and does his business as I set about trying to wipe down my trousers. While washing his hands, he raises an eyebrow at me in the mirror.

"So, you going to tell me?"

"It's a long story and not really one for a public bathroom."

He turns the taps off and dries his hands.

"Please just tell me someone else made her as frightened as a mouse? Because you know what'll I'll do if I find out it was you."

"You know I'm not that sort of man." I reply, staring back at him in the mirror.

"Ok, you need any help let me know. She's a good wife for you."

"Thank you," I offer in gratitude to both his comments. "We need to get back. I don't want to leave her alone for too long out there."

He looks at the door, trying to understand my meaning. His mind working over-time, probably trying to link the breaking of the glass with the arrival of the Cavendish brothers. Sebastian is not titled. He's from a rich family who have never been involved in the society from what my father has told me. He wouldn't understand it, and I'm not about to involve him. I fold my arms across my chest in a gesture that tells him he's not going to get any more out of me tonight.

"Ok. It's best I don't leave Emily alone for long, either. She really is terribly clumsy."

We both leave the bathroom, and the first thing I see is Joanna with Nicholas Cavendish standing next to her. Emily's brows are furrowed together in anguish, and Joanna is white as a sheet.

"Get away from her." I stomp furiously across to them and push Joanna behind my back. Nicholas steps away and places his hands behind his back. His nostrils are flared with rage, but I can see he's trying to control it.

"Theodore. Good to see you again … and married? I'll have to inform your sister. I don't think she's aware yet."

"Your Grace," I show him deference to his title and bow. It sickens me, but I'm the better man, and I won't allow my manners to slip. "I'm afraid we've only just returned from the country. I'll be sure to arrange a meeting with my sister, at the first opportunity. I'm surprised she's not with you tonight."

Out of the corner of my eye, I see Sebastian take hold of Emily and pull her closely to him. I nod to him, confirming he's fine to leave, and he leads Emily away. I really don't want to involve him in what's happening here.

Nicholas watches them go before he replies.

"As you know, your sister had a baby just over a month ago, and Rose takes up most of her time at the moment. I'll be returning home to them as soon as possible."

"So you can abuse them like you did Joanna?"

"I'm sorry?" Nicholas genuinely looks surprised, and I can't help but think of him as a fantastic actor. "The only thing I've ever done to Lady Joanna is to brand her, and that was beyond my control. I've not seen her in over a year. In fact, the second I saw she was here, I came to check on her. I'm amazed to find she's married to you."

I snort a laugh at the utter stupidity of his declaration. We all know the truth, so there's no point in lying about it anymore.

"Do I really look like a fool?" I snarl at him through gritted teeth.

"Do I need to answer that?" Nicholas retorts, and my anger flares enough that I ball a fist and prepare to send it flying into his smug rapist face. At that moment, William and Tamara appear, and Joanna grabs hold of my hand before I have a chance to make a show of myself.

"Please," she whimpers with a cry of desperation.

"Ok." I turn to her as William comes and stands steadfast beside his brother while Tamara stands next to her husband.

"Theo, please. Listen to them," Tamara implores.

"Stay out of this," I bark and focus my attention on Nicholas. "Isn't it enough you have taken my sister and brainwashed her? And now you've wound your claws around Tamara as well. I may have lost them, but I'll not let you take Joanna. You've done enough damage to her. I've seen the scars and heard the screams when she's sleeping. You're sick individuals…both of you."

"Is he nuts?" William exclaims.

"Not now." Nicholas holds his hand up to his brother.

"He must be if he thinks we did that to Joanna. It was his father who bought her."

"William," Nicholas replies tersely.

"Ok. Time for me to do that shut up thing." Earl Lullington folds his arms across his chest.

"Thank you." Nicholas breathes a sigh of relief. "Theodore, I don't know what you've been told, but I've never hurt Joanna, save for the brand. If you just ask her, I'm sure she'll confirm it."

I feel Joanna press closer in behind me.

"Please, Joanna. Victoria desperately misses her brother. She's suffered so much. Now's the time we all need to pull together and support not only her but also help you to deal with whatever you've been through. What I'm trying to do, at the moment, is change the society and make certain there'll be no more sales, and no more demanding of women. This must end. I have a daughter…a beautiful little girl, and I want her to grow up free." Nicholas tries to step closer to us to plead with Joanna, but I hold a hand out to ensure he keeps his distance.

"Enough. Joanna doesn't need to confirm anything to you. I know exactly what you are."

"Let her speak." Nicholas orders with a menacing tone that has several passers-by immediately scatter from the hallway we're standing in. The chandelier lights even seem to shudder with fear.

"He did it." Joanna sobs from behind my back. Her head is buried in my suit jacket, but she pulls away and comes to stand at my side. "Nicholas Cavendish raped me. His brother watched and sometimes joined in. They do the same to Tamara and Victoria. They've beaten and starved me. They are evil and need to be destroyed."

The hallway falls silent, and I take the opportunity to re-form my fist and send it flying into Nicholas' jaw, knocking him off his feet and into his brother.

"Stay the fuck away from Joanna. She's mine, now, and you won't be getting her back. Enjoy the remainder of your freedom because by the time I've finished with you, you'll be rotting in prison for the rest of your lives."

I grab hold of Joanna's hand, and we storm out of the venue and back to the car. I'm itching to return and beat the crap out of the Cavendish brothers, but Joanna's soft whimpers calm my temper. Once we've taken our seat, I bring her into my arms and hold her tightly until she stops sobbing.

"I'm sorry." I kiss the top of her head as the car pulls away, and we commence the journey home.

"Don't be…it's all my fault." She manages to get her words out in between wracking sobs, which break my heart. I vow then and there I will die before Nicholas Cavendish ever lays a finger on her again. This must end. Soon, Joanna, Tamara, Victoria, and Rose will all be free.

CHAPTER EIGHT

JOANNA

The lie that tripped so easily from my tongue last night has haunted me ever since. Thankfully, Theo left early this morning to seek support for what he termed, 'an oncoming battle' with the Cavendish brothers to unseat Nicholas as the head of the Oakfield Society. Theo's father has given him a list of people to canvas, so I'm sure they'll all be people the Viscount has already ensured will support his cause. My father's support of Viscount Hamilton after what that man had done to Victoria, his own daughter, proves to me there are no morals left within the men of the society. I wish I could persuade Theo to leave it behind and disappear to a different country, but I've no chance while he's adamant at clearing his father's name. A name I know is guilty as sin for crimes against me, and I'm pretty sure is equally as guilty on all other charges. Maybe one day I'll be able to persuade Theo of his father's evil actions? But that time is not now. I'm still too scared to tell the truth. The lies are easier since I know I won't be beaten for telling them. It's ironic because in childhood I was punished for the little white lies I told my parents. But these aren't little. They are the sort that could destroy innocent people, and I don't know how to stop them without having to face more of the agonizing degradation of rape and violence I've become accustomed to.

I need to stop thinking this way and start my day. I promised Theo I would try today. Before I was taken, I was learning graphic design in my spare time. I knew I may not have a future so didn't want to specialize, but I enjoyed taking pictures and manipulating them on the computer. Theo asked me the other night what I would like to do, and I told him about the graphics and the photography. The next day, I'd had an all singing and dancing camera delivered to me along with a top specification Mac laptop. I'd also been enrolled onto an online course with the view to doing a degree in graphic design if I wanted too. I was stunned but impressed. I'd spent some time yesterday acquainting myself with the computer, but I want to use the camera today to take photos of the roses in the garden. They really are spectacular and would make a fantastic canvas to work with on the computer.

Retrieving the camera from within the specially laid out cupboard in my bedroom, I check the battery, which is fully charged. I then open the hinged compartment where the memory card is stored and pop a new one in. Theo also bought me several memory cards in spite of the fact each of them probably holds over six thousand pictures, even with high resolution settings enabled on the camera. I'm not sure how many photos he expects me to take.

Placing the camera strap over my neck, I slip on my lightweight shoes and make my way down into the garden. It's a beautiful day, not as hot as it has been over the previous weeks, which is a relief since we're living in a house designed in an era when air conditioning didn't exist. A slight breeze rustles through the leaves of the trees, and I inhale deeply to allow the fresh scents of the garden to settle inside my nostrils. The fragrances are calming and decadent after a year of nothing but four musty walls.

I start walking toward a collection of roses growing over an arbor in the corner of the garden. They are bright red and remind me of blood. Checking the settings on my camera, I look into the viewfinder and start snapping a few pictures. When I'm happy with my first foray into capturing the beauty of the setting, I flick the review mode button on the camera and look at the pictures I've taken.

"Beautiful, aren't they?" The soft feminine voice comes from behind me, and I spin around quickly, dropping the camera on the ground. My heart beats rapidly when I see Victoria standing in front of me, and a memory flashes in my head of our only other meeting. *All of us, in our white linen dresses, standing before Nicholas and the previous Duke of Oakfield while we wait to hear our fate.* She appears to be nothing like the terrified young girl she was back then. She looks glamorous in her tight black jeans and red tunic top. You couldn't tell she'd had a baby only just over a month ago. "The roses are the one thing I miss about this place, apart from Theo of course. I've started a rose garden at Oakfield Hall, but it'll be a few years before they are as beautiful as here. Around by the swimming pool, they are even better. You should take some photo's there."

"What are you doing here?" I ask as I take a few steps back from her. "Nicholas isn't here is he?"

"No. He's not happy I'm here either, but I need to talk with you. We are the only two survivors from the trials, and I need to know what really happened to you. Not the lies you told my brother last night. If Theo is in trouble, I will look out for him."

"They weren't lies," I stutter out before I have a chance to think about what I'm saying.

"Your saying Nicholas and William held you captive for a year, and I didn't know about it?" Victoria rolls her eyes.

"Yes," I try to reply with authority, but I'm shaking so much I have to lean against a nearby bench to support myself.

Victoria rubs her hand against her forehead before stepping closer to me. I jump away from her and find a tree to support me this time, instead.

"I'm not going to harm you. We've both been through enough hurt. I don't know for certain what happened to you, but I know it involved my father. He bought you that day. I saw it with my own eyes."

"No. Nicholas did."

"Joanna, please."

"I need you to leave, or I'll call for help."

Victoria exhales an exasperated snort.

"This is my childhood home. Nobody here will throw me off the premises if I choose to be here."

"Please leave." I muster as much courage as I can and turn away from her and start to walk back to the house. She catches up to me, though, and places her hand on my shoulder. I can't help the scream that escapes from my mouth.

"Don't touch me." I push her away but then cower back when I realize what I've done. "I'm sorry. I'm sorry."

We are by the entrance to the house, now, and I flatten my back against the wall waiting for her fury to explode and the pain to start when she beats me.

"I won't hurt you, Joanna. I'm not my father. He gave me away without telling me anything about what would happen to me. Do you know what I went through because of him? I was degraded in front of the society with a scold's bridle on and nothing else. I was naked, and they beat me until I was left unconscious for a few days. I walked across hot coals, and I saw one of the girls put a pistol to her head and kill herself."

I let out a loud gasp and grip tightly to my stomach.

"No."

I want to cover my ears and shut her out. She was hurt, but now she's okay. She's not a broken liar like me.

"Do you know who saved me?" Victoria asks, but I only half hear her, and she knows it, so she grabs either side of my face and forces me to listen. "Nicholas Cavendish. He saved me. He's a good man and is trying to rid the Oakfield Society of men like the old Duke and my father. He's the father of my daughter, and I've left him alone looking after her at the moment. Would I do that if I thought him capable of doing what you accuse him of? Joanna, we can help you. Whatever it is they hold over you, we can put a stop to it and save you. You must trust me. We have to tell Theo the truth. We have to save him from doing something he'll regret in the long run. Please, you have to listen to me." Victoria is pleading her case to me, but I can't do what she wants. I can't. He'll come for me—my father will know and so will hers. They probably know Victoria's here already. I'll be beaten … raped. I can't. I need the normality of a life with Theo. He's the only one who can take care of me—he's told me as much. I have to support him and what he wants. He's my husband now. He's the only one who can save me, and in return, I'll save him by whatever means necessary—if that requires me telling more lies, then I will. I'll lie to save my husband because he's the only man who's never hurt me. Nicholas Cavendish isn't the good man Victoria is making him out to be. He branded me: he took a red-hot iron and burned his society's crest into my thigh. Would a man trying to put an end to the way his society treats women really do that? Theo can bring the society down. He's the only one. He can get rid of them all, even his father. My brain flits between one fact and another like a washing machine on spin circle. The confusion is rife in my head, but focusing on Theo is the one thing I can do to bring me clarity.

"Nicholas Cavendish and his brother raped and abused me," I tell Victoria.

She lets go of me and steps back, and I see the defeat cascading through her body. She'd expected me to roll over and join her, but I don't know if what she promises is real. *Nicholas branded me*, I repeat in my head to justify my decision. "Please leave."

Victoria nods.

"I'm sorry, Joanna. I didn't realize the full extent of what my father was capable of. He's really broken you. I wish I could save you, but until you realize Nicholas is not the evil in this, there is nothing I can do." A tear tumbles down her cheek, but I turn my head away. I must stay resolute despite the fact a gasp of anguish is caught in my throat, threatening to erupt at any minute. It shouldn't be woman against woman. We are the ones who stay strong and stand together, but not at the moment. We are falling apart because of the society. Victoria continues, "If you ever need me, you know where I am. My door is always open to you."

She starts to walk away but stops.

"I love my brother. He's a good man who knows nothing of what's happened to us. He's the only innocent in all of this. Please don't let it be his downfall. Protect him. Love him. He needs it."

Her heels click along the concrete slabs toward the front of the house. My breathing quickens as they get farther away. A memory hits me of the present the Viscount gave me: the wig made of Tamara's hair.

"Wait." I call, knowing I should keep quiet but unable to silence my tongue from protecting another woman if possible.

Victoria stops and looks hopefully at me.

"It's not what you think. It's just some advice. Watch Tamara closely. I don't know how key she is to all of this, but what he made me do… my captor. His intentions toward her were not honorable. I fear for her safety. Keep an eye on her."

"I don't understand?" Victoria tries to come back to me to ask questions, but I quickly run into the house and don't stop until I'm locked safely in my room.

CHAPTER NINE

THEODORE

The day has been amazing and beyond my wildest dreams. The people I've met on my father's advice have been more than willing to join my campaign against the Cavendish brothers. I feel hopeful we can avenge what they put Joanna through and destroy their stranglehold on the Oakfield Society. As the car pulls up to my home, all I want to do is jump out and run and tell Joanna. She was so quiet after meeting Nicholas yesterday, and I worry intensely it has stirred up all the memories she's tried to bury deep within her. On arriving back home, I allow the driver to open the car door for me, and as I climb out, I see my butler waiting at the front door, holding what looks like Joanna's camera.

"Is something wrong?" I take the steps leading up to the house two at a time, my pulse quickening with worry.

"I don't know, sir. The Duchess of Oakfield visited earlier. Lady Joanna left her camera in the garden when she returned inside shortly after."

I take the camera from him and notice the lens is smashed. In another few quick strides, I've left my butler standing in the hallway, and I'm upstairs and outside Joanna's room.

I knock lightly, three times, before trying the handle. It's locked. Putting my ear to the door, I can hear Joanna crying. Without hesitating I dash quickly into my room and through the interconnecting door into hers. She's lying on the bed curled up into a ball. When she looks up at me, I can see red rims of tiredness and sorrow around her eyes.

"What happened?" I ask as I place the camera on the sideboard and springing onto the bed, I bring her into my arms. She's cold to the touch, so I pull the sheets up to cover her body. "Joanna, talk to me, please."

"Nothing."

"I know Victoria was here. Is she ok? Has something happened?"

"I can't..." she whimpers and then goes quiet.

I pull her farther up the bed, so she has to look directly at me.

"You need to talk to me. I can't help unless you tell me what happened."

She tries to stifle a sob, but it comes out as an exaggerated breath instead.

"Do you ever wonder what it would be like if you were born into a different world, place, or time?"

"Sometimes, but I don't regret the life I live. I know it's honest, and I try to do the best for those around me."

"But what if it's not possible. Because of fear, you're too scared to even think about what the truth is and what lies are anymore. Knowing if you find out what you think is true isn't, then you could be killed for it or worse." I'm deliberately cryptic when talking not wanting to give too much away to Theo. If he discovers the truth of his father's actions, there is a chance he could be killed. I certainly will be murdered for driving a wedge between father and son.

"Joanna, what did Victoria say to you?"

I gently hold her chin with my hand and turn her head from side to side. I'm checking for…I don't really know what I'm checking for, but I have to know she's not injured in any way.

"I want something different," she replies and lifts her head up, so she's looking directly into my eyes.

"What?"

"For tonight. I want to be normal. No hatred, hurt, lies, revenge. None of that. I just want to be husband and wife. We barely know each other. I've told you a handful of things about me. My love for photography and graphics but nothing else. I know so little about you other than you seem to have a passion for philanthropic work."

"But Victoria being here? It upset you."

She shakes her head.

"No. Not tonight. What is your favorite food?"

She shifts on the bed, so she's sitting on top of the sheets. The color returns to her cheeks, giving them a rosy tint. Her eyes are expectant with excitement, and gone is the sorrow and fear that was evident in them before. She has shut away what upset her, and I know I'll never get anything out of her, tonight. In this moment, though, I don't care because I want more than anything to please her and make her happy.

"Filet Mignon."

She rolls her eyes.

"Typical male answer."

I bash my fists against my chest like a caveman.

"Man need meat!" I growl, and she laughs so loudly it fills the room with her delightful sound.

"Woman need chocolate."

She copies my tone while beating her chest.

"I'd never have guessed." I shake my head.

"But do you know how I like it?" she teases playfully.

My brain instantly goes into the gutter, and I imagine her licking chocolate off my dick before I drip the molten delight all over her tits. I'm a hot blooded male, and my wife is sexy as fuck. Not that I'll touch her until she's ready. I compose myself, but I think she's read my thoughts because she blushes.

"With strawberries, raspberries, and blackberries," she quickly adds to dispel all thoughts of my sexual preference for chocolate.

"Nice." I snort a little laugh before reaching out to the phone at the side of her bed and dialing the kitchens. The chef answers straight away.

"Sir?" Despite it being Joanna's room, she'll not use the phone to order anything for herself, so he knows it's me calling.

"Do we have any strawberries, raspberries, or blackberries?" I ask and listen as rustling comes from the other side of the phone while he looks in the fridge.

"No blackberries, but we do have the other two," he replies after a minute.

"Good. What about chocolate?"

"What type?"

"Type?" I query before realizing what he means. I pull the

phone down to my chest. "What type of chocolate do you prefer?" I ask Joanna,

"Dark, please."

I nod and return to the call.

"Dark please. Can you melt it and bring some of those small almond biscuits up as well?"

"I'll bring you a chocolate fondue platter, sir. I believe we even have some marshmallows somewhere."

"Thank you."

I hang up and turn my attention back to Joanna who's moved off the bed while I was on the phone and has gone into the bathroom. Despite it only being around seven in the evening, it appears she's changing out of her clothes and into her PJs. I get off the bed and standing casually outside the closed bathroom door, I shout, "Do you like sport?"

"Sorry?" she says as she walks out in her baggy trousers and top. She's as beautiful in her casual clothes as she is in her smart ones.

"Do you like sport?" I repeat and lead her to one of the chairs in the room. She takes a seat, tucking her legs underneath her, and I pull a blanket off the bed and wrap it around her.

"I do." She laughs as though enjoying a private joke, and I cock my head wanting to be in on it. "I was very much into sport when I was younger. My father got really angry at me, at one point, because he wanted me to do hockey or polo, but I wanted to play rugby. He threw an absolute fit one day when I came home and told him I'd made the school's rugby team. It was all right for the boys at the neighboring boy's grammar school to play but not me. I had to quit after a few games, though, having come home with a black eye. It wouldn't have done if any permanent damage had occurred prior to me being given to the society." She falls silent again, and I'm just about to tell her I preferred rugby as a sport as well, when there's a knock at the door. I unlock it and allow the butler to bring in our food. Joanna stands and bows respectfully to him. He repeats the gesture back before leaving us alone once more. She looks between the food and me, waiting for permission to eat, so I nod my head at her. It's the same with every meal even though I've told her she can start eating whenever she wants. She picks up a big strawberry and dips it into the chocolate before bringing it to her mouth and devouring the sweet treat in seconds. I can't help but smile as I watch her.

"How about favorite animal?" Joanna questions me.

"Animal?" I screw my nose up. It's not something I've ever thought about.

"Yes," Joanna continues. "I don't know why, but I've always had a thing for giraffes. I love their faces, and they seem really cheeky to me. They are majestic. It's silly, but I just like them."

"It's not silly. Don't worry. But I don't know about my favorite animal." I rub my chin while thinking. "I like owls."

"Owls?"

"Yes, they're wise, skilled, and can hunt in the dark. A good animal."

"A prowler!" Joanna chuckles and picks up another strawberry. I do the same.

"What about the future?" She sucks on the end of the red fruit.

"What do you mean?" I swallow my strawberry in one bite and choose a raspberry next.

"Do you see yourself as just the future Viscount or something else?"

I breathe deeply and pop the raspberry in my mouth.

"I'm destined to be Viscount. I've seen how my father has run things, and I'd like to do some of it differently, but until I hold the title, I'll follow his rules?"

"What would you like to do differently?"

Joanna sits forward in her chair, listening intently to me.

"You called me a philanthropist earlier, and I'd like to do more of that. Help people who haven't had the privileges in life that I have. Victoria and I said as children we wanted to set up our own art school for people to learn to paint like all the great artists." I go quiet for a moment and remember my carefree sister. Knowing what Joanna has been through, I'm desperately worried for Victoria. I want to get her and my niece away from Nicholas before it's too late, but I fear I won't be able to.

"I promise you, she's happy," Joanna states out of the blue and picks up another strawberry.

"No one can be happy with a man like that. It's delusional."

She looks down to the ground and places the strawberry back on the plate.

"I'm tired. I think I'll sleep."

Looking at the clock, I see two hours have passed with us talking and eating.

"One final question. This time, I'm asking it."

"Ok."

"After this is all done, do you see yourself still being married to me?"

Joanna gets to her feet and comes over to where I'm

sitting, opposite her. She places her hand under my chin and tilts my head up toward her face. Slowly, she leans forward and presses a kiss to my lips. It's soft and tastes of strawberries and chocolate. I lick my lips wanting more of her taste.

"You'll always be my husband. You saved me when no one else could."

She goes to turn around, but I grab her hand and pull her back to me. My heart is beating so fast. I've tried to keep my distance from her, not just for her sake but also for my sanity. I must be wrong in the head. She's a victim of abuse and doesn't need me forcing anything on her so soon, but I want her. I want her in my bed, I want my dick inside her, and I want to bathe her insides in my cum until my child grows within her. I've never felt emotions this urgent and overwhelming before. Joanna Nethercutt, no, Joanna Hamilton, my wife, has embedded herself under my skin with her beauty, naivety, and a spirit so strong she could fight a million soldiers single handedly if she wanted to. I stand and pull her to me, so she's resting against my body. My forehead drops forward onto hers and rests there a moment while our eyes look directly into each other's. I shut mine and bring my lips to hers again. This time, it's not a brief kiss but one that seems to go on forever. It grows more and more urgent as every minute passes.

Joanna whimpers under my touch, and I instantly pull back. It's not a whimper of pleasure…it's one of fear, and when I look at her, she has tears streaming down her face. I don't say anything to her—I just swoop her up into my arms and carry her over to the bed where I lay her down and climb in beside her, fully clothed. Then pulling her close to me, so her back is against my chest, I hold her tightly until her breathing evens out, and I know she's fallen asleep. I pushed her too far tonight. I have to be mindful of what she's been through, and how it will shape our future life together. She may never get over it. We may never consummate our marriage, but I'll be beside her like this forever. I allow my own eyelids to flutter shut as the exhaustion of the day washes over me.

The next thing I know, I awaken to Joanna screaming and kicking out in my arms. She's shouting, 'no'. I need to rouse her gently, so holding her tightly, I softly tell her it's a dream, and reassure her I'm here. Eventually she stirs and opens her eyes. They are wide with fear, and there are black circles underneath them where her sleep was disturbed. She pushes me away and sits up gasping for air. Reaching over to the nightstand, I grab a glass of water sitting there and offer it to her. She drinks the whole contents in a few big gulps.

"Tell me..." I try to stop myself from asking because I don't want to upset her any further, but I can't. I have to know. "Joanna, tell me what your dream was about?"

CHAPTER TEN

JOANNA

I've not had a nightmare for a few nights now, and as I struggle to get my breath back, I wonder what triggered it. The day had been intense with meeting Victoria again for the first time since I was sold to her father, but I thought I'd relaxed enough with Theo that evening to overcome my anxiety. The only other reason could be the intense kiss we shared. I know I'll be punished by his father for not taking it further, but something inside me screamed at me to stop. Sitting here now, though, looking at him with worry lines etched all over his handsome face, there's a part of me wishes I hadn't. Because despite everything that has happened to me over the last year, my body is calling out for a normality only Theo can give me. Against all the odds, I know I'm falling for him. He's the man I dreamed of marrying: kind and caring with a serious side but not afraid to laugh when it's needed. When I was a child, and I stood in my mummy's high heels, and my Sunday best outfit pretending to be a bride, he was the man I imagined as my future husband. Fate is cruel—it's given me the man I want, but I know he'll end up hating me because of who I am. Life has kicked me and put me down at every opportunity, and I'm already in hell with the knowledge of what I have to do. That's what I spent most of the afternoon crying about: the fact I have to weave a web of lies because I'm trapped with no means of escape. Victoria loves Nicholas Cavendish. He's not the man Theo believes him to be, but if I don't convince my husband he is, then I'll have to watch Theo die, and I'll suffer more torment at the hands of the Viscount. It's an impossible position to be in, and to make a decision either way curses me forever.

"Joanna, tell me what your dream was about?" Theo asks me again.

"My dream was of the first night they took me. I've not reflected on it for a while now. The memories have become clouded in my head, but the dream was so realistic. The smells of the dark room, the pain as I lost my virginity and suffered a beating." Tears pool in my eyes. I don't want to cry them, though. My tears belong to me, and I'll not allow them to fall for Viscount Hamilton ever again.

Lying back down in the bed, Theo pulls me into his chest, and I lay my head on the smattering of hair there.

"Would you tell me more?" he asks, and my head rises and falls with his breathing as he speaks.

"I don't know if I can." I look around my current bedroom—it's a distinct contrast to the room in which I lost my virginity. This room is comforting and inviting. Somewhere I enjoy lying in bed with my husband. It's nothing like the other room, which was hell. It was dark and had a musty smell. The only furniture in it was a bed and very little else. But that wasn't what I hated the most. It was that I had no sanctuary. Lying here in Theo's arms, I feel safe…but in that room. I knew I could be taken at any moment, and I'd be hurt and degraded.

My mouth opens and shuts like a fish on Theo's chest. I want him to know what I went through, but I'm so scared of reliving it. He tightens his grip on me, and it grounds my anxieties.

"It was a few days after Nicholas had chosen Victoria, Elizabeth, and Amelia to go through to the trials. Daphne had disappeared that night, but I was kept in Oakfield Hall for a few days. I was kept away from everyone else, so they didn't know I was there. One night I was woken up, and a sack of some sort was placed over my head. I remember being bundled downstairs and into a car. We drove for so long, and I had no idea in which direction, or where I was going. I think I shook the entire time. I tried to sing some songs to comfort myself, but nothing worked. Eventually the car stopped, and I was pulled out and led into what I assumed was a house. I remember them pulling the blindfold off my head, and *he* was standing there in front of me like a monster with a devilish smile on his face. I knew then what was about to happen." The memory of Viscount Hamilton's leery face causes me to stop and catch my breath. It sends a shiver down my spine, remembering the way he stepped forward and licked my face.

"Nicholas?" Theo asks.

"Sorry?" I'm so lost in my thoughts I don't understand what he's asking.

"Was it Nicholas or William who took you first?"

The need to lie to Theo sits on the tip of my tongue. If I name his father, it could lead to my husband's death.

"He ripped my clothes from me. I wasn't wearing much … just a tatty linen dress like the one I married you in. I was naked underneath as had been prescribed for the presentation of the women." I've ignored Theo's question completely, and he seems to accept it because when I pause, he doesn't ask again. "I tried to pull away, to run, but there was nowhere to go. He punched me in the face, not just once but three times. I was barely conscious, which allowed him with his superior strength to hold me down and push roughly inside me."

I stop and sit up, needing to get air into my lungs. Talking about this, recalling the memories and the pain is leaving me dizzy. I'll still not allow the tears to fall, though. I will not!

"Do you need to stop?" Theo sits up and asks.

"No, I need to continue…I was a virgin and wasn't ready or prepared for the intrusion. It hurt beyond anything I'd ever experienced before. It was even more painful than breaking my arm when I was six, and the bone came through the skin. It felt like it went on forever with him inside me, and his hips bucking wildly as I was torn apart down there, but it wasn't really. In reality it was only a few thrusts and then it was over. He emptied his cum inside me, and he made me his whore."

"You're nobody's whore. No matter what's happened to you. Don't ever say that. You're an amazing, strong woman. You're here, having survived all that happened to you, and you're still functioning. You've not shut down to everything around you. It would have been so easy to do that, but you haven't. You've embraced the new life you have here. I bet if I look on your camera I'll see some amazing pictures. Focus on that, and not on how Nicholas Cavendish made you feel."

My heart beats faster while I listen to Theo as he sets me free from the torment of my mind, but then he utters those two words and drags me back into the depths of despair, 'Nicholas Cavendish'. It wasn't a man with that name who did these terrible things to me. It was my husband's father. I'm a pawn in his game, and the whore he made me. I can't fight against what he wants me to do because I don't have the strength any longer. I'm dying inside with no hope of resurrection.

The tears start to fall. I can't stop them. Viscount Hamilton wins.

"Joanna, please. I meant every word I said. You are a beautiful, strong woman. I'm lucky to be married to you. I don't want to scare you, but I've known since the moment I first set eyes on you I wanted more out of our fake marriage than you'd be able to give me. I'm willing to wait forever for you if I have to, but in these few short weeks, I've known you will be my wife not just for the short term but forever. Damn it!" He stops and pulling me toward him, he wraps his arms around me. I can feel his length hardening against my leg, and the significance of it terrifies me but sends shivers of excitement through my body at the same time. I don't understand what's happening. Sex should repulse me. I should want to run from it. I've just told the man holding me in his arms that when I lost my virginity, I was held down and raped. But he still wants me, and I think I want him too. He continues, "I'm sorry…I've never wanted to put any pressure on you. I've only ever wanted you to feel relaxed and happy around me. Get to know me, but I…I need to leave." He suddenly pulls away from me and disappears out of the room before I have a chance to catch my breath.

I lie there for a moment with a torrent of thoughts running through my head. I'm a victim, but I'm not broken. Maybe I can have a normal life? Theo will protect me. Now I'm away from the Viscount, he can't hurt me anymore. I can ruin his plans without him realizing it's me, and if they don't come to fruition, he can't return to Hamilton Manor. I'll be safe forever. As long as he stays a wanted man by the police, I'm safe from him. I can become a wife to Theo. I can learn to love and cherish him—my growing feelings for him tell me that already. I have to go to him. I have to become a woman again and this time properly.

My legs carry me, stumbling, in a dreamlike state through the interconnecting doors of our rooms. My breath hitches when I see Theo, he's lying naked on his bed with his large hands curled around his dick. He freezes when he sees me.

"Joanna, go back into your own room."

I shake my head, telling him no.

"Please," he pleads, but I don't listen and instead take a step closer to him.

"Show me." The words leave my mouth, and I feel like I'm in a dream. I shouldn't want to see him at his most intimate as he pleasures himself, but my heartbeat quickens with the excitement of seeing this stunning specimen before me. *Men are disgusting creatures who cause nothing but pain and suffering,*…that is what my subconsciousness is screaming at me, but my eyes are telling me something different. They see beauty and the most arousing thing I've ever witnessed. "Show me," I repeat and take a seat on the edge of the bed.

"I don't want to hurt you." Theo's voice is thickly laced with worry.

"You won't," I tell him because I know it's true. I don't

know how, but my heart tells me it is, and it's about time I let it rule, at least for a while. My brain has been switched on far too much over the last year. It's time for it to fade into the background and get some rest.

Theo looks between me and his hand, which is still wrapped around his large cock. In my limited experience, it's a thing worthy of display in an art gallery: straight with a large head, and veins protrude along its length, giving it life and presence. He looks toward me again and then slowly starts to stroke himself. His head falls back down against his pillows, and he shuts his eyes. I watch without flinching as he loses himself in the sensations cascading through his body. I've seen a man experience pleasure in sex and ultimately orgasm before, but there is no malevolence surrounding this intimate act with Theo. He's getting off on stroking himself, but it's innocent at the same time. It's not hurting anyone. His eyes screw up tighter, and his body goes rigid moments before jets of white cum shoot from the head of his dick onto his stomach. He opens his eyes and stares straight at me as wave upon wave of orgasmic pleasure hits him. There is so much happiness and delight behind his eyes. It leaves me breathless, and I can't take my eyes from him. I want that: I want that pleasure, that happiness, and that freedom. His orgasm finishes, and the room falls silent except for the sounds of our rapid breathing. Theo reaches over to the side of the bed and retrieves a box of tissues from a drawer. He starts to clean himself off, but I find myself moving closer and stopping him. I then take another tissue and begin wiping him myself. There's a little bin beside his bed, and I throw the used tissues in there. Neither of us have spoken, yet. We've just shared quick glances between each other as I set about cleaning him, and he lay flat on the bed.

"Make me feel that way." I don't realize I'm saying the words until they've left my mouth.

"Joanna?"

I silence him with a finger to his lips.

"Please." Leaning over him, I remove my finger and replace it with my lips. Now, it is my time to fly free.

CHAPTER ELEVEN

THEODORE

My head tells me to push Joanna away, but my heart urges me to bring her closer. *She's not ready* —it's what I keep reminding myself, but with the way she's looking at me right now, I can tell she is. This feels like the right thing to do. How can you fall for someone so quickly when you barely know them? The heart and mind are strange creatures. So often in conflict but ultimately working together.

"I don't want to hurt you," my mind responds, and I pull my lips away from hers.

"You won't." My wife's plea falls from her beautiful plump lips in a breathless moan of need.

"You really want this?" my heart asks, this time, with a quickening of its pace.

"I want to be normal. I've been a victim for too long now. I don't know why, but when you're near me, my heart beats quicker. I need this." Joanna comes at me again and joins our lips together. This time, I don't fight her. I give in to the need surging through me. Despite having come only a few minutes ago, my dick is hard again already, and I want her.

Pulling back for a second time, I rest my forehead against hers.

"If you want me to stop at any point, you say so, and I will. I won't force anything upon you."

"I know," she whispers with a tremble of nervousness mixed with excitement in her voice. "It's why I want to be with you. You'll take me as far as I'm ready to go and not any further. You'll give me what I need because you already know me better than I know myself."

I bring my lips down to hers. My own breath is hitched and ragged with the need coursing through my body. Pulling her over my naked body, I allow her to straddle my thighs. It gives her the control over what we're doing. If I were in her position, I would want to have that.

I'm naked, but Tamara is still wearing her pajamas from earlier. I can feel the excitement between her thighs, and her wetness against my bare flesh. She really did enjoy the show I'd just put on for her. My dick hardens more against her, and I know she can feel the length of me poking into her through her clothing. She's just witnessed the power of an orgasm, and now I am going to use it to show her the pleasure that can come from taking me deep within her...no, not taking, accepting me willingly without pain or torture into her most private place. One I'll never allow to be abused again.

Leaning forward, I run a kiss over her lips and down her neck. Her PJs button up at the front, so while she supports herself over me, I bring my hands up and start to unfasten them. She lets out a barely audible gasp, and her sapphire eyes shift to watch my dexterous fingers at work.

"One." I undo the first button, the bottom one. Moving my hands up, I loosen the second and third in a swift movement. "Two, three."

Joanna's mouth opens and shuts, trying to bring much needed air into her lungs.

"Please," she begs, but I can not allow her fervent appeal to affect the deep-rooted control which is embedded within my psyche. If this were a normal woman I was fucking, she'd already been on her back with my dick pistoning in to her so fast she'd forget what damn day of the week it is. But this is my wife, my delicate flower, and I need to take this slowly so we can both savor every moment of our first time together.

My hands start to shake a little with the need for rigid control, and they fumble over the final button before finally freeing it from its frustratingly difficult small button hole.

Sliding my hands up to her shoulders underneath the cotton fabric of her pjs, I remove her top and drop it down onto the bed. Her breasts are a perfect fit for my big hands. The cuts and and bruises, which had once marred her skin, have disappeared to leave a stunning feminine form. She's everything I could have wished for in a partner. It's as though she was made for me by the gods, not that I believe in that sort of crap. In my opinion, you make your own way in the world, and by protecting Joanna from Nicholas Cavendish, I've earned her love, and her body.

I lower my mouth down to her left nipple—its peak is already taut with the sensations and emotions running through her body. Wrapping my tongue around it, I lavish it with attention while tenderly massaging the other breast under my hand. The pink flesh smells of the lavender perfume she uses mixed with a slight scent of sweat from the day's exertions. It's purely Joanna, unique to any other woman's breasts in my experience. I'm in two minds whether to linger here or travel lower to discover her other delights, but the grinding of her hips against my thighs shows me where she needs my attention.

"I'm going to lay you down. Is that all right?" I ask and then press another quick kiss to her breast.

"Yes." The reply comes quickly, and I place my hands under her hips and adjust us so she's lying flat on her back on the bed. Her eyes are wild with desire but also mixed with nerves. It dawns on me that together we're giving her a chance at a first time, again…although this time it's with her consent.

"Our first time," I moan into her prickling flesh, sucking and savoring her taste as I move down to her stomach and then even lower.

"Our first time," she repeats and wraps her hands around the thick strands of my hair. With a subtle strength, she guides my head to where she wants me between her thighs. Inhaling deeply, I can smell her arousal, and my dick hardens so much I'm certain I could pound nails with it. I need her, but I have to go slow. I think there's only one thing for it. Times-tables. I need to recite them to stop myself from fucking her too hard.

One times one is one. One times two is two. The words are spoken inwardly as I start to lower her pajama bottoms down her svelte legs. She's had no reason to keep herself trimmed, but the hair on her pussy is shaved into a delicate strip. *One times three is three. Fuck. One times four is four.*

Joanna settles herself back on the bed and opens her legs

wide for me. She gives me the gift of her pussy and the numbers in my head go haywire.

Two times nine is sixteen, no eighteen. Fuck.

"Theo, take me," Joanna begs, but I can't answer her. I can't look at her.

"Three times four is…fuck, fuck, fuck, fuck, fuck!"

"Theo, look at me," my wife demands, and the words pull my head up from looking at her perfect pussy to her beautiful face. "Twelve," she tells me.

"What?" I'm confused and shake my head.

"Three times four…"

Shit. I can't have kept my controlling math as deep within my head as I thought I had.

"I'm sorry." I sit back up on the bed. "I'm completely fucking this up."

She snorts a little laugh and then shakes her head.

"No, you're not. You're a smart man and your using your head to make love to me." She points to where my brain is analyzing every minute detail and coming up with the wrong answer. "But you need to use this, instead," she says, placing her hand over my heart.

"I'm so scared of hurting you, though."

"And that's why you're making love to me like I'm broken. I want you to fuck me. Show me how it should be. Show me the feelings I saw on your face when I watched you come. That's what I need, and you're the only person who can give it to me."

I can't help but feel a total loser at her words. So much for being an alpha male. I've been approaching this from totally the wrong frame of mind. Joanna is stronger than she looks.

I've told her enough times. If I want her, I should just take her and show her how making love can really be.

I nod slowly at her and tentatively reach out to touch her pussy with my left hand.

She gasps, but it's not out of fear. It's pure wanton desire. I run my fingers over her pussy lips and part them to reveal the delicate bud of her clit hidden beneath. It's peeking out from its hood, needing my attention. With my tongue, I taste the length of her warm feminine flesh. It's pure in its innocence and desire. She tastes like my perfect woman.

Joanna moans and grabs the sheets beneath her.

"More."

I oblige, feasting on her pussy. My tongue tantalizes her clit and then dips into her hole to lap at the essence flowing from within her. She's more than ready for me, but I want to give her an orgasm first. I push a finger inside her. At first, there is a little resistance, but that disappears the second I press my tongue to her clit and flick it.

"More," she cries again, arching off the bed. "Make me a proper woman. Make me normal."

I push another finger inside her to join the one already there and hook them up to rub at the sensitive spot within her. My tongue flicks harder and harder over her clit.

"Oh my god. I'm...I'm.... God."

I use my teeth to nip at her clit, and that is all she needs to fly free, for the first time of her own choosing. A broken angel no longer. She cries out with the pleasure cascading through her, her body jerking as she comes. Her pussy clenches down on my fingers, massaging them with the powerful waves of her first pure, beautiful orgasm. It's the single best experience of my life: watching her find herself. I guide her down after and allow her a moment's rest before withdrawing my fingers and moving up and over her to position my dick at her entrance.

She doesn't need to say anything to me. The look of affection in her eyes is her consent, but she knows I need to hear the words.

"I need you inside me, please." A beautiful melody to my ears that has me slowly pushing into her. Her moist heat embraces my dick within its welcoming haven, and I lose my mind and almost my cum like a schoolboy experiencing his first sexual encounter.

"Now you can use your timetables, if you want," Joanna teases. "I want to come again."

"Bossy!" I laugh and slap her backside. I instantly worry it's too much for her, but her pussy clenching around my dick tells me it's something she enjoyed.

"Don't let me lose you now, Theo."

"You're not going to." I withdraw and then slam back in. Joanna lets out a squeal of pleasure.

"Fuck me." Her legs clench tighter around my body as we settle for the missionary position. The traditional position for a newly married couple. I allow my mind to become lost in the movement between us as my hips thrust in and out of her in a poetic motion designed for only one thing…climax. My eyes meet hers, and the stare between us is intense. It's not just the joining of two bodies but of two minds and souls as well. It's perfect.

My orgasm warms in my lower back, and I know I won't be able to last much longer. Reaching between us, I rub at her clit, and within seconds, she's coming again. Her whole body shatters around me in a violent orgasm of nothing but pleasure and desire. Then my orgasm rips from my balls and out of my dick in an explosion, coating her insides.

Shit! We didn't use a condom. I freeze, and she must realize at the same time.

"I'm clean." I offer immediately.

"So am I. They checked me," she stumbles over her words.

We both fall into an uneasy silence with my dick still inside my wife.

My dick still inside my wife.

I realize it doesn't matter about protection as a vision enters my head of her swelling with my child, and I drop down to kiss her lips.

"My wedded and bedded wife." I chuckle.

"I love you, Theo," Joanna whispers before nestling herself against my neck as I say the words back to her.

"I love you, too."

CHAPTER TWELVE

JOANNA

The world tilts on its axis when the sunlight streams through the curtains, and I realize my husband is not in bed with me. The space where he fell asleep last night is still warm, which suggests he left the bed recently. I listen for the shower, but it's silent. I'm disappointed, and my heart instantly deflates. Was I not good enough for him? Is that why he's not here? Does it show down there I'm a victim of abuse. I want to cry, and the tears well up in my eyes but don't fall when I suddenly notice the time on the beside clock. Eleven in the morning! I don't think I've ever slept this late. No wonder Theo isn't here in bed with me. He's an early riser. My body must have been more exhausted than I thought after our lovemaking. Pulling back the bed covers, my hand slides to my flat stomach. I can't help but wonder if Theo and I created a baby last night. It seems odd to me that by being pregnant I'll be safe from a beating, but equally, I'd love a mini version of Theo and me. A baby to worship and give me hope.

"I'm expecting a child in there as well." The deep timbered voice comes from the corner of the room. It's the voice of my nightmares. Please say I'm dreaming. However, as the owner of the terrifying intonation steps from the shadows, I know it's real. Viscount Hamilton is here. "It's taken you long enough to entice my son into that delightful pussy of yours." The monster comes closer to the bed, and I'm scrambling to cover myself with the bedsheets. I'm back in my pajamas, which thankfully offer me some protection. He's stronger, though, and with a hard pull on the cotton fabric of the sheets, they are ripped from my frantic grasp. "I don't believe this is the way I taught you to greet me!"

Next, I'm pulled from the bed by my arm and thrown onto the floor at his feet. I bow my head and stay quiet even though my entire body is shaking, and my teeth chatter with fear.

"My son is too lax with you. He's always been a softy. Sometimes I think Victoria has more balls than Theo does. Let's just hope what he does have are fertile. This has taken far too long. I'm getting frustrated. Do you know what it's like to hide from the police all the time because Nicholas Cavendish thinks he's found morality? Victoria is wasted on him. It's infuriating!" I jump when he stomps his foot on the floor in protest at his perceived injuries. I know exactly what it's like to be running from someone although my someone isn't the law—it's the man standing in front of me. It's exhausting, debilitating, and so very frightening.

I feel him tangle his hand around my hair before it's pulled hard, so my face juts up to meet his.

"You get a baby in your stomach within the week, or I'll come back and put one in there myself. Do you understand?"

My bottom lip quivers, and I manage to stutter cut a, "y-y-yes".

"Good girl."

He bends forward and presses a kiss to my lips. He smells of cigars and brandy—nothing like the fresh and inviting scent of Theo. I want my husband back. Where is he? I say a silent prayer in my head for him to burst into the room and witness his father's abuse of me. My eyes flick to the door, willing it to open and my savior to fill the void.

The Viscount laughs.

"He was called away to a meeting. I'm sure he'll be back later with another vote of confidence in us to take over the society. There are more men like me out there than you'd believe. We aren't all insipid wimps like my son and the Cavendish brothers. We know the real way to treat a woman."

My hair is pulled harder until I'm up on my feet and pressed against his body. I'm so glad I chose to put my PJs back on. Theo wanted me to sleep naked, but I'd told him I wasn't ready for that, yet. I still need the security of my clothing. He helped me re-dress. Maybe if I keep thinking of him, I'll survive what is about to happen to me, and the false hope I had that I was safe here won't be decimated into a crumbling ruin? The Viscount pushes me up against a chest of drawers in the corner of the room. He kicks my legs apart and strokes my pussy through the cotton fabric that's keeping it hidden. 'Theo,' I repeat in my head. 'Remember him doing the same thing. The way he made you feel, the pleasure which cascaded through your body when you came with him inside you.' It's not possible, though. Theo was gentle but dominant when he touched me, having realized

I'm not broken. The Viscount, however, is harsh with his ministrations, prodding and poking in a way that's completely devoid of romance and entirely designed to inflict pain. He pushes his finger hard into me with only the linen of my pajamas forming protection from his calloused hand and jagged nails. I can't keep in the whimper falling from my lips, and I hate myself for giving it to him.

"Always the little whore for me, aren't you, Joanna?"

He thrusts his fingers in a couple more times before withdrawing them.

"You know, when this is all over, I think I'll keep you for myself. My perfect toy who'll take anything I can give her. My cock really enjoys your cries. It makes it so hard."

He grinds his hips into me, and bile rises into my throat at the thought of what he can do with his repulsive member.

"Now is not the time for frivolity. I'm here for one reason alone."

The Viscount finally allows me to breathe by putting some distance between us. I gasp air into my lungs and adjust my pajamas to make my aching private parts more comfortable. That will have to do until I can burn my clothes and shower in scalding water to make myself feel cleaner. I'll never be able to feel completely clean again, though.

Turning around, I watch the Viscount open up a briefcase I hadn't seen before. I don't even want to begin to guess what he has in it, but I know it won't be good. Nothing with this man is ever right. How can I have gone from feeling confident in myself again and strong enough to make love with my husband to having it all destroyed in a matter of minutes? The realization dawns on me there will never be any escape. This is my life until the day I die. Theo may be adamant he'll protect me, but the problem is he's protecting me from the wrong enemy. The burden weighs heavily on my shoulders, and I sink to the floor.

Viscount Hamilton looks at me and shakes his head with a look of disgust on his face.

"Weak… just like all women."

He pulls out an envelope from his briefcase and stomps menacingly back over to me. I cower away, wanting to crawl into my own skin and hide.

"I've already told you I don't have time to play today. You can stop with the whimpering act. I need my dick inside you to make that fun, and I'm only here for this."

He throws the envelope down in front of me.

"Well open it!" he shouts, and it sends a shudder all the way through my body.

My hand tentatively reaches for the envelope, and I open it as quickly as I can while fighting to control the terrible shake coursing throughout my body. I pull something out and notice it's a photo. I instantly recognize the person captured on camera. It's a younger Nicholas Cavendish, and in his hand is a painting. It's vaguely familiar: the vibrant yellow flowers punctured by the glowing red blooms of two poppies. It was in Oakfield Hall. I remember it from the day I was sold. Victoria was staring at the picture for ages, and I wondered why. I never had a chance to ask her, but I've since learned from others she has an appreciation for art.

"I don't understand," I mumble and then shrink back scared I may be punished for talking.

"You don't need to understand. All you have to do is give that to Theo."

I look down at the picture again. It gives me an unsettled

feeling in my stomach. Nicholas is dressed head to toe in black, and the outfit he is wearing is not the clothing of someone who'd be carrying a priceless painting around for any honest purpose.

"It's stolen." The words escape me, and I will my mouth and brain to disconnect. If they keep speaking my thoughts, I could really end up beaten or worse.

The Viscount laughs out loud, the sound filling the room.

"Maybe you are smarter than I gave you credit for." He takes the photo out of my hands and places it back in the envelope. "Of course it's stolen. How do you think we all have the money we do? Looking after old houses and maintaining certain social standards doesn't come cheap. Nicholas Cavendish thinks he can give these things back and get away with it… No, it's not happening."

My tormentor kneels down in front of me and runs his tongue over my face.

"Art equals money. Money equals power. Power equals women, and women equal slaves. That is the future of the Oakfield Society."

A final kiss is pressed to my lips, and I'm thrown onto the floor before the Viscount leaves me lying there, alone. My heart pounds in my chest—its rapid beat is loudly thumping, and I place my hands over my ears willing it to go away, wanting the world to go away. I'm never going to be free. I slide my hands down my body to my stomach.

"Please God, don't let a child be in there. I can't bring another life into this world. It's corrupt and evil. It's hell. Hell is on Earth, and the devil is Viscount Hamilton."

CHAPTER THIRTEEN

THEODORE

I throw my car keys into the pot on a table in the entrance hall where I keep them. Today has been a complete waste of my time. A wild-goose chase around most of London with little result. My first meeting didn't bother to show up, no doubt paid off by the Cavendish brothers, and my second one disappeared halfway through when I mentioned I was married to Joanna. I've no idea what his problem is, no doubt something to do with her father. I've been doing some research on Earl Linton, and it seems he's not as innocent as he makes himself out to be. I wonder if Joanna is aware he was once arrested for rape, but all the charges were dropped when the victim was found dead. A rather convenient death he couldn't be linked to, so he got away with the whole thing. I think I'll keep a better eye on him. It's crossed my mind before he could be a spy for the Cavendish brothers. The last thing I need is for them to know our plans before we're in a position to implement them.

I need to lose the tension in my body, and my beautiful

wife is the only person who can do that for me. I didn't like leaving her still sleeping this morning. I wanted to wake her and take her again, but she looked so serene and peaceful, curled up in a little ball, so I decided not to disturb her. I start for the stairs leading to our bedroom, and taking the steps two at a time, my cock hardens with every step.

"Theo." I spin around when I hear my wife's voice coming from behind me, and in no time at all, she's in my arms, and I'm pressing my lips to hers.

"I missed you." I can't help but notice the way her body tenses, and how her eyes fail to meet mine. "What's wrong?"

"Nothing." The answer is quick, probably too quick.

"Joanna, is it about what happened last night?" My cock rapidly deflates at the thought it was too much for her, and she's suffering because of me making love to her.

"No, no. I promise you. I'm a little sore, but it was perfect." She shuffles her feet on the floor still looking away from me.

"Then look at me and tell me what's the matter because I know something is?" I place a finger under her chin and tilt it up, so I can meet her sapphire eyes.

"I made something for you, but I'm not sure if you're going to like it."

Cocking my head, I raise a suspicious eyebrow.

"What is it?"

She holds her hand out.

"This way."

Following Joanna through the house, she leads me to the busy kitchen. Staff are running around preparing dinner. The mouth-watering scent of roast beef wafts in the air, and my stomach rumbles. If I'm not going to be having sex with my wife, anytime soon, then a roast dinner is the perfect way of relaxing me, especially if it comes with a full-bodied red wine and Joanna at my side.

"Where are we going?"

The staff get quickly out of our way as Joanna leads me into the part of the kitchen that's used for making sweet confectionery. Sitting on a table in the middle of the room is a cake.

"You made me a cake?" I question.

"Yes, it's a Dorset apple cake…my grandmother's recipe. The chef helped me a little bit as I couldn't remember a couple of the processes, but it's been so much fun to do. It felt normal."

I press a kiss to her forehead in gratitude.

"It looks beautiful. Am I allowed a slice?"

"Of course." Joanna reaches forward and pulls a knife from next to the cake and cuts me a large slice. She places it on a plate and hands it to me. My butler enters the room, at that point, with a cup of what appears to be tea in his hand.

"Lady Hamilton insisted this is the best tea to drink with her cake." He places the tea down, bows, and leaves.

I bring the slice of cake to my mouth and take a bite. The apple, cinnamon, and crisp sugar topping elicits a moan of pleasure from my mouth.

"It's delicious." I take another bite and then a sip of tea. "Perfect."

"You really like it?" Joanna stands hopeful on her tiptoes.

"Don't tell the chef, but I think it's better than his cakes."

I give her another kiss to the forehead and quickly wipe away the crumbs I leave there.

"I loved making it with my grandmother. It was something I liked to do whenever I was upset. It's normal, so very normal, and it's just what I need before…" She shuts her eyes when she says the final words. I put the half-eaten slice down.

"Joanna, please tell me what is wrong? It's not just the cake is it?"

She inhales deeply and reaches for an envelope on the sideboard.

"I should have given this to you sooner. I brought it with me when I was rescued." She hands me the envelope, but the shake in her hand tells me something isn't right here. She's keeping something from me. I'm not sure what. I open the envelope and am greeted with a picture of Nicholas Cavendish and a painting. My father told me the society was famous for stealing paintings to fund its activities. If this is what I think it is, it could be the key to bringing down the current leader of a corrupt society, making it good again.

"Joanna, do you know what this is? Is this the only copy?"

She nods and then shakes her head.

"Yes. It's Nicholas with a stolen Van Gogh painting. The photo implicates him in the theft of it. I had another copy made this afternoon. It's stored in my room."

"It does incriminate him. I need to think." I start to pace the kitchen area. My head tells me to take this straight to the police and have him arrested, which would be the best way of bringing him down. But my heart is telling me to use it to do the one thing I've wanted to do from the start, and that is to ensure the safety of my sister, my niece, and my sister's friend, Tamara.

"What are you going to do?"

"I should take it to the police?"

She nods at me.

"You should, but you're not going to, are you?"

I pick up my slice of cake and take a final bite before heading for the door.

"Go up in your bedroom, lock the door, and don't answer it to anyone but me."

I don't wait for an answer. I know she'll do as I ask. Instead, I grip the envelope tightly to my chest and make my way through the house, grabbing my keys from where I threw them earlier and go back out to the car.

It doesn't take long for me to travel across London and into the suburbs, heading for Oakfield Hall. It takes even less time for me to be given an audience with Nicholas because I storm straight past his butler and into the current Duke's office. He is alone and looks up from a pile of paper with a frustrated expression on his face.

"I guess I shouldn't expect you to have the manners of good breeding, considering who your father is," he sneers at me and stands up. "What can I do for you brother-in-law?"

The words linking us together as family have me stomping across the room and pounding a fist into Nicholas' smug face.

"I'll never be a brother to you in any way, shape, or form. You disgust me. I'm here to put an end to your hold over my sister and Tamara, and in doing so, protect my niece."

Nicholas rubs at his cheek where I hit him but doesn't go down or attempt to retaliate. Instead, he looks tired and bored with the conversation.

"How many times do I have to spell it out? I'm in love with your sister. She's chosen to be with me and willingly given me a child. I've put your sister on a pedestal and will worship her forever. I'm not the evil man you think I am. You've been severely misinformed, and if only you'd listened to your sister, you'd understand that."

I cut him off,

"I'm not going to listen to lies instilled into her with violent beatings and rape."

He grabs my shirt.

"I've never once taken your sister without her consent. You need to listen to yourself. Your listening to the diatribe of a man who gave his daughter up to be abused by a society full of corruption. I'm putting a stop to that. Together with your sister."

I push him away forcefully.

"You expect me to believe all that when I have to listen to Joanna screaming and crying every night because of what you and your freak of a brother did to her?"

Nicholas has been calm until now, but my mention of his brother and the stigma that's been attached to him since birth sends him into a rage of monumental proportions. He lunges at me, and despite dodging him, he catches me in the stomach with a winding blow. I cough through the sudden pain and launch myself back at him in a flurry of fists.

"My brother is different to the norm, but he isn't a freak. It's a medical spectrum."

We trade blows as we continue to shout at one another.

"And my wife is forever damaged because of what you did to her."

"I didn't touch her! I didn't buy her that night."

"No, you got one of your old pals to do it instead, didn't

you? Not satisfied with having one woman you wanted them all."

"When are you going to shut up and start listening? It was your father who bought her."

"Liar!"

I send a harsh punch into Nicholas' face, but it misses at the last minute when I'm pulled away. Spinning around, I find William glaring at me.

"You need to listen to him," the younger brother spits out and let's go of me to stand tall beside his brother.

"I don't need to listen to either of you. I've got all the proof here I need to destroy you." I pull the picture from my pocket and hand it to Nicholas. He goes pale and hands it to his brother.

"It captures your good side at least." William shrugs, and Nicholas rolls his eyes.

"This isn't what you think it is."

He looks across to the picture.

"So, it's not you stealing one of the world's most expensive paintings by a very famous artist. One that was stolen in 2010 and has only just been recovered. In London, incidentally."

"He's got you there," William informs his brother.

"Not helping at the moment," Nicholas responds through gritted teeth.

William rolls his eyes and takes a seat at one of the desks.

"All right, it is me who is stealing the picture, but I was also the one who gave it back. I was told to steal it during my father's rule, and at that time, I didn't disobey him.

I shake my head, not believing a word coming out of this

man's mouth. I doubt he even knows what is right and wrong anymore with all the lies he's spinning.

"You've got twenty-four hours to have Victoria, Tamara, and Rose delivered to my house with all their belongings. After which time, you and your brother will leave London and never contact them again. If this doesn't happen, I'll be sending this straight to the police. Your reign of terror is over."

"I'm not giving my wife up." William jumps to his feet, and still holding the picture, he rips it up.

A malevolent chuckle escapes my lips with triumphant glee.

"If you think that's the only copy, then you're not as bright as I've been led to believe."

Turning back to face Nicholas, I stare him down,

"Twenty-four hours. The clock is ticking."

I don't wait for a reply. I simply turn on my heel and leave to return home to Joanna. Soon my sister and Tamara will be free. I know my father would have wanted me to use the ultimatum to take over the Oakfield Society, but the safety of Victoria, Tamara and Rose is more important. I'm sure he'll understand when I tell him.

know Theo told me to go to my room and lock the door, but I can't. A heavy knot sits deep in my stomach. Guilt weighs heavily on me. I don't know for certain what he's doing at the moment, but I know it will involve his sister. He cares deeply for her and will use the evidence I gave him to fight for her. But I can't help fearing that he's rescuing her from the good and drawing her back into the path of evil, especially when his father finds out what he's done. I've made everything so much worse, but what was I supposed to have done? Everything is a horrible mess. I need space to breathe and to clear my head.

I race back through the kitchen, not stopping to talk when a few of the staff ask me if I'm all right. Running up to my room, I retrieve a pair of sandals and a cardigan and put them on, then grab a small handbag I know has some change in it. Theo gave me a mobile phone the other day, but it has a tracking feature in it. Not wanting to be followed, I leave it behind. Making sure the coast is clear, I leave the house by the front door and escape down the long driveway before anyone can see me.

My pulse is racing the entire time. I can't believe I'm being so bold. What if the Viscount finds out and comes after me? Is he watching the house? My eyes dart around me, making sure I can't see him anywhere. I should go back. This is foolish. No, I'm a strong woman. I can do this. I keep walking, and with every step, I'm led farther away from the house. My pulse starts to slow, and I feel normal—if normal is measurable anymore.

The sunlight of the warm September day beats down on me, and tipping my head back, its rays illuminate my pale skin. I'd almost forgotten how bright it can be when the sun shines. Darkness has consumed far too much of my life recently, and it feels good to have a little light in it. Light like I experienced when making love to my husband and feeling complete for the first time. Sadly I was only dreaming when I thought it could lead to a happily ever after. That's not in my future any time soon – probably never.

"Heh," a masculine voice calls out, and following its deep tones, I see a man and woman embracing in the street. He's dressed in a smart suit and carries a briefcase. He looks like he's just come from work. The woman is pushing a stroller with a child sucking on a bottle of milk sat in it.

"I can't believe it!" the woman exclaims with excitement. "How long must it have been?"

"At least five years," the man responds. "I think the last time I saw you was graduation day. My god, I was so drunk at the end of that party. Did you see Timmy Collins? He was dancing on the table with the dean's wife."

"I remember that." The woman laughs. "He was so

drunk. I think there was talk of taking his degree away from him straight after the incident."

They both laugh louder, and the child looks around to see what is capturing his mummy's amusement.

"Yeah, I think he kept it in the end. Along with the dean's wife. They are married now and have a son."

"Really?"

The man nods with wide-eyed delight. Just then the child drops his bottle onto the ground and begins to grumble. Bending down, the man picks the bottle up and hands it to the woman who thanks him. She sucks on the nipple and gives it back to her child who mutters something that also sounds like a thank you in baby language. My hand instantly goes to my flat belly, and I repeat the silent prayer to keep me from falling pregnant until I can find a way out of the mess I'm in.

"Who's this little one then?" the man asks.

"This is Jamie. He's three next week."

"Three. Wow. Big boy!" The man ruffles the top of the little boy's head, but Jamie's more interested in draining his bottle of all the milk. "I see a lot of you in him. I bet his father likes that. I know I've always wanted to see a lot of my wife in any children I have."

The woman's expression changes, becoming dark and furious.

"He wouldn't know. I caught him sleeping with my best friend the week after I found out I was pregnant, and I've not seen him since. I told him about Jamie, but he isn't interested. It's been a nightmare trying to get some child support out of him."

"Jerk!" The man shakes his head, and his face turns red

with anger. "Some men shouldn't be allowed to become fathers." He looks up to where a small café is situated. "Look, can I buy you a coffee, and the little mite a biscuit or something?"

The woman takes a second to answer. I can see her weighing up her options of returning home to what is probably a lonely house with nobody but her and her son, or enjoying the company of another adult for a little while longer.

"Yes, why not."

The man motions for her to go first, and I watch them a little while longer until they disappear into the café. The two of them hadn't seen each other in a long while, but the bonds of their friendship have lasted, and I'd like to think they'll catch up with each other and not lose touch again. There has to be some hope in this world.

A scream off to my left captures my attention, and I start to watch another couple. A man dressed in a tatty T-shirt and ripped jeans is holding a woman by the throat and is shouting obscenities at her. The woman is dressed in jeans and a tunic top, and her pink, orange, and blue hair is scraped back in a pony tail, but as she pleads with him to let her go, it starts to come undone. I take a step closer to them, feeling an insane urge within me to help her. But my heart is racing, and gripped with fear, I'm unable to do anything. Instead, I become rooted to the spot and watch like a voyeur as the scene evolves. I'm not the only one, though. Others around me stop and stare while some continue walking by and even step into the road to get past them. No one goes to help the woman.

"You fucking whore! How long has he been sticking his

filthy dick in your cunt?"

"Listen to yourself, Damien. You've gone insane. I've never once slept with your brother. I'm your girlfriend, for crying out loud."

"I'd believe my own brother over a skanky piece of dick warmer like you. He said you like it up the ass, and I know just how greedy you are when it comes to anal."

The woman tries her hardest to escape from her captor, but he has her too closely held around the neck.

"I can't breathe."

"I should snap your fucking neck."

"You wouldn't." The woman's eyes go wild with fear. "The baby, Damien."

I hadn't noticed before, but the woman's stomach is swollen large with a child growing inside her.

"What? A cracked-up bastard. I've got no idea whose piece of shit your growing. It could be anyone's. If you've opened your legs for my brother, then I want to know who the fuck else you've fucked?"

"No one. It's your baby," the woman screams, and the man slaps her hard across the face. Her lip splits open, and blood starts to drip from it. An elderly gentleman steps up to the couple. I want to tell him not to approach them because I know what could happen to him, and to her for that matter, while this man is so angry. An angry man is a dangerous thing. My mouth opens but then closes again without saying a word. Tears pool in my eyes, and I need to look away, but something forces me to keep watching. It's like a car crash on a motorway: you need to concentrate on the road, but human nature forces you to look at the devastation.

"I think that's enough." The elderly gentleman tries to

stand up tall.

"Fuck off, grandad," the angry man spits at him. "Or you're next."

"Damien!" The woman screams and squirms, her hair flopping all over her face.

"You need to step away from her," the older man continues, but Damien's had enough, and letting go of his partner's throat, he wraps his hands tightly around her multi-colored hair and yells, "I said stay the fuck out of it." He then balls his fist and sends it flying into the face of the elderly gentleman who immediately drops straight down onto the ground and lies there unmoving. A few of those watching scream in shock but no sound comes from my mouth. I've seen men like Damien before. He's nothing but a bully. Sirens wail in the distance, and the woman's still screaming. Damien lets her go and disappears down the street as fast as he can.

"Stupid old man." The woman spits blood onto the unconsciousness form on the ground. "This is all your fault. If he gets arrested, I'll find you. Next time, mind your own business."

The woman takes off running, just as a police car grinds to a halt at the scene. I can't watch anymore. To go from seeing a man so kind and friendly toward a woman and child, and then to witness violence so extreme and unnecessary, leaves me conflicted about the world. Maybe it isn't just me who experiences the hell I'm in? In a bit of a daze, I stumble farther along the street. If the first woman has lost her man, could she find happiness with another? Her old friend, maybe? What about the second? Will she continue to be blinded to the truth about the man she insists is the father of her unborn child? Or is she what Damien said she was? A 'crack whore' who will destroy the life of the child growing inside her. There are always two sides to the story. Heaven and hell.

Someone bumps into me, and I stumble back.

"I'm sorry." The man reaches out to grab me before I fall. My skin heats, and I can feel the palpitations starting. He's touching me. Is he going to hurt me? "Are you ok?" The man's brow furrows, and he looks at me with genuine concern. I can't speak to him, though. I need to put distance between me and him. I push him away and start to run. I've lost track of where I am, and nothing looks familiar. Why did I do this? I wasn't ready. I need to rid myself of the evil stalking me at every turn before I can try to be a normal person again. I'm the only one who can put a stop to this.

In the distance, I'm relieved to see a phone box. They are few and far between on English streets nowadays, and I pray this one is working. Retrieving some coins out of my bag, I feed them into the slot and lift up the phone. It has a dial tone, and I breathe a sigh of relief. My fingers hesitate over the buttons when I realize I don't know the number to Theo's house. Damn it. Why didn't I bring my phone? There is only one number I know: one I had drilled into me since an early age, should I need it. I don't want to call it because I know it'll lead to trouble, but maybe I could use it to my advantage? I need to be smarter. I need to be stronger. I need to be the old Joanna, not the victim of abuse I've become. I dial the number and wait for someone to answer.

"Hello." The deep masculine voice booms down the phone when the call is connected.

"Hello, Daddy..."

CHAPTER FIFTEEN

THEODORE

"I can't believe you've been so stupid. What were you thinking? Actually, don't answer that. I don't think you were thinking. Well, not of anyone but yourself." The angry masculine voice comes out of my lounge as I walk in through the front door.

My stomach is sore from the fight with Nicholas, and I'm sure he got a punch in that will leave me with a black eye tomorrow. All I want to do is go to bed and not have to deal with more hassle. I nod at my butler with a request to let me know what's going on.

"Earl Linton, sir."

"Joanna's father?" I query with bewilderment.

"Yes. From what I can gather, Lady Hamilton left the premises without means of communication and got lost. Thankfully she had some money on her and was able to remember her father's phone number."

"She did what?" I hiss.

"She left the house, sir." My butler cowers down at my sudden angry outburst.

"And you let her?" I stand up tall against him. I'm furious knowing Joanna was out there alone, and at a time when Nicholas Cavendish is probably baying for blood.

"I'm afraid she was rather sneaky in her ability to dodge those watching her."

The angry, raised voice comes again from the lounge, but this time accompanied by a sorrowful whimper from my wife. I loom large over my butler.

"Then you'd better remind everyone that Lady Hamilton does not leave this house without a guard. If it happens again, I'll be looking to change my staff to a set who can follow orders."

I don't pay my butler any more attention. My fury is now focused upon my wife for putting herself into such a dangerous situation. If she thinks the telling off she's getting from her father is harsh, then she's in for a big lesson once I start on her. My heart is beating so fast. Why would she be so stupid? I pound my way across the marbled floor, my dress shoes resonating in a series of eerie clicks. Thrusting the lounge door unceremoniously open, I stomp into the room, and with a growl, I start to admonish my errant wife.

"Is it true?"

Joanna and her father both freeze and look at me with wide eyes.

"What?" her Father stutters at me. The look of concern in his eyes draws me in, and I can't ignore the uneasy feeling I'm getting in the pit of my stomach, telling me he's worried about something other than a daughter with no regard for her own safety. He's like a deer caught in the headlights. I'm about to question his reaction when Joanna steps in.

"I'm sorry." She comes closer to me, and I'm drawn into the sadness in her eyes. "I was stupid. It was such a foolish thing to do. I would have been all right, but a man bumped into me, and I lost my sanity a little."

My anger begins to dissipate, and Joanna's fresh lavender scent calms me. I pull her close and press a kiss to the top of her forehead.

"Did he hurt you? I'll find him."

"No. It was an accident. I wasn't really looking where I was going." Her eyes glass over momentarily, and I know there's more to this story than she's telling me. I won't push her here and now, though. Alone, later, is a different matter. She corrects herself by taking a deep breath and breaking our eye contact. "I promise I won't do it again. I just wanted to experience freedom, having not had any in ages."

"You'll never have it while the Cavendish brothers are breathing," Earl Linton interrupts with his matter of fact response. I'm so captivated by Joanna's beauty I'd almost forgotten he was in the room. She weaves a spell around me and draws me completely into her love.

"She'll be safe soon. The Cavendish brothers will be out of London in twenty-four hours."

"What?" the Earl responds, looking confused.

"Joanna provided me with a piece of information, which will secure the freedom of my sister and niece along with that of Tamara, their friend."

"Freedom? Information? I don't understand. What have you done?" he shouts at his daughter who steps closer into my side, her hands shaking.

"Calm yourself in my house, sir. I won't have you shouting at my wife like that." I place myself between father and daughter as I vent my growing frustration that a good day, which was developing into a triumphant one, is now looking like it's shrouded in more issues.

"I want to know what is going on? If this involves my daughter and can come back on me, somehow, then I need to be informed," the Earl demands.

"It will not reflect on you," I interrupt. My anger previously soothed by my wife is now growing again at her father's arrogance.

"Will you just tell me what is going on?" Earl Linton slams his fist on a table. It rocks, and the glass ornament on it crashes to the floor.

"Calm down!" I yell and motion with my eyes to the smashed glass. "I'll allow you one breakage, but anymore and you start paying for it."

He looks to the floor and then back up at me.

"That piece is of no value anyway. It's fake."

It's my turn to breathe deeply and control my temper. I turn my back to Earl Linton and focus my attention on Joanna.

"Do you want to go upstairs while we finish this conversation?"

She shakes her head and reaches up to my sore eye. I flinch a little when she touches the sensitive flesh.

"You're hurt?"

"Nicholas is worse." I smirk but stop when she steps back horrified.

"This is all my fault." Joanna's eyes start to blink rapidly.

It's like she's trying to understand something that will never make sense. Her breathing accelerates.

"Joanna!" her father barks from behind me, and she looks up at him with so much horror in her face. I'm beginning to wonder whether the fear she feels for the Cavendish brothers isn't only the result of what they did to her but also due to her father's treatment of her whilst growing up.

I turn back to him.

"Did you abuse her?"

"What?" he spits at me.

"As a child, did you hurt her?"

"Never. What do you take me for?" The Earl folds his arms across his chest and resolutely stares me down. "I think you owe me an apology. I would never touch my own daughter."

I back down immediately. My senses tell me something is wrong, but apart from the issue with the alleged rape of the woman who died, I've never heard anything to question Earl Linton's abilities as a father.

"He sold me…" The words come from behind me. They are spoken so fast it takes my brain a few seconds to register them. "For cash, I don't know the exact amount, but it was thousands. He got thousands for me being sold."

Joanna slaps her hand over her mouth when she's finished her accusation. My mind is still struggling to take it all in. It's like I'm wading through deep water with heavy, bulky clothes, weighted down from the saturation. I open my mouth to speak, but her father beats me too it when he lunges forward and wraps his hands around his daughter's throat.

"You lying little whore." He shakes her, and I can only

watch on as my brain struggles to catch up with what I'm hearing and witnessing.

"It's true," Joanna gasps. Her whimpers of pain penetrate into my subconscious, and I grab the Earl by the back of his collar, and with almighty strength, I send him flying across the room and into the wall.

"Tell me again." I stand large over Joanna, my breathing quick and my fists clenched hard.

"W-w-what?" she stutters between hitching in gasps of air. Her father had been holding her so tightly around her neck that already a red ring of inflammation has appeared.

"Say…it…again," I repeat slowly, every syllable pronounced with meticulous precision and definition. I don't want my meaning to be misconstrued in any way.

"He sold me for money. I wasn't given away because my father was forced to. He received payment." Her words are equally as clear. I've learned a lot about her since we've been together. The way her eyes flick with darkness at the corners when she's hiding something—a lie hidden within a story. There is none of that this time. She's being as honest now as she was when she told me she loved me. It's the truth. My nostrils flair, and Joanna sinks down onto the floor.

"Please," she whimpers, and I nod once to her before turning rapidly and once again grabbing her father who has only just begun stumbling to his feet.

"You're never welcome in this house again. If I see you anywhere near my wife, I won't hesitate to kill you." I send a fist flying into his face. He's an older man and not built to withstand my assault. He staggers backward, and his eyes roll in his head before he comes back to his senses. My fury increases, and I send another two punishing blows to his face. His nose cracks, and blood splutters out over me. "You will stay away from everyone we know. You will not move in the same circles as me. You will have Joanna's inheritance plus any money you received for her put into her account before the month is out, or we will report this to the police. And…"—I pause for dramatic effect—"I will find some way of bringing back the previous rape charges against you, and if I have to, I'll plant evidence of you murdering the girl as well."

The Earl who is barely conscious manages to take in what I'm saying.

"There's no proof," he responds, spitting blood in my face.

"I'll make some."

He starts to laugh and looks over my shoulder to Joanna.

"I hope you realize what you've started. The apple never falls too far from the tree."

I've heard enough. I send another quick succession of punches to his face, and he slumps down unconscious on the floor.

Joanna whimpers quietly on the other side of the room with her arms wrapped around her, cradling herself in comfort.

"Theo."

"Did he ever touch you?" I ask and step over the prone body, currently bleeding over the priceless oriental rug my father always loved, but I couldn't stand.

"No. I promise you."

"He just sold you."

She nods and looks down at her feet.

"Head up," I order, and she immediately responds. Tears

are streaming down her face now. She's breaking down in front of me. The shell she's erected around herself to keep in all the real truths of the situation is crumbling.

"More," I demand, but I know instantly from the frightened expression in her eyes I'll get nothing else out of her at the moment. With a blink of her eyes, she shuts down again. I move beside her, and my arms snake around her waist, pulling her into me and the inconveniently timed erection, which juts from my trousers. I can't explain it, but protecting my woman has left me needing the softness between her thighs to counteract the violence of my acts. I have to know she's not going to fall apart at revealing the truth about her father. I need her to know I trust her implicitly and believe in her honesty. My lips press down onto hers in a passionate kiss, which is as intense as the emotion that flooded the room when she spoke her fateful words. I need her, and I want her, but not here. Bending down, I scoop her up in my arms, and we leave the violence of the lounge behind us. I'm heading for the stairs when my butler appears.

"Will the Earl be staying for dinner, sir?"

I snort a laugh. I can't help it. By morning, my bruised knuckles may be as sore as the black eye given to me by Nicholas Cavendish, but I'll never regret inflicting them on my father-in-law.

"No, he won't," I respond to the butler as Joanna buries her head in my chest, her warm breath tickling the skin under my shirt. "I've left some trash in the lounge. Please see it out and ensure it never returns to this house again. If it does, kill it!"

CHAPTER SIXTEEN

JOANNA

I can't quite believe what I just did. I allowed those words to fall from my mouth, condemning my own father. Half a million, that was what I was sold to Viscount Hamilton for. My father wouldn't have received all that money. A fair chunk would have gone to Nicholas' father, but my own would have been compensated well for having a failure as a daughter. He's out of my life, now, but I know I've started a chain of events that could lead to chaos and death. Strangely though, I don't fear death—it's the lies that terrify me more. I don't want to be a part of them any longer.

Theo carries me up the stairs, two at a time, and deposits me tenderly on my bed. His face is splattered with blood, but I don't find it unattractive. It gives him a look of danger and power.

"Are you all right?" My husband kisses my lips and down my neck. I welcome his affections. I want him, need him. I feel strength for the first time in ages, and it ignites flames of desire within my body. It would be dangerous to think this will all end well, but for now, I'll embrace my new-found courage.

"Take me," I plead on a breathless whisper as my tightly coiled body unfurls and welcomes my husband between my thighs. He continues to kiss lower until reaching my breasts, and his hard length presses into my leg as the excitement within him builds. My back arches, wanting to draw him in closer. I need him now… no more waiting or thinking about it any longer. I second guess my decisions too much. I need to go with instinct.

"Theo, please."

"Patience," he replies, and then taking the shirt I'm wearing in his hand, he rips it open, sending the buttons popping and flying around the room. "I'm going to savor my wife. And only take her when I think she's ready." His large hands encase my breasts, and he squeezes hard. It sends a pulse of energy straight down to my clit, and I can feel myself getting wet as I prepare to take him when he's ready to give himself to me.

"Need you naked," Theo growls, helping me to sit up while removing what remains of my shirt. Next my jeans are quickly discarded along with my underwear. "You have perfect breasts." His hands slide around my back and unclasp the fastening of my bra. It's pulled off and thrown across the room, landing over an antique lamp on a dressing table where it swings back and forth. "Damn." Theo sits back on the bed, stroking himself over his trousers. His knuckles look sore. The bruising I can see is the result of the words I spoke earlier, at least in part, when I condemned my father.

I lean forward and gently press a kiss to each of the cuts on Theo's hands. The metallic taste of his blood gives an erotic edge to the vision in my head of me kissing away his injuries. He's protected me more than any man has ever done before. He twists one of his hands around my hair and pulls my head up so our mouths can meet. They combine in a tumultuous tango of emotion and lust, crashing together like rough seas breaking over land. I'm tasting him: his masculinity encapsulated in a spicy mixture of the scent of oaky wood aftershave and the flavor of coffee…his favorite drink. This is my Theo, my husband.

He pushes me down until I'm lying on the bed and looks at me again. When my eyes follow his hand as it travels over the contours of my breasts, I see blood is smeared onto my skin from his shirt and face.

"Never again." His vow needs no explanation. I know he means my father will not be allowed to harm me again.

He shifts from the bed and quickly removes his clothes. His hard cock springs from the captivity of his trousers with an excited bounce, glistening already at the head with pre-cum. He strokes himself a few times before lying back down on the bed.

"Up," he orders, and I willingly obey my husband. From under my hooded eyelids, I look up at the intensity in his face. His commanding presence framed by the soft lighting in my bedroom. He's pure sex on legs with a strong jaw, deep chestnut eyes, and full lips swollen from our passionate kissing. He reaches out and wraps his hand around my hair before pulling me down so I'm level with his dick.

"I want you to suck me."

I hesitate momentarily, but it's enough to worry my husband. He immediately releases my hair and brings me up to lie against his chest.

"I'm sorry. You don't have to."

"I do," I respond into the small covering of hair there. "I want to. I have bad memories of oral, but I want to replace them with good. Just like I replaced the vision of losing my virginity with our first time."

"Joanna."

I free myself from his embrace and move back down, so I'm lying next to him on the bed at his groin. I slide my tongue over his body and toward his dick. Little nips with my teeth ignite his flesh, and I can feel it heat to an inferno.

"Fuck!" he exclaims out loud when I wrap my hand around his dick and bring it to my mouth. My tongue darts out and licks up the salty taste at the tip. There is something intrinsically masculine in his flavor. He's nothing like his father or any of the other men I've been forced to service before. He's sweeter, fresher, cleaner, perfect. I swirl my tongue around the tip a few more times before drawing it into the warmth of my mouth.

"Fuck." Is the only word Theo appears to be able to utter at the moment because as I draw him in farther the expletive is repeated a few more times. "Fuck, fuck, fuck!"

Circling my mouth around his length, I draw him to the back of my throat. I was forced by his father to deep throat. The first time, it scared the life out of me, but with Theo, I'm not afraid. I want to please him. To show him I'm here for him only. That I'm not a damaged soul, but the sexual goddess of his dreams when I allow myself to live.

I swallow his length and hold him there for a few seconds before pulling back and expelling his length from my mouth. Saliva drips from my chin as I repeat the process accompanied by a loud moan of pleasure from my husband. I can feel my own excitement drip from between my thighs. My clit thuds with its own need. I'm getting excited from pleasing a man and making my husband happy.

Theo jolts me away from his dick.

"I'm going to come if you carry on doing that."

"Then come," I purr, having newly found the sex kitten within me.

Theo laughs. "There will be plenty of time for that another day. For now, I need in your pussy. I want to be immersed in you and pumping my hips so hard you're screaming my name as you explode underneath me."

I let out my own little laugh at the mild-mannered gentleman, and his dirty sex talk. I think I'm not the only one finding their inner self in this relationship.

"Do it then," I offer and lie back on the bed. He places himself at my entrance and pushes straight in, in one long thrust before settling and allowing me to adjust to his intrusion.

"Wet as always. Are you like this whenever I'm around?" Theo rubs a finger over where we join. He then captures my legs and pulls them up to rest on his shoulders so he can drive deeper within me.

"I have to go and change my panties whenever you walk into the room."

"I think you should just stop wearing them. I can have you whenever I want, then."

"I'll hold you to that if I do."

The bantering between us is carefree and easy. It's a normal couple in love. That's what we are. Here and now, we are free from all the oppression and fear created by the Oakfield Society.

Slowly, he starts to move, and the mood between us shifts. Our playfulness dissipates, and silence fills the room with the seriousness of what we are doing. We are making love. My legs are lowered to the side of his thighs, and we settle into a missionary position, Theo's eyes meeting mine as we move as one. We have years ahead of us to explore the many different ways you can have sex.

"Tell me what really happened the night my sister was taken to the society." Theo leans forward and presses a kiss to my lips as he breathes the words into my mouth.

"I can't." A single tear falls from my eye and weaves a path down my cheek. I want to tell him and end all of this, but the fear within me is still ingrained. I'm not ready to jump over that final hurdle yet.

"I'll protect you. Nobody will hurt you."

"You can't protect me from the monsters you can't see."

"What does that mean?"

Another tear falls, and I shut my eyes as Theo continues to undulate his hips, thrusting in and out of me.

"Joanna."

"I love you," is the only reply I give before an orgasm bursts out of me from nowhere. It erupts deep within me and cascades through my body with a powerful surge of pleasure. I'm shuddering and shaking underneath him. I'm calling his name and milking him to his own orgasm. His affirmation of the love we share is spoken on a final groan as his cum explodes into my inner warmth.

We both go still and silent. The sounds of our rapid breaths the only noise filling the room.

"Theo."

He pulls out of me and gets off the bed. His shoulders are

slumped, and he looks defeated. He's no longer the tower of strength I rely on to protect me.

"If I go to Victoria, will she tell me the truth?"

The question causes my breath to hitch. It's not something I've ever really thought about. I thought he would have already asked her, and she would have told him. I just thought he didn't believe her because he thought she'd been influenced by Nicholas.

"Haven't you spoken to her before about the right she was given to the society?"

He shakes his head and looks down at the ground forlornly.

"I think I feared the answer, and then later when she tried to tell me, I chose to believe her mistaken. I was convinced she'd been brainwashed by her husband."

I can't believe the words I'm hearing from him. The walls he has built, based on a solid belief in what is right and wrong, are breaking down around him. I should open my mouth and tell him it was his father who bought me, but I can't. I try, but nothing comes out. In the end, I pull the sheets up around me and curl into a ball in the bed.

"Go to her, Theo. Listen to her. She's your sister. She can tell you what I'm too scared to admit. She's the only one who can save us, now."

CHAPTER SEVENTEEN

THEODORE

I make sure Joanna is safe when I leave her alone, this time. She's sleeping in our bed with the sheets tangled around her as the early morning sun floods in and illuminates her now flawless skin. I've given her the means to protect herself, if necessary, with an illegal hand gun next to her bed. Before leaving, my father gave it to me as a means to protect myself after Elsie's death. Joanna's from an upper class family, so I've no qualms about her knowing how to use it. It's the sport of the elite to shoot small discs for fun. She'll be more used to a shotgun, but the principle is roughly the same. Instinct will kick in should she need it. I know most people would say I'm insane to leave a weapon with a victim of the horrific abuse she's suffered, but I know she's free from most of the torment from her bad memories. I don't fear her hurting herself, even for a moment. Silently creeping from the room, I leave my butler instructions that no one is to leave or enter the house while I'm absent. Nobody at all, no matter who it is. At this point in time, I don't know who I can and can't trust any more, but something in the lines of worry crisscrossing his face tells me this gentleman, who's been with me for most of my life, will protect my wife. He's aged as much as I have over the last few weeks.

It doesn't take me long to return to Oakfield Hall. It's early in the morning, and the streets are still empty. The imposing gothic style manor sends chills down my spine. This place holds so many dark secrets, which those around me seem to be a part of while I've been kept in ignorance. Or has it been that I've not wanted to hear the truth? No matter what the reason is, I need to know, now. I need to discover what is really happening around me, and what type of pawn I've become in a game I fear is about to turn deadly. My sister according to Joanna is the only one who can give me answers. I need to listen to her.

I knock loudly, and a butler appears at the door.

"I'm sorry, sir, but you are no longer welcome here," he informs me and makes to shut the door. I place my foot across the threshold just in time and curse when the heavy wood slams against it. Damn, English oak! That's going to hurt for a while.

"I want to see my sister."

"She doesn't want to see you. Please move your foot, or the consequences will be upon your own head."

"Victoria!" I shout through the crack in the door. I can just about see my sister on the stairs behind the butler. Nicholas is standing beside her with his arms wrapped around her. His face is as bruised as mine feels.

"Go away, Theo," she informs me with a voice I can hear is close to cracking.

"I need to speak with you," I shout back.

"I'm not leaving Nicholas. You can do whatever you want with that picture of him carrying the painting. We'll fight you every step of the way." Her resilience breaks on the last word, and a whimpering sob fills the cavernous hallway.

"Leave," Nicholas orders with murderous tones.

"I need the truth," I try one last time. "I need to know what happened the night our father gave you to the Cavendish family." Victoria's hand flies to her mouth, and she bends over sobbing, trying to bring air into her lungs. Nicholas rubs her back. "I know Joanna's father was paid money to give her to the society. I know I'm being lied to, Victoria. I need the truth no matter what it is." I pause, my vehement pleas for information are leaving me exhausted. "I want to save my wife. I love her."

Nicholas waves his hand at a butler, and the door opens.

"You'll listen to her?" He steps toward me as I'm admitted into the hall.

"I just want the truth. No more lies. Joanna is terrified of something. You, I think, but I'm not certain." Confusion laces my tone. "All I do know is I want to protect her, and she tells me my sister is the only one who can help me do that."

"I'm not going with you, Theo," Victoria repeats. "You say you love Joanna. Well, I love Nicholas. He's not the monster you think he is. What I have to tell you is going to hurt. It's going to destroy you."

"I'm ready." I take a step closer to my sister and hold my hand out to her. I can tell she's been crying for hours. Her eyes are red-rimmed, and she looks exhausted as if she hasn't been sleeping and not only because she's the mother of a newborn.

With some reluctance, Nicholas lets Victoria go, and taking my hand, she leads me into the lounge where I assaulted her husband earlier.

"Do you need me with you?" Nicholas looks terrified to let her out of his sight.

"I need to do this with Theo on my own. We are at fault for not telling him sooner. I wanted to protect him from the truth, but he's become embroiled in it anyway. We need to do this as siblings together."

"I'll wait outside. Leave the door open."

She nods at him, and we enter the lounge. She leads me to the sofa, and we sit on it. Her hands feel cold, and I wrap mine around hers to warm them.

"I won't leave him, Theo. I love him in just the same way as you love Joanna."

I look at the door where Nicholas stands guard while we converse. He looks tired. His demeanor does not appear to be that of a man who is filled with confidence in regard to his power nor does he seem capable of being the demon I've been led to believe he is. His look is that of a man who's frightened of losing his wife and daughter. The truth finally dawns on me. Nicholas acts exactly the way I do when I'm around Joanna. His eyes always light up when Victoria is with him. He's protective of her but only because he loves her.

"He loves you, too." I turn to my sister. "I see it now. Victoria, you have to tell me what happened. I can't be kept in the dark any longer. When I married Joanna, I was brought into whatever fight it is you're embroiled in. I'm confused, and I don't know what the truth is anymore. All I do know is my wife is terrified, and I can't protect her unless you tell me. Please."

"It will hurt, Theo."

"I'm ready. Tell me what happened the night you were brought here."

She shuts her eyes,

"I want you to listen to everything, please. Before you speak, you have to listen."

I nod acceptance of her terms.

"Father came and found me the day I was given to Nicholas. He told me it was time for my debut in society. I was dressed by Elsie in a white linen gown, and she styled my hair in a French plait."

"A white linen gown. Joanna wore one to our wedding." I realize I've interrupted her already and bow my head in apology.

"We all wore them…five girls in total. All born during the same year, and all given to Nicholas on his thirtieth birthday"

I nod because my father has told me about this being a requirement of a centuries old society our ancestors were forced to join.

"I was led into the room and introduced to another couple of the girls. I remember Joanna well. Her father was telling her off because she had frizzy hair. She looked terrified. I, on the other hand, was confused. I didn't really understand what was happening. Eventually Nicholas and his father appeared, and we were brought forward one by one and branded with the Oakfield Crest."

Bile rises in my throat. I've seen the mark on my wife's thigh: a vicious scar in the shape of an Oakleaf.

"After that, everything became crazy. We were lined up and inspected by Nicholas. He was told to choose three of us to carry on further in the trials to select his wife. The other two would be sold."

"Trials?" I ask, and she nods, and then looking sorrowful, she lowers her head.

"I endured some of the trials, and they've shaped me into the person I am today. Nicholas seems like a bad man when I tell you all this, but he isn't. He was under the influence…no, the control of his father. I saved him from that, and he saved me in turn."

"What trials?"

"Theo, please."

"What trials?" My response is terse, my hands pull away from warming my sister's, and I clench them into fists.

"I was placed in a scold's bridle, for one, before I was led around naked while being whipped."

"A scold's bridle?" I can't believe I'm hearing this from my own sister. She's suffered just as much as Joanna has, possibly even more. What type of people do things like this in modern society? What type of organization is the Oakfield Society? "Who did this to you?"

She looks up at her husband, and I don't need her to answer. I know exactly who it was. Without another thought, I'm out of my chair and racing across the room with my fists held up high in front of me.

"Theo, no!" Victoria screams. "Please."

My fist is inches from Nicholas' already bruised face when I pull it back before landing a punch.

"You monster. How could you do that?" I spit at him.

"I regret it every day," he responds, and I see the guilt in his eyes.

I spin around, pulling at the ends of my hair in frustration.

"He did that to you, yet you love him?" I can't understand my sister's reasoning, and I'm doubting her sanity at this point. Has she been brainwashed? "Does he still hurt you?"

"No." Victoria is on her feet and pleading with me to understand. "Never. He's not the man he was that day, and that's why we're being attacked. He's trying to change the society from what it once was and eradicate the evil element within it."

"The artwork?" I question.

Nicholas responds, "We are returning it all. Since the inception of the society, art has been stolen to fund it. The eldest son of the leader is taught the skills needed to continue providing for the society. I stole the painting, but I also returned it along with several others."

"So, you're a thief and an abuser! Yet my sister says you're a good man."

"He is, Theo. He's the best. He's trying to make things better, but he's being thwarted at every turn."

"I'm not buying this, Victoria." I reply, shaking my head. My skin heats with fury, and a bead of sweat forms on my brow. "He's not a good man."

"Nicholas may have done wrong. He'll pay in eternity for some of the things he's done, but he is a good man in a society full of evil," Victoria hisses at me through her clenched jaw.

"Evil…that's all I keep hearing from you, but the only evil I see is him."

She shakes her head and slumps back against a table. "That's because you are too afraid to look closer to home."

"What's that supposed to mean?" I query, fearing the answer.

"Our father." Victoria replies.

It's my turn to shake my head in a furious denial.

"He saved Joanna from Nicholas."

"No, Theo. Nicholas never had Joanna. Remember I told you two girls weren't chosen and were sold instead. Joanna was one of them. The night after I was given to the Oakfield Society, Joanna Nethercutt was sold to our father for five hundred thousand pounds. The day you introduced her as your wife was the first we'd seen or heard of her in over a year."

"No. He took me to her in the middle of the night and said the only way to save her was for me to marry her."

"It's all part of whatever plan he has to take over the society." Victoria holds her hands out to me, willing me to believe what she's saying.

"No." I'm done listening to their lies. My father's a good and honest man. He'd never do anything like this. He's been trying to save Joanna, not hurt her. "I'm not listening to this anymore. It's all lies. Nicholas has brainwashed you. You've admitted yourself that he paraded you around naked and had you beaten. He's the bad man, not our father."

"Theo."

"No." I push past Nicholas and into the hallway where William and Tamara are waiting. Tamara holds a pile of papers in her hands.

"Out of my way," I tell them, but neither move. Instead, Tamara steps forward and hands me a printout from an ancestry website.

"Remember you did a DNA test once, hoping to find a link to royalty? I know you didn't find that, but you did discover a link to a half-sister."

"Not this again." I throw the paper on the floor not wanting to hear her fabricated tales of how we are brother and sister. It's nothing but lies designed to ruin my father's reputation.

"Your father raped my mother, Theo. He killed her, and when I get the proof, I'll see him rot in jail."

"Lying bitch."

"It's the truth." William bends down and picks up the paper. He holds it directly in front of my line of sight, and I can clearly see the results identifying Tamara and I as half brother and sister.

"This is fabricated."

"I'll do a proper DNA test with you, if you want?" Tamara offers.

"No!" I shout with fury.

"Theo, please listen. You promised me you would. I know you love Joanna, and we are just trying to save her. She and I are the only two of the five girls left." Victoria places her hand on my shoulder. "Please, listen."

"I can't." I'm shaking so violently now. It's too much to take in. Tamara is my half sister. My father bought my wife for five hundred thousand pounds.

"Show him." Nicholas steps around to stand next to Tamara. She still holds one piece of paper in her hand, which she offers to me, but I'm too scared to take it.

Nicholas continues, "Your father is no longer Viscount Hamilton. He desires a greater title. My own. One which my death would lead to under the terms of a treaty he and my father signed before my father's death." Nicholas takes the paper from Tamara and thrusts it into my hands. I look down at it. The words blur, and I struggle to read them, but gradually the truth finally sinks in. My father is the man behind all of this. He's lied to me from the start. Nicholas Cavendish never abused my wife. He never had her, but my father did all along. The words become clearer on the page, and I'm able to see my name identified as the current incumbent of the title of Viscount Hamilton.

"I'm the Viscount?"

"Yes." Tamara nods. "I've checked the documentation twice and had a friend check it as well. It's all legally binding."

"I don't understand why? If he's after your title, why give me this and not tell me?"

Victoria wraps her arms around me, and I allow her sisterly affection to calm the confusion I'm feeling.

"He's setting you up, brother. He's given you his name to take the fall for everything."

I open my mouth to speak, but I can't.

"Do you know where he is, Theo?" Nicholas asks me, and all I can do is nod. "Then you need to go to the police and tell them."

"I'll come with you," Victoria offers.

"I will as well," Tamara also confirms.

The shock of everything finally overwhelms me, and I drop to the floor. Victoria comes down with me and cradles me in her arms as I struggle to get breath into my lungs. I'm trying to understand everything I'm hearing. From the foggy haze of my brain, only one thought emerges though. If Nicholas Cavendish didn't rape and abuse my wife, who was it? I don't really need to ask myself that question though for I already know. It was my father.

CHAPTER EIGHTEEN

JOANNA

I know the instant I wake Theo isn't in the bed with me. He's gone to see Victoria. I'm sure of that. Part of me is terrified at the thought of him finding out the truth, but the other part rejoices in the fact we could be at the end of the torment. Is it possible to dream of a life outside of the dictatorship of Viscount Hamilton? Could it be a reality? What if Theo doesn't believe his sister? What if the words my father spoke about the apple not falling too far from the tree are true? Have I been blindsided all along, and Theo's in league with his father? My heart aches at the thought of that. I don't want to believe it as the truth. I'm a good judge of character. Surely, he's the kind and protective man I've fallen in love with. The thought I might have got him wrong sends a shiver down my spine, but I dismiss it as quickly as I think it. No, I trust my husband. He'll come back and save us from the nightmare we've found ourselves engulfed in. A war between members of a society we know little about. How can it be that an agreement made between a group of gentlemen in the eighteen hundreds has defined my future in such a violent way? Did the men who signed up truly understand what they were condemning future generations to suffer? I know little of Nicholas Cavendish, who's coming of age was the catalyst for my torment, but what I've seen and heard from his wife, suggests he really is trying to change the future for generations to come. Will it be possible in a society where there is such deep-rooted malevolence, and where there are members who still believe they have a right to behave as their forebears did? Theft, abuse, lies, it's all second nature to the generation my father belongs to. Can our generation, Nicholas, Victoria, Theo, William, Tamara, and I really change it, or is it a dream which will end in defeat and stricter rules for the future to prevent an insurgency again?

I shift from the bed and wrap a dressing gown around myself, despite the warmth of the last few days, there is a chill in the air this morning. Perhaps it's the first frosts on the way, or a sign of impending doom bearing down upon us at a frantic pace. I can only pray for the first option.

My breath hitches when I notice the gun beside my bed. Theo must have left it there for me to protect myself, I don't even want to question how he came to have it because I know it must be illegal. The thought chills me to the bone that in order to ensure my safety when alone in this house where I'm supposed to be mistress I need a weapon capable of bringing death. It's not right. I open the drawer and put the gun inside. I won't be scared in my own home. I need to find the strength within me to help Theo end this.

I pick a change of clothes out of my wardrobe and head into the bathroom. A quick shower refreshes my senses, and

I'm feeling a lot more relaxed than before. It's a new day, and a new start. Everything will be all right.

With a yawn and an exaggerated stretch of my arms, I blow away the final cobwebs of sleep and head downstairs for breakfast. The house is quiet. It's normally a hive of activity with staff milling around doing jobs to make sure everything runs properly. I was brought up believing a woman's place was to run the household. I'll have to speak to Theo about taking on some of the responsibility. I call for his butler, but nobody comes. An eerie feeling passes over me. This is not normal. Maybe Theo had his butler travel with him to see Victoria? No, he would've had him stay here to protect me. I tentatively push the door open to the dining room and am greeted by the horror of Theo's butler lying unmoving on the floor with a bullet hole in the centre of his forehead.

"Did you really think you'd get away with pulling a stunt like that against your own father?" The deep voice from behind me chills me to the bone.

"It wasn't a stunt." I turn and drop to my knees. The words leave my mouth when I know I should be silent. "I had to give Theo something, and it was the only thing I could think of."

Viscount Hamilton steps forward with several men flanking him on either side. I recognize the majority of them. They are members of the society. Men who were there the night I was purchased. He pulls me to my feet and pushes me hard against the wall.

"Lying little bitch." He whacks his hand hard across my face. My ears ring with the force of it, and my head spins. "Your father came to me, barely alive. He was one of my biggest allies, but after my son did a number on him, he was questioning whether this is all worth it. I couldn't have that." The Viscount's lip curls up at the corners in a demonic smile. "Well, Lady Hamilton, now Countess of Linton, I hope you're happy? You caused the death of your father."

I try to feel guilt at the death of the man who was supposed to love and protect me, but I can't. He gave me away to a monster for money, and I'm unable to grieve for him. All I can do is wish him a speedy passage into hell. Another punch comes to my face, and my legs struggle to hold up my failing body.

"You've spoiled my son. He was supposed to be strong and a great leader, but you've made him weak. He wasn't supposed to take the photo to Nicholas. He was supposed to lead a riot against the Oakfield Society's current leaders with it. Get them sent to prison where I could finish them off. But no, you made him into a fool. Why would I want Victoria back? She's shown her true colors. I can't believe she succeeded in becoming the Duchess and making Nicholas a wimp at the same time. The women around me are conniving little bitches. They'll all get theirs though. A Duchess will fetch a good price."

The laugh that comes from the Viscount scares me more than the thought of being raped by him again. I can deal with that. I can shut my mind away from his torment because I know he's the one who is inadequate and wrong, not me. But to hear him talk of his own daughter in a way that describes her downfall brings bile to my throat. The ends of my hair are pulled hard, and I'm dragged across the room and thrown to one of the men who accompanied the Viscount.

"Take her to the car. She'll fetch a good price as well."

I'm handed over to the other man, and he wraps his arms around me, over my breasts, with his filthy digits digging into my flesh.

"Remember, Joanna, what happens now, you started. We end Nicholas and William Cavendish tonight. My daughter will be sold, and Theo…he dies. He's served his purpose and has now been misguided by his willful whore of a wife. I made an error marrying you to him. I thought him stronger than to fall for your sorrowful eyes and magical pussy, but I was mistaken." The Viscount sneers at me. He's talking about selling his own daughter and murdering his son. This man isn't human. He's a devil, walking the Earth. I can't take in what I'm hearing. The person holding me lowers one of his hands down to the cleft between my thighs.

"Can I sample this magical pussy while we wait?"

As he heads toward the stairs the Viscount replies.

"Do with it what you want. Don't break it though. That's my job."

The man who's haunted my nightmares since he bought me disappears, and I'm dragged out of the house and toward the back of a waiting car. I try my hardest to free myself. I can't believe this is happening again. I want the nightmare to end.

"Theo!" I scream, willing him to appear, but I know in my heart it's a miracle that won't happen. If I'm to stop this chain of events, I need to save myself.

The man holding me slaps his hand over my mouth to prevent me from screaming. I bite down into his flesh until I taste blood, and he yelps in pain.

"Fucking bitch." He throws me onto the ground and sends a kick into my stomach. I curl instantly up into a ball and groan as an explosion of agony cascades through my body. *Think Joanna, I tell myself. You need to be sensible and strong.*

The man kicks me again, this time in my head. I see stars, and the pain in my body is bordering on the limit of what I can cope with. He lowers himself to the ground before flipping me over, so I'm on all fours, and pulling me back against his hard length.

"I was going to let you have it in the softness of the car, but I think a gravel driveway is better for you." He lifts the skirt up I'm wearing and fumbles to remove my underwear. *Strength Joanna, strength.* He leans over me, and I sense an opportunity. Throwing my head back, I connect with his face. I hear his nose crunch, and he loosens his grip and falls to the gravel. I may have just killed him, but I've no time to think about that. My entire body hurts, and I need to get away. Thinking quickly, I search around in his pockets for the car keys. Finding them, I rush to the car and start the engine just as one of the other men comes out and sees what's happening. I don't have time to think. I've not driven in so long, but it all comes back to me, thankfully. I push my foot down on the accelerator and speed down the driveway. The second man rushes at the car in an attempt to stop me. I don't stop, though, not even when he goes flying over the bonnet. I speed out of the driveway and onto the road.

Think Joanna…Police? I need to go to them. No, I can't. I have to warn Theo and Victoria. I have to get to Oakfield Hall. I've only been there once, but I remember the journey and how to get there. Trying not to draw attention to myself, I keep my driving as normal as possible. There must be a large dent in the bonnet of the car where I hit the man, so I drive sensibly.

It's still early, but the roads are starting to get busy with yet another commuter rush hour. I take a few wrong turns on the way with my hands shaking violently on the wheel, and my eyes flicking into the rear-view mirror every few seconds to make sure I'm not being followed. I don't know how long it takes me to make the journey, but eventually I make it to the Cavendish's house and slam to a halt in the middle of their driveway. Nicholas appears at the front door with William behind him. Both have a look of concern on their face. As I get out of the car, all the adrenaline I've been feeling dissipates, and I fall to the ground as my tears start to fall.

"Theo!" I shout at them as they both run to my side. Nicholas picks me up and carries me into the house while William calls for hot water, brandy, and bandages.

"Joanna, what happened?"

"Where's Theo?" I ask again.

"He's gone to the police with Victoria and Tamara?"

"No." I break down in heaving sobs again. "You have to find him."

William hands me the brandy brought in by the butler, and Nicholas moves back to allow a maid to step up and start cleaning my wounds.

"Speak slower. What happened?" Nicholas questions.

"You have to go after them. The Viscount came for me. He's going to end this today. He's going to destroy you and William, sell Victoria and Tamara, and kill Theo. Please, you have to save him. Save everyone. I want this to end."

CHAPTER NINETEEN

THEODORE

The car is silent for most of the journey. All of us are lost deep in our own thoughts. I'm struggling, and I'm not afraid to admit it. The man I grew up worshipping as my father is nothing but a fraud and a liar. I don't know for certain if it was my father who hurt Joanna. I've not heard it directly from her lips, but my heart already tells me it was. I don't know how I can ever make it up to her or rid her of the pain she must be feeling. Does she even really want me as a husband? A constant reminder of the man who abused her. I can't think about that, now. As we draw nearer to the police station, Victoria nestles in closer to my side. Tamara rubs at her stomach.

"How are you feeling?" I nod at where her hand rests upon the baby growing inside her.

"Is it that obvious? I'd be fine it it wasn't for William fussing over me all the time." She rolls her eyes.

"William is a little over protective of her at the moment,"

Victoria adds. "You'd think she's made of glass and could break at any moment."

"He's a good man. He's just looking after you." We all become silent again at my words. "So's Nicholas." I kiss the top of my sister's head. "I'm glad you both found the two of them."

"We wish it were under other circumstances, but I wouldn't be without Nicholas," Victoria responds.

"Nor I without William," Tamara adds.

I reach out for my other sister, how strange that sounds, and squeeze her hand.

"I'm just glad you're both married, and I don't have to worry about the two of you out partying together."

"Protective big brother," Victoria teases, but the smile on Tamara's face is what I really notice. She's gone from having no family to being in a loving relationship with her husband and the middle child in a sibling sandwich between me and Victoria.

"Don't you know it, sisters," I reply before turning to look out the window as the streets of London flash past. I look back at Tamara. "I'm really sorry about your mother. She was a special person in our household. I'll miss her."

Tears pool in Tamara's eyes, mourning the loss of a woman who, I now know, had to deal with so much but came out the other side still fighting for her daughter.

"She's at peace, and I'm going to continue her legacy. Victoria is as well."

"Yes, we are." Victoria smiles at her best friend and sister. "Nicholas is changing the society. We're going to be looking to do more philanthropic work. Nicholas is in the process of setting up the Elsie Bennett fund to provide grants for children to study art."

"That sounds a fantastic idea," I reply with enthusiasm. It's something I've always been interested in doing but have been hampered by my need to learn how to be a Viscount. A title, which I've found out today, I've been the holder of for a few months. It's just another thing to take in. I wonder where it's all going to end?

The car suddenly screeches to a halt, and we all jerk forward in our seatbelts. I manage to stop myself from banging my head on the seat in front of me, but Victoria isn't so lucky and rubs her head in a daze. Leaning forward, Tamara begins to open the partition between our compartment and the driver's. Suddenly, a blood curdling scream comes from her, telling me something is seriously wrong.

"Run!" she shouts as she frantically tries to undo her seat belt, but her hands are fumbling against the release button. I undo mine and set her and Victoria both free. We jump out of the car, but before we can run anywhere, guns are pointed directly at our heads.

"You had to allow your cock to do the thinking, didn't you, son?" My father gets out of one of the vehicles surrounding our own. A bullet hole has broken the glass of our windshield, and behind the shattered mess is the bloodied face of our driver. Now I know what Tamara was screaming at.

"What is going on, Father?" I decide to try and play dumb until I can formulate a better plan. My father is obviously a dangerous and volatile man. To hold up a car in daylight with people around is a sign of desperation, and a last resort.

"Don't play dumb. I know the little whore of yours has told you everything."

"What?" I screw my face up trying to feign confusion. "I've just collected Victoria and Tamara from Nicholas. I've got them back. He's taken Rose somewhere, but I'm working on that."

Victoria must catch on to what I'm doing.

"Please, Father. He has my daughter. I don't know where he took her. You have to find her. He'll hurt her I know it."

My father hesitates for a minute, his eyes narrowing as he tries to make sense of the scene unfolding before him. I can see the questions as to the validity of it running through his head.

He motions with a wave of his hand and his men step up to us and search us. My phone is removed from my pocket. Victoria's and Tamara's are taken as well. They are handed to my father who drops them onto the ground before smashing them with his feet. Victoria and Tamara both scream.

"What was that for?" I protest.

"First lesson, Theo. Nicholas doesn't give up anything easily. He'll have them tracked."

I lower my head to show deference to his superiority and acknowledge my mistake.

"I'm sorry, Father. I was just so glad to get them away from him. Joanna has told me things about what he's done to her. I couldn't bear to think of him hurting my sister in that way."

"No." My father steps forward toward Victoria. I can see her hands shaking as she struggles to maintain her compo-sure and keep up the web of lies we're weaving. I hadn't thought about it until now, but this must be one of the first times she's seen our father since he gave her away. I've always visited her alone because she never wanted to see him. Why didn't I question everything sooner? I've been so blinded by the affection I have for this man who doesn't deserve it.

"Did he hurt you badly, my little one?" He strokes his hand down Victoria's face, and she lets out an anguished cry.

"He was horrible, Daddy," she whimpers, and he pulls her into his arms. "Shush, my darling girl. It'll be better now. You'll never have to see him again."

"Thank you." Her voice cracks as she replies.

Next, he turns to Tamara.

"And you?"

My father steps toward Tamara, and I say a silent prayer for her to continue our charade until I can figure out a better way to get us to safety. Someone must have heard the gunshot and reported it. Police must be on the way. We just need to buy more time.

"They spin lies and draw you in to the point where you don't know what the truth is anymore." Her voice is almost robotic, but the tears trickling down her cheeks tell of the emotions crashing through her body.

"Lies. You've been surrounded by lies all your life, haven't you?" My father is in front of Tamara, now, and he reaches out to touch her cheek.

"Far too many."

"Hmmm." My father hums as he strokes down Tamara's cheek and across her shoulder bone. "Lies about your birth, lies about your friends, and lies about your mother." The last word is said with such malevolence it freezes even my own blood. It has the opposite effect on Tamara though. It ignites her blood into a fiery tirade directed at our father.

"You bastard, don't you dare mention my mother. I know what you did. I know just who you are." She brings her fist up and aims it at him, but he catches it and twists her around, so she's pulled close against him. "It's time for Daddy to take what's his," he says as he leers at her, and I realize for the first time the true level of his depravity. When Joanna told me William called her Tamara, it's now obvious to me that it wasn't William who said it but my father.

"No." Victoria reacts before I can. She lunges for her friend and sister but is pulled back by one of my father's men. She punches and kicks out at him until he knocks her over the head with a gun, and she falls as if lifeless into his arms.

"Get them in the car," my father orders. I try to step forward, but I am prevented from doing so by a gun raised in my face and two men pulling me back. My strength can't match their numbers. The man holding Victoria drags her to the car. Tamara is handed over to another man and is hauled screaming toward the same vehicle. They are pushed into the backseat, and it speeds away.

My father steps toward me.

"Such a disappointment. You could have ruled at my side, but I won't have the weak with me. I'll be the King of Oakfield by the end of the day, and you…" He looks at the man pointing the gun at my temple. "…will be dead. You shouldn't have fallen for the whore. Mind you, her pussy is wonderful. I'm the one who took her first, and I'll continue to take her for as long as I allow her to live."

Despite being held at gunpoint, I lunge for my father but

never make it. The men surrounding him stop me and throw me to the ground. A hail of fists thump into my body and face as I watch my father get into a vehicle and depart in a screech of tires. He's won. I've lost my sisters and possibly my wife if my father's words mean he's also taken her. I should've listened sooner.

Everyone steps back, and the man who originally held the gun to my head then steps forward. He points it down at me, and I know this is the end of my life. I've failed in my pledge to my wife. More car tires screech, and the man pointing the gun at my head suddenly flies into the air and lands with a thud on the ground. His body twisted and broken. The two men remaining, set upon the new vehicle, and I see Nicholas and William emerge from it. Both have weapons drawn and make quick work of disposing of the two men. Nicholas throws his phone to William,

"Call Matthew Carter and get him to send in a clean-up squad."

William nods and flips open the phone.

"Where are Victoria and Tamara?" He looks past me at the car.

"My father took them, a few minutes ago. They went that way," I respond indicating the direction I saw the vehicles take.

Nicholas curses but still helps me to my feet. I lean forward and cough up a little blood from the beating.

"Get Matthew to trace Victoria," Nicholas orders William

"He broke their phones," I inform him.

"My wife is a walking tracker. Do you think I'd let something so precious be left vulnerable? Don't worry. I'll have a location for her in a few minutes, and we'll go and get her.

Let's get back to the house and clean you up. There's someone waiting to see you there."

"Who?" Nicholas helps me into his car as several other cars sweep into the section of the road we've just committed chaos in. The occupants of the vehicles emerge and eagerly set about cleaning up. This is all alien to me, and it feels like I've suddenly become embroiled in a James Bond film.

"Your wife." Nicholas smiles at me. "She escaped your father and probably saved your life."

"What?" I stumble into the car, and we drive back to Oakfield Hall with me sitting in a daze of disbelief. My wife survived—we have a chance. We just need to save my sisters to get our happy ending.

CHAPTER TWENTY

JOANNA

I don't think I've ever begged time to go so quickly. I just want to know what's happening as I pace up and down the living room of Oakfield Hall. My hands are shaking, and I keep humming to myself to settle my nerves.

The soft murmurs of a waking baby in the bassinet beside me draw my attention. Nicholas left in such a hurry he entrusted the care of his daughter to me while supervised by a stern looking butler at all times. Apparently, it's the nanny's day off, but she's making her way back from visiting her cousin in Oxford as a matter of urgency.

Little Rose coos after her sleep before getting a bit more disgruntled when her mother doesn't appear. I look at the butler, and his eyes widen in fear of the tiny human in the crib.

"What's wrong with her ladyship?" he asks, and I try to stifle my amusement that a young baby is being formally referred to as 'her ladyship'.

"I suspect she needs changing and feeding." I go over to

the cot and dangle my hand in. I've taken a quick shower after my assault and wrapped myself up in one of Victoria's dressing gowns, so I'm clean. Little Rose looks up at me with a squint, trying to focus. Her crying becomes a little more panicked when she realizes I'm not her mother or father.

"It's all right, little lady." I bring her up into my arms and rock her gently. "Daddy has just gone to get your mummy and Uncle Theo. They'll be back soon." I pat under her bottom to feel her diaper, and it feels full.

"Is that uncomfortable? Let's get you changed while Mr. Alfred arranges for your bottle to be brought up." Before she left, I was told Victoria requested some milk for Rose. Alfred quickly disappears to retrieve it, and I'm left with a grumpy baby. I carry her over to the changing table and quickly make her more comfortable. We then settle down in a chair and wait for the milk. I can't help but fall instantly in love with her. A perfect angel born into a world of chaos. I can only hope she'll have a better future than the one her mother and I have experienced.

The door to the nursery opens and a tired looking Nicholas walks in with a bottle. I stand and hand him his daughter. He looks like he needs her.

"What happened?" I'm too afraid to ask, but I know I must.

"The Viscount has taken Victoria and Tamara. We saved Theo, though." A noise behind the Duke distracts my attention, and I see my husband leaning against William. He's been wounded.

"Theo." I run to him and fling my arms around him. I'm trying my hardest not to cry, but an anguished sob leaves my throat.

"It's ok. I'm all right." He kisses the top of my head. "You did so well escaping and getting here. I'm so proud of you."

"I'm sorry," I whimper into his chest.

"I know the truth now. We can put a stop to this," Theo reassures me. I feel the room close in with the tension, and the three men surrounding me look urgently down at the phone in William's hand.

"What is happening with Victoria and Tamara? Have you called the police?"

"No," Nicholas replies curtly.

"We'll deal with it our way," William adds, and I don't dare ask what he means even though in my heart I already know, and it won't be pretty.

The mobile in William's hand rings, and we all freeze and stare at it for a few seconds before he answers and puts it on speaker.

"William Cavendish."

"It's Carter."

"You got them?" The conversation is clipped and straight to the point.

"We've got an issue with the tracker. Hamilton must have his own people with links to MI5. Only they could block the signal ." The dominant voice from the other side of the phone explains.

William looks at his brother. Nicholas comes closer and asks,

"What are you doing about it?"

"Everything I can. I wanted to give you a quick update. Ryan and I are going to go and get some answers from the grid itself. You'll have to give me another hour, and then I'll have a location."

"I don't know if we have an hour." Nicholas cradles his daughter who's happily sucking on her bottle, unaware of the tension in the room.

"I'll have to bash heads together harder, then."

The phone goes dead.

"Who's that?" I question.

"A friend," Nicholas replies, not giving me anymore than I need to know. "I'm going to sit with my daughter. Fetch me when he phones back." The Duke turns away, effectively dismissing us from his presence. William directs us out of the room and down the hall to a spare bedroom.

"You can freshen up in here, Theo. There's a change of clothes in the wardrobe as well. I'll be downstairs in the study. I'm going to go through all the papers Tamara has on the Viscount. Hopefully there'll be something in them that can give us a clue to their location."

Theo nods at him, and says, "I wish I could give you more. We've already checked the one location I knew about. I'll keep thinking of others. We'll find them."

William doesn't say anything. He just flicks his ear and nose before marching off down the corridor while Theo leads me into the room.

"We should be doing something," I plead with him, but he shakes his head.

"Nicholas and William know what they're doing."

"But they are so calm, and with what he's capable of…" I falter on the last words. Does my husband truly understand what his father can be like?

"William and Nicholas are anything but calm, believe me. They are prepared to end this to save their wives. Don't mistake deadly intentions for calmness." Theo pulls his shirt off over his head, and I notice the bruising on his chest. He rubs a hand over it and looks at me.

"I'm starting to learn what my father is capable of. I think you need to tell me the rest."

My stomach drops. I knew this moment would come but the thought of reliving my nightmares in front of my husband scares me more than the actual abuse itself. I'm scared of losing him. What if he doesn't love me anymore as a result of what his father did to me? I slump down into a nearby chair

"Why didn't you tell me?" Theo shakes his head at me. "My own father!"

"I wanted to. I don't know if I can explain it. I was kept hidden for a year for a reason. He had to condition me, so I couldn't think for myself." I get up from the chair again, finding it really difficult to talk about what happened. I've been instructed not to say anything and accept I'm the Viscount's property to do with as he wants. I no longer have a right to a thought of my own, but I do have thoughts, I'm having them now, and it scares me so much

"I have to try and explain this to you, don't I?" I say pacing the room.

"Yes," Theo replies despondently.

"When I was brought to the house, the same one we were married in, I was placed naked in a small basement room. I was left there for weeks with nobody to talk to. Food and water were thrown my way, but I wasn't addressed. I had to do all my business in a small bucket, which was occasionally emptied. I had nothing to read, and no concept of what night or day was. The only sounds around me were the noises of the building itself. Do you know how noisy an old house can be? It's deafening at times." I stop pacing by a window and stare out at the green pastures below. "Eventually your father started to visit me. He didn't speak to me. He'd just stand there at the door staring at me. This went on for another couple of weeks. Everything was starting to blur by then. It could have been days, but to me, it felt like weeks. I was starved of the sound of humanity…starved of the sound of a voice no matter what it said. I would have begged to be called a whore if it meant I heard something other than the creaks of the house. One day, he did talk to me, and it was like a choir of angels rejoicing hallelujah. Do you know what he said?"

I shift position, so I can see Theo's face. His breathing is even, but I can tell he's trying to control his emotions. His fists are tightly clenched, and there is a tic in his jaw.

"I don't."

"On your knees." I lower myself down to kneel before my husband. "I couldn't believe what I was hearing. I was stunned. I just stood there, so he shut the door and disappeared. He didn't come the next day, or the day after that. I craved for him to return. How sick is that?" I allow my hands to fall at my sides and hang loosely while bowing my head, so I'm looking down at the floor. "He came back after three days and said the same three words, 'on your knees.' This time, I obeyed. He'd won and broken me. Over the next few weeks, months, I don't know how long, the same treatment was repeated. If I didn't do something he wanted, I would be left alone in the darkness until he reappeared, and I obeyed. The first time he wanted me to give oral, I didn't hide my teeth enough, and he thought I was going to bite him. I was beaten black and blue and left alone for so long. I thought I'd been abandoned, and left to die. Food was minimal during that time, and I rationed the portions I was given. I remember when he returned I was so grateful to see him, especially as he brought me a small bar of chocolate. It's stupid." I can't stop the tears. I'm sobbing now, but they are freeing and needed. "I allowed him to come down my throat three times that day. I swallowed every bit of him and was rewarded with a speech of how I was a dirty little whore, and that the next time he came to see me, he would be taking my pussy over and over again. I should have hated what he said to me, but I didn't. I wanted more. I wanted him to call me every degrading name in the world. I didn't care because at least someone was talking to me."

It's Theo's turn to get up, this time. I don't look up from my bowed position. I just listen to the sound of his feet as they march to the bedroom door before hearing him furiously pull the door open, and then slam it shut behind him as he leaves.

I let out an anguished cry and collapse down into a ball on the floor. I knew he would hate me. I'm disgusting. How can anyone crave the sort of abuse I did? A loud masculine roar comes from the hallway, and I shrink further into myself. A deafening thud pounds into the wall, not once but twice, and is followed by smashing glass.

"I'll kill him," Theo yells, and there are more sounds of breaking glass.

"Enough." There is another deep voice, and I recognize it as Nicholas'. "Save the anger for when we find him. Between the three of us, we'll tear him apart limb from limb."

The hallway goes silent for a few minutes, and then the door opens again, and Theo re-enters the room. He comes straight to me, and sweeping me up into his arms, he carries me to the bed where he brings my face up to meet his.

"You'll never bow before anyone again. You'll stand proudly upright as a strong woman. I'll fill our entire house with noise. It will never be silent again. I'm sorry…I'm so sorry I didn't realize the truth sooner. I'm just glad he arranged for us to marry, so I was able to get you away from him for a while."

I can't stop the whimper on my breath.

"No." Theo shakes his head. "Please tell me he didn't."

"I wish I could. He came to me the night after we first made love. It was him who gave me the photo and demanded I give it to you. He's been playing games from the start. He told me I had to get pregnant with your child."

Theo pushes away from me in disgust.

"That's why you pleaded with me to take you on our wedding night."

"I was so scared. He told me what would happen to me would be worse if I didn't do it. Then he started threatening your life. I'm scared of him, Theo. He's a monster, and I don't know how to get out from under his shadow. Even now if he walked into this room, I'd fall to my knees and let him do to me what he wants. I don't know how to say no."

Theo places his head in his hands. When he looks back up at me, I can see tears in his eyes.

"Don't you see. You've already saved yourself. You did get away from him. You came here. That was you beating his rule. His spell on you is broken."

He comes back to me and kisses my lips passionately and then places his hand over my heart.

"This is what gave you the strength to beat him. Love…

our love. You are free, Joanna. You've just got to start believing it yourself. There is no more silence in the world. Even if it's quiet, you'll hear the sound of the beating of your heart entwined with mine."

"I'm free." The concept is alien to me. I test it on my lips and like it. "I can be your wife?"

He nods.

"Yes, but only after you learn to be yourself."

"I thought you'd hate me."

"Never." Theo pulls me into his arms, and we settle back against the bed. My eyelids grow heavy with the exhaustion of telling him everything. Theo continues, "No, the person I hate is my father. He's gotten away with too much for too long now. As soon as we find out where he is, we're putting a stop to this. His reign of terror is over. It's about time he learned the correct way to treat a woman."

CHAPTER TWENTY ONE

THEODORE

Joanna and I rest for no longer than half an hour before the need to find my sisters gets the better of both of us. We make our way down to the office where William is surrounded by papers, which he's frantically searching through for any evidence of where my father could be hiding. Nicholas follows us down with a baby monitor in his hand and immediately picks up a pile of his own papers. He looks exhausted, and I can see the love both men have for my sisters. They may be quiet and tired of waiting, but they'll be vicious when it comes to the rescue. A mobile sits next to William within easy access for when the call we're all longing for comes through. In total, the girls have been missing for an hour, and it's been the longest hour of all our lives. I know what my father is truly capable of, now. I would like to think his paternal nature would kick in and protect Tamara and Victoria, but after hearing the way he treated Joanna and ordered my execution, I know he's incapable of compassion.

"I'm going to see if the chef can get us all a sandwich and a drink." Joanna stands up on tiptoes and kisses my lips. "We need to keep our energy up."

Nicholas looks up from his papers and signals it's a good idea before asking, "Would you mind checking on Rose as well? She's sleeping but is unsettled. I think she knows her mummy is missing. A feminine touch might help."

"Of course." Joanna lets go of my hand and leaves the room, shutting the door behind her.

"How is she?" William looks up from where he's been studying a piece of paper that looks like a bank statement.

"Ok." I pick up a couple of the sheets he's yet to examine and start looking over them. "It's going to take a while, but she's strong."

We fall into silence for a short while. Each of us are lost in our own thoughts as we search for something, anything, to tell us where my father could be. The paper I have lists financial transactions from his bank. Different amounts relating to donations, household expenditures, and a couple of costs for properties he owns.

"Has someone checked our property in Yorkshire?"

"Yes," Nicholas replies. "It seems he moved Joanna's keeper, Camilla Fentress, up there. She's dead, killed by a bullet to the center of her forehead. He's obviously been cleaning house, getting ready to take over from me."

I remember the woman who was there when I was married to Joanna. She seemed kind, but I know better now. I won't mourn her death. I hope she suffered.

"We've got to be missing something." William throws down his pile of papers. "I need to get Tamara back. She's pregnant, and Joanna warned Victoria about the Viscount and his fascination with her."

"He made Joanna dress up as Tamara," I blurt out.

"What?" William is on his feet and thumping his hands on the desk.

"She told me it was you, and you had a wig made like Tamara when she had long hair."

William and Nicholas look at each other.

"Fuck!" Nicholas exclaims. "He's sicker than I thought."

"What?" I question.

"Tamara was taken by an old associate of the society, a perverted man named Lord West. We were late rescuing her, and the Viscount got there first. I didn't understand it at that point, but I do now," William explains.

"Sorry you've lost me?"

"While she was kidnapped, Tamara's hair had been chopped short, but we never found the hair that was removed. We assumed it had been thrown on the fire, but I've now got a feeling perhaps it was taken by the Viscount." William goes over to the corner of the room and pours a glass of what looks like brandy. He waves the decanter at me, and I nod to say yes.

"Perhaps what he did to Tamara's mother twisted his mind. I wonder if it was the first time he'd raped a woman?" Nicholas joins us, and William pours him a glass.

"First time?" These two brothers know so much more of what is happening around me than I do. I've been kept in the dark and am catching up quickly.

"When he raped Elsie and conceived Tamara," William informs me, and we all remain silent for a moment and take a sip of drink.

"I can't help but think it was more. Possibly a result of the trials and what his parents put him through. If it wasn't for Victoria, I'm not sure my mind would have survived what our father ordered me to do." Nicholas muses into the bottom of his glass.

"I don't understand how they've been able to get away with treating women the way they have for so long. When my father bought Joanna, he just assumed the marriage between me and her would take place." Nicholas shrugs at me. "And it was never suggested I should be allowed to choose my own bride. Have generations of our families been so warped that they haven't been able to see right from wrong?"

"Eight generations," William mulls into his brandy glass.

"How many women have suffered at their hands?" I query and take another mouthful of the amber nectar.

"That we know of? Over the centuries, the sum total of the chosen ladies given to a Duke on his thirtieth birthday is…forty-three." Nicholas answers before shutting his eyes as the pain of the number sinks in with William and me.

"You know?" The younger Cavendish is shocked at his brother's answer.

"I went through all the papers shortly after I took over as the Duke. I learned the name of every single girl. Our mother,"—he looks at William and then at me—"your mother. They are both on the list. Nearly all died young. Your mother, Joanna and Victoria are the only survivors."

"My mother was one?" I can't believe what I'm hearing. I know my parents have never been a romantic couple, but it makes sense now why she's never really been around. She escaped as soon as she could, and my father was too busy tormenting other women to care. "Tradition was followed in my father's case and in mine. A rejected girl bought to marry?"

"Yes, every Hamilton is descended from one of the girls since the inception of the society." Nicholas shakes his head at me.

I stand there dumfounded at what I'm hearing.

"I can't get my head around this. How have they got away with it for so long?"

"By having the right people in their pockets. People who'll turn a blind eye to what has been happening. Judges, police, senior politicians, even members of the royal family in the past. The aristocracy has been rotten for years, but I won't let it be that way for Rose." Nicholas slams his now empty glass down onto table in a defiant response.

"Too much sex of the wrong kind, if you ask me," William adds, and that earns a chuckle from Nicholas. "Small dicks with no ability to please a woman properly."

"You always have a way of putting things, brother, that lightens the mood." Nicholas slaps his brother on the back.

"I'm just saying it takes a real man to treat a woman properly and earn her respect. You don't get that by abusing her or ordering her around like a dog. You worship her and love her with as much affection as you can give even though men are shit at stuff like that, and they'll make mistakes. Or as in my case where their brain doesn't work the same as everyone else's, and they'll end up telling their wife she doesn't look good in the new dress she's just bought." William smirks

"Some women will say that's a good thing," Nicholas points out, and I nod in agreement.

"Not when you say she looks like the bride of Frankenstein, because the outfit was far too black for my liking." William screws his face up and then finishes his brandy.

"You didn't," I gasp.

"She thought I meant her hair and make-up as well as the dress. It was an honest mistake. I make them often. She should know by now."

"She does. Don't worry." Nicholas slaps his brother on the back again, and we all go quiet, hoping Tamara will get a chance to spend more time being told the honest truth about her outfits by her husband.

"I'm sorry I doubted you two." I finally break the silence. "I can see you both adore my sisters. I'm glad they have you. What you're trying to do for the society is going to help so many people. It will help to right the wrongs of the past."

"It will." Nicholas pushes away from where we are congregated and goes over to a safe in the wall. He punches in a code, which I don't see, and pulls out an old parchment.

"Is that what I think it is?" William cocks his head.

"The original society deeds. I think it's about time we wrote a new one."

Nicholas places the aging paper down and scribbles through the middle of it with the words, 'Null and Void.' He then turns it over and starts writing.

It is hereby claimed on the eighth day of the eleven month of the year twenty nineteen that a new charter for the society of Oakfield is to be adopted. From this point forth, all violence against women will result in summary expulsion from the society.

The purpose for the society will now be to educate future generations of women who wish to learn the creative arts such as painting, literature, drama, and music. We will all work together to ensure they have the necessary skills to help them find their own way in life. Past wrongs will be righted. Hope is our new motto.

Underneath, he signs his name, Nicholas Cavendish, Duke of Oakfield, with a flourish and hands the pen to William, who signs as the Earl of Lullington. William hands me the pen, and I look at him.

"You were born a part of this, remember. Together, we are the ones who can change it."

I take the pen and sign my name, Viscount Theodore Hamilton, Earl of Linton.

A soft clapping comes from behind us, and we turn to see Joanna standing there with a big smile on her face.

"I love the idea. I hope I'm going to be allowed to help." She comes over to us and stands at my side. I look down at the pen, then back to her, and then to Nicholas. He nods. I look to William, and he does the same.

"Woman are now a part of the society and not in the way they were before." I hand her the pen, and she looks at me confused.

"I don't understand?"

"Sign it."

"But?"

"Sign it," Both William and Nicholas tell her at the same time.

"There are no more unequals in this society. We are all one."

Joanna takes the pen from me, and next to my name she signs, Lady Joanna Hamilton, Countess of Linton, and then places the pen down.

"Now we just need to bring the Duchess of Oakfield and Countess of Lullington home to sign it as well."

At the same time, we all turn our heads to the mobile phone sitting on William's desk. It must hear our silent prayers because it starts to ring.

CHAPTER TWENTY TWO

JOANNA

"They're at Seven, Winchester Place. My men are on the way. See you there."

The phone goes dead, and I watch Theo as he stumbles backward and down into a chair. He knows the address—I'm certain of it.

"Theo?" I stroke his shoulder while Nicholas and William retrieve guns and other weapons from within a locked cupboard. "What is it?"

"My mother."

He's gone as white as a sheet and pulls his phone out of his pocket. Nicholas grabs it off him before he has a chance to call anyone. The elder Cavendish brother drops the phone onto the floor and stamps on it with his foot. "Don't be stupid."

"Hey." Theo scrambles to pick up the pieces of his broken mobile. "I need to warn her."

"They've been there for over an hour now. It'll be too late." Nicholas hands Theo a gun. "The society girls all die young. Let's hope your mother is the last one, and we can save my wife and your sister before it's too late."

I'm looking between the two men, wondering what's going on. What has Theo's mother got to do with this? William appears at my side and hands me a gun. I look down at it and back up at him as if to say 'what am I supposed to do with this?'

"Seven, Winchester Place, is just down the road. It's where Theo and Victoria's mother lives…lived. We've got to hope he sent her away rather than the alternative." He nods at the gun in my hand. "You know how to use it?"

"Yes," I say, stunned. The Viscount has spoken to me a few times about his wife, Lady Celia, during my time in his captivity. I know she was one of the ladies who was given to Nicholas' father. She wasn't chosen and was sold to the Viscount's father. Apparently, they were instantly married that night. She never had to experience the year of being hidden away and tortured like I did. No, she was taken the first night and conceived Theo. I remember the Viscount telling me about how he planned Victoria's birth to ensure she was one of the chosen for the next generation. She was nearly not born. The Countess had fallen pregnant with another child, originally, but an early test showed it to be a boy. She was forced to have an abortion, and then the Viscount had spent all his time 'fucking her hard', his words not mine, to ensure she conceived a girl. He took great delight in being rewarded with Victoria a month before the cut-off. His wife's job done, he set her up in her own house, so he could continue with his business of being a Viscount and raising his daughter to be as virtuous as possible, ready for her debut into the society. He told me he hated his wife. She was weak and cried for her lost son all the time. She'd found out about Tamara as well and had berated him so much he'd been forced to break her jaw, so she'd shut up until it was fixed. Prior to him taking me, I don't think he'd seen her in years. He'd told Theo and Victoria she'd met another man, and she'd limited her contact with them. This will be another story I'll have to tell my husband—another truth I'll have to deliver to him, which will break even more of his spirit. He looks a defeated man at the moment, standing there looking at his gun as if he'd rather point it at his own head than anyone else's.

William breaks me out of my thoughts by handing me spare rounds and a bulletproof vest.

"What are you doing?" Theo steps forward and grabs the vest.

"Making sure she's safe during the assault." William looks at Theo as though it's obvious what he's doing. It is really, but I can see my husband has other ideas.

"She's not coming with us. She can help look after Rose along with your nanny now she's returned." Theo takes the gun from me, and I stand there compliant. It's still my nature not to argue. I think that will take a long time to recover from.

"We don't have time for this." Nicholas, who has finished preparing, sticks his head out the door to the office and calls for his car to be readied, "Let's go."

William places his hand on the document we've all just signed and points out the signatures. "All for one, Theo. She needs this more than we do. She needs closure. Don't stop her from getting it." The younger brother goes to stand with his sibling, and they both look impatiently back at us to make a decision.

"Do you want to go?" Theo asks me.

I hesitate over an answer. I want to see the Viscount die. I'd love to be the one to kill him, but what if I get in the way or get captured again? I realize I'm scared, but that's only natural. There's a bigger picture here than my fear: Tamara and Victoria. They need to be rescued, and my joining them may be the distraction needed.

"Yes," I respond to Theo and hold my hand out for the weapon and vest. He sighs heavily but hands them back to me.

"Stay close to me."

"I will." We follow the Cavendish brothers out of the house and into a Range Rover. Nicholas drives, and his foot is instantly put to the floor, and we speed out of his estate and onto the roads of the suburbs of London. It's almost lunchtime now, but it seems like so much more time has passed since I woke this morning and found Viscount Hamilton in the house and Theo's butler dead. God, I haven't even told him about that yet. Turning, I squeeze his hand, and he looks down at me, his brows furrowed in concentration.

"Your butler is dead."

"I know. A clean-up crew has been to the house. He was a good man. I'll make sure he gets all the honors he deserves."

"Good."

We all fall silent again and contemplate the possible outcomes of the next few hours. Eventually several other vehicles join us. I don't need to ask, but I know these are the men who work for the mysterious Matthew Carter. I hope they are as well trained as those of the Viscount. I think we're going to need it. I try my hardest to think of the men around the Viscount. I've been with them, and I've seen them all. I could be of help here but remembering them means remembering my time with him. Sitting next to Theo, knowing we're heading to save Tamara and Victoria from the same fate, helps me conquer my fears, though.

"I remember him normally having two other men he kept with him all the time." William turns around from the front seat to look at me.

"Go on," he encourages, and Theo, who's sitting next to me, squeezes my hand.

"They aren't all properly trained, not the men closest to him, anyway. I think they are society men." I bite my lip. "One of them was old, very old. He has other people, ones he calls dispensable for better protection. They'll probably be outside. I remember seeing them from my window when I was transferred to a proper bedroom." I look to Theo. "After about nine months, he decided my training was complete, and he trusted me enough to move me out of the basement because I wasn't a flight risk. It's true, I wasn't. By that point, I didn't remember a life before being beholden to the Viscount. I do now, and I want it back."

"Do you remember the names of any of the men he kept close?" Nicholas asks while keeping his eyes on the road.

I shake my head and swallow down the rising bile. I don't know the names of any of the men. I blocked out what they called each other. I had to after they gang raped me.

"I'm sorry. I…" My voice breaks.

"It's ok." Theo brings my hand up to his lips and kisses it. "We'll make them all pay."

"I'm sorry to ask you, Joanna, but is there anything else you remember? Anything that could be helpful regarding the way he works."

I take a deep breath and try to think, but only one thing comes to mind.

"I think they'll be kept somewhere dark in the house… maybe a cellar if it has one. It's his way of disorientating you. He'll want Tamara and Victoria confused and scared. It's the way he breaks you."

William nods his thanks at me and pulling out his phone, he dials a number. It comes up on the Bluetooth in the car.

"Carter."

"Do you know the layout of the house?" William asks.

"It's in front of me. What do you need?"

"Does it have a basement or cellar?"

"Yes."

"That's where they are."

The cars stop outside a large country house in the middle of a busy area of London. It's surrounded on all sides by other properties. Two men stand guard outside. Within seconds, the people in the other car are out, and the two men are disarmed and secured. I'm shocked at the speed of it all. One of the men, a massively built man with a commanding look mixed with dreamy brown eyes, nods at Nicholas.

"Clear," he mouths, and we all get out of the car and follow behind the large man and three others. I'm surrounded by William and Theo. My gun is in my hand, and in my head, I'm running through all the things I need to do to ensure it works properly if I need to shoot it. The tension in the air is palpable. The door is kicked in, and two men standing in the hallway are shot with silenced guns. I pull my lips together tightly to stifle the scream threatening to escape. We need to be quiet.

"Please, let them be ok," I whisper a prayer to myself as we make our way through the house. We reach the kitchen via the entrance to the hall, and there, in the middle of the floor, lies a woman with blood pooling around her from a wound to the head. Her eyes are open but dead. I instantly grab hold of Theo's hand. I know who the woman is. His mother. A single tear tumbles down his cheek before he mouths.

"Let's end this. My father dies today."

CHAPTER TWENTY THREE

THEODORE

I try my hardest not to look down at my mother. I know she's a person who for many years I've held hatred for because I thought she'd abandoned Victoria and me, but it was all lies. She was escaping the real villain in this story. I need him gone.

Matthew Carter presses a device against the door of the cellar and holds a finger up to silence us.

"Three men, two women," he relays back to us. "We need to go in quickly and hard. It's my guess the men will be armed. Two of them will make a grab for the women and use them as shields. They won't kill them, yet. They lose the bargaining chip if they do. Hamilton will no doubt have one of the ladies. Give me a few seconds, I want to try and ascertain their positions better."

We all nod in agreement with him, and he goes back to listening at the door. A few minutes later, his eyes go wide with fear, and he drops the listening device and pulls out his gun.

"We go in now. One of the women is about to be raped."

"Tamara," Joanna gasps from beside me, and Nicholas and I both step in front of William. I can physically see a change come about him. He's been calm and collected, up until this point, but his pupils darken to the point where I'm unable to see the color of his irises. He surges forward, but his brother and I hold him in place.

"Out of my way," William growls.

"Joanna sing hush little baby. Quickly, if he loses it when we go down there it could be the end of Victoria and Tamara," Nicholas orders as Matthew prepares his men, and they smash through the door into the cellar.

"Wh-What?" Joanna stutters in confusion.

"Do it!" Nicholas shouts.

> *"Hush, little baby, don't say a word,*
> *Mama's going to buy you a mocking bird.*
> *And if that mockingbird don't sing,*
> *Mama's going to buy you a diamond ring."*

Joanna sings, and William goes limp in our arms. His pupils shrink back, and his brown eyes reappear.

"I want my wife," he informs us, and both Nicholas and I step aside and allow him down into the cellar. I pull Joanna to my side and follow them down. The basement area is damp, and the smell of mold invades my nostrils. Is this similar to the place Joanna was hidden away? I turn back to her in the dim light of the stairway and can see the hesitance in her eyes, but then it's instantly masked with a determination so strong I can't help but feed from it.

We reach the bottom of the stairs and are faced with a

stand-off. Matthew and his men are pointing guns at two men: one my father and another I recognize from visiting him. They each hold one of the women. My father stands behind Tamara, and the other man is behind Victoria who looks dazed and confused. A third man lies unmoving on the floor—blood has started to pool around him from a wound to his chest. I'm left in no doubt that he's dead or nearly there. It's a fatal wound, but I feel no sorrow for his death.

"You've changed your hair," William speaks first and cocks his head to where Tamara stands, wearing a wig of thick black hair.

"It wasn't my idea." She tries her hardest to struggle against my father's hold, but he's too strong for her, and there is a hesitancy in her movements, probably because of the child within her stomach.

Nicholas takes control of the situation with his commanding presence.

"It's over, Hamilton. Let the ladies go."

"It's not over until the blood in your body flows all over this floor," my father retorts and moves his gun from where it's pointed at Tamara's head and aims it straight toward Nicholas. He doesn't pull the trigger, though. He knows the speed of the men who have guns pointed at him is far superior to his own. He'd be dead before the bullet leaves the gun.

I push Joanna closer to William, and he tucks her behind him, so I can step forward to join his brother.

"It's over, Father. You've made too many mistakes. Put the gun down."

A lecherous sneer crosses his face.

"I see you've brought my little whore with you. I underestimated her ability to escape the way she did. I guess I'll have to work harder at breaking her when you're lying dead next to the Duke. So many titles for me to take. A whole new world to rule over."

"You sure it's only cigars he smokes and nothing a little stronger?" Matthew raises an eyebrow over at me.

"I'm beginning to wonder." I shrug my shoulders.

"Enough." My father steps forward with Tamara in front of him. His weapon is pointed at us, and we perform a dance around the room. He's working his way toward the door to escape. The trained men in our entourage try to prevent this, but there's little they can do with my sisters in the line of fire.

"We have to stop them," Joanna whispers behind me, and I look carefully over my shoulder to reassure her it'll be all right, but she's already moving forward to where my father stands. I instantly want to stop her, but Nicholas prevents me from moving.

"Give her a chance. She needs this."

Joanna walks between Nicholas and I and slowly lowers herself to her knees in front of my father. She bows her head, and a triumphant smirk crosses his face.

"Maybe I underestimated my skills, after all. Once a slave always a slave. Tamara and Victoria will make great pets for their new owners. Come here." All I can do is stand by and watch whatever Joanna's plan is unfold. She gets to her feet with her head still bowed and makes her way to stand next to him. At the same time, I see out the corner of my eye one of Matthew's men step closer to where the second man has Victoria. He's the weaker of the two and will be easier to take down. Nicholas slightly nods his head, and in the blink of an eye, the man holding Victoria is on the floor and dead with a bullet hole to his head, and she is free and in her husband's arms. With the distraction, Joanna pulls her weapon from where it was hidden in her thick jumper and points it at my father's head.

"Drop your gun," she orders. He doesn't move at first, but William and I descend on him with our own weapons drawn.

"It's over," I repeat. "Drop you weapon."

It seems like an age, but eventually my father accepts defeat and lowers his gun. He lets go of his hold on Tamara, and she runs to William while I take the weapon from my father.

"Why?" I ask him.

"Because I could," my father replies.

I shake my head and turn to give the weapon to one of the trained MI5 men in our group. My father uses my distraction and pushing past me, he tries to race up the stairs. He's not quick enough, though. A weapon fires, and the bullet goes straight into his leg, causing him to collapse down onto the ground. When I look down, there's smoke emerging from my own gun. It was me who shot him. Joanna comes quickly to my side while Nicholas and William leave Tamara and Victoria to drag my father back into the center of the room. He's screaming in pain. Nicholas removes the tie my father is wearing and stuffs it into his mouth to shut him up.

Matthew comes over and secures my father's hands with cuffs.

"I'll leave you six to finish this. We'll start cleaning upstairs. What do you want done about the woman?"

Nicholas looks at me, and Victoria lets out a cry.

"With Theo and Victoria's permission, I'd like to bury her with my mother and Tamara's. The three women who've given birth to the new generation of the society all together. While the three men: my father, Joanna's, and eventually the scum at my feet, who gave nothing but their sperm, will be forgotten for the evil deeds they committed."

"Please, Theo." Victoria begs as she slides down to sit on the floor. She looks exhausted and weak.

"Of course," I reply instantly and go to help support her. Joanna comes with me and sits down next to her.

"Is Rose ok?" Victoria asks immediately.

"She's fine. She has more guards around her than we have here." Joanna smiles weakly. She's exhausted as well.

While Matthew and the other men leave the six of us alone with my father, William and Tamara speak quietly in the corner of the room. Pulling the wig from her head, Tamara drops it onto the floor. Then William places his hand over her stomach, and she reassures him she's all right and wasn't hurt.

Nicholas stands over my father and addresses us, "I don't think I need to tell you what happens next. In order to put an end to this, I need to send a message. If you don't want to be involved, then you may leave with no questions asked. Victoria?"

She shakes her head. "I need closure."

"Tamara? William?"

"I want to see him suffer," Tamara announces through gritted teeth.

"I'm with the wife," William smirks.

"Theo? Joanna?"

I look down at my wife.

"I want to stay." She gets up from her position where she's sat beside Victoria and goes to stand in front of my father. He looks up at her and spits. Nicholas kicks him in his wounded leg, and he lets out a scream of pain.

"On your knees," Joanna commands, standing tall in front of him with her shoulders pulled back, and her head held high. He doesn't move, so she repeats her order, "On your knees."

Nicholas grabs him and pulls him up so that he bows low before her.

"If I could keep you here and subject you to what you did me, I would, but I don't think any of us want to keep you alive for that long. You don't deserve a moment more of our pain and worry. I will, however, thank you for one thing. For giving me Theo. My soul mate, and my savior. Despite who his father is, he's the kindest man I've ever met. I know we'll be gray and old, and in our bed together when we die. It will be peaceful and painless. Not like your death."

Tamara comes to Joanna's side and takes her hand.

"You stole my mother from me, and in a brutal way. She should be here to see the child I'm carrying welcomed into the world. You are a sick old man with twisted views on what is acceptable. In no way would your depraved thoughts about me ever be reciprocated. I'll enjoy your death. I hope you rot in hell." She pauses a moment. "But I also have to thank you. You didn't give me William. Well, I suppose you did in a way with your treatment of Victoria, but no, my thank you is for something else. You gave me an education, and one I'll use to ensure every trace of you is removed from the records. You'll be nothing. A nobody for eternity."

I help Victoria to her feet when she holds her hand out to me and assist her over to where the other two women are standing. With Tamara on one side of Joanna, Victoria stands on the other side of my wife and takes her hand.

"You stole my innocence from me, and my belief in a world that was better than the one I lived in. You destroyed my past so you could have a future. It's a shame you never realized how strong the daughter you raised actually is. I survived being given away like a possession to a wicked and ruthless society. I found my husband and my love, and as the Duchess of Oakfield, I'll bring peace for generations to come. That is what I thank you for. For being my father, in just the way you were. You created what you see in this room right now. Every action you've ever undertaken has led to this point. The point of your death and our triumph." My sister looks to me. "Do you want to say anything, Theo?"

I look at my father who has managed to spit out the tie that was stuffed in his mouth and is now starting to beg,

"Please, Theo, you can stop this with one word. I'll do whatever it takes. Don't be the monster these people have tried to turn you into."

I let out a laugh—it's a long barking one, and the entire room falls silent.

"You still believe after all of this you're innocent, don't you? That what you did was for the good of a future where women would be preyed on and abused." I pull my fist back and send it slamming into his face. My knuckles are still sore from my attack on Joanna's father and instantly smart. But I don't care when I see my father's nose break.

"Pull his shirt off," I order Nicholas who eyes me suspiciously. But when I unbuckle my belt, he realizes exactly what I mean to do. He strips my father of his crisp white shirt, which has been marred with a splattering of blood, and

I take my belt and bring it crashing down on my father's back. He yells out and tries to shift, but William comes forward and holds him down. I repeat the process twenty times, harder and harder each time until his back is littered with cuts, oozing blood.

"Is that how you think a woman should be treated?" I ask my father, and he spits at my boot, so I kick him in the face. "Did you do that to Joanna?"

My wife comes to my side and places her hand on my shoulder.

"Yes," she tells me.

"Was there more?"

There are various sex toys littered around the room, which the men had planned to use on my sisters. I grab a large one and ram it down my father's throat.

"How about that?"

Joanna nods.

"Maybe I should go further? Make you truly understand what it's like to be a woman in your world."

William bends down and picks up a particularly large phallic shaped object.

"If you do, I say we use this one."

I shake my head.

"It's not something I particularly want to see, thank you. No, I think he gets the message. His actions have created a better man in me than he ever was, and that's why Joanna is now free. She's learned what happiness is, despite the demonic actions of a mad man who has half the balls I do."

"Phew." William wipes his brow. "I was worried. I've seen some sick things, but I'm getting too old for this shit. I'd rather just go home and fuck my wife senseless."

"William." Tamara whacks him on the shoulder.

"Sorry, can't help with the truth."

Nicholas coughs.

"Are we done?" he questions, and we all nod yes. "Who wants the honors?"

"Me." All three women say in unison. It's like a melody in my head. The three women left distraught at the hands of my father are ready to take back their power.

Joanna pulls her weapon back out while William hands Tamara his, and I give Victoria mine.

Nicholas positions my father on his knees and steps away from the path of any possible ricochets.

"Arthur Hamilton, former Viscount. I, Victoria Cavendish, Duchess of Oakfield and founding member of the new society of Oakfield find you guilty of offenses against our charter including the rape and murder of Elsie Bennett." Victoria points her weapon at our father.

"Arthur Hamilton, former Viscount. I, Tamara Cavendish, Countess of Lullington and founding member of the new society of Oakfield pass sentence of death upon you for offenses against our charter." Tamara follows suit.

Finally, Joanna steps up and points her weapon at my father.

"Arthur Hamilton, former Viscount. I, Joanna Hamilton, Countess of Linton and founding member of the new society of Oakfield strip you of your name and power by acting as your executioner."

Three guns fire and hit their target. My father slumps down to the ground—dead. Each woman places the gun down on the floor and walks over to their respective partner. Joanna nestles into my chest.

"Can we go home, now?"

I bring my lips to hers.

"Yes."

As we all leave the room, I turn around and take a final look at the man who I worshipped for most of my life. It'll take a long while to absorb everything that has happened over the last few weeks, but with my loving wife at my side, I know that what she said about us growing gray and old together won't just be a dream. It'll be a reality, and a new Oakfield will emerge with me, Joanna, Nicholas, Victoria, William, and Tamara at the helm. A place of sanctuary, not violence. The past is dead. Long live the future.

EPILOGUE

Rose Windsor, Duchess of Oakfield

Thirty years later

Hello and welcome to Oakfield hall. I want to thank you all for coming here today. My name is Rose Windsor and today I turned thirty years old and inherited my father's title and became Duchess of Oakfield. Thank you, daddy." I smile down at my father where he sits in the front row of the audience with his arm wrapped around my mother, he leans over and gives her a kiss and she kisses him back. I know that despite being sixty my father will take my mother back to their bedroom soon and I doubt they'll surface for the rest of the evening. It's a big embarrassment to me and my younger sister and two younger brothers how in love with each other they still are. Twins, Amelia and Jonathan, and little Reggie named after my father's childhood butler, all sit beside my parents. Amelia is engaged to be married to a man from New York and is only here for a few days before she returns to her fashion career in the states. She was recently asked to design the wedding dress of the actress Bethany Jolie when she married my dad's friend, Prince John. Jonathan runs the Oakfield estates for my father while Reggie is still at university studying finance and unsure what he wants to do with his future yet. Next to them sits my husband, Henry Windsor, we were married last year after being introduced at an art exhibition three years ago. I'm carrying our first child at the moment, but we've not told anyone yet as it's still early days. I know mum and dad will be thrilled when they find out. I'm ex cited to tell them. About ten years ago, mum sat me down and told me about how she and dad met. I've always known she had the Oakfield crest burnt into the skin on her thigh. I've never asked about it before, but it just felt like it was time. She told me how her father had given her to my dad as part of an old pact within the society. She'd been subjected to terrible trials by the previous Duke but her and my father had fallen in love and eventually managed to triumph over the man who would have been my grandad. It took me a long time to come to terms with what had happened. I'd packed my bags and travelled around the world for a few months as I allowed it all to sink in. It was the best thing I'd ever done though as it helped me when I eventually took over the new version of the Oakfield Society.

That is the other reason I stand in front of an audience on my thirtieth birthday. It's because I'm handing out grants to a new intake of candidates to our scheme to help assist those who want to succeed in the world of art, drama and music.

I finish handing out the last certificate and step down from the plate. My cousin, Daphne stands their clapping her hands. She's the daughter of my Aunt Joanna and Uncle Theo. She's a few years younger than me and I've brought her into the society as my assistant because her knowledge of marketing matters is second to none. My aunt and uncle had difficultly conceiving her, I was told his was due to scaring, it wasn't until after my mother had told me the story of her meeting with my father than she told me how my aunt and uncle met. To have one grandfather who was a devil is unlucky but two, shameful. I can't believe what happened to Joanna and the fact it left her unable to conceive a child without IVF. Thankfully they had Daphne and then adopted three more children, Sebastian, Chloe and Frederick. You would never know that the last three aren't biological to them, they are loved just as much and told off when wrong in the same way. My uncle Theo can be a bit domineering and over protective especially of the girls, but my aunt Joanna seems to like it. She often calls him her saviour when I've been around. My uncle runs his estates which have been combined with the title of Linton which Joanna inherited from her father. Joanna spends a lot of her time doing photography and even has a gallery in London where she sells them from.

"You were so good." Daphne applauds me, "How are you feeling? Any sickness?" She hands me a flute full of water not champagne.

I roll my eyes at her. I can't keep a secret from my cousin. It's impossible.

"I'm good. Where is your mum and dad?" I laugh.

"Mum had a headache, they send their apologies. Dad was going to come but he said he better stay with mum in case she needed anything." Daphne doesn't need to say anything else, Uncle Theo and Aunt Joanna are just as amorous as my parents.

Henry comes to my side and brings me close to him kissing me passionately.

"I love it when you come over all boss lady. Maybe you could speak to me that way later." He winks and I run my tongue over my lips. I wish I could take him to bed now, I think I've inherited my parents passionate streak.

"I don't need to hear that about my niece." My uncle William coughs from behind us.

"Sorry Uncle William." I give him a welcoming kiss on the cheek.

"You did amazingly." My aunt Tamara joins him and congratulates me, "Your mother was feeling a little tired. Your father has taken her for a rest. They'll be back down to congratulate you later."

William lets out a loud snort.

"Not if he takes one of his Viagra tablets. He'll be fucking her all night."

Daphne and I both screw up our noses and stick out our tongues.

"Yuck! Uncle William."

"I know." He grabs a flute of champagne from a passing waiter. "One of those things I'm not supposed to talk about."

"Yes." Tamara whacks him on the shoulder and shakes her head.

"How about I say I'm going to wash some Viagra down with this champagne, so you better get that cute backside upstairs."

"You are just saying things to cross out the children now. Katherine and Oscar hate it when you do that." Aunt Joanna refers to my other cousins, their children. Katherine is an actress in Hollywood while Oscar still lives at Oakfield Hall.

He is on the autism spectrum like my Uncle William, but I've never seen two parents so devoted to giving him love and reassurance over his diagnosis.

"Is it working." They both laugh together before disappearing and I know I won't see them again this evening. This party is now mine. A new generation is taking over. The sins of the past are dead, our futures are bright, and we have the power to make our own decisions. Everyone is happy. Everyone is free. That is what Oakfield is now, our sovereignty complete but no longer one of darkness because it is only filled with light and sex, lots of consensual sex.

THE END

Thank you for reading the Dark Sovereignty Series.

———

Ready for more dark romance? Then keep reading for a sneak peek at a brand new stand-alone dark romance, **Mine**.

I will get my pound of flesh.
I will make her suffer.
I'm the devil she thinks I am.

So why do I find myself starting to care about her?

Get **Mine** today at
www.AuthorAnnaEdwards.com

———

If you love romantic suspense, you'll love the internationally bestselling: **The Control Series:** A complete, dramatic, witty, and sensual suspense romance set predominantly in London.

FIVE STARS — "Beautifully written story that keeps you gripped from page one and keeps you on your toes. Would you Surrender control to James?? GOD I already have!!" — *Amo & Sarah's Book Corner*

Get **Surrendered Control** today at
www.AuthorAnnaEdwards.com

————

Interested in paranormal romance? Be sure to check out my bestselling, fan favorite, the **Glacial Blood Series.**

Welcome to the Glacial Blood series, a world of shifters and witches, magic and mayhem, unforgivable lies and unbreakable love. A world where family is born not only through blood, but bond. With plenty of the threats to come—and a secret that remains untold.

Pick up **The Touch of Snow** today at
www.AuthorAnnaEdwards.com

————

Keep reading for a peek at:
Mine,
Surrendered Control,
and **The Touch of Snow**…

MINE
USA TODAY BESTSELLING AUTHOR
ANNA EDWARDS

A SNEAK PEEK AT MINE
A STAND-ALONE DARK ROMANCE

Eaton and Shelby must navigate the sins of their parents and hope one of them survives.

Our parents decided our future before we were even born.

We've no say in what happens now.

Well, she doesn't, because she's mine

I will make her pay for what was taken from me.

All her dreams of a normal life are about to vanish.

Replaced by a hellish nightmare.

Death might be the better option.

But I won't let that happen.

I will get my pound of flesh.

I will make her suffer.

I'm the devil she thinks I am.

So why am I starting to care for her?

————

Chapter 1

Shelby

I put the the plate of biscuits and gravy down in front of the customer and can't help but look up and notice *him* standing on the sidewalk again. He's been there, in the exact same spot outside the supermarket, every lunchtime for the last week.

With his crisp suit and tie, he looks out of place among the poverty-stricken, local inhabitants. The area of Pharr where I live has a rundown, small-town vibe; its struggling residents occupy the most mobile homes per capita in all of Texas.

I shrug his presence off. Whatever he wants, it'll have nothing to do with me. A handsome, rich man, rescuing a poor, city girl from a living hell only happens in fairy tales.

This is real life, and I've got customers to serve.

"What can I get y'all?" I ask a man and woman who appear to be a couple.

They are obviously tourists; the maps spread over the table and the fanny pack are a dead giveaway. I don't know why they've chosen to eat at the run-down diner I work in. The red leather chairs are tatty and in desperate need of re-covering, and although the white plastic tables are clean, they've seen better days.

Why the fuck anyone would want to visit Pharr is beyond me.

"Could you recommend a local delicacy?" the man responds, his strong British accent sounding cute. "My wife and I want to try as many new dishes as possible on this holiday."

"Wow. You're from England!" I exclaim. Like it's the first time I've ever met anyone from there.

"We are. We're from Kent. Just outside London," the man replies with a smile.

I'm glad he added the last bit. I wouldn't have a clue where Kent is, but I've heard of London. Having never left Pharr, I don't know much about the rest of the world.

"What y'all doing after this?" I question.

"We're driving from here to Los Angeles, hoping to take in as much of the country as possible along the way. It's just so vast, and there's so much to see," the man replies.

"Well, you've just got to have biscuits and gravy," I recommend. "It's a favorite around here."

In truth, it's pretty much the only food on the menu that's edible. We're not exactly five-star dining here, but in a city where most residents live below the poverty line, we provide food at cheap prices, along with a generous helping of grease. Let's face it, when you're hungry, you'll eat anything.

"That sounds perfect. Bring us two plates, please," the woman requests, and I scribble the order down on my pad. "We'll have two cokes as well."

"What type?" I ask. "Coke, to a Texan, is any carbonated beverage."

"Coca Cola, please," she confirms.

"I'll get that out for you straight away," I say with a nod.

As I walk away, I pass by the diner window and notice the man has disappeared. He's probably returned to his wealthy, privileged life.

The rest of my shift passes without any drama. The friendly tourists leave me a big tip, which I'm very grateful for. It means, Mom and I won't have to rely solely on the scraps from the diner kitchen for the next few days, not that Mom eats very much anyway. I might be able to afford some fruit or maybe some vegetables that haven't been deep fried. Even a fresh apple would be nice.

"See you later, Fred." I grab the bag of leftovers I've collected over the course of the day and wave goodbye to my boss.

It's past ten pm, and when I step outside, the cool air of the late evening hits me even though I'm still wearing my diner uniform, which consists of black leggings and a long-sleeved red shirt. It's cold for this time of year. I inhale deeply, clearing away the stench of fries and burgers. The polluted town air fills my nose instead, but it's still smells fresher than the odor of grease I've been breathing in for the last eight hours.

Clutching my bag of scraps in one hand, I make my way through the busy streets toward my mobile home that sits on the outskirts of the city. The home I share with my mom is rundown and hasn't been decorated since the seventies, but with my mom's issues after my dad died, it's all we've got to live in.

The one-bedroom, mobile home is in darkness when I arrive, which suggests my mom is out. I'm kind of grateful for that as I don't want to have to handle the shit that comes with her, tonight.

After opening the door, I step inside and flick the switch to turn on the lights.

Nothing happens.

"Fuck's sake." I grumble, running my free hand over the top of my head in frustration.

This is just what I need!

I place the bag of food on the kitchen counter and go back outside to check the generator; it's out of fuel. I drop my head into my hands. There goes my big tip, and with it the happiness I was feeling at the prospect of a meal that didn't comprise solely of leftovers. I'll have to use the extra money to buy fuel tomorrow, instead.

I make my way into the kitchen area and grab a couple of candles and the bag of scraps before heading back outside. Tonight, there'll be a candlelit dinner for one.

I've got a little seating area out front with a log of wood I use for a seat and a small planter containing a few herbs I've cultivated from stolen cuttings. I place both candles on the ground and light them. It's all very peaceful out here and a little bit zen.

Opening the food package, I see it looks quite appetizing for once. One of the customers left their salad untouched. The leaves are a little wilted, but as I shovel them into my mouth, I savor every bite. There's also some chicken wrapped in cheese and bacon and a few fries. I hadn't realized how hungry I was after my shift, until now, so I gulp everything down quickly.

"Meow." Betty, my little cat friend appears by my side, obviously attracted to the smell of food.

"Evening, Betty," I greet her as I break off a small piece of chicken and throw it toward her.

Betty's not my cat. She's a stray that I look after and feed. I throw her another piece of chicken, and she rolls over onto her back for me to stroke her stomach and purrs when I tickle her tummy.

"Have you had a busy day sleeping, Betty?" I ask.

"Meow," she answers, as though she understands everything I'm saying.

I guess you could say Betty is my only friend in the world. I didn't make any friends at school. In my last few years of high school, I wasn't there a lot. I grew up early; I had to with a mother addicted to heroin and a father who died far too young. I wish I could say I remember him. But I was only two when he was shot and killed.

My mom doesn't talk about his death. I think it broke her, and that's the reason she lost herself to her addiction. I can't count how many times I've tried to help her quit. Now, I guess, I'm just waiting for the day I wake up and she's overdosed. It's a tragic waste of a life.

Headlights flash as a car pulls up in front of me. My heart deflates. I know instantly who it is. My mom's home, and my worst fears are realized when she stumbles out of the passenger side of the car.

Betty, as if sensing trouble has arrived, scampers away in a hurry, growling as she goes because she wasn't able to finish the chicken.

"Shelby." My mom waves at me.

The driver of the car gets out. He's one of Mom's regulars. He makes my skin crawl.

"Hi, Shelby." He nods my way. "Is tonight going to be the night you join us? You know you want a piece of me."

My stomach turns, and I hope I'm not about to bring up the contents of my second-hand salad and chicken.

"Leave her alone," my mom quips and pats at her client's fat stomach playfully. "I'm woman enough for you."

"And I'm man enough to handle both of you. One day, you'll be desperate enough to spread your legs for me,

Shelby. Like mother, like daughter. Your mom is a whore for her heroin, and no doubt, you'll follow her down that path eventually. After all, you've known nothing different."

The man's smirk is cruel and twisted, just like his words. He's right, though. I may still be a virgin and determined to stay that way for as long as possible, but prostitution is one way to make money. And it's the destiny of many women, and even some men, in this city[st1] .

I turn my back to the two of them and respond, "But today won't be that day. By the way, we've got no power indoors, so you might want to go elsewhere. With or without my mom."

He laughs. "I only need your mom's pussy to get my dick wet. I never want to see her drugged up face while fucking her. I won't have to do her from behind if it's dark. It'll be a welcome change."

His words sting. This is my mother he's talking about. I've tried to do everything to help her, but her addiction is too far gone.

A lone tear tumbles down my cheek as I watch them go into my home, and not long after, the rhythmic sound of fucking starts. I don't want to be here. I don't want this life. But it was the one that was chosen for me. So, I guess I must suffer through it. I'm only nineteen, and I keep hoping I can save enough money to escape. Who am I kidding? My life's a mess. And it's always going to be this way.

"He's got it all wrong." A deep masculine voice comes from behind me.

Startled, I spin around on the log before getting to my feet, and I'm stunned at what I see. The man in the designer suit stands before me, the one who's been lurking outside the diner every day this week.

"Who's got what wrong?" I mumble.

Illuminated by the candlelight, he looks even more handsome up close. His jawline is square, his eyes a bright blue, and his dark hair is neatly combed back from his face.

What is he doing here?

"That man with your mother. You don't just start banging a pussy straightaway. You must warm it up first. It makes the experience so much more pleasurable for both participants," he answers and then winks at me.

I open my mouth to say something but can't find the words. He's shocked me into silence. That wasn't the response I was expecting to hear from him. Then again, I wasn't expecting him to be here in the first place.

"Who are you? What are you doing here?" I finally manage to ask.

"My name is Eaton Armstrong. And I've come to collect what's mine."

———

Get **Mine** today at
www.AuthorAnnaEdwards.com

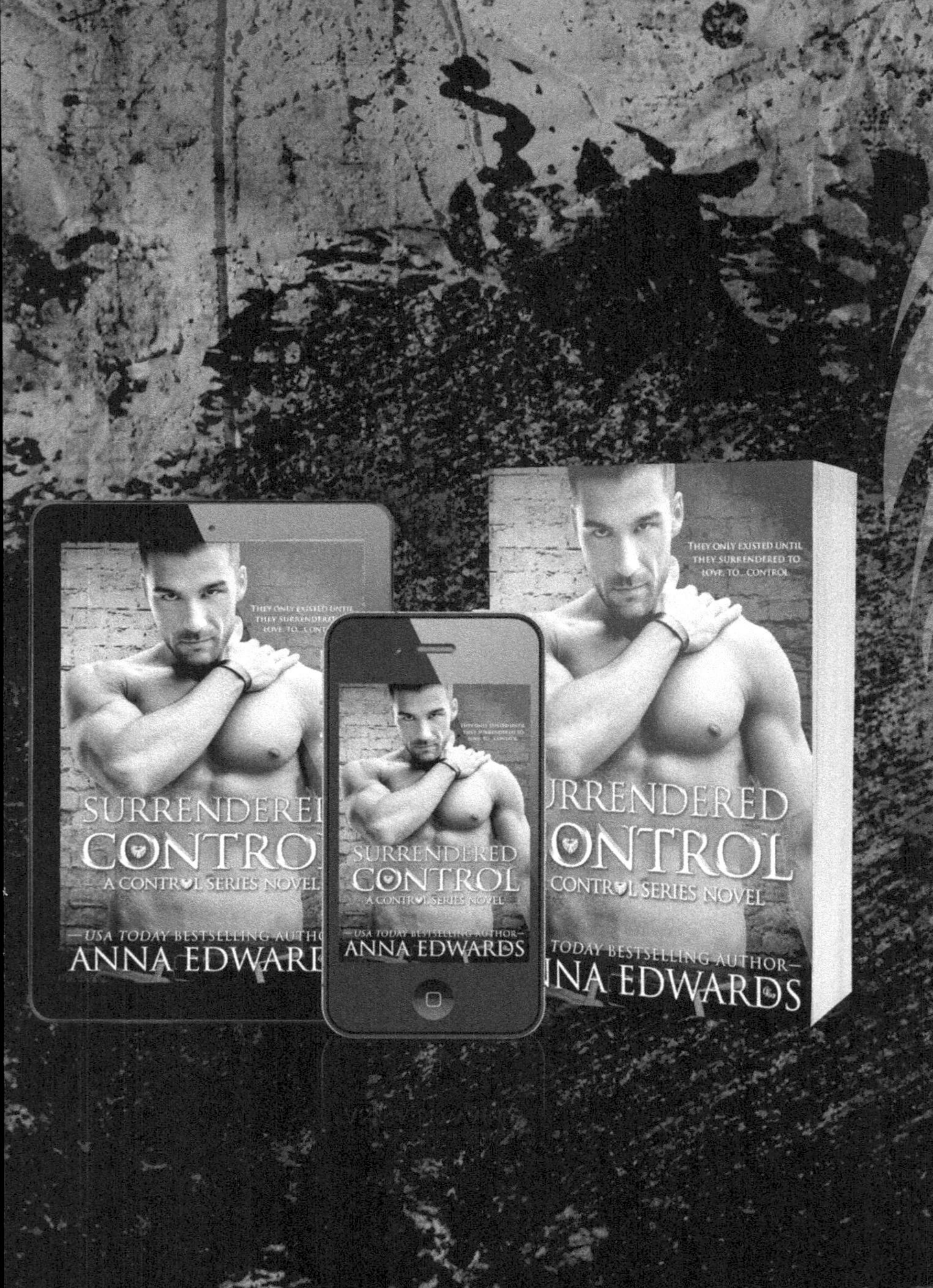
THEY ONLY EXISTED UNTIL
THEY SURRENDERED TO
LOVE. TO...CONTROL.
SURRENDERED
CONTROL
A CONTROL SERIES NOVEL
USA TODAY BESTSELLING AUTHOR
ANNA EDWARDS

A SNEAK PEEK AT SURRENDERED CONTROL

THE CONTROL SERIES, BOOK 1

Innocence and naiveté make Amy Jones a rare breed among exotic dancers. She does the job reluctantly…but there's no hesitation when she meets a mesmerizing, sophisticated stranger while on holiday. Under his skilled hand, she'll learn the depth of her own strength even as she surrenders to his masterful control.

Successful businessman James North avoids a dark past by hiding behind an enviable career and rigid control—over his business and pleasure. One night with blonde goddess Amy, however, and the blazing attraction that erupts between them throws his ordered black-and-white world into multiple shades of ecstasy.

When innocence and experience collide, the volcanic explosion may burn everything in its path…including the couple's fledgling love.

CHAPTER ONE
AMY

The full moonlight glistened over the endless volcanic sand as Amy emerged from the water. The bright illumination shone on her honey-blonde hair and she brushed her fingers through it. The day of travelling had left her tired and the warm water had eased her aching muscles, cramped by the budget flight. This was her first holiday for many years. Aspiring writers didn't tend to have the money to travel. Nor dancers in a gentlemen's club, forced to work just to make ends meet. But it wasn't as bad a job as it sounded; she was well protected, as her uncle ran it and made sure she was sheltered from the seedier side of the profession. And she enjoyed the dancing side, in fact, it was her second passion. Her uncle Stephen had paid for this holiday to Lanzarote as a twenty-first birthday present. Ever since her parents had died in a car crash two years ago, he had always looked out for her. He was the only family she had left, and she looked up to him and trusted him implicitly.

As Amy took a towel and wrapped it around her body, the aroma of the freshly caught fish being cooked was everywhere and made her mouth water in anticipation. She decided on a small taverna that was filled with more locals than tourists. Amy wasn't big on the mass-market tourism of the island--she preferred places of culture and history--but as the holiday was a gift, she couldn't refuse it. She ordered the grilled catch of the day with salad, and a glass of the local *La Geria* wine. As she watched the sun slowly set over the shimmering waves, the tension in her shoulders began to dissipate.

When she had finished her delicious meal, Amy ordered another glass of wine and pulled out a little notebook from her bag to begin writing down some of the details of the island so far. She liked to bring her personal experiences into her writing, and she wanted to get everything noted should it be needed for future stories.

She had just finished a passage on the chaotic wait for her luggage at the airport when an uneasy tingling warmed her skin as though she was being watched. Looking up, she met the alluring sky blue eyes of a man sitting across the room. Had he just arrived? Or how had she not noticed him previously? He too was sitting alone with just a glass of wine for company. Upon making eye-contact, Amy couldn't help but blush. He was exquisitely handsome. He had a rugged yet smart look, a defined jaw line, and short dark hair that he ran his fingers through as he watched her. The top few buttons of his blue linen shirt were undone and revealed a muscular upper body that oozed a primal masculinity. His stare was intense, and she felt herself being drawn into it even more. When his lip twitched at her blatantly checking him out she pushed the other chair at her table out with her gladiator-sandalled foot and looked up, smiling at him with a cheeky grin that masked her excitement. For a moment she thought he wasn't going to move, but then he got to his feet. Even the way he walked was sexy, she was glad she was sitting down as her legs felt like jelly at his presence. He took a seat and held his hand up to the waiter, who promptly took his order for a more expensive bottle of wine. Neither of them spoke at first, they just continued to take each other in.

"James." His voice was deep and inviting, and she was pleased to note he was speaking English.

"Amy." Her voice was smooth and possibly a little bit to sexy when she spoke.

Silence.

"Well, if this isn't awkward." He ruffled his hands through his hair again. The bottle of wine arrived, and the waiter poured them each a glass.

"Shall we start again? I'm Amy, I'm twenty-one, I come from London, and this is my first holiday in a while. I have come away to finish writing my first novel."

"I am James, I am twenty-eight. I also come from London, well Kent initially. I haven't had a holiday myself for a while. I tend to be a workaholic."

"What do you do?"

"I work in property. It is all very boring, I am sure you don't want to hear about it. So; a novel. Is it all hush-hush or can you tell me something about it?" He sat back in the chair, his left leg resting over his right, the wine glass tantalising-ly resting at his full lips. Lips that she couldn't tear her eyes away from. She wondered what they would taste of if she kissed him? He seemed happier to be asking questions than answering them so she decided to answer him to continue that line of conversation.

Amy chuckled and took a mouthful of her wine. "It is a classic. Boy meets girl, boy loses the girl, boy wins the girl back forever."

"Interesting. So this boy? What is he like?"

"Tall, dark, and handsome."

James nodded with genuine interest.

"And the girl?"

"Pretty, slim."

"Blonde?"

"Blonde."

"I like this story already."

"Told you it was a classic."

"Certainly, is." He raised his eyebrow as he spoke. "So, is the man proficient in the bedroom?"

"That is a little presumptuous isn't it?"

"Why?" He chuckled now as he refilled the glasses they both seemed to have drunk rather quickly.

"They have only just met."

He shrugged, "Why should they waste time, if there is an attraction between them?" James reached forward, took Amy's hand, and their eyes met in an intense stare as sparks of electricity flowed through them both. She wasn't drunk, so it wasn't that. "Are you staying nearby?"

The question hung thickly in the air between them.

Amy had had only one previous partner, and that was a boyfriend of four years. Strange as it seemed she felt she knew James, which was odd since they had only set eyes on each other not fifteen minutes before. "Yes, the Rivera apartments."

"Do you want me to walk you home?"

She didn't doubt from the look on his face that this would turn to sex if he did. But something about him, something about the mystery of his tone prevented her from saying no. He had a presence about him that drew her under his spell.

"Yes."

James pulled out his wallet and put forty euros on the table. The walk back was short, and they talked a little more. Just general facts, where they grew up, favourite foods, drinks, and a particularly funny story about an encounter that he had had with a flock of seagulls in Brighton. Amy didn't tell him she worked in a Gentleman's Club.

When they entered her apartment, she was suddenly nervous. James took a seat on the cream sofa, and Amy went to look in the kitchen for a drink. She found two glasses and a semi-chilled bottle of wine and returned to the lounge. His big body was so commanding in the small lounge.

"Sorry, it isn't more. I only arrived today."

"It is fine. I still haven't bought any wine for my apartment so you are a step ahead of me."

"How long have you been here."

"A week now. A few days left. How long are you here?"

"Only a week."

"Not long to finish that novel then."

"No. Not really. I will have to forgo sunbathing and do lots of writing."

Amy put the bottle down on the table; she needed a corkscrew to open it. "I won't be a minute. Just have to figure out which drawer the corkscrew is in." She turned back to walk into the kitchen but stopped as James called out 'Wait'. It was the way he said it -- it sent shivers of anticipation down her spine. Slowly she turned and looked at him, her eyes wide. He had risen from the sofa and was walking towards her.

"Take your dress off."

"I...."

"Take your dress off, Amy."

She had no answer. Her mind was telling her this was crazy, but her body was doing as he asked, completely disobeying the part that was telling her to tell him to fuck off. She reached down to the hem of her dress and pulled it over her head. Amy wasn't big breasted so, underneath the summer dress, she hadn't worn a bra. She stood in front of him in just a pair of white lace panties. He walked around her, studying her, taking in every inch of her prickling flesh. She could feel the heat of his gaze marking her. Amy was never *naked* in front of the clients at the club, but she wore revealing clothing, and none of that could prepare her for what she was feeling right now. He leaned over her and took a deep breath, he was smelling her.

"You are beautiful." His tone was calm but had a stern undercurrent to it.

"I was supposed to be getting you wine."

James laughed. "I am going to kiss you now. Are you sure you want to do this?"

"I don't think I would be standing in front of you in just my panties if I didn't. Now are you going to remove some of your clothing?"

"Eager. I like it. But we will do this my way." James pulled his shirt over his head, and Amy noted she was indeed correct about his superbly toned chest. She couldn't see his back, but she saw on his left arm he had a tattoo. It looked like the tips of wings.

"What is your tattoo?"

His face went momentarily blank. He didn't answer but pressed his body closer to hers. He leaned in and kissed her. Tender at first, and then with intense passion. Amy could feel her knees weakening as she was pushed back against the wall. "Place your hands above you head and don't move them." Again with the authoritative tone.

"Why?"

"Will you do as I asked, Amy? Or should I leave now? I told you, we will do this my way. You will enjoy it. Don't worry." A hot kiss was again pressed to her lips and without thinking anymore, Amy moved her hands above her head. "Good girl. You will be rewarded for that later."

Rewarded? James moved his mouth from her lips down to the peaking tips of her nipples. His tongue swirled around the sensitive buds and she let out a yearning moan. He looked up at her, a mischievous look in his eyes and began to travel down the flat line of her stomach until he knelt on the floor in front of her. He placed his hands on either side of her panties, and in one fluid motion ripped them from her body. Amy was breathing fast now. This whole experience was so damn intense it almost seemed like a dream, her body was on fire, and she longed for him to touch her.

James put his hands between her legs and parted them to reveal her neatly trimmed sex. He groaned. "I haven't even touched you yet, and you are ready for me. Have you been like this all night? I can even smell your arousal."

Amy sure as hell wasn't going to let him know that he was turning her on more than she ever had been before. "You know how to kiss a lady and get her excited. It is a good start, just depends on what skills you have now."

He gave her a little tap on the top of her thigh which brought a scream from her and then ran a finger over her displayed folds before moving it slowly into her inner channel which was already slick with the need for him.

"If you doubt my skills again, I will put you over my

knee." Amy's body writhed against his hand as she found herself being excited about having her bottom spanked.

Holy hell. Where had that come from?

His thumb found the hidden bundle of nerves between her thighs and teased it. She could feel the heat within her starting to build. "If you don't stop doing that, I am going to come all over your hand." James abruptly withdrew his finger and got to his feet with a tutting sound.

"No. Not yet. You will come when I tell you that you can." He looked her in the eyes, and it was almost like he was controlling her body with his words.

"You are not in charge of me you know that right?"

He didn't answer, only sniggered, reached into the pocket of his trousers, brought out his wallet, and retrieved a condom from it. The wallet was then tossed aside, and Amy watched as he lowered his trousers and pants to reveal a substantially thick cock and covered it with the condom. It was jutting up towards his stomach and was a work of art. It should be framed and hung in an art gallery it was that perfect. She was panting now; she was terrified that the length and girth of his manhood was going to hurt, but at the same time she needed him buried deep inside her. She wanted to know what he felt like. Amy pulled her hands down and reached out to touch the muscular sinews of James' shoulders.

"No. You don't touch me unless I give you permission." He slammed her hands back against the wall and held them there with one hand. With the other, he lifted her leg from the floor and in one slow thrust pushed inside her.

"Oh God." Amy groaned. He was nothing like she had felt before. Her ex-boyfriend wasn't small, but sex between them had always been something that they seemed to do because they were boyfriend and girlfriend. This was different. It was raw, and it was dangerous. James began to move slowly. Their eyes locked together as with each long movement he stroked against the sweet spot deep within her.

Their lips tangled in a tumultuous tango of passion. James' hand still held her in place, and she was glad for it because she was barely able to support her weight as she felt the build-up of her climax again. She tried to suppress the feeling. James had told her that she couldn't come until he had told her she could, and she wanted to please him.

Jesus, what was this man doing to her? This was her body. Why was it responding to his control like this?

James seemed to know she was close and trying to control herself; she could tell by the little curl of his lip. She wanted to hit him. She wished he would let her release. He finally let her out of her misery when he leaned forward and collected her lip between his teeth. He nodded consent, and Amy exploded around him. Wave after wave of cataclysmic plea-sure rolled over her shaking body. She called out and James joined her over the precipice as he released himself into her.

They were both covered in sweat, breathing rapidly, their legs quivering. James lowered her leg to the floor and with-drew from her, checking the filled condom as he did.

"Are you alright? I didn't hurt you, did I?" Amy shook her head; she couldn't find her voice just yet. "Good." He pressed another kiss to her now-bruised lips and looked into her eyes. At that moment, something within him changed. Amy saw it. Gone was the dominantly splendid lover he had been; he withdrew into himself. He pulled up his trousers, quickly found his shirt, and put it on. "I am sorry. I shouldn't have done that." And with that, he left Amy confused, standing naked, covered with the scent of the best sex she had ever had, and her hands still above her head.

Get **Surrendered Control** today at
www.AuthorAnnaEdwards.com

The TOUCH
of Snow
GLACIAL Blood
ANNA EDWARDS
USA TODAY BESTSELLING AUTHOR

A SNEAK PEEK AT THE TOUCH OF SNOW

THE GLACIAL BLOOD SERIES, BOOK 1

Selene Harper awoke in Death Valley with no memory of who—or what—she is. Capable of reading thoughts with a single touch, she's unnerved by her ability, until it warns her of imminent danger. When an alluring man comes to her aid, neutralizing the threat, Selene can't read his mind. .but the stranger's touch sets off a series of events that finds Selene a captive of the mysterious Glacial Blood Pack.

Shape-shifter Brayden Dillion, a deadly pack assassin, can only become a sentinel if he finds his mate. A miracle that seems less and less likely…until a favor for his mother puts him on a collision course with Selene. With help from the pack, they discover she's a preciously rare breed of shifter who can absorb the form of any creature she touches. Brayden knows she's meant to be his, but mating Selene is impossible unless she learns to control her immense powers.

Or until those powers are taken from her…

Welcome to the Glacial Blood series, a world of shifters and witches, magic and mayhem, unforgivable lies and unbreakable love. A world where family is born not only through blood, but bond. With plenty of the threats to come—and a secret that remains untold.

———

Chapter 1

The barren desert wasteland with its hues of gold, orange, and red sped past the car window. The rock formations were a testament to years of erosion, beaten down by forces greater than he could understand. As a shape-shifting snow leopard, Brayden Dillon knew a lot about the ways of Mother Nature. Considering he spent most of his time exploring the snow-capped peaks of The Glacial National Park he already had the air-conditioning turned up as high as it would go. The brand-new Ford Mustang he drove had been a gift from his alpha, Kas, in recognition for a job done well; so was the break from duties as pack Enforcer. Why his mother had to live just outside Death Valley was beyond him. You really couldn't get a hotter place on Earth. She'd told him it was because his father had always lived in the snow. When he died, she decided to get some sun. She hadn't looked back.

He pulled his Mustang up outside the café and shut off the roar of the high-powered engine. The disapproving looks from the locals soon vanished when he climbed out of the car. His height of six foot five silenced any potential disagreement. He purred to himself in contentment, but that was quickly lost when the heat of the midday sun hit him. He was not designed for this weather. He had all the usual snow leopard attributes: thick black hair with smoky gray flecks, small ears, and big feet that helped with balance. He was pale because he rarely spent time sunbathing like the lions and tigers in his pack. Dusk to dawn was when he was the most active. He made quick steps towards the café and into the air-conditioned building.

He didn't see his mother, only a fresh-faced waitress. She wore the café's uniform: a barely-there skirt and a tank top that was almost a second skin. She was pretty, in a timid sort of way. Every time someone came near her she flinched, and he could smell her fear. Well, he assumed it was fear. His judgment was slightly clouded by the fact that he needed a drink, preferably ice cold and dumped over his head. She approached the seat he had taken near the counter.

"Hi. Welcome to the Last Stop. I'm Selene, and I'll be your waitress today. Can I get you an ice water to start with? It sure is a hot one out there today." Any sign of her nerves had disappeared, replaced with a business-like smile.

"Yes please, lots of ice. In fact, just bring me a big bowl of ice."

She laughed, her tiny nose crinkling up and dimples appearing in her cheeks. Up close, she was even prettier than he'd originally thought. "Let me guess." She took a step back and looked him up and down. "Well, the fact you seem as if you're melting, I take it you're not a southerner. The lack of a tan confirms that but I can't quite place the accent?"

"Montana."

"No wonder you're hot. I'll bring you ice cream as well."

She spun around in her little ballet pumps and started to stride off. Something stopped her. She turned back and took another long look at him; an eyebrow raising in question.

"Brayden?"

"Yes." His reply was tentative. Not many people knew who he was. It was his job to be secretive and stay in the shadows.

"Your mother said you were coming. She had to go to a meeting in Pahrump. She should be back soon, but she said that you could go up to the apartment if you wanted. My God, now I really look at you, you look like the pictures she has of your father. God rest his soul." She bowed her head. Brayden couldn't help feel a little unease. This girl, she couldn't have been more than eighteen from the looks of her, knew far too much about him. He just hoped she didn't know everything. His mother would never tell her that, would she? "You head on up. I'll get your water, ice cubes, and ice cream, and bring it to you. It's my lunch break, I'll keep you company till she gets here."

He did as instructed. Mainly because he was freaked out by the insistent waitress, but also because his mother had the biggest freezer known to man. If he didn't get cold air on him soon, he was going to dissolve into a pile of fur on the floor.

His mother's apartment hadn't changed one bit from when he visited last year. It was decorated in a minimal style with clean lines and equally clean surfaces. She had always liked the latest trends in interior design. It had apparently annoyed his father, to no end, because he preferred to take things as they came, which, in his case was usually wild and chaotic. While he waited for Selene, Brayden opened the freezer and stuck his head in it. The blast of icy, cold air surrounded him, and his inner beast jumped for joy at finally getting away from the inferno that was the Mojave Desert. It was definitely scolding him for coming to this place. He'd introduce it to a snack of jackrabbit later. That would keep it happy.

"Damn, you are hot." Selene's voice came from the doorway. How had he not heard her? She blushed. "I mean..."

"I know what you meant. I spend a lot of my time in the mountains in Montana. I'm more acclimatized to snow." He watched her while she placed the food on the table.

"Come on and sit down before the ice cream melts. You look like a cookies n' cream guy. I hope you like it. I'll turn up the AC."

"I can do it."

Surprised, she dodged out of his way when they both reached for the air-conditioning remote control. It was such a quick movement, almost cat-like.

"Please sit. I've already got it."

He took a seat at the table and downed the glass of ice-water in one mouthful. Its cold liquid reduced his body temperature. Selene pressed a button on the remote control, and another icy blast hit him. He purred, as he finally felt relaxed with the cool air washing over him. Thankfully, it was quiet enough that the young human female would not hear him.

"Your mom called when I was downstairs. She shouldn't be long. There was an accident just as she came on the route one-ninety by Death Valley Junction. That's less than half an hour away."

"Great." He needed to have a few words with his mother.

"When was the last time you saw her?" Selene took a seat

at the table with him, with a small salad she'd brought for herself. No wonder she was tiny if that was all she was eating. The ice cream was good, but he couldn't wait for his mother to cook him a steak, or three or, hell, he was on holiday, make that four. Who was he kidding? He wanted the whole cow laid out on his plate. His inner leopard approved of that idea with a smacking of it's lips.

"It must have been a year now. I don't get here as often as I would like."

"She said your job keeps you busy; park ranger, isn't it?"

"My mom seems to talk about me a lot," he chuckled.

"She's really proud of you." She shrugged. "I think I've pretty much seen all your baby, kindergarten, and graduation pictures, as well as all the school reports. I love the mullet you had going on in high school." It was her turn to laugh.

"Puberty hit me hard."

"You've still got a bit of a mane to you."

"This is nothing in comparison to my friend." He ran his fingers through his hair. He kept it long because it did its own thing most of the time. "He has the full fluffy thing happening, no sooner does he style it, than it goes poof into a mess again."

"Poor guy."

"What about you?"

"My hair? It does as it's told." She tucked a strand of chestnut hair behind her ear.

He raised an eyebrow at her.

"Oh, you meant who am I?"

"I did. I feel at a disadvantage. You seem to know a great deal about me."

He finished his cookies n' cream, placed the spoon back in

the bowl, and popped an ice cube into his mouth to suck.

"There isn't much to know. My name is Selene Harper. I've been working for your mother for six months now, ever since I arrived in Death Valley. She's given me a room in the apartment with her. It means I can look after the place when she needs to go out."

"How old are you?"

"Twenty-one."

Throughout their entire conversation she'd been keeping eye contact with him, but now she looked down at the salad. Was that a lie? He took a deep inhalation and felt a shift in her scent. She was nervous again. There was something this human was not telling him. He would play along, for now, but when his mother returned he would be demanding answers. Who was this woman living with his mother? Was she safe with her?

"Where did you live before?" Brayden asked.

Selene put her fork down on her plate.

"Look at me stuffing my face and all I've given you is ice cream. I'll tell you what, I'll go and get a burger for you. I'm sure the chef knows how you like it." Was she deliberately avoiding his question?

"There's no need."

"No, no I insist. My lunch break is over anyway. I'll send someone up with it when it's done." She hurried out, leaving him alone with his thoughts.

His mother had emailed him a few months back asking if he would visit her, when he could get away. Brayden was the pack's lead enforcer, basically the assassin for the Glacial Blood pack. A pack, well a family really, brought together by choice, not blood. He was damned good at his job. Recently, he'd been kept busy enough that, this was the first chance he'd had to get away.

He'd bet money that whatever his mother wanted to speak to him about, it was related to the waitress. Brayden wasn't going to sit around in his mother's apartment, he was going to go down to the café and observe. His instincts were telling him something was not right here, and he'd learned at a very young age to trust them.

Brayden had just sat in the café, with his burger, when his mother arrived. He gave her a great big hug, and a contented thrum left his throat. He heard her own hum of pleasure at having her son close.

"I'm sure you've gotten even taller," his mother exclaimed and took a seat opposite him.

"Compared to Kas, I'm like an ant."

"He always was freakishly big. Your father always said it was the seal blubber. I remember the day I roasted some for him with my grandma's secret spice mix. I don't think I've ever seen a grown man drool so much with anticipation."

"Which reminds me… he wants me to bring another packet of the mix back with me. He's got a hunting trip planned."

"Please tell me he is not going to eat it raw again?" Jane raised a questioning eyebrow.

"He likes it that way," Brayden huffed.

"Philistine." His mother rolled her eyes in disgust.

Their conversation quieted when Selene brought his mother a coffee. "Thanks, Sel. How have things been?"

"No problems at all," Selene said. Brayden sat back and started on his burger while the ladies spoke. A perfect medium rare, just as he liked it.

"I see Stuart is in." His mom nodded her head towards a table full of jocks. Their team jackets were thick, despite the high temperature.

"Yes, he wants me to go out with him tonight." Selene stood with her shaking hands clasped in front of her.

"Hi, Mrs. Dillon," one of the men called out. His hair was slicked with gel into a fashionable style and he had a smug smile on his face.

"Hi, Stuart," his mom shouted back, before reverting her attention again to Selene. "I thought we might have a nice meal with Brayden?"

"I turned him down last week. I can't really say no again."

"You don't have to go out with him."

"He is good to me," Selene stated quietly.

Brayden could tell by the sudden look of disgust on his mother's face that she didn't believe that.

"And besides, you and your son probably have a lot to catch up on."

"We will do dinner tomorrow. Don't make any plans, please." There was a hint of desperation in his mother's plea.

"You have my word." Selene turned her attention to another patron who had arrived.

"What is going on, Mom?" Brayden asked.

"We'll talk tomorrow, please. Here isn't the place."

"You are worried. We'll talk now."

Someone from the table, at which Stuart sat, loudly called over to Selene. She timidly went over to them.

"Can we get another round of sodas, please? We better get them to go. Don't want to be late for practice. Why don't you see if you can get off and come and join us?" The loud-mouthed idiot, Stuart, grabbed Selene's hand and ran his other hand up her naked leg. Instead of looking like she enjoyed it, the panic-stricken girl looked like she would be sick. A growl formed in Brayden's throat and his fingernails started to shift to claws.

"Brayden, no. She knows what she is doing." His mother placed her hand over his, hiding the sharpened talons. All he could do was watch and keep the reverberations in his throat as quiet as possible. It was his natural state; he couldn't help it. Selene nodded toward where he and his mother sat.

"I wish I could, but Miss Jane needs me." Selene removed Stuart's hand from her leg and kissed it. "But I'll be there when you finish practice, and you can show me that lookout point you wanted to. How about that?"

All Brayden could think about was, how could she be all sweetness and light when it was evident, to anyone with half a brain, that this man made her skin crawl?

"I suppose that'll do. Make sure you wear a short skirt and show me some skin. That gothic stuff you wear is awful. I never get to see anything with those long skirts."

"I think after a day here it will be a little dirty, but I will see what I can find." With that, Selene disappeared into the back and Brayden could relax. He sheathed his claws again.

"Talk, Mom." After the display he'd just witnessed he wasn't in the mood for arguments.

"I can't here." His mother was panicked.

"Well then let's go upstairs."

"I need to check on Selene."

"Mom. What is going on?" He reached out to grab her hand but she was too quick and got to her feet. He could see tears forming in her eyes.

"Later Brayden. Please, I need you to trust me."

"You know I do, but I can't help if I don't know what is going on." He was on his feet and round to her side of the table pulling her into his arms.

"I will tell you later, but for now, I need you to do one thing for me." She looked up at him. His mother was upset. It ruffled his leopard's fur that she was not telling him how to help.

"What?"

"Tonight, when Selene goes on her date. I need you to follow her," she asked.

"Follow her? If she wants to date that dickhead, why do I need to follow her?"

"You just do. Damn, why are you Dillon males so stubborn and need to know everything? Please, can you do what I ask for once?" This final plea was frantic.

"Ok. I'll follow her," he replied.

"Thank you. Let whatever happens, happen, but he mustn't touch her."

"Touch her? They are going to a lookout point. I'm pretty confident he plans on doing a lot more than just giving her a kiss."

"He mustn't touch her Brayden, please." His mother was serious; she was worried for this girl.

He held his hands up in surrender. "Alright. He won't."

Get **The Touch of Snow** today at
www.AuthorAnnaEdwards.com

ABOUT ANNA EDWARDS

Anna Edwards is a *USA Today* Best-selling British author from the depths of the rural countryside near London. When she has some spare time, she can also be found writing poetry, baking cakes (and eating them), or behind a camera snapping like a mad paparazzo. She's an avid reader who turned to writing to combat her depression and anxiety. She has a love of traveling and likes to bring this to her stories to give them the air of reality. She likes her heroes hot and hunky with a dirty mouth, her heroines demure but with spunk, and her books full of dramatic suspense.

www.AuthorAnnaEdwards.com
Newsletter: http://bit.ly/NewsletterAnnaEdwards
Facebook, Friend: TheAuthorAnnaEdwards
Email: anna1000edwards@gmail.com

facebook.com/AnnaEdwardsWriter
twitter.com/Anna__Edwards
instagram.com/authorannaedwards
bookbub.com/authors/anna-edwards
pinterest.com/authorannaedwards
goodreads.com/anna__edwards

THE CONTROL SERIES

A complete, dramatic, witty, and sensual suspense romance set predominantly in London.

Surrendered Control

Divided Control

Misguided Control

Controlling Darkness

Controlling Heritage

Controlling Disgrace

Controlling Expectations

Controlling the Past

Also available:

The Control Series Boxset

Surrendered Control audio

Binge read ready - completed series!

THE GLACIAL BLOOD SERIES

A world of shifters and witches, magic and mayhem, unforgivable lies and unbreakable love. A world where family is born not only through blood, but bond. With plenty of the threats to come—and a secret that remains untold.

The Touch of Snow

Fighting the Lies

Fallen for Shame

Shattered Fears

Hidden Pain

Stolen Choices

A Deadly Affair

Power of a Myth

Banishing Regrets

Binge read ready - completed series!

DARK SOVEREIGNTY SERIES

A complete dark and suspenseful series set amongst the elite of a London society intent on finding power in the wrong place.

Legacy of Succession

Tainted Reasoning

A Father's Insistence

Legacy of Succession audio

Binge read ready - completed series!

ALSO BY ANNA EDWARDS

Beauty's War - Gods Reborn with Claire Marta

Apollo's Protection - Gods Reborn with Claire Marta

Oliver - Part of Blaire's World

Cruel Angels with Dani René

Happily Ever Crowned with Lexi C. Foss

Happily Ever Bitten with Lexi C. Foss

Zhànshì - A Mulan retelling

Mine